SHERLOCK H
THE CASE OF
THE UNDEAD CLIENT

~ *BEING* ~

BOOK ONE OF THE UNPUBLISHED CASE FILES OF
JOHN H. WATSON, M.D.

M.J. DOWNING

Burns and Lea Books

LOUISVILLE   NEW YORK

Burns and Lea Books
7919 Niemann Drive
Louisville, Kentucky 40291
www.burnsandleabooks.com

Layout by www.formatting4U.com

Publisher's Note: This is a work of fiction. Names, characters, places, and incidents are a product of the author's imagination. Locales and public names are sometimes used for atmospheric purposes. Any resemblance to actual people, living or dead, or to businesses, companies, events, institutions, or locales is completely coincidental.

Sherlock Holmes and the Case of the Undead Client/ M.J. Downing. -- 1st ed.
Ebook ISBN: 978-0-9995083-2-9
Paperback ISBN: 978-0-9995083-4-3

For Amy, the light in my life, without whom, I am lost.

*"Alack, there lies more peril in thine eyes
Than twenty of their swords."*

—William Shakespeare

Today dawned cheerless, dreary, despite the hoped-for warmth of the month. The morning greeted me with the news of the identity of the Swallow Gardens victim, another casualty of this dreadful business. She had finally been identified by the popular press as Frances Coles.

The name jolted through my memory, taking me back to a night near the beginning of this case when I stood yet in the light. Her face had been pert, framed with ringlets of bright red hair. As I recalled, she'd had an insolent manner, and I'd hoped her anger might save her from this darkness. My steps in life and my mood had grown darker since the time of our only brief meeting.

The article, a report on prostitution entitled "The Great Evil of the East End," said that Frances Coles's throat had been horribly lacerated with a dull knife some three months before, her body left below a railway arch. Holmes has said that we may expect more of these grim reminders as the press composes the picture of the Whitechapel murders, one grisly brushstroke at a time.

The influenza is on the rise, as Moriarty promised it would be long before he fell with Holmes into the Reichenbach chasm, but my new work, outside my medical practice—the new work to which I dedicated myself after the terrible events of the year before—goes on.

Reading of Frances Coles's so-called murder threatened to make me lose my breakfast. The police would file her case away, but I knew that she was just the latest victim in the case I have called "The Undead Client." I shuddered to think of the fresh horrors that could yet rise to the streets of London, with Holmes now gone.

I cannot imagine a time in the future that this case could or should reach the eyes of readers, since everyone will have been led to accept the fictional "Jack the Ripper" as historical fact. I am again dismayed at the memories I call upon to set this one down to paper. However, it is my role in this weary life to chronicle the exploits of my esteemed friend Mr. Sherlock Holmes, even in memoriam. I shall endeavor to pen the details of this many-sided, horrific case as I have others, though they will harrow the heart of any reader and likely stand forever in testimony against my character. This tale will have readers crying out in disbelief at its contents—at least I pray that it does.

For me, the record of these events begins in early 1888, just before my marriage to Mary. Holmes bade me withhold this account until all prominent parties mentioned herein should die, and I trust that my solicitors have done so. If Mary should survive me and should still live when and if these pages come to light, I hope that she can find some place in her generous heart to forgive all that I put her through during this, our darkest year.

I doubt that I shall ever find that forgiveness for myself.

Part One.

"The East End Evil"

CHAPTER ONE

I rose rather late one frosty January morning after fevered dreams of the Battle of Maiwand, which had nearly claimed my life before I'd ever met Holmes. The nightmare that woke me, of being overrun by wild Afghani tribesmen, had me tossing to and fro in a tangle of bedclothes. I forced myself to rise, desiring only to escape before the fateful Jezail round tore my flesh again.

I woke to a cold, quiet flat, donned my dressing gown, and sought warmth by the fire in the sitting room. Because I had slept awkwardly, my old wounds ached in the chill air. I poked the low fire to life in the grate and rang Mrs. Hudson for my breakfast. Fresh coals on the hearth warmed the room as I sought to put away the dreadful memories of my soldiering days, memories that are never far away.

"I had wondered when either of the two of you would stir," Mrs. Hudson claimed, bearing my steaming breakfast tray and the morning papers.

"Do you mean to say that Mr. Holmes is still abed?" I caroled in mock horror, hopeful that my protests might awaken him, much to his chagrin. Holmes, ever the model of industry, was almost always up before I was, chiding me for my tendency to sit up late at night and rise, leisurely, at midmorning. But this morning he was nowhere to be seen. In fact, I had seen little of Holmes in recent days.

Mrs. Hudson smiled at my jest and looked toward my friend's door. Silence greeted us.

"Well, Doctor, I don't believe he's there, for he would never fail to rise at such a suggestion, would he?"

A sudden worry clouded my thoughts. "No, my dear, I don't suppose he would," I muttered, heading toward Holmes's door. I knocked and, receiving no response, opened it. The room stood cold and empty, the bed neat and tidy, unused for the night.

"He appears to have deceived both of us, Mrs. Hudson. I think that he has been out through the night," I said, wondering what fit of work had driven my friend out into the abysmal cold.

I returned to my breakfast as Mrs. Hudson left me. "Tsk, tsk," she muttered on her way out. "Such a careless, wandering man. No good can come of it."

Putting Holmes's absence out of my mind, I lit an after-breakfast bowl of ship's tobacco and settled into my chair with the morning papers. These revealed the usual complaints about Parliament and reports of the empire abroad—the usual muddle of policy and the resistance of native populations. I soon put it aside, lost in a brown study of my own time in Afghanistan, enacting imperial policies as the wild tribesmen fell upon us like mad beasts.

"Better, maybe, to leave them all to their own devices," I said aloud to the empty room, though I knew better than to think that an empire can leave anything well enough alone. I remembered Mary's father and the dreadful cost he had paid for bringing home the foreign horror of the Agra treasure. I prepared a telegram to Mary, arranging dinner that very night, hoping that I would be able to protect her from any future threats.

Then a pounding on the front hall door, like to wake the dead, startled me into action.

I pulled open my desk drawer and retrieved my service revolver, jamming it into the pocket of my dressing gown. Then I heard Mrs. Hudson's stern remonstrances from the door to the street change to shocked cries of concern, then to panicked cries of my name which resounded in the corridor and up the stairs.

Before I could reach the door, it burst open to reveal an alarming sight, one which sparked even more memories of my own time in service. I wondered for a split second if my foul dreams had not been a premonition.

A large, flamboyant figure of a Royal Marine passed into the room, his tunic undone and his helmet gone. He half carried Holmes, one brawny arm around my friend's waist. Holmes's fist clung to the soldier's shoulder as to a lifeline.

Holmes's garments were those of a dockworker, and they had suffered rips and tears which looked fresh. One sleeve of his coat hung to the floor in shreds, as though talons had ripped at it to get to the flesh beneath the disreputable garment. His cap was gone, his hair awry. His face had nasty, bruised swellings, and two savage cuts, one above his right eye and another on his left cheek, had left it a mask of blood. I knew such cuts had been caused by heavy blows, as though Holmes had been in a prizefight and lost. Each was severe enough to require stitches.

Obviously this attack had been brutal and ruthless. I could not imagine what intrigue Holmes had gotten into that had led to such a beating.

"My word, Holmes!" I cried. "What have you been up to?"

But Holmes was in no shape to answer.

The marine with him had close-cropped black hair and a mustache, both within military trim. His strong, lean features bore little evidence that he had taken similar damage as had Holmes, though I noted bruising on his heavy chin. His face showed that he had seen service recently in the tropics, and his wide, dark eyes showed determination. His hands gave evidence that he had conducted himself manfully in the melee, as did Holmes's, whose own formidable hands were crusted with dried blood from battered knuckles.

Mrs. Hudson, ever ready to respond in a crisis, came through the door with a bowl of chipped ice and some tea towels. The marine moved Holmes to the chair beside the fire from which Holmes conducted most of his cases.

"Your consulting detective work has taken a rather grim turn," I said to Holmes under my breath.

"Consultin' detective, is 'e?" the marine said, in cockney tones moderated by long military discipline. "I'd 'ave thought 'e was a middleweight contender, sir, the way 'e used 'is mitts. Most capable man I've ever seen in action, this 'un."

Holmes seemed to recognize that he was home then, for his eyes fluttered open and he said, "Watson. Thank God." Then his eyes closed again, and his head fell back onto the chair.

"Mrs. Hudson," I said, "please apply the ice to the bruises first. We must get that swelling down before I can stitch up those cuts."

"Has someone taken a knife to him, poor dear?" she fretted.

"No knives, but a lead pipe, or maybe a hammer," I said.

I turned to the marine and looked at the chevrons on his bright sleeve. "Sergeant—your name, sir?"

"Oh. Guthrie, sir. Sergeant Magnus Guthrie, sir."

"Excellent man, Guthrie. We owe you a debt of gratitude. Do fetch my medical bag, on the table beside the door, while I wash my hands."

"But it wasn't a knife attack, sir. 'T was all bare knuckle," Guthrie said, snatching hold of my dressing gown sleeve. "No lead pipes or 'ammers, either. Just the fists of some 'alf a dozen men, though they were about the 'ardest lads I've ever seen."

He moved to fulfill my request as I ran to the basin in my room and gave my hands another scrubbing. I wondered for a second why Guthrie had not added the name of his unit and posting to his name and rank, as was customary. Such matters would have to wait, though.

Holmes groaned from his chair and sought to push the ice packs away as he rose to consciousness. "Keep them where they are, Mrs. Hudson," I said, moving to Holmes's side. "And you, sir: kindly desist and let me tend to you."

Ice compounds the pain of swellings, and Holmes came around to restless consciousness as it worked. In moments, he mastered his hands and did not try to push it away, letting his gaze wander to the familiar surroundings of our flat. Mrs. Hudson held the ice in place. I thought of Holmes as the most capable man alive, but I looked upon a man who had returned from the brink of disaster, and it shook me.

"Do I surmise that you are lucky to be alive?" I asked, frightened and agitated by Holmes's condition, probing his battered head with none-too-gentle fingers.

"Yes—Ow! Damn it, man. Be careful," he cried, coming back finally to full volume and attention.

"Ah, grand. 'E's finally comin' around," Guthrie observed, peering over my shoulder. "MacGuire and I got nothin' from 'im at first but an address. We took 'im there, a place near the docks, as soon as we could. We got your name and address from a preacher fella who 'ad the rest of the 'ouse as 'is 'ome and chapel, I reckon.

"So, you are Doctor Watson, then? Might I learn this gentleman's name as well?"

"Yes, certainly," I returned, still looking at the raw edges of the gashes on Holmes's face. I worried about the bones beneath, especially above Holmes's eye. "This pathetic victim is none other than Sherlock Holmes, consulting detective, and I am Dr. John H. Watson, late of Her Majesty's Fifth Northumberland Fusiliers; Captain, though retired."

Guthrie snapped a salute without thinking, and I gave it back in some haste, wishing to know more of what had happened to Holmes. "At ease, Guthrie. Can you tell me where you found him?"

"Yes, sir," Guthrie replied, going into report mode as I stitched Holmes's cuts. "Be'ind a pub in Mitre Square. We—that is, Corporal MacGuire, my mess mate, and I—'ad just nipped be'ind the pub to take a—" He shot a glance at our landlady and chose different words. "To relieve ourselves, sir, when we 'eard the sounds of a struggle. Quite dark it was, and we saw Mr. 'Olmes 'ere as 'e was bein' set upon by some six men. 'E looked like the very picture of old General Gordon surrounded by the 'eathen devils at Khartoum, I'll warrant, but Mr. 'Olmes was fightin' 'em off like mad, sir."

"What the devil were you doing there, Holmes?" I asked, Guthrie's description taking my dark thoughts back to my dream. I shuddered and struggled to compose myself.

"I was in the pub investigating a murder. I sought the secrecy of the alley behind the pub to escape notice," Holmes said, impatience clipping his words. "Oh, never mind numbing the damnable things, just stitch them up, Watson," he growled in surly tones, pushing the ice away. I moved to treat him.

"And you were randomly set upon by six strangers?" I replied, still agitated. "Pull the other leg, Holmes. It's got bells on. You were less careful than you should have been, weren't you?"

Holmes did not reply.

"Do either of you have any idea of the identity of these men?" I asked, thinking that the Metropolitan Police should take note of this incident. Just the sketchiest report of it had set alight my fears, though I suspected this was partly because of my recent nightmare.

Holmes glared at me in silence while I stitched. Clearly he would say nothing more in front of Guthrie or Mrs. Hudson. I turned to the marine.

"Me, sir? I've no idea, but they weren't normal blokes, sir, not just some rowdies from down the pub, sir. Why, they said not a word, sir. Silent as a grave, 'cept for their moanin'. And 'ard, sir, as 'ard as coffin nails them lads were. I saw Mr. 'Olmes 'ere stomp one fella's knee completely backwards, and that cove just kept on comin'. We weighed in on Mr. 'Olmes's side, of course, pullin' them off of 'im. It looked for the world like they were tryin' to get close enough to sink their teeth into 'im, sir.

9

"MacGuire treated one of them blokes to the old Glasgow Kiss, smashed 'is nose flat to 'is face. Now, MacGuire's a big lad, sir, eighteen stone at least, and when 'e 'its a fella, that fella stays 'it. Not that 'un, though. I couldn't believe my eyes. 'E came right back at Mac as though that vicious 'ead butt were a tap, sir. I've never seen the like of lads that could fight on with such damage to 'em."

"But you gave it back to 'em in spades, didn't you, Mr. 'Olmes?" Guthrie went on, proud at having seen my friend in action. "That's why I thought you a pugilist by trade, sir. That, and the way you were dressed."

"Desperation and need, Sergeant Guthrie," Holmes replied. The swelling had reduced around both cuts, enough to let my stitches close the uneven gashes. "But I wonder, sir, if I am not keeping you from your posting. I am most grateful for your assistance in this matter, and I hope to see you rewarded for this action on my behalf. I'm sure that I would not have escaped that alley without you. Where is MacGuire, by the way?"

"Oh, I sent Mac back to the *Icarus*, where we are billeted, sir. I am be'ind my time returnin', sir."

"Watson, we should not keep this man from his duties. Perhaps, when you are finished, I could freshen up a bit, and you could provide him with a brief note to his deck officer, attesting to his assistance. Such a thing might help your return to the—the—"

"The *Icarus,* sir," Guthrie replied. "And thank you both. Cap'n Suffield would 'ave me in irons without it, like enough, though 'e's a fair man. But I'd appreciate the 'elp, seein' as 'ow I missed the launch for returnin' to the ship this mornin'."

I saw that Holmes wished both the marine and Mrs. Hudson gone before he would reveal any further details. My agitation grew then, for if it had been a casual matter, he would have been more forthcoming in his thanks. Whatever had occasioned this dreadful assault, he wished it kept quiet.

"Was there no police involvement at all?" I asked, thinking that keeping quiet would be in no one's interest with a gang of such deadly ruffians wandering London's alleys.

"No, sir," Guthrie replied, "not a Peeler in sight, and that preacher fella said that Mr. 'Olmes would likely not want 'em involved, though I don't know why. That's why I brought 'im straight back 'ere, as soon as I could."

10

"I see," I said, taking in Holmes's steely look, which urged me to caution. "Very well. I'll tend to the note for you while Mr. Holmes cleans himself up a bit, shall I?"

Mrs. Hudson took her cue to leave at a quick glance from my friend, with a shake of her head. "Such a wandering, careless man. No good can come of it," she said, repeating her earlier assertion, for it held even greater meaning in light of Holmes's condition.

***

"Is the *Icarus* at the West India Docks, then?" I asked Guthrie as I stood with him at the outside door, the wintry air blowing around us.

"We came in through the East India Docks, Cap'n, sir, but she's flyin' no flags at present," Guthrie said with a wink, trusting my military background to convey the idea that his ship was not officially in port yet. "She's at anchor in the estuary," he added.

The Royal Marines were often billeted aboard ships bound on sensitive or secret missions in various parts of the realm, moving in to different outposts to quell disturbances or carry out some design ordered by the Admiralty. I would get no more from Guthrie on that subject, but it added to my growing agitation about this business.

"Well, sir," I said, cupping a ten-pound note in the handshake I gave him, "I trust that this will help defray your expenses and serve as a small token of our esteem."

"It isn't necessary, sir."

"Nonsense, Sergeant. You've earned it," I replied.

Behind me, Mrs. Hudson, grumbling about my letting the heat out, bore another breakfast tray and a fresh pot of tea up to the sitting room. Guthrie seemed loath to take his leave.

"Very well, and thank you," he replied, looking at his feet. His dark features clouded over in a deep frown, and he went on, "I just want to say, Cap'n, that them blokes meant to kill Mr. 'Olmes, sir, if I am any judge. I 'ope you will both keep that in mind. As a detective, 'e will want to get to the bottom of it. That could well be a mistake. If you ask me, them lads was waitin' to waylay 'im, sir, and get 'im out of the way. Someone knew 'e would be there, I reckon."

"Thank you, Sergeant," I replied. "I will make sure that he keeps it in mind."

And, with a dark look back at me, Guthrie took his leave, hurrying down Baker Street after a hansom cab that rattled by.

My steps shook as I mounted the stairs back to the sitting room, where I found Holmes clean and dressed in his own clothes again, giving his attention to the hot porridge Mrs. Hudson had brought him. She filled his teacup and buttered toast for him.

"Our patient looks better, at any rate," I said to her. "I'll see to him now, ma'am."

I took a seat opposite Holmes, filling my own teacup.

"Cluck, cluck, mother hens," Holmes muttered in protest, causing our land lady to "tsk, tsk," out the door with a shake of her gray head. When the door closed behind her, I said,

"Mother hens, nothing, my man. You nearly met your death this night. I should think you'd be more grateful."

"Ah, Watson," he replied, "I am grateful, to all of you. I just... well, I don't know what to say about it all."

"Guthrie believes that you were waylaid, and he urges you to drop the matter. I cannot say that I find much fault in that," I said, wondering if the great Sherlock Holmes had gotten himself mixed up in something that was beyond even his capabilities to handle. The story I had heard, though I might have been more alarmed at it because of my dreams, had quite unnerved me, and I told him so.

For once, he did not put off my concern. "I think that he is right, Watson. Somehow, those beastly fellows knew I'd be there. I cannot think otherwise, when I consider the savagery of their attack. I seem to have run afoul of someone's plans, and I was targeted."

"I am quite shaken, Holmes. Can you, will you, not tell me more about this horrid business? Cold-blooded murder in an alley is one thing, but these, these... assassins, quiet, seemingly invulnerable— wishing to tear at you with tooth and nail—do not sound like simple thugs. How did you come to have them on your trail?"

I waited for Holmes's response, but it was slow in coming. He shook his head and gave his attention back to his breakfast, and I thought it good to let him take nourishment.

When he had finished the last cup of Mrs. Hudson's strong buttery tea, he returned to his chair by the fire. I walked to stand next to him. Plucking his old, oily briar from the mantel, Holmes filled it from the Persian slipper in which he kept a supply of Bradley's Black

Shag tobacco, a noxious mixture of perique and dark-fired leaf. I replenished my pipe, too, and waited on him, taking my chair.

"Do you recall the news of a week or so ago, just after Boxing Day? The so-called Fairy Fay incident?" he inquired. I nodded. The respectable papers had not touched it, though Holmes had shown me articles concerning it amongst the rag sheets.

"The vicious murder of a young woman, as I recall," I said. "Some say that no such person ever existed and that the rumor mill merely made up the incident as another way to call attention to the poverty question in the East End." I kept my voice calm, but a connection to another murder served only to stoke my own dark fears.

"Indeed, some have said so, but this murder fascinated me for several reasons that I thought worthwhile to investigate, if only to satisfy my own curiosity," Holmes said, stretching his long legs toward the fire.

"Murder is commonplace among many of our poorer residents in this city, and the law is scarcely aware of it and rarely, if ever, involved. Amongst the gangs of poor, the rag and bone merchants, costers, crossing sweepers, and tumblers, matters of rough justice are meted out on a daily basis. Every cockney lad or lass knows the score and wouldn't 'peach' on a neighbor. No, Scotland Yard has little to no knowledge of what occurs in those dark warrens, and if I had met my end there, they would be hamstrung in their investigations. No one sees anything in the East End, I have found.

"However, my friend, the press is an engine of discernment. True, one must sift its information with care to identify matters of true worth. Yet reports of unexpected murders, especially of innocents in that populace, usually fall outside the bounds of such rough justice, and when they reach the press, they usually have some basis in fact, even if the evidence is hard to come by. The Metropolitan Police, as you know, are Scotland Yard's worst asset where preservation of evidence is concerned; by the time the official investigators arrive, little remains to be seen of the original crime scene."

"Which I assume is the case with Fairy Fay?" I asked, trying to follow the logic of his tale.

"Indeed. It is as bungled as any crime report I have encountered. I dare say that Scotland Yard will disavow any knowledge of it, in time. But you see, the popular account actually suggests two—possibly three—different crime scenes, and no one seems to have actually known the young woman who was murdered. That, in fact, was the chief factor in my desire to look into it."

"And what have you found, having looked into it, other than a sound thrashing?" I joked to cover my uncertainties.

"Ha! Indeed, my efforts have turned up no facts to confirm that there was a local woman murdered not far from Mitre Square, and in simply being there, I put my life in danger unknowingly, collecting only hearsay and the battering you have tended. No one could have experienced greater surprise than I, old fellow. My life would have surely been forfeit if not for the intercession of Her Majesty's forces."

"So you poked about and fell afoul of the 'rough justice' you spoke of, eh, Holmes?" I chided him, thinking the lesson in precaution would do him good.

"Come now, old fellow. You know how cautious I am. And you have the testimony of your own eyes to know that I went there in a safer guise. Gentlemen's attire stands out in that field like a red flag. No, my friend. I was there as a known resident. The tracking of a tiger requires a thorough knowledge of the jungle. You see, in those parts of London I'm known as Bert Tiller, a simple dockworker, emphasis on 'simple.'"

"Ah, yes. Guthrie mentioned taking you back to your flat, I believe. A regrettable necessity," I added, disliking some of the secretiveness of his profession. I mistrusted his ability to mix with the lower classes so freely, and now I had greater reason to.

"My 'bolt holes,' scattered across London, are a necessity in my work, which you will note has kept me out for the bulk of many days. And it is overgenerous to call it a flat. It is a very humble room, I'm afraid, yet one which has had heavy use of late. I rent it from a Methodist minister by the name of Hepplewhite. I have spent the past week or so using that room as a base of operations whilst cultivating Bert's reputation as a good hand on the docks. Bert works a good, hard day for pennies. He is known as a simpleton who is not above buying a pint or two for a friend when the work day is done. Men talk freely around Bert, and he is glad to let them."

"But how do you get the work? Isn't your employer suspicious of any new man?" I asked.

"Dock work is hardly dependable or steady, Watson. New fellows show up daily, especially when a ship or two comes in. They fight like dogs for the meanest jobs. But I have cultivated some help in the matter. Several men in the stevedores' growing union know me—or, rather, they know Bert, and they know that Bert gives good, steady work.

"And Reverend Hepplewhite, for whom I have done a good turn or two in my time, lets me keep a room off of the back of his lodging. Separate entrance, of course. He also helps me with a letter of introduction to any dock area enterprise I might wish to infiltrate, since Bert's powers of speech are rather less than eloquent."

"So you have been working on the docks these past days?" I replied, wondering if his intended murder was a matter of some dark intrigue of the dockworkers' situation, which often erupted in violent clashes.

"Indeed. It is good, honest labor, though often dangerous, especially for those who will not use their heads. Work there keeps me in touch with the toshers, mudlarks, and other young ruffians, who know how to read those streets better than any Scotland Yard bloodhound. Besides, it keeps me fit. I think it would do most men substantial good to work with their backs on a fairly regular basis," Holmes said, with a smile and a nod at my stout form.

"Nonsense. I'm as fit as a fiddle."

"In any case, I worked my plan, affected a blank stare, and put myself in the midst of the people who were most likely to talk about the local goings-on. I was just another pair of hands on the ropes and two willing ears to listen to any tale that came my way. You'd be surprised how freely men will talk around a fellow they see as simple."

With this, Holmes sat up straight in his chair, stretched his neck, and put on such an expression of emptiness that I could scarce believe what I saw. He turned eyes upon me in which the light of his fierce intellect no longer burned. The transformation extended to all his person, as he stood and took shuffling steps across the oriental carpet in my direction. I could imagine him in his heavy jacket and boots, pushing a barrow along the docks or lending a strong hand at a cargo rope. He turned from me and walked to the hearth, whereupon he resumed his typical bearing and stirred the fire, feeding it from the coal scuttle.

"Holmes, I am astounded," I whispered. "I wouldn't have known you."

"Please forgive my bent toward the theatrical, old fellow. An actor who nearly got himself buried in his role, I couldn't help but put on one more performance," he said with a smile.

"I am amazed at your ability," I said. "Were you found out, then? Is that why the ruffians set upon you?"

"Not at all. My identity as Bert Tiller remains secure," Holmes replied, lighting his pipe again.

"But the men with whom you fought," I cried, "how did they come to choose you as their victim? Who, in the business of this Fairy Fay murder, wants to see you eliminated?"

"That, I cannot say," said Holmes. "Those moaning, savage men were as strange to me as the fauna of the Antipodes.

"After I left the pub in Mitre Square, having overheard men discussing the murder as having occurred on a street in Spitalfields, I made my way into the alley behind the pub, seeking to keep my movements secret. The nameless lane I was on was very dark, and these men emerged as one from an equally dark alley and set upon me with such odd, determined ferocity, like predators, that I soon found myself in a fight for my life. You know me as capable of handling myself against two or three men, as long as I can maneuver to set them in one another's ways. But against so many..."

"Yes," I said in a quiet voice. I could tell by his reflective glance that Holmes still bore a sense of surprise, which I seldom saw in him, he who is usually so poised, so ready for any action. How he could remain calm after such an encounter, I did not know.

"There was very little light to speak of in that alley. It was likely only the sounds of my efforts to preserve my skin that drew the attention of those two stout marines. I know that I broke several of my attackers' limbs, Watson. Indeed, as Guthrie reported, I crippled one of them, and I'm sure I fractured at least two men's jaws before my comrades joined the fray. I had no time to marvel that those men kept at me even with broken bones."

"The Assassins of old were said to be able to sustain even serious injuries and keep fighting, through their use of hashish. Viking berserkers of an even older age, too, supposedly fought on with debilitating injuries."

"Indeed. But something else was strange," said Holmes. "My attackers did not speak. They uttered nothing, not a word, only animal grunts of effort and low moans, as they sought my life. Any locals who set upon me would have made their intent clear in boasts or other such remonstrances that would inform me of my crime. These men said not a word. And they possessed a smell of a tannery, a smell like old blood, decaying.

"Yet I have no facts other than the witness of my own senses, and you know that I refuse to speculate with no evidence. I cannot account for what I saw and heard, given what I know to be true. I am merely thankful that those two doughty marines came to my aid.

"And there was yet another odd thing," he added, "which I must investigate."

"You cannot think to return to the investigation, Holmes," I cried out at the idea of another fresh horror in Holmes's encounter. "Someone means to kill you. That much is clear. You cannot possibly think to take up an investigation even Scotland Yard considers unimportant, especially now."

"True enough, old man, but some aspects of the event are of such a singular quality that I cannot just ignore them. I will let the matter rest for a time, as reason and recovery warrant, but I must return to it at some point.

"And there is that added element. You see, an eerie piping from the near distance, faint, tuneless, yet distinctive, seemed to call off those attackers. I heard it just after Sergeant Guthrie and Corporal MacGuire entered the fray," Holmes said, his eyes closed to hold the specific memory in mind. "My attackers left quickly at the sound of those tones, dragging themselves back into the shadows from whence they had come. I believe that those devils would have killed me, Guthrie, and MacGuire, had that eerie tone not called them off. Whoever wishes me out of the way, he is not ready to complicate the matter with the deaths of others just yet."

"And you have no idea who this person is, a person who would set assassins upon you just because you investigate a murder that is not an official police matter?" I replied. His use of the phrase "just yet" implied that someone might yet try to kill him again, and perhaps to kill his associates, of whom I was number one. Again, my nightmare of being overrun by savage foes at Maiwand came to me like a premonition of some worse disaster to come. My reason told me that I would never face such an onslaught again, but Holmes's story suggested otherwise.

"Not as yet, old man," Holmes replied. "Though I have my suspicions, which I will keep to myself, I think, for now." Thereupon he gave his attention to his pipe and to his deep speculation, leaving me to my own.

"Just be sure to stay wakeful today, especially while your head aches," I told him. "I'm sure that you have sustained at least a mild concussion, to say no more about this brush with death."

***

My familiarity with Holmes's methods told me he would not speculate without facts before him to consider. As his closest associate, I was forced to hold further questions, despite my agitation. I knew that, with Holmes, I must be satisfied with the knowledge that all would be revealed soon enough, for if anyone is capable of bringing the light of reason and certainty into the darkness of human criminality, it is Holmes. Thinking back to my soldiering days again, I found another deep and horrible memory stirring in me, a memory which would not abate, though it was slow in rising to my clear recollection. When it did come to me, it was as unwelcome as my nightmares had been and not as easy to escape.

I once had a mess mate in my old regiment, a stout fellow—an amateur pugilist, in fact—who regaled me with stories of his victories. This fellow, one Lieutenant Kerry Barnard of County Cork, had been garrisoned in Jamaica briefly before joining the Berkshire regiment, in India, to which I was attached.

Barnard once spoke of a time when he had run afoul of a witch doctor in a dispute over a local beauty. After besting the fellow with his capable fists, Barnard had sought to return to his barracks, but he had been attacked by a slave of the witch doctor, who set upon him before he reached the garrison and nearly killed him with his bare hands. It was a ghastly encounter, as Barnard related it. His assailant, though not a large man, fought with amazing strength and ferocity, taking punches which would have felled any man.

Remembered, this tale gave me a clue about the nature of Holmes's attackers, who shared so many similarities with the man who had attacked Barnard: nonverbal, preternaturally strong, relentless. And I remembered that Barnard had called his assailant something peculiar. An odd term it was, sounding curiously trivial, like the name of a child's game. A name Barnard learned from native servants in the garrison. A name which sounded so innocent and yet was associated with an inhuman monster.

"Zombie," Barnard whispered, long ago.

I'd thought it a silly name at the time. In fact, I'd thought the entire story silly. I'd called it bosh, ridiculous, that a man could fight on with such damage to his skull as Barnard had inflicted on his attacker. Barnard said it had taken a rifle shot to the head of the zombie to keep it from battering him to death. Barnard feared no man alive, but he feared the memory of that man. His story left me in terror, a terror that rose again in me at the thought of Holmes's attackers. The thought of a foe who is not daunted by anything except the most extreme measure—shooting him in the head—called forth in me an unreasoning panic.

Though the idea of such assailants made me shiver, especially in light of how much damage Holmes had sustained in his brief encounter with the men in the alley, I dismissed it again as ridiculous. We were in London, not some barbaric backwater. In time, I thought, Holmes would find a plausible explanation for the actions and attitudes of his attackers and would come up with a name for the person or persons who wanted him out of the way. At least I hoped he would, for the alternative was horrible.

***

As to the matter of Sergeant Guthrie, our request for an interview with Captain Suffield of the *Icarus* was denied. He would not meet with us, though he thanked us in a brief letter for the good report we had given of Guthrie and MacGuire. Suffield was glad his men had rescued Holmes, but he advised that we would all be well served to forget the incident, especially in light of the Royal Marines' involvement. He closed his response with the idea that, as far as he was concerned, the matter had never occurred.

I wished that we had the power to make it so. Though the adventure of the men in the alley grew quiet in our conversations for a time, I must report that it stayed ever in the back of my mind. I even wired Barnard, having found his current address from another old mess mate, but I received no word back from him.

Holmes surmised, as I had, that the *Icarus* had been on a clandestine mission, and that this was the reason she had come no further into port than the Thames Estuary. Such a practice would have kept her crew's mission status from public record, and Suffield likely wished to keep it that way. We thought it best to take the captain's request to heart, for the good of Guthrie's and MacGuire's future standings. While I disliked the idea of those men not being rewarded for their bravery, I knew well that a soldier's future status depends on the success of his missions and on his officer's good opinion.

Holmes appeared indifferent to the matter, but I had yet to master the fear in me that Holmes's account had evoked. At last, at Holmes's urgings for reasonable restraint, I concurred with my friend. We agreed to let the matter of Guthrie's and MacGuire's rewards rest, though nothing about this incident would rest easy in my mind as long as the name "zombie" stayed with me.

CHAPTER TWO

Soon we had other cases to which we gave our full attention, such as the matter of McParland's misadventures with the Molly Maguires in the American coalfields. It was a devilish affair, one I will call "The Valley of Fear." The investigation of a local murder introduced us to one Professor James Moriarty, a clever and resourceful criminal who remained well-insulated from the charges he ought to have faced. On our own, we lacked the resources to plumb the depths of Moriarty's influence or abilities.

With the McParland adventure behind us, we moved on. As much as I sought to maintain my equanimity, a dark foreboding still accompanied me when I thought of the attack in the alley. I remained fearful of that silly-sounding term, "zombie," when it rose in memory. However, though it was often in my thoughts, I never mentioned the word or the incident to Holmes during this time. I thought that Holmes would deride it as so much superstitious piffle, as I once had.

Holmes said little about his "zombie" attackers—as I always thought of them now—for some time.

Not long after the McParland adventure ended, Mary and I married and moved into a modest home in Paddington to begin our life together. I looked forward to the peace of married life and to building my medical practice, which should have been enough to occupy any man's future.

***

Mary and I set our efforts toward building up the medical practice I had purchased. Mary created a comfortable home for us, and her cheerful demeanor created a wonderful atmosphere for my new patients. The medical community dealt with a measles outbreak at the time, so many of my days were spent with patients in darkened rooms, my hands smelling of carbonate of ammonia. It was tiring work, though easily managed with proper medical care.

Yet, one fine afternoon, I gave over the cab ride back to Paddington in favor of a long stroll through Kensington Gardens. At the beginning of June, the weather had turned cold and rainy. Many of my older patients greeted it as another year without a summer, as they had experienced in their childhoods after the 1815 eruption of Mount Tambora.

This summer, I had been possessed of an especially gloomy spirit, perhaps due to the burden of building up my practice. Mary had commented on it over breakfast, suggesting, rather, that I missed the adventurous life with Holmes. I had denied that as nonsense.

Whatever the cause of my bleak mood, on the day of which I speak, the gloom lifted from me with each step I took. I enjoyed watching swans gliding on the water and listening to the happy cries of children at play on the lawns. Feeling energized, I marched along at a brisk pace. London itself glowed, scrubbed clean by the rains, and the gardens were crowded with her denizens, young and old, seeking the balm of sunshine.

As I approached a stand of spreading oaks through which the footpath ran, I was greeted by a salutation from their shadows that quite caused me to start.

"Cap'n Watson, sir! It canna be," the voice called to me.

I turned and saw the familiar look of tropical fatigues, covering a tall, gaunt form. His cap low, he approached me. For a moment, I believed I looked upon my former orderly, Murray, the man who had carried me to safety after the Battle of Maiwand.

"Good God. Is that Murray?" I cried, delight and surprise giving strength to my voice. He strode toward me, hand outstretched. "I heard from the regiment that you had opened a pub in Edinburgh. What brings you—"

"Sorry to mislead you, old man," said my friend Sherlock Holmes, whose eager face I now saw clearly beneath the slouch cap. He carried a much-abused grip in his left hand. The leather of his cartridge belt was cracked and faded with long wear. His khaki tunic he wore open at the neck, with the tattered remains of decorations over his breast pocket. He wore the look of a down-on-his-luck pensioner, but the bright gleam in his eye revealed my friend Holmes, a sight as welcome to me as Murray would have been.

"Hol—"

Holmes shushed me sharply, then added, "Could ye no' stand an auld soljer a pint, sir?" in a loud voice, for the sake of those who passed around us.

"Er, certainly, Murray, old man," I said. "I believe there's a fine establishment not far from the park that will suit our needs quite well!"

With a tip of his cap and a crooked smile, Holmes strode off with me in the direction of the pub. Once there, I procured two pints of London's finest and joined Holmes, who had retired to a dark corner in the back. When I sat down, Holmes was in more normal clothing and was just folding the old Sam Browne into his valise.

"Are we working a new case, Holmes?" I asked, sliding his pint across the table. "Can you give me the particulars?"

"A mere suspicion, Watson. I keep tabs on a number of criminals through my connections with beggars and street urchins, and I was doing so today. I also wanted to meet you on your return home."

"What? You knew that I would be walking across Kensington Gardens this afternoon?"

"I reasoned that it would likely be so, given the turn of the weather. I called at your practice earlier in my disguise. One or two well-placed questions to your housemaid informed me of your rounds today, though I doubt that she will recall. She suggested that you would return from Kensington before tea. As I had business amongst the beggars who come out on fine days, trusting to the warm sun to increase the mood for charitable giving, I simply placed myself in your path. If you had not come, I would have sent you a letter."

"Do you have an urgent matter at hand?" I asked.

"Not immediately urgent, I think, but it might well touch on that attack I suffered in the Mitre Square alley last January," Holmes replied.

"Have you learned more about your foes? I will certainly come, if I can help you clarify what occurred there," I assured him. "Can you tell me what to expect?"

"More of a related matter, perhaps. I'd rather you judge for yourself. Until tonight, then." He rose and made his way out the rear entrance of the pub, leaving me to my scarcely touched pint and a resurgence of my fears.

"Such is the nature of life with Sherlock Holmes," I muttered, taking up my pint, determined to enjoy it. Sudden meetings, cloaked in mystery and disguise, had been my daily fare when I shared rooms with him. Those occasions had decreased in my married life, of course, but I missed their energy, the urgency of action.

And yet this case seemed different. Those men in the alley, those "zombies," were not merely criminals. I had read that they were occult creatures, dead men who live on in dreadful service to some master of dark magic. I shuddered at having to consider their reality, that they might be abroad still, lurking in dark places, part of some evil plot. I hoped that Holmes's new case would help shed the light of reason on this ghastly business and end my fears.

I drained my pint with a hopeful sense that my fearful response to the men in the alley was at an end. Clearly, as Holmes liked to say, the game was afoot.

***

That night, I took my leave of Mary and told her that I would be back late. I even asked my old friend Dr. Jackson if he could take my calls the following morning, in case the evening's interview necessitated some action in the late hours. Naturally, my revolver went with me.

When I arrived at the appointed hour, I found Holmes already in conversation with two persons who stood upon my entry, casting wary glances in my direction.

"Ah, Watson," Holmes cried, "I'm afraid we have begun without you. Would you allow me to recap our conversation thus far?"

"Certainly, sir, if your guests find it agreeable," I answered, looking at the pair. One was a tall, well-formed, elderly man whose face registered with me in an instant: William Ewart Gladstone, once prime minister of the United Kingdom. I scarcely knew what to do or think at the presence of such an eminent figure in Holmes's sitting room.

Then my eyes fell upon his companion, a young woman near my own height, wearing the uniform of a nurse. Her almost coal-black hair and translucent skin would have garnered any man's immediate attention. However, the icy blue of her wide eyes, which held mine in an open, frank gaze, caused me to stumble. A touch of color rose to her cheeks as I gazed back at her, and she turned her smile away. In that instant, I had forgotten that I was in the presence of a former prime minister.

"If you think it wise, Mr. Holmes, though I would have no one else endangered by our business with you," Gladstone intoned in his sonorous voice.

"Dr. Watson, aside from acting as my Boswell," Holmes returned, pulling up a chair for me, "knows my methods and is the soul of discretion. If your business is as serious as you say, I will have need of his aid."

It was my turn to color at the cheeks. I sat down quickly, trying to keep my gaze from wandering to the strong profile of the woman next to me. Though she bore the signs of having worked the day through, with stained cuffs and a stethoscope hanging from her pocket, her posture showed her supple strength and vitality.

Mr. Gladstone nodded toward me, with a mild scowl. The woman cast a curious glance at me before she said, "If you would choose to act for us in this matter, Mr. Holmes, I cannot think that we would question your choice of associates." The soft Scots burr in her voice caught my attention, as did the voice's tone, surprisingly soft and feminine in one with such obvious strength. I could tell that she sought to correct her Scots pronunciation, with mild success. Its warm tones drew my attention, as I imagined its soothing sound would bring comfort to her patients.

I forced my eyes away from her.

"Watson," Holmes began, "Miss Prescott is a new acquaintance of Mr. Gladstone, whom you no doubt recognize. He is not here as a representative of the state but as a private citizen, acting on behalf of a populace whom he fears has no voice. They have brought to my attention matters occurring in the East End which, they think, have a nefarious air: Men from certain charity wards in Spitalfields and Whitechapel are going missing, some of whom had seemed to be on the mend. One of these men was Tom McHugh, a man of Miss Prescott's acquaintance.

"Mr. Gladstone, as you know, makes a practice of walking the streets of the East End, looking to help members of the poorer classes, especially young women who are in danger of falling into disrepute."

"I merely do what any good Christian man would do, I assure you, Doctor," interjected Mr. Gladstone. "I try to get these unfortunate women into charitable programs wherein they might reform and find a noble profession, such as that of Miss Prescott here—not that she—"

"Indeed, no, sir," said Miss Prescott. "I first came to London to find my sister Katie Rose—Kathleen, I mean to say—who had turned to a life such as Mr. Gladstone has described, after the man she had taken up with cast her aside. He later had her arrested as a woman of the streets."

Another blush rose up in Miss Prescott's cheeks. Whether it was caused by anger or by embarrassment, I found it endearing, though I knew I should not.

"And have you found her, Miss Prescott?" I asked.

"No, sir. That I have not," she murmured. "I fear she must have met with foul play. I have asked after her at Cwmdonkin Shelter, Urania Cottage, and Magdalen Hospital so often that each has offered me a nursing position."

"And have you taken any of those positions, Miss Prescott?" I asked, desiring to hear her voice more.

"No, sir, not as yet. You see, the pay at my present billet is better, although Dr. LaLaurie has us work such long hours that I scarcely have time to look for Kathleen anymore. It was only God's hand that brought me to Mr. Gladstone's timely attention and rescue."

"Indeed," the Grand Old Man exclaimed, "if I hadn't liberated Miss Prescott from the clutches of those ruffians, I fear they'd have taken advantage of her, if you take my meaning, despite her being obviously in the garb of her noble profession. Why, Florence Nightingale herself would not be safe from such wanton advances. I tell you, the young men of this city, nay, of this country, have fallen into a moral laxity, which—"

"Yes, Mr. Gladstone, we all acknowledge the depravity of the age," Holmes interjected, stopping the orator.

Gladstone scowled and muttered, "Yes. And so, on with this business."

"Miss Prescott," Holmes asked, turning his attention to her, "is your sister's middle name Rose?"

"Ah, no, sir. It's only we call her that because of a rose-colored birthmark on her right arm," she said.

"Thank you," Holmes replied. "Now, if you would be so kind as to tell us of Mr. McHugh's disappearance."

As she began, Holmes closed his eyes and tented his fingers before his face, leaning back into his chair, an attitude of intense listening that I had seen numerous times in our short history together. He heard more in one sentence than I could glean from a whole speech. My fervent hope was that he could help Miss Prescott, for my heart went out to her for her earnest sincerity as well as her beauty.

"Tom, with whom I walked out when we were younger, wrote to me when I first came searching for my sister," Miss Prescott said. "He was apprenticed to a dairyman on Commercial Street, in Whitechapel. We had made plans to be married this year. But as so often happens, he lost his position, for that cruel dairyman found he could do better hiring children whom he could abuse rather than a man who wished to learn the business. So Tom took to the docks, finding work whenever he could.

"Then he came down with a case of influenza, and I arranged for him to get treatment at Dr. LaLaurie's clinic, just to keep him out of the workhouse hospital. The doctor assured me that Tom was responding quite well, as he was a strong young man. The last time I saw Tom, Mr. Holmes, was the very night before he was to be released from care. We both thought it was a new beginning for us. We even hoped that we would find Katie soon.

"But when I came back the next day, he was gone. When I questioned Dr. LaLaurie, he said that he had released him shortly after I'd left, the night before. 'Did he not seek you out?' the doctor asked. 'No,' I replied, 'nor did he have anywhere to go.'"

"'Like as not, m'dear,' he said, 'he went where many young men will when they are at liberty. If he does not seek you out after a while, you'd be best served by forgetting you know him.'"

"But, Mr. Holmes, I know Tom McHugh," Miss Prescott said in earnest tones. "I cannot think that he would abandon me the way that army officer abandoned my sister. And I don't believe he can have come to harm through drunkenness, for he was not a man given to drink, beyond having a pint with his mates now and then.

"What's more, many of my fellow nurses have reported similar sorts of departures from our hospital and others in the East End. I was shocked to discover this happening to others, and not just my poor Tom, with no notice to the authorities! When I raised the issue with my employer, Dr. LaLaurie treated my concern prettily but informed me that such disappearances were common. Many men go directly to the workhouses by their own choice, he said. But I knew of no such plans from my Tom."

"And you haven't seen him for how long?" Holmes queried, his eyes still closed.

"A month at least, sir. And none of our people in Glasgow have had word from him, according to a recent letter from one of my cousins," she said, hugging herself tight across her slender waist. She regarded Holmes with a fierce look as he stayed relaxed behind his tented hands.

"Can you, will you look into the matter, sir?" she pleaded. Her voice, earnest and full of hope, would have drawn lost souls across the abyss, I thought. Gladstone's wide forehead creased in a frown as he looked on.

"Certainly, certainly," Holmes said, springing upright and seeking the eyes of each of our guests. He took two quick strides to the mantel to retrieve his black clay pipe and the slipper of shag, then turned to regard us all as he filled the pipe.

"The case has intriguing possibilities. However..."

"I assure you, sir, that if you are about to refuse because of Miss Prescott's reduced financial situation," Mr. Gladstone exclaimed, rising to his feet, "you know that I have considerable resources to put at your disposal. We cannot countenance such crime—"

Holmes held up his hands.

"I would take the case without thought of remuneration," he said. "I would appreciate some avenues of your support as well, Mr. Gladstone, though I acknowledge that this is not an investigation sanctioned by Parliament or on behalf of the Crown. You and your associates are only involved because of Miss Prescott's needs, yes?" Holmes added with raised eyebrows. I gathered that his question had a hidden part to which Miss Prescott and I were not party.

"Yes, Mr. Holmes. This does not involve our mutual friends," the old man replied, adding, sotto voce, "yet."

"Indeed, your efforts on behalf of our less fortunate citizens are well known," Holmes said, moving to place his long hand on the old man's shoulder.

"I was about to say," continued Holmes, "that I cannot hold out much hope for the fortunate return of Mr. McHugh, nor of your sister, Miss Prescott. I'm sorry to put it to you this way, but I think that you would be well served to consider the need to grieve your losses. It would be unkind of me to hold out false hope. I am sorry."

She bore the news like a soldier, I thought, with a quick nod of her head and hands clasped, though Holmes had obviously shocked her with his sudden claim. Surely Miss Prescott must have considered her fiancé lost to her before she had sought our help, but, like all of Holmes's clients, she had visited him with high hopes. Tears formed along her lower eyelids. I would have gone to any lengths to stop them, had it been in my power. She brushed them away.

"Can justice be done for them, then?" she pleaded in strained tones.

"That, indeed, will be my concern, dear lady," Holmes offered in a solemn voice. "And now, Mr. Gladstone, if you would be so good as to convey this lady safely to her lodgings, I will be in touch. I trust that a telegram will bring you to our need?"

"Indeed, sir, you may contact me through our usual channels," Gladstone replied. "Whatever you need, please do not hesitate to call upon me."

Miss Prescott rose along with Gladstone, and I escorted them to the door. "Whatever Holmes says," I said to her, "you should consider, but even Holmes does not know all outcomes. Things may yet come to light. I have seen him do wonders."

She turned a sober glance to me. "I thank you for your kind words and your support, Doctor. It means a great deal to me to have men of such caliber acting on my behalf."

***

When the outer door closed on our visitors, Holmes was already drawing deeply on his pipe, sending up a brown cloud, which hung in the air above his head.

"Could you give her no hope?" I asked, waving the haze away.

29

"It is not my position to give hope, Watson, only a clear understanding about the dark deeds which occupy criminal minds. I leave hope to you—and, of course, to Providence."

"And what of the men in the alley?" I asked. "How does this concern them?"

"If I am correct, they, or some like them, killed Mr. McHugh and may also have killed Miss Prescott's sister," Holmes replied gravely.

"Now, please leave me to smoke on it for a time," he added, dismissing me with a wave of his hand. "However, I think you had better see if you can find a heavier caliber of revolver for our next meeting, that or a kukri knife such as the Gurkha were wont to use in the Indian Army."

I started to protest at his outlandish suggestions, not knowing what to make of them, but I saw that he had spoken in all seriousness, and my dark fears returned. Holmes piled his black shag on the table next to him and made ready to concentrate. With his pipe alight and the haze forming around him, I saw that he was already lost to any human contact. I retired and made my way home early, troubled at heart.

***

When I walked into my study, I found Mary waiting for me at my desk, reading Wilkie Collins.

"My dear," I said, "this is an oddity. How often do you sit up at night in my office reading?"

She smiled and lay the book aside. She was dressed for bed and had donned my heavy dressing gown as protection against the chilly night air. With her hair down, dressed as she was, she had the appearance of a young girl wearing her father's clothes.

"I was just missing you," she said, rising to embrace me. "You have discovered my secret. When you are away late, I often do this. You caught me at it, for you are early in your return."

"My dearest angel," I said, kissing her forehead, "I didn't dream that my absence would grieve you so. I must make it a point to refuse Holmes's requests."

Mary broke away from my embrace and held me at arm's length, her bright eyes wide with alarm. "You will do no such thing," she replied. "Holmes needs you, John, and when he needs you, England needs you. I knew this when I accepted your proposal of marriage. Do not take away my fancy that I am married to a heroic knight errant. My only regret is that I can offer so little help."

"Nonsense!" I protested. "You are ever at my side."

And I embraced her again. In my heart, however, I knew that she was in the right. I had to hold her fragile body with care; too strong an embrace and she would take injury. For a moment, I imagined what Miss Prescott's strong body would feel like in my arms.

"In your heart, yes," she assured me. "However, when you are away with him, confronting evil, the only way I can feel close to you is to sit in your office, wear your dressing gown, and read a mystery. And pray for both of you. Someone must."

"Thank you, my love," I said. My tone was grave. My mood had been dark when I returned from Baker Street, but my guilty conscience over my thoughts of Anne Prescott had made it worse. Mary's words heaped coals of fire upon my head.

"Clearly, I am not deserving of the love of such a woman as you," I said.

"You might be, if you will excuse my habit," she whispered.

"Your habit?" I echoed. A sudden wondering at what dark secret she might have hidden from me sparked through my mind.

"Yes. I'm afraid that I will also hold one of your pipes while I sit and read, just to have the scent of you around me."

I laughed at the thought of her doing so, again so childlike and trusting, and asked with mock sternness, "And whatever am I to do with you?"

"Just come home, John. Please, no matter where you go or what you do—what you have to do—just promise me that you will do your best for Holmes and then come home," she pleaded, looking into my eyes.

"Yes, I will. I promise," I said, hoping that I would always be able to keep that promise.

CHAPTER THREE

As the hansom cab bounced over the rough cobbles of Commercial Street, Holmes broke his silence about Anne Prescott's case. I had pestered him with questions upon my arrival, but Holmes had put me off with his warning that he needed facts to work with before he could draw any meaningful conclusions about the case. I had, only that morning, on Holmes's recommendation, procured a Webley & Scott revolver, which chambered a .476/.455 round and featured a five-inch barrel. It was too large for a pocket, so I carried it under my light jacket in a shoulder harness, which chafed my underarm and side.

"I trust, Watson, that the chafing will be worth it, if that Webley of yours has more stopping power than your old bullpup," he said, as I twitched my shoulders to settle the straps into a more comfortable position.

"I am assured that this weapon will stop anything that goes on two legs and most things under pachyderm size that go on four," I replied. "I just cannot think of a need for such firepower in London. Would I not be better off to be armed with a Martini rifle than a revolver?"

"Not if I am right in my conjecture, old fellow," Holmes said, his eyes glinting in the dim cab. "I think, if combat ensues, you will be too close for rifle work."

"But will you tell me no more? I deduce that we are heading back to the area where you were beset by those ruffians from whom the Royal Marines rescued you." My memory of Lieutenant Barnard's story stirred dark and foreboding.

"Very good, Watson. I'm gratified that my methods of observation are becoming your habits as well. You have a marvelous adaptive facility, my friend."

"But, like you, I require facts, do I not?" I said, desiring something sensible to remove Barnard's story from my imagination. Holmes nodded, as though to remind himself that I could be trusted to hear his conclusions, however incomplete they were at present.

"Thus far, Watson," he said with a sigh, "I have only the most tenuous threads in my grasp. But tell me, do you have any knowledge of voodoo and its practices?"

"Little, but enough," I whispered, knowing at that moment that my intuition was right. A shiver ran through me. "So I think that I can put a name to a horror, perhaps the same that set upon you in that alley. Holmes, I have seen fascinating feats—men lying on beds of nails with no harm to their skin, others climbing ropes which rose into the air like charmed cobras from a wicker prison—all explained as magic and performed by swamis and fakirs in the bazaars of Calcutta and Delhi. Those I came to see as tricks, sleight of hand, nothing more. But since winter, I have thought about those men who attacked you, and I believe I have a name for them."

"I am intrigued. Would you share your conclusions with me? I might yet be able to corroborate them," he said.

"As I recall from a fellow I knew in the army," I replied, "that word is—and I beg you to avoid laughing at me as I say it—'zombie.'"

Holmes's eyes grew wide, and though he smiled, he did not laugh. "Watson, you have outdone yourself! I am amazed. Pray, tell me how you came upon this curious but most apt name."

I sketched out Barnard's story in a quick, clear account, to which Holmes nodded and listened with eyes closed, as though he recalled his own experience alongside Barnard's harrowing tale.

"This is marvelous, Watson!" he cried. "If any man maligns you as merely my Boswell, I shall knock him down for the insult." He offered me his hand and shook mine in earnest vigor. "You are quite right, and I hope that you will not let the quaintness of that name deter you from appreciating the worth of your speculations, for though you might think that you lack a factual basis on which to speak, I remind you of your own reliable witness to the event."

I was so gratified at Holmes's support that it put away from me, for a moment, the horror of the subject, and I was silent.

"As to that term, 'zombie,'" he continued, treating me as a favored pupil, "it is perhaps a compound word from several terms in

33

West African Kikongo: their words for a god and a magical charm, 'nzambi' and 'zumbi.' It concerns the practice of reanimating the dead for the purpose of enslaving them. I do not think that any mesmerism could work so on an unwilling subject; I fancy it works by dint of pharmacology, some concoctions of intoxicating plants and herbs known through native practice and ritual. Or so it would seem to a rational mind. After all, a shaman's knowledge of the plant and herb extracts with which he works comes from a dark history, thousands of years old, of patient trial-and-effect research. Our Western science cannot know all the properties of the local flora."

"I cannot conceive, though, of any natural compound that could bring the dead back to life," I returned. "Nothing apart from sheer alchemy, I should think, could explain it. It is preposterous to the scientific mind."

"Not, perhaps, to scientific minds of a certain bent," Holmes said.

Then he changed tack. "Watson, I must ask something more. Does the name LaLaurie have any meaning for you?"

"Miss Prescott mentioned that he is the physician for whom she works. Other than that..." I searched my memory. "No. I have no other recollection of it. Do you mean to suggest that someone of that name has attempted such arcane practices as Miss Mary Shelley described in *Frankenstein*? That is madness."

"Not in the manner of Shelley's stick-at-naught physician, but LaLaurie is a name of infamy in the American South, Watson, particularly in the voodoo-haunted streets of New Orleans," Holmes claimed in low, dark tones. "A physician called Louis LaLaurie and his wife Marie Delphine LaLaurie, several decades ago, were an affluent couple, the toast of New Orleans society. The lives of their servants, though, were horrific beyond description. After widespread reports of the atrocities the couple visited on their slaves, their neighbors rose in revolt against them. But those neighbors only knew a part of the terrible truth. Louis LaLaurie's vile surgical practices were only an adjunct to Delphine LaLaurie's voodoo rituals, through which she tortured her servants and manipulated her friends.

"Of the slaves who survived to tell their tales, and from the accounts of the neighbors who were present in the aftermath, it was learned that many of the LaLauries' slaves had been surgically mutilated and maintained in putrefying conditions, seemingly to see how long they could survive. Flayings and eviscerations, as well as voodoo rituals such as zombification—if I might coin a term—were their common lot. One woman in particular had been made to move about on all fours like a spider, her bones broken and reset in a horrid mockery of that creature.

"Some of Madame LaLaurie's enemies, after witnessing these horrors, took action to make them known. As a consequence, outraged vigilantes burned the LaLaurie home to the ground. What became of the couple and of their offspring is not known, though it is believed that they escaped to France, from which Louis had emigrated."

"How deplorable! What a ghastly inheritance in that name! And you tell me that the authorities did nothing to punish them?"

"Their society languished in the grip of slavery, Watson. Slaves were personal property; they had no rights under the law. Thus, the law could do little or nothing to the deplorable LaLauries. It was a grave societal injustice. The vigilantes tried to enforce a punishment, but the LaLauries and their children escaped. I had not heard they had a male child."

"The horrors of medical mutilation are bad enough," I cried, disgusted that a man trained in medicine could be so depraved in his quest for knowledge that he would break the first law of medicine: do no harm. "But it was Madame LaLaurie who brought the dark arts into it, yes?"

"It is a matter of historical record that the beautiful Madame Marie Delphine LaLaurie, known to her intimates as Delphine, was the real power in that couple. Having been married to wealthy men at least twice before and enjoying her inherited riches, she used occult and economic power to control public opinion. In Louis LaLaurie, she seems to have met her dark soulmate. Her husband's practices might have been equally cruel, to the point of calling them human vivisection, but her occult practices were more matters of magical compulsions. For instance, she bound her servants to her so unnaturally that some killed themselves for having displeased Delphine. And we know she was the source of these practices, because some of her personal journals survived the fire, and there one comes across the term 'zonbi' or 'zombi.'"

"But why, Holmes," I cried, my mind rebelling against such barbarities, "would a powerful couple stoop to such... such indecencies?"

"Why, indeed," Holmes replied, "would any man subject his fellow creatures to any criminal conduct, any wrong, be it as simple as armed robbery? To fill his needs. Needs for power, control, domination. The human soul is a dark labyrinth, Watson. It is up to just men to stop such things. I follow the LaLaurie name with some energy in that cause," he added in steely tones.

"Suffice it to say that the LaLaurie name stands for an unspeakable sort of slavery, a complete enthralling of a human's mind, removing his will, making him dead to all human faculties. Do not the disappearances our client has asked us to investigate speak of something similar? And so, the history of that evil name and the nature of our client's request are the reasons why we are going to pay a visit to Dr. LaLaurie. I hope to ascertain if any connection can be made between him and that nefarious family."

As I contemplated the idea that a mentally and spiritually twisted physician had undertaken the business of making London's poor into zombies, I found myself arrested by a sense of how ridiculous it would sound if reported in one of London's better papers. We would certainly be laughed out of countenance if we took this matter to the Metropolitan Police. The nightmarish fear of the undead, however, seemed very real to me at that moment.

"This will do, driver!" Holmes called out. He sprang from the cab, holding the door open for me, as though this night's work were just another investigation of a common criminal. If Miss Prescott's employer had any connection to the LaLaurie story which Holmes had just repeated, however, we would be seeking out a diabolical madman. For a moment, I was frozen by dread, and the cascade of degenerate images he had set free in my overactive imagination took my breath.

"Watson? Will you be joining me?" he called back into the cab, and I realized I would have to force myself to step into this great task.

"Yes. Certainly. Coming, Holmes."

He tossed our fare to the driver and tugged my arm to hurry me along. "I appear to have given you rather a nasty setback, old boy," he said.

After a few steps, I apologized for my seeming reticence.

"No need. No need," he replied. "It is a shocking business, but it is a first-rate case, don't you think?"

"What?" I shot back, startled by a fit of coughing that broke out from what I had taken to be a pile of sodden rags in a doorway. I began to look about me with greater care, seeing a few feeble lights flickering in filthy windows and observing huddled figures who rose in doorways and fled at our approach. We walked along a narrow passage through a squalid street as a thin rain dampened our hats and macintoshes. Smudges of low-hanging smoke from cooking fires threatened to choke me. I heard muffled voices, raised in anger or savage joy, I could not tell which. Hell, I imagined, would look and sound something like this.

"I think it is a wretched business, at best, Holmes," I said at last, "especially since we begin with two missing persons whom you see as already lost. And, now that it comes down to it, I am distracted by my own fears, especially if we are going to confront a physician in a charitable hospital about a diabolical voodoo practice and cold-blooded murder."

"I realize that, from the outside, our search tonight may appear desperate and nonsensical," replied Holmes. "But I fear that these zombie appearances will yet claim a higher toll in human lives, and if so, I cannot—will not—stand idly by. Furthermore, I am compelled to find out whether my suspicions are correct regarding Dr. LaLaurie's parentage. However revolting their actions, the story of the LaLauries is a fascinating one."

I strode along at Holmes's side, wondering how our client would greet our supernatural speculations.

"Can you truly offer Miss Prescott no hope about Mr. McHugh?" I asked after a moment had passed.

"I think not. If an honest man disappears through the agency of nefarious persons, and a month or more has gone by with no word from him, I must presume that his life is forfeit. Even the naval press gangs of the previous century left better word than that following Mr. McHugh. As for Miss Prescott's sister, the night that I was beset in that alley, I heard two loungers in a pub swear that the 'Fairy Fay' victim had a pretty little rose-colored birthmark on her arm. Hearsay is not fact and coincidence is not causality, but such facts as we have in the Fairy Fay case and McHugh's disappearance give rise to strong suspicion which warrants investigation. I'm sorry that I cannot be clearer."

"I would rather trust to your guesswork than anyone's," I said with a grudging nod, "and I'm sure Miss Prescott will benefit from it. As to this Dr. LaLaurie, Holmes, though what we have discussed fills me with doubt and dread, rest assured that I will aid you in any way I can." I was determined to see the matter through, for his sake... and for hers.

"I work with patterns of behavior, Watson. I don't need to consider what LaLaurie thinks or believes he is doing. It is a cardinal error to believe I can know the thoughts or beliefs of a man. I only need to predict with reasonable accuracy what he will do. And I have the proof of my senses to inform my speculation.

"I think I can say that my attackers in the alley behind Mitre Square were almost certainly zombies, or men who were given to think that they were. This line of thinking you have corroborated with the story of Lieutenant Barnard's exploits. Patterns of behavior, Watson. Those I must pursue, and zombies in London speak to me of a terrible pattern behind which we must find the hand of the evil master."

"However reluctantly, I must agree," I admitted. "Zombies, then. So it is a good thing, my purchase of this cannon under my arm." In fact, I wondered if even the Webley & Scott would be any use against such creatures.

Holmes nodded his head and pulled a kukri knife from a scabbard slung beneath his Mackintosh. "Preparation, Watson. We have no substitute for it. And if it comes to it, I think the only way of truly stopping a zombie, or a man who believes himself to be one, is to separate this"—he tapped my bowler with the awful blade—"from this," he continued, lowering the blade to rest it on my shoulder. The kukri knife had a ghastly weight I remembered well from my service in India. I knew such a knife could take the head off a man in one stroke.

Holmes put the blade away as we entered a pool of light in front of a crumbling brick edifice. We stopped there for a moment, inspecting the building's newly painted sign, which read "St. Lazarus Infirmary." I shivered at the thought that someone who worked in that building—who might be there at this moment—might be able to raise a man from the dead.

CHAPTER FOUR

"I suggest that we introduce ourselves as Miss Prescott's relations, uncles, or cousins, perhaps," Holmes whispered. "In such a way, we may find it easier to gain an audience with her employer."

We entered the front door and found a clean, spacious triage. Miss Prescott was there, wrapping in gauze the hand of an elderly man.

Her eyes went wide as she saw us enter. Holmes swept around the chairs and across the room to take her hands in his with a merry greeting.

"Ah, dear cousin Anne," he cried, twirling her around once and eliciting from her a sudden, lighthearted laugh. "Surely you know us? It is Cousin Jack"—gesturing to me—"and me, Oscar."

"Oh, my," she chuckled, a happy smile transforming her handsome features into rare beauty. She fussed with her hair, knocked loose by Holmes's embrace, as I strode up to her and also embraced her in a familial hug. I heard her swift intake of breath, and she withdrew from the embrace, blushing.

Besides the elderly man, there were two women in the triage area. All three persons looked up at us quizzically as we greeted one another.

."I hardly know what to say," said Miss Prescott, her trembling hand still on my arm. "I had not expected to see you again so soon."

I sometimes forget that Holmes has a past on the stage. In this instance, gratitude filled me for his improvisational talents. I knew that any success I could contribute would hinge upon keeping my mouth shut as firmly as I could.

"We were told by Great-Aunt Kate that you were here, and with the opening of our new warehouse on the West India Docks, we could

39

not resist paying you a visit," Holmes said. "We will only be here a day or so, and then it's back to Liverpool."

"And you are certainly welcome," said she, picking up the thread of story which Holmes had given her. "Pray, give me a moment to finish Mr. Coles's dressing, and I will give you a better welcome."

We stood back as she taped the gauze into place and gave instructions to Mr. Coles to keep his hand clean and, if at all possible, avoid using it for a day or so. The older woman at Mr. Coles's side had a dull-eyed, detached manner, as though she suffered from excessive drink. The younger woman, red-headed, more animated, reacted to Anne's suggestion.

"He can get no work, then?" she cried. When she spoke, I smelled alcohol on her breath. "We can't make it on what I brings in alone, can we?" Her face flushed with anger. "He's my old dad, true, but he needs to be able to turn out or he'll end up in the workhouse."

"Yes, Miss Coles," Anne replied to the younger woman, "but the wound needs time to mend before he puts it to use, if only for a few days. Perhaps, Frances, if you and Emma—"

"Emma Smith is just as useless as he is," Frances Coles exclaimed, "since you lot have been treating her. Without the few pennies Dad brings in, we're all bound for the workhouse, and do you care? Can you get him work?"

"You are a cobbler, I believe, sir," Holmes interrupted, drawing out his pocket notebook and jotting down an address.

"T-True," the old man said, his eyes widening. "But how did you know that?"

"A lucky guess," my friend replied, handing the fellow the slip of paper, "based on that stitching awl you have in your vest pocket. If you will go to this address in two days' time and inquire after Milton Weisskopf, you might have a chance to put that awl to good use. And this," he said in a lower voice, handing Mr. Coles a sovereign, "will keep you and your daughter in victuals until then."

His daughter heaved a sigh of relief but turned her eyes away from us. She placed her hands around the old man's shoulders and pulled him to his feet, making for the door. Emma Smith rose and followed after them as though tethered to them, her feet dragging over the threshold.

Watching Frances Coles as she departed, I thought she had likely been an attractive woman a few years ago, before hard drink and harder work had brought her to desperation. Today, though, desperation seemed to be at her very core. I wondered if she would take Holmes's money and leave the other two to fend for themselves.

Miss Prescott watched the trio leave with troubled eyes and a sad shake of her head. I could not read her thoughts, but I recognized her awareness that people like the Coles and Emma Smith faced a desperate reality, one which Kathleen Prescott had also known before she had disappeared.

After a second or two of worried silence, Miss Prescott turned to Holmes and said, "I didn't even see the stitching awl, Mr. Holmes."

"Nor did I," I said. "The man's coat was closed."

"Your observational skills are improving," Holmes replied, turning his bright gaze upon me. "I saw no such awl, either, but I inferred its presence. The particular callus patterns on the man's right hand, the many injuries to his left, and the discoloration of his trouser legs all speak of a man accustomed to repairing shoes. I counted on the tools of his trade still being on his person, especially a tool that could have made that laceration between his thumb and index finger. Simple observation."

"Now, Miss Prescott," he continued, "would you consent to show us the establishment and, if possible, give us an opportunity to meet your employer, Dr. LaLaurie? And do, pray, remember that we are your cousins."

Anne nodded and showed us around the triage area, with its desk and patients' chairs, two narrow beds, and stock of first aid supplies on shelves behind the formal entry point. I remarked on the room's cleanliness.

"Yes," Anne replied, "Dr. LaLaurie insists that the place be kept immaculate. Any patient who stays with us, we move to the floors above, by this," she said, showing us double doors obviously set recently into the brick of the back wall, the new casements in place and painted. The rough wood of the doors, despite the coat of white paint, suggested a recent, hasty addition to the old building.

Holmes pulled open the doors to reveal the empty lift shaft. Off to the side of the shaft, a set of ropes revealed the means by which the lift could be operated.

"Do you operate this lift, my dear?" Holmes asked.

"Oh, no, sir, though I've thought I am strong enough to do so. But the doctor insists that it would be too hard on a nurse's hands, so he employs his man to do the job." Her face darkened at the mention of this man, I noted.

"Are there doors similar to this one on the lower level, Anne?" Holmes asked quietly as he kneeled near the opening to the lift shaft, leaning forward in a precarious way.

"We do not go down there," Anne whispered. "Dr. LaLaurie says that we should remain on this floor and the two above, so that we do not carry contamination. Fumes from the sewers sometimes rise up into the cellar, he claims, and he fears that we might bear on us something to harm his patients. Why?"

Holmes motioned for me to lean over the edge with him. "Do you smell it, Watson?" he whispered. As I bent down beside him, my head in the dark, the pungent scent of the sewers did come to me through the door on the cellar level, along with a smell like that of a tannery and an odd, pungent scent, for all the world like the smell from within a workingman's boot. I pulled my head back, wrinkling my nose.

"What is that other smell, besides the sewer?" I whispered.

"I am almost certain that it is jimsonweed, the Devil's Trumpet," he said. Then he backed away from the shaft quickly as the sound of the lift platform descending came from several floors above us. "I will explain later."

I knew well enough that jimsonweed was a member of the deadly nightshade family. Medical literature identified it as able to induce hallucinations or euphoria if eaten. In India, I had run across native shamans who used it to induce trance states, and I knew that it could be lethal if taken in large enough amounts. I knew it grew native in Britain, where it was regularly removed from gardens, but I had never encountered in Britain a variety that had such a powerful odor.

Still, I waited for Holmes's explanation, trying to remember that I was "Cousin Jack" as the lift descended toward us with a creaking of ropes and grinding of pulleys. Soon the platform came within view, lit within by candles. We all stepped back as it came into view, showing us first the feet of two men, one in well-shined shoes and pressed trousers and the other in heavy work boots of enormous size.

The men were revealed to us slowly. As he saw us, the doctor, his profession obvious from his attire and the stethoscope draped around his neck, smiled in greeting. Slightly below the common height, Dr. LaLaurie had a fresh, angular face with keen, close-set eyes. His blond hair was well cut, and he held his trim body straight.

His companion was his antithesis: a black man who looked like a giant who had been crushed. With its deep widow's peak in close-cropped hair, his head stood lower than the doctor's, but if his stooped figure were to stand straight, I could tell he would reach well over six feet in height. His hands, which hauled the lift rope, were twice the width and length of mine, and the muscles of his powerful arms, coiling and elongating like serpents, strained the fabric of his shirt to the breaking point. Though his bent back looked for the world like the result of a disabling injury, I surmised that his strength was titanic.

My thoughts ran back to the unnecessary surgeries that Louis LaLaurie had performed on his slaves.

When the platform came level with the floor, the black man threw a lever at his side, locking the lift into place.

"Ah, we have guests!" the doctor cried, in a soft French accent and with a brittle smile. "Dear Miss Prescott, won't you introduce me to these men? Oh, thank you, Alcee," he added, turning to the black man. "You may take the lift back up to my quarters and prepare for me my bath."

As the doctor closed the doors behind him, Alcee nodded and set a hand to the rope, though he lingered, his large brown eyes studying Anne Prescott.

"Dr. LaLaurie," Anne said, sketching a quick curtsy to him, "these are my cousins, Jack and Oscar, just in from Liverpool." She looked at Holmes in a sudden panic, having found little else to say and likely forgetting which of us was Jack and which was Oscar.

Alcee's muscles bunched as he began to raise the lift.

"Oscar Newton," Holmes said, extending his hand to the doctor, who bowed to him but did not take his hand. "And this is Jack Dodge, my relation and business associate." In turning to wave in my direction, Holmes let his bowler hat slip from his hand, and it landed within the slowly-rising lift. Alcee held the lift in place with one hand, scooped up Holmes's hat in the other, and offered it back to him.

"Oh! How terribly clumsy of me," Holmes cried. "I thank you, sir." Dr. LaLaurie moved with care out of Holmes's way.

I knew that the preternaturally graceful Holmes had merely pretended to drop his hat. He had some reason for his seeming clumsiness, likely to see which hand Alcee used, or something of the kind.

"Please forgive my not taking your hand, sir," the doctor said. "My specialty in medicine is infectious disease. And so I have given over the custom of exchanging grips. Particularly at a time like this, when I have just come from a patient's side. But I am delighted to make your acquaintance. Miss Prescott, I did not know that you have family."

"Quite all right, sir. But to be fair, sir," Holmes-Oscar said, "We are distant cousins of Miss Prescott, not immediate kin. But we knew that she had come to London and were compelled to seek her out, though we will not be in London long, just now. We have bought into a shipping concern out of Liverpool and are only here for a brief visit to see to our local interests on the West India Docks. We are greatly attached to our great-aunt Kate, who desired us to seek after the welfare of Anne and to inquire after Anne's sister, our aunt's namesake, if we can."

"So busy are we," Dr. LaLaurie said, strolling to the desk, "that I had forgotten the reason for Anne's relocation to London. Her services to me are indispensable, but I fear that I have kept her from her objective. You should be proud, though, of the work your cousin does here."

"Oh, we are," I said. "We will convey that to all her family."

"Miss Prescott," Dr. LaLaurie said, turning to her, "I recall now that you claimed to have no family."

I cast a quick glimpse at Holmes, worried that Dr. LaLaurie would sniff out our little pantomime and perhaps take actions against our client. She managed well, though.

"Nor do I, except for my sister. My parents and their parents died long ago," she said. I reasoned this was the truth.

"Yes, we are all scattered to a variety of concerns, and truly, Great-Aunt Kate is the last of her generation, which is why she sought for news of Anne and Kathleen," Holmes said, employing his best Oscar joviality. "But tell me, sir, about the treatments you use here. Do you import your medical supplies or use those of a local— homegrown, so to speak—variety?"

"We use what we need and get it from such places as we can afford, since we treat here mostly the injuries of poor men who work on your docks. Simple exhaustion from overwork and other maladies are our common fare, like influenza, when it breaks out. I think that the conditions in which these men labor are deplorable, causing all manner of illness as well as damage to their backs and limbs," LaLaurie said, fixing Holmes with a hard stare.

"Indeed they are, Doctor, and Jack and I would be delighted to support your work here, when our profits allow us to," Holmes replied, seeking to ingratiate himself with LaLaurie. "We trust that the growing union movement on the docks will take hold, so that our workers will have the benefit of good treatment and regular pay, as do your staff.

"I noticed that your man, Alcee, looks to have been injured at one time in the past. Was that injury dock-related?"

"Ah, no," LaLaurie replied, taken off guard enough to smile. "Mr. Alcee Sauvage's condition results from other, inherited causes. He has been with me for years. He is like my family, so I take him with me and employ him where I can."

"A fine and charitable attitude, eh, Jack?" Holmes-Oscar said, turning to solicit my nod of approval.

"Are any of your current patients dockworkers, then?" Holmes-Oscar asked LaLaurie. "If any have come to harm in or near our establishment, Jack and I would be delighted to assist in their recovery. Perhaps we could speak to—"

"Alas, no," LaLaurie demurred. "I insist upon the absolute tranquility of those in my care, Mr. Newton, Mr. Dodge, but I will have Anne and the rest of my staff take up this inquiry for you. What name do you give your place of business? We can send you notice if we treat men of your employ, yes?"

"Indeed, sir. We share an office space with another agency for the time being, but you may contact us at Sumatra Imports on Brick Lane," Holmes replied, reaching again to shake the doctor's hand and again being rebuffed. "Please excuse my overfamiliarity. I am often excessively enthusiastic when the moment takes me. Isn't that right, Jack?"

"Yes. Since we were boys, Oscar has always been headstrong," I replied, with what I hoped was a believable shaking of my head.

I observed Holmes sidling toward the door and Miss Prescott's readiness to leave with us. "If your shift is over, my dear," Holmes said to Miss Prescott, "we would be delighted to escort you safely home."

"Yes, do go with them, Miss Prescott," LaLaurie said, smiling. "I have finished my nightly rounds, and Louisa is still upstairs. She can attend to the one or two duties left. You should have time to enjoy the company of your cousins."

"I would hate to impose upon you or Louisa, Doctor," Anne replied, a worried look coming over her face.

"But I insist," Dr. LaLaurie exclaimed, making for the stairs which stood near the entry doors. He stopped before he had gone very far and called back to us, "And, gentlemen, please do not keep her up too late with family memories. She must be here early tomorrow, yes?" He flashed a strained smile at us and mounted the stairs.

***

When we were all on the street, far enough away from St. Lazarus not to be overheard, I spoke to Miss Prescott.

"I could not help noticing that you regret leaving. Will the good Doctor dock your pay?"

"No," she replied. "It is just that none of the nurses like to be alone with Alcee. His—his ways are strange to us. And when the doctor isn't around, Alcee is too familiar; he stares at us so."

I was glad of the dark to hide any blushing on my part, for I, too, stared at her.

"Tell me the layout of the place, if you can," Holmes said, changing the subject quickly, to my relief.

"Yes, sir. The topmost floor is the doctor's residence. Below that is his surgical suite and then a floor with beds for patients. Then, of course, here, is the reception and first aid area, the triage."

"Is any cooking done on the premises?" Holmes asked.

"No, sir. Any soups, or whatever small meals we give, are brought in from outside, from a chophouse on Commercial Street."

"And there is a cellar," Holmes added, drawing a nod from Anne. "That leaves the top floor, as well, for LaLaurie's activities; plenty of room for secrets. The hospital has five stories. That leaves two whole floors unknown. I would have given much to see them. Still, though our quarry is quite careful, we have learned a great deal."

"But, Holmes," I said, "we have learned nothing, that I can see, of any use!"

46

"Ah, Watson, you judge so harshly and do not use your God-given faculties," Holmes replied. "We know the general features of his residence, where to find him, his base of operations, so to speak. And we know, Watson, that Dr. LaLaurie has in his possession, likely stored in the cellar, a fair supply of that substance we know as jimsonweed. Do you never go to the cellar at all, Miss Prescott?"

"No, Mr. Holmes. It is forbidden, as I said. We keep the lift door closed much of the time. The doctor and Alcee are the only ones who use it. The other nurses and I use the stairs, since we never have call to move more than one or two floors at a time. None of us nurses have set foot in his surgery or in his quarters, so far as I know, nor has he invited any of us to do so. He only goes there alone or with Alcee," she said, eagerness in her voice, anxious to answer Holmes's queries.

"Do you often hear the lift moving below and above the patient wards and the triage?" Holmes asked.

"Why, yes, sir. It moves above or below us at all hours of the day."

"Watson, we have the first link in the chain," Holmes said, turning and placing his hands on my shoulders. "We have knowledge of evidence which will connect LaLaurie to the business of last January in Mitre Square."

"How, Holmes? Simply because we detect the presence of jimsonweed on the premises? I know it is dangerous, even deadly, but I fail to see how that helps you leap to the conclusion that LaLaurie—" I halted at Holmes's swift cautioning glance at me, warning me to avoid bringing up the matter of LaLaurie's past in front of our client.

"Think, Watson, about what you know of that plant and its uses. True, we do not know all of the materials LaLaurie uses to effect his horrible ends, but we have the first link in the chain of reasoning, the first clear indication of a pattern."

Anne looked on, perplexed, though not wishing to interrupt Holmes's thoughts. He turned from us and took two idle steps away, musing.

I nodded my head, acknowledging what I knew of jimsonweed and its uses in native practices. It had no useful applications to treatments, as far as I knew. But I was less than convinced that LaLaurie used it to create zombies on the premises of St. Lazarus Infirmary.

"But Holmes, if it is sufficient evidence to think—to think LaLaurie is up to something criminal," I said, reminding myself that Anne would be more incredulous than I at the mention of zombies, "at the very least, you've exposed Miss Prescott to danger, since you've connected us, her so-called cousins, with a nonexistent business. Surely LaLaurie will inquire after the business to see if it is legitimate. You heard his admission that he thought Miss Prescott had no family. He seemed insistent upon it. Was that a requirement of your employment, Anne?"

"Well, not as such, but so far as I know, all of the nurses in his employ lack family," she said.

"Hush, please, Watson. I am forming a plan," Holmes replied, taking no note of my agitation. I started to offer apologies to Miss Prescott for putting her in danger, but Holmes added in a scarcely audible mutter, "Miss Prescott is in no greater danger than she was before our visit. As to your other worry, Watson, any inquiries which come to Sumatra Imports will be dealt with. I have an office there of which I have told you..."

Then, with quick energy, Holmes changed the subject. "Watson," he said, "will you see Miss Prescott home? I have need to find some associates before tomorrow morning.

"My only other hope," he cried as he hurried away from us, "is that I can honestly come by an injury that is serious enough to need treatment, yet mild enough to keep me moving. I'll be in touch."

And with that, he turned into a hidden alley and was gone from our sight, lost in the fog that rolled up from the mysterious Thames.

**

"Well, Miss Prescott," I said, "if you will point us in the right direction, I'll do as Holmes suggested. For his last, odd comment and sudden departure, I pray, let me apologize. I am often left with the task of explaining his odd ways. The truth is, I hardly know where to begin."

"You could begin instead by telling me of the crimes you think to lay at Dr. LaLaurie's feet," Anne said, holding my gaze with her frank expression. "What situation in January in Mitre Square is linked to him?"

I paused. "I do not wish to keep you in the dark," I said finally, "but I think that we had better wait to see what proof Holmes finds to corroborate what we have discovered tonight. At this point, Holmes is likely to discover no connection at all. I am sorry. I wish I could give you more definite news about your loved ones."

"I see. I will take the matter up with Mr. Holmes as soon as I can. Thank you for your courteous care of me, Doctor, though it is not warranted," she said, giving me a smile.

"I have a room two blocks from here," she added. I should have been thankful that her residence was close at hand, but in her company, I could think of little other than the desire to remain with her despite the prohibitions that should have sent me happily to my own home and wife. As we made our way past shops closing up for the night and chophouses where men dined, I told myself that my actions toward Anne meant nothing, not even innocent flirtation: I was merely escorting Holmes's client safely home. But I could not keep my eyes from seeking out every expression on her face.

"Dr. Watson, I am glad for this brief walk," she continued when we had walked for a time. "I could use some time alone with you."

"I beg your pardon?" I sputtered, taken aback.

"To find out more about this curious man who is your partner," she said, in earnest tones. "He is quite the oddest man I've ever known."

"I grant you," I said, thankful to keep the conversation off of me, "Holmes is an acquired taste. But I assure you he is a man of many parts. I've not seen a mystery that is beyond his power to solve. His energy is inexhaustible, as far as I can tell, especially when he is on a case. As odd as they are, you may trust his ways."

"And he says that I should trust you," she said. "Which I do, for you make me remember my Tom. He wasn't a professional man or a gentleman like yourself, but he was a steady fellow and a hard worker. I don't know if I have yet accepted the fact that he's gone, though you and Mr. Holmes suggest that I ought to do so."

"If Holmes thinks it is likely, I'm sorry to say that you should take it for granted," I said. "But, Anne, I don't know that I recognize in myself those qualities you mentioned."

"No. But I see them in you, and that is why I do trust you, Dr. Watson," she said. "And, as sudden and as odd as his energies are, I trust Mr. Holmes. Will you or he feel sure enough about me to trust me with your suspicions about Dr. LaLaurie's endeavors?"

"Yes, Miss Prescott, I will," I said. "And as to your question, the answer is yes. As soon as I digest this new information, and as soon as Holmes has finished the rest of his investigation this night, we will try to explain, though it will be much for you to take in."

"But I have taken in much already, and I need to know the truth," she said, turning to face me. We had been walking at a steady pace, for her stride matched mine with ease. I could not think why we had stopped, but my head was swimming with the touch of her hands on my arm.

"Miss Prescott," I began, uncomfortable with my reactions to her standing so near, "why have we stopped?"

"I live here. Ah'm hoam, as they'd say in Glasgow," she said. "And I wanted to thank you—and Mr. Holmes—for bringing some hope into my life, though it is a dark hope, a hope for justice rather than for reunion with Tom and with Katie. I know Mr. Holmes holds out no hope for my seeing Tom or Katie again, but your sudden appearance at the infirmary has lifted my spirits. Someone is working on my behalf. I've not had that feeling since I was a girl, which I am no longer, sir." She gazed into my eyes and squeezed my hands. I could feel the wedding ring on my finger, a cold reminder to me of my responsibilities.

She smiled as though she too recognized the touch of that band.

"Good night," she said, dropping my hands and running up the steps to her rooming house.

"Sleep well, Anne," I called up to her. "I hope to see you again—with good news about your case, I mean," I added.

She smiled again, nodded, and entered the dark doorway. I stood for a second or two, uncertain of what to do, wanting mostly to call her back to me.

"Get hold of yourself, Captain Watson," I whispered through gritted teeth. I turned on my heel and started to march along as best I could, despite the discomfort that grew in the joint which had been hit by that Jezail bullet. I used the pain as a reminder that if the owner of that musket had been a better marksman, I might not be here now, able to return home to a loving wife and a growing medical practice. I decided to walk the rest of the way home, thinking that my aching muscles would be fit reminders that I am not a foolish young man anymore.

CHAPTER FIVE

The need to drive thoughts of Miss Prescott away from my mind, largely unsuccessful, made me ever ready to assist Holmes in his other cases. Apart from a brief adventure concerning Bavarian royalty and an American adventuress, however, Holmes needed little of my time. Mary insisted that I keep calling at Baker Street, though Holmes was often out. I assumed that he had become Bert Tiller again to seek clues amongst the dockworkers about Dr. LaLaurie's clinic.

Holmes broke his silence with an invitation to Monsieur Toulouse's restaurant near Harrods on the early April bank holiday, promising me news of all the facts he'd gathered in his investigations of LaLaurie's movements and motives. I joined him, excited by such news but equally, I'm afraid, wanting to hear anything of Anne Prescott.

"May I assume you have found evidence that will allow authorities to arrest or detain that vile doctor? How is Anne?" I stumbled over my words as he stared at me over his aperitif.

"Patience, Doctor. Wait and see. I have little doubt that the men who become zombies are made so in the cellar of St. Lazarus Infirmary. That is all I am ready to report to you. I have no intention of reporting this matter to the Metropolitan Police, for fear of being laughed at. It is too outlandish a charge. But we know that Dr. LaLaurie and his servant Alcee Sauvage have enacted a voodoo ritual on the premises of St. Lazarus. "

"We do? I thought we only suspected that jimson weed was on the premises. Have you been back there? What other evidence have you found?"

"No, I have not been back," Holmes replied. "But nothing is quite as effective for gathering dust as a felted hat, Watson. Thanks to my seeming clumsiness on our last visit, we know that there are sufficient quantities of jimsonweed on LaLaurie's premises to warrant suspicion. Moreover, it is not your typical British Devil's Trumpet or thornapple. LaLaurie's strains are from India or South America, I believe. They are stronger, more toxic, than local varieties and are more likely to be of the sort used in voodoo rituals. I have also been looking for dried reptiles and amphibians that have come into England this year and last, for there are trace elements of marine life in the dust I tested."

"We can conclude absolutely that LaLaurie is making men into zombies? Holmes, your logic is based on hasty generalizations. You—"

"I have identified patterns, possibilities; not certainties, Watson. Investigations are ongoing. LaLaurie seems quite careful. The very fact that my research has shown no imports of jimsonweed or marine specimens bound for St. Lazarus, especially when combined with the details of Miss Prescott's case, ought to tell you something about the suspicious nature of LaLaurie's operation."

"I confess that mere suspicion about the elements I found on his premises does not suggest the presence of a master criminal conspiracy, though I am more likely to accept because of it that LaLaurie is up to no good. I concluded that just by observing his manner and his attitudes toward us, Miss Prescott, and his own servant."

"And I am being less than logical?" Holmes retorted, peering at me over his menu.

I scanned our surroundings, concerned about our outlandish conversation being overheard. Holmes followed my glance and kept his voice low. "Simple evil intent might make a man create one slave or two, but I suspect from the evidence we have seen that LaLaurie has created at least six men who behave like zombies: those men who attacked me in January, and likely more, if Miss Prescott's fiancé is now under the Doctor's vile control. Granted, we cannot connect my assailants to St. Lazarus Infirmary—yet. However, someone was able to control them, set them on me, and call them off. This suggests a hidden organization, as does LaLaurie's clandestine collection of jimsonweed, dried amphibians, and obscure fish, with which, research shows, the zombie ritual is enacted. Obscure, yes, but my actions remain logical: I seek to know why LaLaurie and Sauvage turn men into zombies."

"But do we know, then, how he turns men into zombies?" I demanded, desiring a clearer sense of LaLaurie's culpability. "Do we know the aim of this great and terrible enterprise? Have you broached this subject with your client Miss Prescott?"

"No, no, and no, in order, Watson. As I said before, I am looking for patterns I can track, and I do not concern myself with questions to which there are no clear answers, such as how, exactly, a man can be turned into a zombie. As for ways to turn men into zombies, I have researched many methods from several native traditions. All of these are bathed in superstition, not science, and they all result in much the same outcome: enslavement. It is enslavement of the most nefarious type, using a man as a tool or weapon. If I am right, the doctor's family passions, though, suggest that he will probably keep engaging in this vile practice as long as it suits his needs.

"I do not think we can do anything now for Katie Prescott and Tom McHugh. I believe they are past help. Now I care only about stopping LaLaurie and Sauvage... and bringing them to justice."

I ordered and ate my lunch in silence then, as did Holmes. Though I did not speak, the revolting subject matter of the case, as well as my obsessive curiosity about Anne, kept me agitated.

At length, Holmes looked at me over his cup of coffee and said quietly, "Clearly your infatuation with Miss Prescott has you out of sorts, Watson. But I beg of you, be patient. Also, be ready to respond to my summons. If LaLaurie gets wind of my activities—or of Miss Prescott's—he may retaliate, and I simply do not know what his resources are or how vigorously he will respond. I have only you to rely on in grave need."

"Yes, of course, Holmes," I sighed. "I beg your pardon for acting in such a rash manner. I just—"

"I have every confidence that you will act honorably where Anne Prescott is concerned," Holmes said.

"Yes. Quite," I said, looking up into his intense gaze. He nodded, though I could tell that this case worried him as it did me, though for different reasons. He also needed time, and I needed to respect that, though granting that need taxed my patience. I stared at Holmes, thinking about all he had told me, all we had learned thus far about this dreadful business.

"For when you do call on me," I said slowly, "it will be to face more than just the six zombies who assaulted you in the Mitre Square alley... for by now he has likely made many more of them."

He nodded.

"Indeed, Watson, you have hit it. Your perspicacity has triumphed again. I would congratulate you, but I would not wish to be in your shoes, nor would anyone wish to be in mine."

***

The next afternoon, 4 April, I sat in my study, going over the notes from my rounds. My measles patients were showing progress, fevers abating. Most of the parents showed sense by isolating their children and limiting the spread of the infection, as I had ordered. In my own small way, I considered my work progress in fighting the tendencies of epidemic diseases, yet it made for little joy during that time of waiting for Holmes's summons. I knew in my bones that it would come soon. A poisonous thing like LaLaurie's experimentation cannot be contained.

I jumped at our housemaid's knock at the surgery door. She entered and handed me not one, but two, telegrams. The first was a brief message from Holmes, which read,

"My thoughts be bloody or be nothing worth!" Stop. Consult the *Times* about events in the East End last night. Stop. Meet Mr. Miller in the rear of 23 Brick Lane at sundown. Stop. Bring Mr. Webley and friends. End. S.H.

The words of resolve from Prince Hamlet came from Act IV of the great tragedy. Hamlet had cause, in that instance, to pursue his revenge against the usurper King Claudius. Holmes, by using the quote, signaled the need to spring into action. The game was certainly afoot.

I opened my desk drawer, broke open the top of the Webley & Scott revolver, and loaded the heavy, hollow-pointed cartridges. Then I slammed the weapon closed, a sound that foretold action and stirred my blood like the sound of pipers on a battlefield. Once I had settled the harness around my shoulders, I scribbled a note to Mary, who was doing the shopping, informing her that Holmes needed me. I would be very late.

Having started my rounds early that morning, I had yet to take a moment to myself to peruse the papers. I did so then, with the second telegram still clutched unread in my hand, seeking word of the crime in the East End to which Holmes alluded.

"Horrific Gang Assault in Brick Lane," read the headline. A woman identified only as a prostitute had been attacked and savagely assaulted by three or four youths, the account read. She had been admitted to the London Hospital, in shock from battery and from blood loss.

Throwing the paper aside, I prepared to depart. With my heaviest walking stick in my trembling hand, I started along the streets that ran toward Regent's Park, where I hailed a cab.

Once in the hansom cab and on my way, I noticed the second telegram folded and crushed against the stick in my hand, where I gripped it fast. Thinking it might be further instruction from Holmes, I opened it, and its contents almost stopped my hammering pulse.

Sir, I have seen Tom. Stop. He is alive. Stop. St. Lazarus suddenly closed. Stop. Desperate for help and cannot reach Holmes. Stop. Please. End. Anne

I opened the trap and told the driver a different address.

"Twenty-two Arnold Circus, driver. The need is grave," I said, and I sat back in anxious silence as he whipped up his horse. Delayed by traffic going toward Commercial Lane, I tried not to fret, for there was over an hour until sunset, when I was supposed to meet Holmes. The distance to Miss Prescott's rooming house was not great, so I determined to go to her aid first, though I confess that my stomach knotted at the thought of seeing her and of helping her regain the society of Tom McHugh. I, who have loved women on three continents, ought to have been proof against such a response. But soon I had to admit to myself that my need to see Anne—already, somehow, I thought of her by her Christian name—was obsessive. My efforts to stay aloof had failed.

The moment we arrived, I threw some money in the driver's direction and ran up the steps of the large rooming house. In answer to my brisk knocking, I was greeted by the angry face of an elderly woman with eyes the color of gunmetal. Anxiously, I inquired as to the whereabouts of Miss Prescott.

"Who might you be, sir, and what do you want Miss Prescott for?" she snapped, her thin face framed between the door and the jamb.

"I've come at the request of Miss Prescott," I started, brandishing Anne's telegram.

"You Johnny Hopper? The Old Bill?" she demanded, revealing further traces of an Irish brogue.

"Who? Oh," I said, recognizing one of the street monikers for the police. "No, madam. I am a doctor. Miss Prescott is a client of my colleague. She summoned me within the hour."

The steely eyes regarding me did not waver or soften.

"What she need a doctor for, then? She never 'ad a sick day what I can tell," the old woman insisted.

"Perhaps, madam, if you could bear to Miss Prescott the message that I have come at her request, she can explain to your satisfaction," I said, desirous to avoid wasting more time in conversation with this difficult woman.

"No better than you ought to be, I'd bet," she muttered, slamming the door in my face.

I paced the small porch for a moment or two. Then the door swung wide open, and the frowning woman beckoned me in.

"In, then, Doctor," she growled, ushering me into a dark, stuffy hallway. She slammed and bolted the heavy door behind us as though she expected an armed assault. Pinching my sleeve, she dragged me to a dimly lit sitting room. Spindly chairs and tables of the previous era cluttered the room. Given the delicate nature of the furniture, I elected to stand.

Soon the old woman ushered Anne into the room within her protective arm, though she was many inches shorter.

"Now, my love," the old woman crooned, "I'll leave you to your visitor, but if you need me, I shall be less than two steps away. With a stout broom handle to hand," she added, directing the words at me.

"Thank you, Mrs. Cromarty," Anne replied, favoring her with a wan smile.

Even with my wide experience of women, I stood shocked to see the strength of Anne Prescott. Where I expected to greet an agitated woman who demanded my help, as one of the two trustworthy males she knew to call upon, I met the eyes of an equal. Clearly, she had not slept or even rested well, but her native resilience stood her in good stead. Having put aside her nurse's uniform, she wore a dress of a generation before, an afternoon dress in a deep purple hue. True, it obviously had often been repaired, and the hem, which reached the floor, was stained and faded in spots, but its narrow waist accentuated her figure, and the coil of her thick, black hair fell over her right shoulder.

I had not yet seen Anne with her hair down, and the sight will remain in my memory. Despite the awful shock she'd had, her beauty—regal, powerful—made her a vision which fashion would never accommodate or define. I'm afraid I stared, which drew the accustomed blush from her cheeks.

"Miss Prescott," I said, my voice suddenly husky with emotion, "I've come to assist you in whatever way I can. We can meet Holmes in a little over an hour. Please, tell me how I can help you."

"Dr. Watson—Jack," she said, dropping her gaze to the floor, "I'm sorry to call you away from your home and your—your family. I went round to Baker Street, but Mrs. Hudson said Mr. Holmes had been out all day. She didn't know when to expect him back. I would have contacted you even if she hadn't insisted. I'm sorry, though, that I revealed my desperation. I—I'm not accustomed to asking for help, especially of those whom I have not known for long."

"Nonsense, Anne. I have done similarly for other clients of Holmes's, persons whom I held in much less regard. Can you tell me the facts of what you found out? Your telegram said that you saw Mr. McHugh. Do you need my assistance in finding him again? I was on my way to meet Holmes, in any regard, and perhaps he could be of more help."

She turned to sit in one of the small chairs. I chose a slightly larger settle, facing her. Its entire structure emitted an ominous groan as I let most of my weight sink onto it. I winced at the sound and tried to perch more on its edge, making Anne smile a little; I returned her smile in kind.

"I'm afraid Mrs. Cromarty doesn't encourage male visitors," she said. "You are a dear man to take trouble over me. The more thought I give it, though, the more I think that Mr. Holmes is right: my Tom is... gone." Her lips quivered, and a single tear rolled down her cheek. Her eyes had already been red-rimmed, so I knew these were not the first tears she had shed tonight. Nor, probably, would they be the last.

"Yet you did see him?" I insisted, repressing my desire to ask about the closing of the infirmary as well. She nodded but looked away.

"Two nights ago, it was," she said. "Dr. LaLaurie requested that I fetch an order from the bakery on Commercial Street, for the bank holiday would mean we couldn't get our usual Monday order from the chophouse. Since we only had two patients over Easter, we wouldn't require much to tide us over. Having learned the back ways, and having helped so many of our poorer neighbors, I felt secure in taking a shortcut. Generally, my nurse's uniform grants me safe passage.

"Along the way, I saw the bent form of Alcee dart into a doorway. I had thought it unusual that Dr. LaLaurie had not sent him on the errand, but I hadn't questioned it at the time. I went with some caution then, for that man frightens me, and I did not want to be surprised by him.

"Slowing down, I passed a cellar window covered by a heavy grate, and there, staring up at me—at the air, really—I saw Tom. I would know that face anywhere, Jack, in the half-dark, even only seen for a moment: I loved him."

"I understand, but if he was down in a cellar, it must have been awfully dim. Can you be sure?" I insisted.

"Yes. It was Tom. There was enough light from the street that I saw him quite clearly. It was just that..." Her voice broke in a sob. "His eyes, though they looked at me, did not know me. His eyes were empty. Tom was a fair man, with high color and very light hair. I used to think that he glowed, so healthy and strong, those eyes, so bright..." She let her face fall into her hands and wept again, very quietly, as though it pained her to have me see it.

"There, there," I murmured. "I'm sure you saw him. I didn't mean to doubt your story."

"It's not your doubt that causes me to weep, Jack," she cried, reaching out and gripping my hand with a formidable strength. "When he did see me, he lunged, thrusting his hands through the bars, grasping at me. So sudden it was that I jumped back, and when I took his arm by the wrist to keep him from harming himself against the rough grating, other hands grasped at me. Jack, they would have dragged me through those bars. Their grip was like cold iron. And the look in Tom's eyes, Jack... he would have delighted in dragging me through those bars, though it would have killed me. And never a word from him or the others whose faces pressed around his. Just the most dreadful moaning."

Listening to her account, I recalled Holmes's struggle with the men in the alley behind Mitre Square.

"Was there a foul smell? Were these men only, or men and women? Were they exceedingly strong, inured to pain?" I asked.

Her eyes widened in surprise at my seeming prescience. "Yes, their grips were hard, and the smell that came from them choked me. And Tom's flesh was torn by the rough iron of those bars, but he did not flinch. If I hadn't kept to my feet, I would have been dragged in pieces down past those bars. I could swear that he wanted to draw me toward his mouth, though never a word out of him, just moans and that horrid stench."

"What did you do then?" I asked.

"I ran back to the infirmary, so scared I was," she said, shivering at the memory. "Louisa fetched the doctor when she saw my tears, and I repeated my story to him, though he seemed less than alarmed or—or even interested, Jack.'"

"Do you remember the details of his reaction?"

"Yes, clearly. He smiled at first, then he put on an expression of concern, examined the bruises on my wrist and ankle, and said he was sorry about my discovery, but that it was about time to take the experiment out of the laboratory. Then he asked Louisa to make sure I got home all right and told us that he would see us in the morning."

"Take the experiment out of the laboratory?" I repeated.

"Those were his very words," Anne said, fixing me with a calmer gaze. "Could he have meant those men in the cellar? My Tom?"

"I fear that is the case, though it turns my stomach to think so," I said, shuddering, "but if Holmes is correct in his understanding, Dr. LaLaurie may well have done that very thing. But when you went back to work, you found the clinic was empty?"

"That it was empty—of people, records, medical supplies. I cannot say about the upper floors or the cellar, for I don't have keys that open the doors to Dr. LaLaurie's flat, nor does Louisa."

"Have you been back to the place where you saw Mr. McHugh and Mr. Sauvage?" I asked.

"Of course," she said. "I went straight there, with due caution. But there was no sight of them. Only the foul sewer smell remained, the smell of filthy bodies and decay."

Here she paused and took a deep breath.

"As I've thought of it," she said sadly, "I'm convinced that my Tom is dead. And I'm forced to believe that Dr. LaLaurie is somehow the one behind the disappearances I've reported to you and Mr. Holmes."

"I think you are correct," I replied, wondering how much to reveal to her of Holmes's discoveries, "on all accounts. I know that

Holmes works on this complex matter even now. I have his summons that he is ready to act. As for me, I am sorry that it has resulted in personal losses for you as well as in the loss of your position. What will you do now, Anne?"

She returned my searching gaze with one of somber reflection. Her sadness as well as her strength drew me to her, yet I recognized that I could do little to help her, not emotionally and not financially: my practice was growing, but that had not made me a wealthy man by any stretch of the imagination. Still, my one desire was to help Anne Prescott in any way I could, though I knew I must be careful not to become even more involved in her life.

A slight blush colored her cheeks, as though she had followed the direction of my thoughts. She smiled again. "I am not totally helpless, Jack," she said, her soft voice taking on a harder edge as she continued, her anger showing in the brief return of her broad Scots burr. "I have friends at Cwmdonkin Cottage, and I have had offers from Magdalen Hospital to join their staff. I may well turn there for help, but I have taken such a scunner to this city that I hope to return to Glasgow, or Edinburgh, perhaps. London is a bitter, brutal place, and it has consumed those I love. I even begin to fear for those whom I have just come to know and care for, like Louisa and some of my patients."

Nodding my understanding was all I could do, since the thought of her leaving London filled me with relief that she would no longer be a temptation for me, though I would grieve never seeing her again.

"For the best, perhaps," I said.

"But I do not wish to leave," she replied, taking my hand, "until I have seen justice done for those I love—or, perhaps, those I loved. Do you think it is true, as Mr. Holmes said, that there is no hope of finding my Katie, though Tom's loss seems assured?"

"I trust Holmes's conclusions that her life is forfeit, but I pray, let me spare you any details he has shared with me," I answered, hating that I had to be the bearer of such bad news.

Anne bowed her head, allowing her lustrous hair to fall and hide her face. We sat in silence for several minutes, her hand still grasping mine.

"We must go and find Holmes, Anne," I said, trying to take her thoughts off of her grief. "And, along the way, I would like to see this place where you last saw Tom."

Lifting an intense gaze to me, she squeezed my hand and said, "Of course. I am at your disposal. Pray, give me a moment to make myself ready."

CHAPTER SIX

Shortly thereafter, with Anne wearing a flat straw hat and veil and a lightweight purple jacket against the evening air, we set off at a brisk walk back toward the warren of small alleys that ran off Shacklewell Street, toward the defunct St. Lazarus Infirmary. Once she was in motion, Anne's energy grew focused, and she allowed no traces of her sadness and loss to remain on the face she turned to the city that had become hateful to her. Many of the poorer denizens of that quarter called greetings to her, bearing testimony to the good work she had done amongst them. She returned their greetings with a quiet smile, not stopping to converse.

Soon, leaving the main thoroughfares, Anne turned down a dark lane of mud-covered cobbles. Indicating a heavy wooden door in the side of what appeared to be an abandoned rag and bone shop, she drew to a halt.

"This is the door into which Mr. Alcee entered, and you can see the gratings that cover the windows into the cellar," she said, pointing to two openings along the blackened alley. "The one farthest back is where I saw Tom."

I searched them both, peering into the darkness within, which was complete. Imagining myself as Holmes, I sought any signs that might reveal some clue but came up with few details except one: the barred grating over the window was bloodied, and tracks of Anne's shoes in the alley's gritty mud were clear where she had sought to keep her former fiancé from dragging her through those bars.

"Other than the stench arising from the cellar, I can detect little," I said, looking at the blood and bits of skin left on the rough iron bars.

"You were right that Mr. McHugh—or perhaps others in there—injured themselves as they grasped for you."

"The stench is less, Jack," she observed. "It was nearly enough to overpower me, especially when those horrible faces appeared at Tom's side."

"I think that we can do little here now," I said, "and I am not sure how to proceed. We do need to inform Holmes of this development, so we might push along to meet him at the Brick Lane address. Perhaps you know where we can get a cab? We still have a short time before nightfall, which is when he desired me to come."

"Follow me," she said with a nod, and we were off at a brisk pace again.

***

On Shoreditch High Street we hailed a hansom cab, after several minutes of hard walking through the growing mist. Soon, despite the immediate protests of the driver, who didn't think much of the quarter of Brick Lane to which I had directed him, we were deposited before a disused storefront, standing dark and still. It bore a hand-painted sign, which read "St. George's Methodist Chapel," with the times of services listed below.

Persistent knocking at the shop door brought a small, thin man in a clerical collar. Light from an upper room fell on his bald scalp. His round face broke into a smile as he opened the door to us.

"Welcome, friends," he called to us, ushering us into the storefront. It featured a battered piano near the back wall and a variety of chairs standing in neat rows across the room. A large, unadorned cross was fixed to the wall behind the piano, and a small lectern—his only pulpit, I supposed—stood beside. "I'm afraid you've missed the evening hymn sing for today. We will have a later one tomorrow evening, with a communion service, however, in case you can return. I'm Adam Hepplewhite. Is there any way I can assist you?"

"Ah, yes, sir," I returned, taking the man's hand in greeting. "I'm Dr. John Watson, and this is Miss Anne Prescott. We were given this address as the offices of Sumatra Imports and were asked to meet one Mr. Bert Tiller here at dusk. Are we in error?"

His smile widened. He closed the door behind us, chuckling to himself. "No, indeed, Dr. Watson. You have come to the right

63

address. Mr. Tiller—that is, your Mr. Holmes—will be along shortly, if he has appointed this time to meet you. Please, allow me to take you to the Sumatra Imports office," he called over his shoulder, as he turned his back on us and began to bustle across the room.

"Please forgive the state of my lodgings," he cried, beckoning us to follow him through a door at the rear of the room, below the stairs. "I am a bachelor and a deplorable housekeeper."

Mr. Hepplewhite muttered and chuckled to himself as he led us through a small kitchen at the back of the house. To my eye it was as neat as a pin. We saw only the remnants of a small tea eaten in haste at a plain wooden table barely big enough for one.

"I left my repast in haste, you see. An idea for Sunday's sermon just came to me, and I hastened upstairs to draft it out," he said, gesturing to the chipped cup and pot and the scant crumbs left on his plate. He turned to a narrow door in the back wall of the kitchen, took a key from his vest pocket, and opened it. "The offices of Sumatra Imports, my friends."

We had to take turns walking through it, so narrow it was. Within the windowless room, we saw a cold water tap and sink to our right, corresponding to the wet wall of Reverend Hepplewhite's kitchen. A heavy, wooden door to the right of the sink opened into the alleyway, I supposed, and along that alley wall stood another plain wooden table on which rested one of Holmes's oldest pipes and various bottles of theatrical makeup. Dimly seen at the back of the room were a camp bed and two chairs, of the same varied vintage as the furnishings in the sanctuary.

"If you care to wait," the Reverend Hepplewhite said, lighting a small oil lantern on the wall beside the sink, "Mr. Holmes will come through the side door soon, I think, though you may not know him to look at him. Would you care to have me wait with you?"

We both shook our heads, declining the offer. "Though your company would be grand," Anne said, her Scots burr drawing a delighted smile from the Reverend, "we do not wish to keep you from such important work. Might we ask for your prayers?"

"Indeed," he said, taking Anne's hand in his own for a moment. With that, he departed, though he gave us a final look as he did so, a look of grave, quiet concern.

My own faith was never something I practiced openly, considering that I did so with my hands every day. Anne, taking a seat near me in silence, appeared to be considering her own prayers, so I kept silent.

Within a mercifully brief time, the side door opened. The tall, spare form of Bert Tiller shuffled through the door, his shirtsleeves rolled to his elbows, his slouch hat pulled low, his rough clothing soiled from work. He turned a slack expression toward us, causing Miss Prescott to rise from her chair in alarm, a startled cry escaping her lips.

"My dear Miss Prescott," Holmes said, sweeping the hat off of his head and abandoning the visage of Bert Tiller, "I am delighted to see you, though it is unexpected. Watson, clearly you have had additional calls to duty today. I perceive that Miss Prescott has been with you upon some errand into the warrens off Shoreditch High Street. I'm glad, as well, to see that you are well-armed."

Anne uttered a nervous laugh, looked from one of us to the other. I shook my head, as though despairing.

"It is his way, my dear. Doubtless, both of us bear an otherwise undetectable speck of something or other about our persons, which tells him all of our movements for the past three days," I said, feigning tiredness at his demonstration.

"Indeed," Holmes replied. "Now, pray, do give me the particulars of your day." He drew a basin of water and washed his face, neck, and hands. Then, moving a plain wooden screen away from the wall where it had stood unnoticed by either of us, he ducked behind it and began to change his clothing. Anne told him about seeing Tom McHugh and about the closing of St. Lazarus. Holmes listened, casting glances over the top of the screen, as Miss Prescott related her experiences.

Still buttoning his vest, and glancing at his watch, he emerged with a look of fierce concentration burning in his eyes. He bore, slung over his arm, the long Gurkha blade in its black leather scabbard. I saw Anne's eyes widen at the sight of it.

"Did you walk here?" he asked, placing a hand, shaking with vibrant energy, on my shoulder.

"No, we took a cab. Time was short," I replied.

His face grew suddenly pale.

"I assume that you could walk a great distance at need, Miss Prescott?" Holmes said to Anne. At her curt nod, he pressed on, handing me several banknotes from his pocketbook.

"Watson," he said, "You must help Miss Prescott get to a place where she can stay, a place whose identity and exact location you will not know about. You must go on foot and with great care. Avoid main thoroughfares as best you can. The presence of many people would normally provide protection, but in this case, I hope that secrecy will provide us with some advantages."

He thrust two soiled raincoats into our hands, gave a dun-colored bonnet to Anne. To me, he gave Bert Tiller's slouch hat, while he took my own bowler, saying, "There. That should help."

Glancing at the heavy stick I carried, he patted my side to find evidence of my revolver. Then, with an appraising glance at Anne, who was tying the bonnet over her luxurious hair, he fished a worn leather blackjack from his side pocket and pressed it into her hands. It dangled loose in her grip as she looked with mouth agape at its deadly shape.

I was still thinking of a plan. "I—I suppose that I can take her to—"

"Do not tell me where," Holmes cut in, "in case I am taken captive. And do not tarry. You might have twenty-four hours or one. I cannot tell. I will get word to Mary and to Mrs. Hudson. Does Mary have a hotel or residence where you will know where to find her?"

"Y-yes," I said, Holmes's urgency making me stammer.

"Good. I will tell her, in your name, to repair there at once. I can send Adam. Tell me a name of endearment that only you use for her."

Blushing crimson, I whispered, "My jewel," which drew a smile from him.

"Really, Watson? Could you be more obvious?"

"I, well, after the matter of the Agra treasure..." I muttered.

"Never mind, old friend. I'm sure it will do."

"But, Holmes—" I started to protest this sudden need to run out into the night. He cut me off with a vigorous shake of his head.

"Trust me, Watson. We are in a brief calm, after a horrible onset. Emma Smith"—upon hearing the name, Anne's eyes opened wide— "has been murdered within the past twenty-four hours. This signals, I think, a desperate change in Dr. LaLaurie's operations, and I do not know what he will do next. Our enemy is moving against us, testing our strength, and we cannot take the field against him, for we do not yet know the strength of his numbers. In two days' time, if we are all able, we should rendezvous at a disreputable pub not far from here, the Ten Bells, at nine o'clock sharp. Do you understand?"

"Yes. We must prepare to be waylaid," I said, wanting to make clear for Anne the possibilities of a physical assault. She nodded in response.

"Indeed, my friend. It may be that none of us will make it to our destinations tonight," Holmes muttered, drawing a ring of keys from his pocket and pulling one loose for me. "If need be, return to this place and leave again at first light. Your return here will be unexpected, I think, and two people might well defend this place long, if they bar the outer door."

As Holmes moved to leave the room, Anne called to him. "Mr. Holmes, I know we must leave with all speed... but can you not tell us first, however briefly, what happened to poor Emma?"

"Yes. When was the last time you saw her, Miss Prescott?"

"She was discharged just yesterday morning, though she hardly seemed well. The doctor had been treating her for flu-like symptoms. Do you recall? She was there the night that you both came to visit the clinic."

Holmes nodded and said to us both,. "Emma Smith's murder was so violent that I will not harrow your imaginations with its details. It may be an isolated incident, but I do not think so, and I will take no chances at the risk of other lives. If I am right, then Dr. LaLaurie, whom I hold responsible for both your fiancé's and your sister's deaths, Miss Prescott, has enough of his hellish servants on hand to take his plan to its next level, whatever that may be. All of us are in grave danger.

"More than that, I will not take time to say now. I beg you to remember that, if all goes well tonight, we should meet in two days' time at the Ten Bells, where I will bring you all up to date on the business of this case. Now, are we agreed? I must hasten to ask the good reverend for another favor."

"Yes," we both replied.

Holmes grasped each of us on the arm. "Protect each other," he said.

We nodded our heads, accepting gravely the demands set before us. Letting go of us, Holmes ducked into Adam Hepplewhite's kitchen.

***

"I wonder how you are to escort me to a safe place," Anne said when we had left and were rushing away from the meager lights of Brick Lane, "if I cannot give you its name?"

"I can take you near a friend's house, or perhaps in the vicinity of another infirmary," I suggested, taking a left turning in the warren of lanes. I made my way instinctually toward the Thames, that great, trackless thoroughfare.

"As of now," she said in a fierce voice, "I have only two friends, and I am squeezing the arm of the best of them." Her grip trembled. "Can we trust that Holmes is right? Are we in danger?"

"Holmes's hunches are more trustworthy than the deliberation of so-called experts," I said. "We should proceed under the assumption that we are being hunted and go to ground like frightened prey."

"I—I've never had cause to use one of these," she said, lifting the cosh into the meager light of the alley.

"With adequate knowledge of the human skull, which I assume you have had in your training, you can strike those places most likely to cause lethal damage," I returned, "not merely pain."

I heard her mutter a mild oath as she thrust the weapon into the raincoat pocket.

We hurried on, taking turns always toward the river and away from the lights. The people we passed, often couples, took little notice of us. They were on their way to more carnal engagements, judging by their overheard conversations and drunken progress. In the misty darkness, most of the ways we took had very little traffic. We skirted all establishments that would lead us into the light. As we entered an area of warehouses, seemingly abandoned by industry, I began to think that we had slipped the net and made good our escape.

"So, what area, my dear?" I asked.

"Shepherd's Bush," Anne said. "Whitehall Street."

"My dear, you cannot go to the police yet," I said, recognizing the location of Scotland Yard. "They would provide us no safety from Dr. LaLaurie and his associates."

"I have no intention to, Dr. Watson," she began, and then she broke off. "What is that whistling sound?"

I pulled us into the shadow of an arched doorway, drawing my revolver and gripping my walking stick by its middle. Anne produced the blackjack, holding it close in both hands. She pressed to my side, shivering.

Then, I heard the high, tuneless piping. It had a sleepy, eerie air, designed, I thought, to lull yet disturb, perhaps to compel. Its insistent, erratic highs and lows made my skin crawl. Nearby, I heard coughing, ragged breathing, and the scuffing of many feet. We pressed as far back into the dark as we could, our backs to the heavy warehouse doors.

Across the alleyway, a rusted metal ladder ran up a solid wall, disappearing into the misty night. It reminded me of the enchanted rope of a fakir, rising into the air, propelled by the eerie piping. It offered the fastest means of escape, but I knew we could not reach it in time.

We saw them coming from either direction in the alley: they shambled toward us, heads hanging or lolling side to side. Some of them dragged horribly injured legs or held mangled arms close to their bodies. They emitted low moans and ragged sighs through raw throats. Several came from the direction in which we had come. Four, at least, came from the direction in which we had been headed. Their stench came with them all, sickening, making my gorge rise with this, my first sight of zombies.

"Dearest God in Heaven, Jack," Anne breathed at my side, as they converged on our hiding place. "What is wrong with these people?" They looked as though they had taken no notice of us, but they were clearly being driven toward us by something, and I wondered again if that atonal piping sound had anything to do with it.

"I don't think you'd believe me if I told you. Also, I think we should run, back the way we came," I whispered, pointing with my pistol.

At that moment, the tune stopped. For a breath or two, the zombies did not move, but they grew quiet, and their heads swung in awful unison toward us. I grabbed Anne's hand and took a step that would skirt the zombies on my right, but I was too late.

The zombies surged in our direction, hands extended, some to arm's length, some held crooked but grasping still. Their swift change into focused, murderous intent made them close on us in a second, in eerie near-silence, without a cry of anger. Anne screamed, and I lashed out with the heavy stick in my left hand, swiping at the grasping arms and hands. My Webley & Scott roared in my right hand, the shocking concussion ringing in my ears. The heavy round struck one of the foremost attackers in his forehead, bursting out the back of his skull to shatter the shoulder of the man who pushed behind him.

Anne wailed "Tom!" in a horrified scream as she recognized the remains of her former lover, who had fallen to the alley with my first shot, tangling the feet of the others who swarmed behind him and tripped over his now-limp form. A brief wave of nausea hit me as I realized that just seconds before, I had killed Anne Prescott's fiancé, or what he had become. Would I—would she—ever forget the sight of Tom McHugh's head exploding?

I could not pause to think on this, for even as Tom McHugh fell, others surged forward, claw-like hands clutching. Anne kicked them away, while I yelled "Back, you devils!" I shot twice, lower this time. My shots found their marks in the hearts of two of the creatures, driving each back several steps. But they did not stop.

Despite her harrowing loss, I watched Anne strike out twice with the deadly blackjack, defending us. I heard the butcher shop sound of bone cracking under a heavy blow as the blackjack struck one creature in the temple and the second in the cheek, smashing the mandible. The first zombie went to its knees, but the second, jaw hanging loose, surged on. In seconds, they would smother us with the weight of their bodies, and then, I felt sure, we would die.

One of them carried a long kitchen knife, another a jagged piece of wood, perhaps the broken leg of a dining table. The zombie with the club grasped my right arm in a bone-crushing grip, even as it swung its club at Anne. Anne dodged the blow, moving behind me, and the club struck another of our attackers, breaking his collarbone with little or no effect.

Placing my stick before me, I cried, "Help me shove!"

I placed one foot against the brickwork and forced my whole body forward, Anne's weight added to mine. We knocked three of them over by sheer strength, but several more remained on their feet. One fell upon Anne, grasping her arm and drawing it toward his mouth. Turning, I brought the brass head of my walking stick down across his neck, but still he managed to tear through the fabric of her coat and dress, lacerating her arm with his foul teeth. I fired at his head and watched him drop.

The door behind us began to shudder and buckle. Its heavy wood broke asunder, and yet more hands reached toward us from the breach as the rest of the door fell in ruins.

"How many are there?" I yelled in disbelief, thinking that we had vanquished half of them. I had counted on there being no more than the ones reported by Holmes in his first attack. At least six more, however, were behind the door and closing on us. Already, in the split second it took for my horrified remark, three hands had caught my right arm and shoulder. They pulled me away from Anne's side, though she saw it and took hold of my jacket as more of them closed upon her. I caught her eye, desirous to express my sorrow at leading her to a horrible death.

Then a flashing blade caught my peripheral vision, and the meaty "snick-snack" sound of a razor-sharp blade slicing through flesh and bone came from my right. Two of the arms pulling at me were shorn of their hands. Holmes whirled into the attackers' midst, the kukri knife flashing. More zombies fell. I dragged Anne after me, out of the reach of the men coming through the ruined warehouse door.

"Shoot them in the head!" Holmes cried with a sweep of his lethal knife. I heard him grunt as the Gurkha blade swept through the neck of one man who surged forward from the pack. The head spun for a second in the air above the creature's torso, and a weird giggle escaped my lips at the sight.

I used my last three bullets to shoot at three of the zombies. One head exploded, and its body fell to the alley, encumbering those behind it. And in the next second, we were free.

CHAPTER SEVEN

One look at the alley in either direction sent Holmes scurrying to the ladder opposite us. More zombies shuffled toward us, and for the first time I saw that some were—or had been—women. I shuddered.

"Up, Miss Prescott," Holmes ordered, and Anne obeyed him without question. I reloaded while Holmes worked with his stick and knife to keep the fiends off us.

"Heads. Point blank, Watson," Holmes cried, scurrying up the ladder. I anticipated their surge as best I could and strode toward them, barrel forward, blasting each in the forehead as it came to bear under my gun. Soon the gun's barrel was wet with the blowback, and my ears rang with the hellish din, but the zombies were silent, implacable, grim as death. Six of them fell to the ground, giving me time to holster my weapon and make my own ascent as the weird trilling rose again, seemingly under my feet. I fought the urge to turn and see whether they were climbing after me.

When I turned back at the top of the ladder, aiming my Webley back the way I'd come, they were all gone. The gun smoke, with its sharp smell of cordite, and the piping sound were both growing fainter, but the terrible stench of the undead remained.

"Holmes," I cried, "they've vanished!"

Strong fingers grasped my sleeve as Holmes urged me farther onto the rooftop.

"They've gone back to their holes, like the vermin they are," he said through gritted teeth. He brought me away from the roof's edge to where Anne stood, pressing her right hand onto her left forearm. The bonnet hung low over her face, the raincoat in tatters down her left side, and her dress and foundation garments were a ruin. I couldn't help but take in the sweep of her bare left leg, trembling from our exertions. My own garments were in similar condition: my hat was gone, I knew not where, and my right coat sleeve hung in shreds.

"Are you both able to move?" Holmes asked, drawing us into a loose embrace. "I was sure I had lost you, when I saw your predicament. You both fought bravely, but we are not safe yet."

"Wh-where did they go?" I asked, still breathing hard. Holmes, I noted, wasn't winded at all, though he had fought with the ferocity of a wounded leopard.

"The sewers, Watson. The sewers. I only learned from Jimmy O'Doole—he is the leader of a local gang of toshers, Miss Prescott— minutes ago that they were on the move. O'Doole's lads in the sewers had knowledge of the zombies' movements for several days but did not know what to do about it. O'Doole knew I was in Whitechapel working this case and warned me. Would that we had known sooner. I ordered O'Doole and his friends out of the sewers, and I pray to God that they heeded my orders."

"He mentioned," Holmes continued, "that a huge man, matching Alcee Sauvage's description, was with them."

Her voice shaking, Anne asked, "Did you say 'zombies'? I've heard the term, but surely they are not real? Who—what—are they? If I had not seen Tom's face among them, I'd have sworn they were not human."

"They are, or were, quite human, not long ago," Holmes replied. "But what they are now, I have no name for, except 'zombies.' Anne, Tom McHugh ceased to be a man when he left the infirmary under the control of Dr. LaLaurie. And he was not Dr. LaLaurie's first or last victim."

"Forgive me, but... this all sounds more than a bit mad," Anne returned, the strain of terror showing in the drawn lines of fatigue in her face and her confused, panicked glances around her.

"Miss Prescott," Holmes said, "given what you have just experienced, and whatever awaits us yet, I daresay that name will become somewhat useful, even though—"

The sound of something striking the rooftop drew Holmes's eye away from us, and in the next instant he propelled us forward to the far side of the roof, hauling us behind the wooden bulk of an air vent shaft.

"Take cover! Someone is shooting at us," Holmes cried, pushing us down.

More shots splintered the wooden slats behind us. The distant reports of a rifle came to my ears.

Peering into the dark of the air shaft, Holmes yelled,

"Quickly! Down the rope! Watson, you first, so that Anne might cling to your back. Anne, hold as much of your weight as you can on the rope."

As wood splinters showered us, Holmes set my hand to the stout hawser attached to the top of the air shaft. I hardly dared think what I was doing, slipping into that unknown darkness, my grip tight on the worn rope, wondering what marksman had shot at us. Whoever he was, he was deadly. Anne clambered onto the rope above me, clamping her long legs about my middle and grasping the rope above my hands.

We made our descent as quickly as we could, gasping and groaning with our efforts. I suspected that her hands were no better equipped than mine to take such rough work, but we hastened to provide Holmes with the same opportunity, as more wood shattered on the structure above him. What glass had formed part of the roof of the shaft was hit, as though the marksman had planned to send shards of it down on our heads.

"Eyes down!" I cried, hopeful that we could keep the shards away from our faces.

Our hasty descent ended when I lost my grip and we tumbled two feet to the floor. Anne rolled away from me. Holmes dropped down at our side.

"Well, my soldiers," Holmes breathed, "we must push on. Can you make it?"

I nodded and saw Anne's head move in unison with mine.

"We must find a way out of here so that we are not fired upon again," said Holmes. "I think the mist from the Thames saved us this time. We were not clear targets."

"Who else is trying to kill us?" Anne asked, struggling to contain the confusion that clouded her thoughts as it did mine.

"I do not hazard to guess," Holmes said.

"Those shots came from a considerable distance and in a mist, and if they did not hit us, they came awfully close," I said, my incredulity rising. "Surely a zombie cannot use a rifle. Is this some other voodoo magic?"

"Doubtful, Watson," replied Holmes, "but I have no facts with which to work, other than the effect of those rounds, so expertly aimed at us. Nor do I have time to reason it out. We must make haste. Quickly now. Stay on my heels."

***

The instant we emerged through a door which Holmes kicked down, the tuneless trilling arose around us again. Holmes cried, "Follow me, at the double," and he was off like a shot, away from the river and back toward Limehouse. I caught Anne's hand and began to run. She kept pace with me, tearing off the encumbering remains of her bonnet as she ran, her knees lifting high, freed from the entangling dress. She ran like an athlete, keeping up with Holmes's pace, at which I struggled.

The alley was a long one. A hasty glance over my shoulder showed me that we were being pursued by a pack of the zombies, moving inexorably toward us, slow but determined in their pursuit. I doubted that they would stop to rest, but I feared we would need to and soon. I could not hear Holmes's breathing, but both Anne and I were breathing hard.

Ahead of Holmes in the alley, figures emerged from cellar windows and grates of dark houses on either side. One, then two, rose to their shambling feet. "How many of these damnable creations does he have?" I yelled.

Holmes was upon them before they could take their first steps.

A double sweep of his flashing knife, and the grasping arms of an approaching fiend flew off. It stood there stupidly, looking at us as though it were wondering where its arms had gone. Anne bowled it down with her shoulder. With a heavy blow from my walking stick, I smashed its skull as I ran by, watching with fierce glee as Holmes brought his heavy blade down through the skull of the next zombie to cross his path.

Then two more emerged from cellars on either side of us.

"More speed," Holmes yelled back. "We dare not stop to fight them!" But one lunged at Anne's legs, grasping her ankle. With a panicked cry she fell, her head bumping on the cobblestones. Immediately, the zombie began to drag her toward him, though he had scarcely lifted himself from the cellar. Leaping, I brought my weight down on the creature's wrist as my walking stick caved in its skull.

Anne lay stunned on the pavement as another creature rose behind me. I pulled the Webley, broke it open, cast aside the spent shells and quickly plugged in six more as the thing walked toward me. I let it come. More were behind it, though I had not seen them rise. I stepped forward, muzzle level with the thing's face, and fired. Then I emptied the chamber at those following until I heard Holmes yell, "Not now, Watson!" at my back. I jammed the pistol into its holster.

I ran to Anne and picked her up, slinging her over my shoulder as Murray had done for me at the Battle of Maiwand, and trotted after Holmes. Inside the structures around us, the backs of dark houses and ragged businesses, I heard screams here and there. Underneath them, I could hear the trilling sound again. I did not check to see if that meant that the pursuit was over. I simply ran, with Anne, toward Holmes.

He took some of her weight from me, turning her face-up and catching her legs as I held her under her arms. We made the best speed we could down the alley, falling into stride with each other, left, right, left, right, as best we could.

"We must... get her... someplace safe, Holmes," I panted.

"I fear there is no safe place near," he called back to me. I could scarcely believe it: Holmes wasn't even breathing hard.

In the mist behind us, in the alleys around the warehouses we had just left, I heard the blasts of several policemen's whistles. To my relief, Anne moaned, and her eyes fluttered open.

"Holmes, she stirs," I panted, and we halted. I propped Anne on the back steps of an alehouse—judging from the smell—and she leaned back against the brick wall, panting. I ran my hands through her thick hair, my fingers searching along her skull, and found only one small lump on the side.

"Och, ma heid," she muttered, lapsing into her home dialect, wincing as my fingers probed the lump.

"And a grand, thick, Scots skull you have, Miss Prescott," I said, breathing a sigh of relief. Holmes squatted at her side, peering at her.

"My dear, you are perhaps the bravest woman I've ever met," said he, smiling and squeezing her hand. To me he said, "Watson, lend me your pistol and look after her. I think we are out of immediate danger, so I think it best if you both stay put until I return."

"What a preposterous idea, Holmes," I complained, handing the Webley to him, butt first. "I need to get her somewhere safe. This alley is too exposed, and you saw how those things crawled out of every dark hole we passed." I found the unspent bullets in my pocket and passed those to him as well, though I worried that I would need the Webley before he did. "And it would be suicide for you to go back!" I added.

"Not to face them, old fellow. Just to do some reconnaissance. But perhaps you are right. Take her someplace safe, then," he said, flashing me a fierce grin. To my lasting shock, he planted a kiss on Anne's forehead before saying, "Stay with the doctor this night, then; to ground with the both of you, yes? And then, in two nights, should we survive, I will meet you at the Ten Bells."

We nodded, and with that he was off, despite my misgivings. His fleet steps bore him away from us into the dark, grim alley through which we had made our narrow escape. I prayed that the zombies had withdrawn; if not, I feared that they would overwhelm him before he got too far. But I saw none, heard none, and the air held only its normal East End stink of raw sewage and impoverished lives.

"Will he be all right, do you think?" Anne asked, rising to her feet.

"We can only pray that he will be," I answered. "But do not worry. This is Holmes's milieu. He has done countless deeds of daring in the pursuit of justice, deeds which no one, not even I, will ever hear about. Never, not even in Afghanistan, have I seen a kukri knife wielded with such power and grace. He is wonderful and terrible."

"That he is," she breathed. "I can see why you love him so."

I could only smile and nod. I just needed to act on my own. "Let's go back to the Sumatra Trading Company offices and get you patched up."

***

Though the walk seemed to take hours, I'm certain that it did not. Still, we took extra precautions to avoid being seen, which added time to the journey. And we were exhausted, so our movements were slower. Anne clung to my arm in silence as we passed through the stinking recesses of Whitechapel, which were sweeter, by far, than the stench of the zombies.

Once I had locked and barred the outer door of Holmes's room, the supposed offices of the Sumatra Import company, I lit the oil lamp and searched the supplies on Holmes's makeup table.

Behind all of the powders, coloring agents, and various facial hair appliances, I found alcohol, gauze, and tape, enough to help me. I turned to look at Anne. She was standing in the middle of the floor as though lost, a bitter smile on her face. Fatigue, I thought, had pushed her too far. I was wrong.

"All right, soldier," I said in bluff heartiness. "Let's have you out of that kit, so that I can dress your war wounds."

She cast away the remains of her coat. The afternoon dress in which she had started our venture nearly fell away of its own accord, as pulled and ripped as it had been by our encounter. She tugged at the chemise under it to cover herself, though much of her midriff and her legs were exposed. Cruel hands had torn all of her clothing to shreds. She shivered as her eyes met mine, and that bitter, wry smile appeared again.

"Sit here," I said, drawing two chairs to face each other. She complied, turning her eyes away from mine.

I turned her face back to me, though, to study her pupils, looking for any sign of dilation, which would signal a concussion.

"I don't think I have a concussion," she murmured through nearly closed lips, since I held her chin in my hands. Turning her gaze away from mine, still blushing, she forced my fingers away from her face. I scooted my chair back a few inches, curious as to her mood.

"No. You wouldn't think you had a concussion. Few do think so, until it's too late. We mustn't court such a dangerous chance, though," I said. She flashed a fierce glance my way and again showed that half-smile.

"Now, let's have that arm," I said, reaching for her left arm. She winced as I touched the red, inflamed area.

"May I call you Jack?" she asked. "It seems fitting, given what we've been through, especially now." She glanced down at the tatters of her undergarments.

"Yes, Anne, you may," I replied, feeling my cheeks redden. I gave my attention to her wounded arm.

"Do you like it, then, Jack?" she asked. When I looked up from her arm, I could see she still had that fierce look in her eyes and that wry smile, and she was shivering with more than cold. Was it anger?

Her words took me aback. I wondered if she questioned my approval of her body, since so much of it was exposed to my view. I didn't know what to say.

"Do I like what, Anne?"

"Killing them. Fighting these—these zombies, as you call them," she returned, looking at the bite mark on her arm.

"Of course not," I protested. "I am a doctor, after all. I abhor the idea of killing—anything."

"Do you, Jack?" she asked, and she leaned toward me, bringing her face close to mine. Her vulnerability and her beauty of face and form drew me to her. Even her sudden defiance spoke of her strength and fire, which made me desire her more. "You appear to do it well, to relish it, in fact. Do you delight in killing them?"

"If you mean in defending myself and my friends, why, I—" I began, confused and affronted.

"I mean the way in which you stood stock still as they approached, killing them one by one, almost daring them to come for you and meet their deaths. Did you like that? Was it as exciting as looking at me like this?" she asked, standing, holding her arms out to the side so that her chemise threatened to fall away. I confess that I desired to reach for her, but I fought against that impulse. Her mood confused me, since she seemed to entice me even as she questioned my motives.

"Anne," I began, rising to my feet and turning my back on her. Her challenging words touched a part of me that I did not wish to talk about. I was embarrassed, as well, by her description of my actions, for they revealed my foolish behavior, this need in me for action. Trying to rationalize, I told myself that I had been forced to kill them.

"I'm sorry if my actions have offended or upset you," I said. "I did what I think any man would do in defense of those he... those for whom he cares."

"You killed Tom," she whispered. "I watched you put a bullet through his skull. Did you do that to protect me or to possess me?"

I closed my eyes and gulped. I wanted to say how ridiculous she was being, that Tom McHugh would have killed either of us, but she was also right. And, strangely, my response had been right, for it had helped save us. However, I had not hesitated to kill Tom, to kill any of them. Earlier, reading her telegram, I had harbored a sudden regret that she had found her missing lover. As to my actions in the alley, I tried to reason that Holmes had prepared me to fight, to defend myself and Anne. He had convinced me that we were fighting for our lives, and the cold, murderous actions of those creatures had validated my actions, or at least I thought they had.

But she was right. Killing them, battling them in a life and death struggle, freed me to act without thinking. A part of me needed such action. I craved it, as I craved her.

"Was it wrong to do so, Anne?" I asked, somewhat defensive. "You may well be right that I exulted in it, but was I wrong to do it? Tom McHugh was lost to you when you saw him in that basement. He would have killed you, and... and done God knows what." I turned to face her then, and she collapsed back onto the chair and buried her face in her hands. I took my seat again and pulled her wounded arm to me.

"Please," I said, "let me clean this."

"It aches still," she mumbled, sagging into the chair as one spent, "and where they grabbed me still stings and burns."

"Yes. I have that sensation too," I said, relieved that the conversation's focus had shifted.

Her wound was a laceration, and I knew that it would be extremely painful. I cleaned it with water from the sink, gently washing away the dried blood. "I'm sorry, Anne, but I have to clean this, and it will hurt almost as much as the bite that caused it."

"Go ahead," she said, raising her eyes to meet mine. Thankfully, her expression had grown soft. All traces of anger had left her face, and fatigue had drained its color.

I sprinkled alcohol onto the laceration and held her arm tight as she reacted.

"Agh!" she cried, her right hand catching me around the back of my neck and pulling her head toward mine, touching her forehead to mine. She shook violently. "Oh, d-d-damn!" she hissed through her clenched teeth as the burning liquid found every tender, exposed nerve. Our heads together, she held onto me and let me search the wound with a gauze pad, while I crooned, "There we go. Not long now, not long."

When I was done, she released my neck, falling back against the chair in a swoon, exposing her white, tender throat. Her breathing was regular, so I did not try to bring her around again. Besides, though she had one small goose egg on her scalp, I thought there was little chance of a concussion, having studied after the attack the unwavering, fierce blue of her eyes.

I closed the laceration as best I could, satisfied that it had been cleaned out well, and taped an alcohol-soaked layer of gauze over it. It needed stitches, but I had no needle, no sutures. I would trust that the tape would hold it until some other remedy could be made tomorrow.

Once again, I paused to look at Anne. Even disheveled, her hair a ruined tangle, her strong, tender body marked with bruises and abrasions, her beauty astounded me, sent waves of desire running through me.

The very force of her uniqueness, I thought, emanated from her and drew me, though every thought in my head told me that it was wrong. Perhaps I had indeed killed Tom McHugh because he had a claim upon her, I admitted to myself, though I did not know what alternative there could have been.

Her passion, her bravery, the very fire of her, wove into my desire to abandon myself in action, to lose myself in her as well. On the battlefield, I had seen grown men cry out like children at the sort of treatment she had endured, and I marveled again at the strength of this lass. For a young lass she looked, her long hair streaming down, her fine limbs pale but strong before me.

I forced my thoughts into healing her hurts. The abrasions on her legs and arms, like those on my own, were far less serious than the laceration. I swabbed them with cool water and daubed alcohol on them as well. She was unconscious through it all, and the pain did not reach her. Soon I lifted her in my arms and placed her as gently on the camp bed as I could, covering her with the old, coarse blanket. When she stirred and pulled the blanket around her, I knew that she had passed from swoon into natural sleep, the greatest healer of all.

***

In the night, I woke, feeling her stir and sit up on the bed next to me. I had been dreaming fitfully of hands grasping at me out of the darkness, and my head was still muddled with fatigue.

"What is it?" I whispered as she reached for me.

"Please just hold me, Jack," she whispered, and lay her head on my shoulder. I turned toward her and put my arms around her. As I did so, she let out a sob so deep that I knew it could only come from a heart which was truly broken. I let her cry as she needed to, whispering to her that all would be well, stroking her hair. She cried harder, like a bereaved child, without holding back. Then she pulled out of my embrace and turned her stricken face to mine, seeking something from me, I thought.

"No! No, all will not be well," she sobbed, searching my eyes. "It will never be well again. To have seen what I have seen leaves me empty. I have never felt so alone."

"But, Anne, you are not alone," I cried, placing my hands on either side of her face. Even streaked with tears, her face drew me on, and when our lips met, I tasted the power of her passionate response to my kiss. She wanted me as much as I wanted her.

Her tears replaced by soft moans, she returned my kiss with raw desire. But when my hands fell from her face to her bare shoulders, she drew back from me, holding me at arm's length. I pulled my own hands away, startled at my actions, and sat back, shaking. She did the same, pulling back onto the cot, taking up the blanket to cover herself.

She stared at me, her face pale and wide-eyed with shock at her actions, at mine. Tension, like a burning cord, tied us to each other. I knew that I had been prepared to take her in the passion of the moment, and I was chastened by her recognition that I was bound to another. I turned to the door, half in anger, half in fear, and stepped out into the pre-dawn dark.

Outside, I stood shaking, seeking to master my foolish blood, to exercise some responsible control over myself. I tried to think of Mary, or at least of my duty to Anne as Holmes's client. My thoughts rioting, I paced the alley.

At length, I decided that it would be best not to be away from her side, and I re-entered the room on soft steps. She was asleep, and I let her be.

Part Two.

"Risky Ventures and the Bedeviled Captain"

CHAPTER EIGHT

The tiring trip back to Paddington, which I took on foot even in my tattered clothes, found me ruminating about my need to remain true to Mary, yet wondering when I would see Anne again. I had escorted Anne, who by then was dressed in Holmes's Bert Tiller clothes, to Shepherd's Bush, so I was alone with my thoughts as I walked home.

I chided myself that even as a schoolboy I had never been so foolish in matters of love. I wanted to see myself as a man of the world, capable of dealing with such a simple decision: I was married to Mary and would not give in to any wrong-headed desire to take Anne as a lover, though the vision of her, the memory of her in my arms, would not depart, even in the face of cold logic, even in the recognition that Anne might not wish to return my affections. The whole of it left me in a muddle.

Gaining the refuge of my own home in the late morning, I found word from Mary, as I'd thought I would, stating that she was with Dr. Jackson and his wife, not terribly far from our home. Truepenny that she was, Mary was flustered but not overcome by the sudden change of household.

Having cleaned myself up and gotten into fresh clothes—my others had been as torn and shredded as Anne's had been—I went to find Mary. As always, she greeted me with joy and concern, but this time her good-natured smile scored my heart like acid. I told her that Holmes and I had been in a deadly struggle, trying to protect Holmes's client. It was true, if not just, given what passed between Anne and me.

***

Two days later, at the appointed hour, dressed in the roughest clothes I could manage, I made my way to the Ten Bells in Spitalfields. I understood that it took its name from the bells in the church across Fournier Street, but the clientele I saw as I entered at its Commercial Street door made me doubt any other ecclesiastical connection. Working harlots and rough men filled the smoky interior. I shouldered my way to the bar, wondering what our next steps in this case might be, wondering what Anne would say about our experiences two nights before.

I had just cause to be fearful about the case, but my heart foolishly anticipated seeing Anne again. Would she regret, as I should, that brief moment of shared passion? Would she return to that angry diffidence from which she had questioned my need for violent action?

And what would Holmes say to it all? I had not heard from him since he had sprinted away from us into the darkness of that alley. I chided myself, thinking that he might not make this meeting at all if he had fallen prey to those foes he sought. Surely, I would have heard of it if he had. Then again, within the secrecy of our operations, much might happen which would never meet the public eye.

I stood at the bar, nursing a pint I had ordered from the surly barman. Then a hand tugged at my sleeve. I turned to look at a dark-haired youth, bright of eye.

"Beg pardon, guv, but there's as pretty a bloke as you'll want to meet in the far corner," he said, nodding to his left, where the old oak bar turned into the darkest part of the smoky room. Nodding to him to lead the way, I trusted that he would lead me to Sherlock Holmes and Anne Prescott in disguise.

Jostling through the rough crowd, the lad led me to a table where a young man in a flat cap and old coat—Anne, I presumed—sat with bent head, talking to none other than Holmes as Bert Tiller. I'd last seen Holmes dressed as Bert in the small room at the rear of Hepplewhite's chapel and lodging, the room that purported to be Sumatra Imports.

I pulled up a chair, my back to the squalid room. Bert/Holmes turned his vapid expression on me. The striking blue of Anne's eyes greeted me beneath her cap bill, pulled low on her forehead.

"Thank you, O'Doole," Holmes said in his own voice, which sounded odd coming from Bert Tiller's slack face. "You may take up your guard post."

"Cor, sir, but couldn't I stay with Miss P.?" O'Doole asked, his eyes as hungry as mine for a full look at Anne's face.

"You will take up your post, if we are to leave here as planned in a few minutes. But you may look forward to escorting Miss Prescott through the sewers to Magdalen Hospital. You may count yourself lucky in that," Holmes said in tones of warning.

O'Doole winked and smiled at Anne, who favored him with a grin as he walked to the front corner of the room, within sight of the front door and our corner. We were well-placed, I saw, to make a hasty exit behind the bar if need be. And if any curious eyes were turned our way, they would see only three dockworkers muttering together over their pints, though they might note that the youngest one, in the large cap, possessed the smile of an angel.

"Jimmy is a bright lad—one of the brightest—but he is a hopeless admirer of feminine beauty. I hope you will excuse his indelicacy, Miss Prescott," Holmes said, vapid eyes staring at nothing. Anne smiled and nodded.

"I hope that he will make a fine police detective," Holmes continued. "But what of you, Watson, Miss Prescott? Have you both survived your brush with death... and passion?"

I choked on my beer and lifted my eyes to Anne's, wondering if she had revealed details of our brief encounter in Bert Tiller's room. Her wide-eyed look returned my questioning gaze. She wondered the same about me, I supposed, and I shook my head, as did she. Then we both cast imploring looks at Holmes.

Holmes went on in quieter tones. "Given the attraction which draws you to one another, I would be surprised if you had not shared a much more, er, involved moment of passion, given what you had just been through. I urge you to see it as a trivial matter, one that can plague you only if you let it. Rise above it, my friends, for we are in greater danger now than ever before."

Anne and I could only exchange mute stares. Holmes had it right: we both needed to concentrate on the dangers at hand.

"If I may," Holmes continued, "our recent encounter with LaLaurie's forces revealed that he has a more extensive plan as well as a network of support. I know of no other explanation for that rifleman shooting at us from the distance he did. Later, in my search of the area, I found some of his shell casings, which I assume he missed picking up in the misty darkness. He was a good three hundred yards away. Few men would even attempt such shots under those conditions. LaLaurie has the financial support to give him access to such a gunman.

"And LaLaurie is able to move his forces in ways which we have yet to discover, likely through the sewers, though not always. Moving that number of zombies through the sewers, O'Doole assures me, would have attracted notice earlier. O'Doole, self-appointed King of the Toshers, prides himself on his knowledge of what goes on in subterranean London, and he assures me that no zombies moved through his sewers before two nights ago."

"Then where have they all come from?" I demanded. "They cannot all have come from St. Lazarus."

"No, indeed," Holmes said, maintaining his Bert Tiller expression. "And this, too, points to a more expansive base of operations. LaLaurie has the means to hide and transport impressive numbers of his creatures at will, making this a much more dangerous business than we first considered it. This has gone far beyond a missing persons case and far beyond one man's evil tendencies."

"But what is his aim?" Anne asked, her voice low but strained.

"I do not know yet, Miss Prescott, but I will find out," Holmes replied. "And the obvious extent of his plans means that we must take greater precautions than we have heretofore. LaLaurie must think of us as inactive, frightened off. We need to become as secretive in our motions as he is and not draw his attention again until we know how to best him. We must prepare in the greatest secrecy and learn as much as we can of LaLaurie's strengths.

"To do so, I will need each of you to undertake some training with an associate of mine so that you will be better equipped to deal with the forces that counter us. They will be as horrible as those that almost claimed your lives in that alley, and you must prepare physically and mentally to deal with the threat," said Holmes. We both nodded our heads in acceptance.

"Have we no help, Holmes?" I asked, wondering how many zombies I could kill before being overrun.

"Not for the encounters with his creatures that will likely occur if we pester him further. But if we can act as though we have given up our pursuit, we can hope that his secretiveness will keep him away. I count on help from sources I cannot reveal at the moment, but we cannot risk police involvement. We cannot possibly equip and train even a picked lot of constables to deal with this threat. There would be too great a loss of life, and one cannot easily explain the deaths of multiple constables. With your commitment to see justice done in this case, you two are the only allies I can risk asking to take the field against LaLaurie.

"Please, both of you, consider this as your last, best chance to remove yourselves from this action. Truly, it would be prudent for any of us to do so, but I will not abandon this case until I see justice done to LaLaurie, official or otherwise."

"Nor will I," Anne said, just above a whisper. I wanted to warn her away, but I saw that she was adamant about seeing this business through.

"I cannot," I said. "I will not abandon either of you."

"I have taken a position at Magdalen Hospital. Send word there about where I report for this training, Mr. Holmes, and I will be ready," Anne said, rising and leaving with O'Doole.

I turned an imploring glance to Holmes.

"Watson, she has just cause," he said, watching her stride away. "I will not stand in her way, even if it means risking her life."

"But Holmes," I whispered harshly, "you cannot let a woman expose herself to such dangers. She will—"

"She will have to be abducted, tied up, and sent away under guard, if we are to keep her from her chance to see right prevail. She will see it done, and I will aid her. It is high time, Watson, that we treat women as our equals, especially where justice is concerned. Miss Prescott is not helpless, as you well know from seeing her in action."

His clipped words, coming from Bert's slack face, challenged me, and though my feelings for Anne would have had me spare her from any danger, I knew he was right. I also desired to give her the chance to avenge her sister and her lover, even as I feared the outcome. I hated the thought of not seeing her again, as foolish a notion as that was. I shook my head at the impossibility of the situation.

Holmes lowered his face, and for a moment, he looked at me with something like his normal expression. "Poor old Watson. She really is something, isn't she? Has she captured your heart so thoroughly? Should you stand down, old friend? You need not follow me on every adventure, you know. You are free to return to Mary, your practice, a more placid life."

I looked hard at him, seeking any sign that he might be testing me. I saw none, though that was likely because he had taken on, again, Bert Tiller's lackluster expression.

The bar noise rose around us, and Holmes stood. "We had best leave separately," he said. "I will send word about where you should meet us, but it will be covert. Disclose all this to Mary, if you must. Consider your wisest choice in the matter. If you arrive at the appointed hour, I will count that as proof of your commitment to the balance of this case."

CHAPTER NINE

Holmes's sudden eloquence about women's equality notwithstanding, I left the Ten Bells that night with an even greater level of anxiety, looking to rooftops, expecting the shock of a rifle round tearing into me. I believe the saying is "pins and needles," which I cannot remember feeling before, despite all my encounters with danger. The call to stealth and secrecy left me chafing for action yet fearful that I would be shot before I could meet my foes. Knowing that I could put faith in one of Holmes's plans did not help me adopt a greater patience. I also longed to keep Anne from danger.

Yet with equal strength I longed to see her again, just to be near her. The idea that I was to see Anne Prescott on a regular basis sent a thrill through me, which I recognized as foolish. I was like a boy, delighted and in terror of his first love. My warring thoughts argued that I had freedom to have feelings about Anne or anyone, so long as I did not act on them. I told myself that we would not become lovers, that we would have a chaste sort of love, like something in a courtly poem. The thought of not touching her, though, was as grim to me as the thought of facing another zombie.

Unlike Holmes, I could not—cannot still—simply free my mind from the grip of my emotions. Yet if I looked without passion at my readiness to shoot zombies down, Anne's questions about my seeming relish in moments of conflict played over and over in my head. Was I not as bloodthirsty as those I called my foes, even if I saw that law and right were on my side?

Yet I knew that I would answer Holmes's call when it came.

Seeing no way forward for me except through the path of our investigation, I settled myself down as best as I could and returned to home and to Mary. There, I spent much nervous energy avoiding windows, with the thought of rifle bullets finding their mark in my skull.

***

In the next days, Holmes, with the help of O'Doole and of William Wiggins, self-appointed leader of Holmes's band of street Arabs, worked out a series of sewer and alley routes that would take each of us from a spot where we were expected to be to either the training site in Soho or to a central location on Oxford Street where we could rendezvous and carry out our investigations into LaLaurie's movements. We would have to add a sense of randomness to our "regular" movements, but Holmes assured us that for the length of time the investigation was likely to last, we could manage this task. To help, O'Doole offered to escort Anne Prescott personally through any stretch of his underground world. Later, in confidence, she claimed his was the sweetest invitation to wander the sewers that she could imagine.

When a letter purporting to be from a "Colonel K. Barnard," in Surrey, no less, came for me two days later, I knew that Holmes's plan was in place. I had sent my earlier telegram to Barnard's home of record in Ireland, not Surrey. Colonel Barnard asked me to pay a visit to his old regimental batsman, Anderson, whose host of maladies left him in need of the constant attention of a physician, a role which Barnard hoped I would take on, at least for the foreseeable future.

Not only was this Colonel Kerry Barnard from Surrey, but the letter addressed me as Jack, a name Anne had begun to use for me even in Holmes's presence. Holmes counted on this knowledge, and on our private discussion of the real Kerry Barnard's exploits in Jamaica, to help me see his subterfuge. He evidently feared that LaLaurie and his confederates could intercept the mail. The very idea frightened me even more.

However, at a time appointed in the letter, I took my leave of Mary after dinner and journeyed the short distance to Oxford Street. I found there a venerable, clean block of flats. Anderson's name appeared on the label of the basement flat. I went down the stairs and knocked, wondering what disguise Holmes would take on to appear to be Anderson.

When the door opened, I gasped, for Anne Prescott stood before me, dressed in the loose-fitting dungarees of a laboring man, her voluminous hair tucked up into a flat tweed cap that she had pulled low over her eyes. She raised a finger to her lips to signal my silence and gave me a glowing smile.

A deep voice from within the darkened room called out, "Is that the doctor? Pray God it is! Come in here, my good man, at the double!"

Entering, I noted that the voice had come from a large man sitting in the far corner beneath the glow of a gas lamp, most of his person hidden by an open copy of the *Times*. A full glass of claret at his elbow winked in the dim light. The shirtsleeves, trousers, and shoes, all of excellent make and rather new, suggested that he was no pensioner.

Holmes sat closer to the door, away from the lamp, at a bare wooden table. When Anne closed and bolted the door, Holmes stood and shook my hand.

"Well met, Watson. I must congratulate you on reading through my subterfuge and coming so promptly," he said in soft tones. "Welcome to one of my bolt holes. The pub next door has wonderful fish and chips, which I can recommend if you need sustenance. Or would you rather see to your new patient?"

"I am at your disposal, sir," I said. Then, turning to Anne, "And miss—or should I say 'sir' again?"

Anne smiled and whispered, "If you can think of me so, maybe 'sir' would be better."

I returned her knowing smile, then turned to Holmes and said, "And as to this other gentleman?"

"Our compatriot here has volunteered only to voice your invalid batsman, Anderson, for a period of four visits, which he thinks is the extent to which we can use this bit of trickery. I tend to agree. Of course, we will adapt to changing needs. He will answer to the name Anderson for the foreseeable future; is that not right, sir?" Holmes said, turning to the figure by the fire. In return, we received a general nod of the paper, which I assumed was in concert with the head behind it, and a brief "Umpf!"

"I had thought to be treated to another of your false identities, Holmes," I said, "another of your garrulous old soldier routines."

"This fellow is garrulous enough, in his way," Holmes returned, earning a forced bark of laughter from the newspaperman. "And for now, I will forgo introductions so that we may be off." As used as I am to Holmes's caprices, I followed him, as I always do.

With Anne, we left that basement flat via a trap door in the floor of its kitchen and entered noxious sewer tunnels for several blocks, keeping to the main line, which ran toward the Thames.

"If LaLaurie can use the sewers and underground crypts of old London, so can we," Holmes said, free now to speak in normal tones. "O'Doole has several routes for us to use, with the Oxford Street entrance to which you came being the one most directly connected to the Soho address to which we repair. I trust, Watson, that you are ready to begin the training phase of which I spoke? Tonight we meet one of our great allies in this cause, Mr. Takachi Uyeshiba, a master of the sword and of a system of hand-to-hand fighting upon which I have come to rely."

"Mr. Holmes," Anne said, hurrying along in the small pool of light that surrounded us, "surely firearms will suit the task better than swords. What purpose will we serve blundering around in tunnels and dark alleys with long, unwieldy weapons?"

"If I may, Anne," I answered, "pistols run out of ammunition, and carrying a great many extra rounds, even for a light weapon like a pistol, would encumber us."

"The doctor is correct, Miss Prescott," Holmes added. "However, Mr. Uyeshiba's training methods also have the benefit of inuring one to the fears associated with combat. His system is economical yet extremely effective, and I hope that exposing you and Watson to it will prepare you better for the coming encounters."

"If you mean the horrors of facing zombies, I'm afraid that even a year of training would do me little good," Anne said.

***

We left the sewers and entered a sub-basement, which Holmes told us was on Carnaby Street, beneath a small tea shop. A set of five broad stone steps led to a stout wooden door near the top of the sewer tunnel. Knocking on this door, we were ushered into the training room of Mr. Uyeshiba, a short, thickset Japanese gentleman who greeted Holmes with warm enthusiasm. Soon, all of us down to our shirt sleeves, we started our training.

Grueling does nothing to describe it, nor the aches and pains I took home with me that night and for many nights after.

The Japanese gentleman complained bitterly of my stoutness and inflexibility but praised Anne for each action she took. Mr. Uyeshiba, it seemed, had found a star pupil. I had to give him credit, for even distracted by the pain of strained muscles, sore joints, and bruised extremities, I thoroughly enjoyed watching Anne's movements, full of power and grace as they were.

The rigors of stretching, punching, kicking, and grappling left me red in the face and gasping during the first lesson. Mr. Uyeshiba, with his frequent criticisms, soon had me ready to give up. Only Holmes's interventions on my behalf seemed to placate the taciturn Japanese.

That first night, we were there for an hour before we returned to Anderson's flat, but I had the sensation that more like twelve hours had passed. As we made our way through the tunnels on our return, I said, "Anne, I think you may have been right that this is unnecessary. I, for one, would be willing to carry as much extra ammunition as will be required."

"Oh, no, Jack," she answered. "I quite liked it, and I'm sure that it will do us both much good." At that point, she delivered a light punch to my ribcage, as though to punctuate her assertion.

***

Another week or so went by, me visiting Mr. Uyeshiba's dojo on my own and then repairing to the tea shop above for ache-filled luncheons. I was nowhere near the level of mastery Anne and Holmes had already attained, and yet I soldiered on, if only because my sessions merged with Anne's. She was marvelous to watch. Graceful, powerful, fluid movements came easily to her, and I could see changes in her physique from the exercise: her comely shape grew more slender, and she walked with an even greater vivacity, head proud and erect as a result of even a short amount of training.

For me, the changes were to my heart. The aches and pains of stretching and training were as nothing compared to the tender agony of growing even closer to Anne. Though she would often chide my failing efforts to adapt to Mr. Uyeshiba's Jiu-Jitsu, she let her natural warmth spread freely to me, encouraging me and calling me "Jack" in a soft voice she used with no one else. My weaknesses in the training appeared to draw her to me, though her excellence gave her cause to ridicule me.

I tried hard not to fall harder for her, and I mentally renewed my commitment to loving her in name only. For Mary grew as solicitous of my condition as Anne did. Indeed, in some ways, she was more so. When I told her that my present case with Holmes required a higher level of fitness, Mary saw to it that our meals offered leaner fare. And she grew more solicitous in our moments of intimacy, showing how much she appreciated the slow changes in my physique, the hardening of my body. Taking on a program of mild exercise herself, she delighted in the changes we both experienced, and she did not even offer a protest to my restricting her from my training sessions on the grounds of her frailty. I simply could not countenance the idea of bringing Mary and Anne together, showing my wife the growing bond which I experienced with another woman.

Making love more often to my wife, as gratifying as it was, still did little to remove Anne from my mind. At the very least, though, the intimate moments with Mary did help me stay true to my commitment over the long weeks of our training during that cool summer, though my closeness with Mary formed the nexus of an acute, bittersweet pain when I was near Anne. For I could see that Anne's caring for me grew with each occasion of our meetings. Madness. I had the distinct feeling of being tested, and I sensed my impending failure.

***

As those summer days passed, LaLaurie seemed to withdraw from the field. Wiggins's street Arabs reported no sightings of him or of Alcee Sauvage in their old haunts. Holmes even allowed some of O'Doole's lads to make careful trips into the Whitechapel sewers, but with no result.

Soon, Holmes, Anne, and I began more serious training with the long, curved swords which Mr. Uyeshiba called "katana." Things proceeded as usual: Anne and Holmes, with their lithe bodies, wielded those incredibly sharp blades with grace and precision, while Mr. Uyeshiba took to calling me "ham-fisted butcher boy." At least, I thought ruefully, I perhaps was the cause of his growing proficiency in English.

In our first sword lesson with Mr. Uyeshiba, he showed us a legendary weapon. It bore a strange name, "Mustard Seed," because in the hands of the warrior for whom it was made, it had sliced a mustard seed in half in midair. Even to my touch, trained to the scalpel, its edge was unequaled. I believed Mr. Uyeshiba when he said it was the sharpest blade ever made.

Other than during our brief introduction to Mustard Seed, it remained at the top of Mr. Uyeshiba's sword rack, untouched in its midnight-black scabbard. Mr. Uyeshiba claimed, with great sincerity, that it was searching for a new master. After our first session with katana, he expressed the hope that it would not choose me, for I was inept with the long blades.

In the second session with katana, we were interrupted by a frenetic knocking on the dojo's secret entrance.

"This cannot be good," Holmes muttered, sheathing his sword and rising to open the door to a panting Jimmy O'Doole.

"Mr. 'Olmes, Mr. 'Olmes," the lad panted, "it's Spots and Bothers, sir. They been done for, sir. Oh, God, 'ow they been done for. It's—it's—"

"Easy, Jimmy my lad," Anne crooned, moving to the boy's side. She stroked his damp hair. "Take a good deep breath and tell us. Who or what are Spots and Bothers, and what has happened?"

"His very good friends, Anne: Hector "Spots" Edgwick and Seanine "Bothers" Brothers, both fine lads, inseparable. Jimmy," Holmes said, placing a hand on the boy's trembling shoulder, "were they patrolling in the East End as you told me they would be?"

"Yes, sir. Like you said yesterday, small patrols, not roamin' at night, just lookin' in on the big tunnels in that dock area where you three was attacked," Jimmy said, trying to regain his composure. "I missed 'em at evenin' check-in down at the Fryin' Pan, and me an' Brewer went for a look and found 'em, sir."

O'Doole gulped, wiped his streaming eyes and nose, and continued in a whisper, shifting a sorrowful glance at Anne. "They was 'alf et, sir. Those dirty bast... devils din't jus' kill 'em, Mr. 'Olmes, sir. They fed on 'em. Even—even the insides of their 'eads, sir."

"How long ago, Jimmy?" I asked, hiding the shudder his words had caused.

"They ain't been dead more'n three hours now. Not even stiff, like, the poor mites."

"LaLaurie must have his own bolt holes, too, Holmes. You recall the dwellings from which some of those vile things attacked us when we were running away from that most recent attack," I observed.

"Indeed, Watson. I have been into most of those dark pits, but I found them now deserted," Holmes said. "Perhaps LaLaurie is moving his creatures from one holding area to another. In any case, we must have a look as soon as we can. This attack on Spots and Bothers will seriously change our plans, though. We may well risk our secrecy in moving to investigate this atrocity. I think it wise to assume that LaLaurie keeps watch on our movements. Breaking away from them now may cause him to react."

"And therefore increase the risk to ourselves of LaLaurie's or more immediate retaliation," I added, thinking of the unknown marksman.

"Agreed. We must adapt to the change, but we must first look into the deaths of young Spots and Bothers, both sterling lads, in their own ways. I do not ask either of you to accompany me, for it will be grim at best," Holmes added, putting his coat and tie back on.

Anne did not hesitate, however. She jammed her hair up into her cap and stood grim-eyed, ready to move. I could only follow, though my heart misgave me.

CHAPTER TEN

We quit the sewers and hailed a cab on Brewer Street, reckoning that no rooftop rifleman could track us, though I would have to return to the Oxford Street flat in order to retain my cover. We made an entrance to the sewers again half an hour later on Montague Street, a block above Whitechapel Road, and were not long in finding the channel where the boys had been killed.

I expected the worst and found it. Even before we reached the dead boys, the flickering lights and eerie shadows caused by the narrow beams of our dark lanterns, together with errant splashes of noxious water, set my nerves on edge. My stomach threatening to heave, I looked with Holmes on the scene first, with Anne coming behind me. Holmes sought to hold us back—to search for clues, I knew—but when Anne saw the bodies of those poor boys, she would not be restrained.

She pushed past me with a gasp and hurried with O'Doole to where Spots and Bothers lay. The only parts of the poor lads which were recognizable were their pale, thin legs. Anne and Jimmy sank to their knees beside the grisly remains, which lay in sequence on a ledge above the rank water. Only shreds of their clothing still clung to them. Their torsos had been stripped, hacked, or pulled apart, and partially consumed. Anne's sweet voice trembled with each groaning "no" she uttered.

"This one was Spots, miss," O'Doole muttered in a cracked voice. He lifted into his lap the shattered torso and the remains of the head, half of the lad's pimpled face staring at us in the light of my lantern.

"Oh..." Anne gasped, reaching out to touch Spots's face. She ran her fingertip down over the open eye and closed the lid, whispering, "Shh, shh, oh, poor lamb, sweet little lad" in a voice so tender that tears welled in my eyes and dropped down my cheeks. She looked to the remains of Bothers and rested a shaking hand on his leg. Then she broke down in tears. Holmes, his head bent, may have cried, too, for the love he bears for all his lads.

And then, God help me, Anne's weeping turned into heaving, wracking sobs, so hard that I worried she would never stop. The hat fell from her head, and her hair cascaded down as she turned her face to the heavens.

Holmes, taking her shoulders in his hands, sought to quiet her, but she would have no solace. Shaking him away from her, Anne rose slowly to her feet, and her weeping escalated into a scream of such fierce rage that both Holmes and I backed away. O'Doole clamped his hands over his ears and cowered before her. The tunnels rang, echoed, and increased the power of her cry, as though the darkness itself responded to her anger and sent it back a hundredfold.

I felt that all of the East End would hear it, that Anne's rejection of this wrong would echo down to the very roots of England itself and cast back upon the world a recognition that retribution for all of the wrongs done in the dark was at hand. This was no shriek of fright or pain which I might expect from feminine lips. Raw, primal, it was a battle cry which promised revenge, and it took all my strength to keep from adding my voice to hers, though it could have had nothing like the same power.

Her breath running out, Anne gently picked up the body of Bothers and turned like Niobe, all tears, yet with the countenance of one of the Furies, to make her way past me. O'Doole picked up the remains of Spots and followed her into the darkness.

As the two, with their dreadful burdens, passed out of the reach of our lights, I stammered, "Anne, can I... can I do anything to... to help?"

Her eyes met mine, and I saw no anger then, but a deep anguish, which tears could never heal.

"They were just wee lads, Jack. Would any loving heart not break, seeing them so?" she asked in a cracking voice. Turning her eyes back to the pitiful form in her arms, she went on her way. I could only follow in her slow steps.

***

After I'd witnessed the power and depth of her emotions, my appreciation for Anne Prescott rose. I watched her gain greater and greater levels of skill with the sword and Jiu-Jitsu, growing to match Holmes's abilities and surpassing anything I could accomplish. Anne Prescott simply unfolded before my eyes into the most complete woman I could imagine: generous heart, sharp mind, powerful yet feminine physique, kind soul, and a capacity for love so great that it could become fierce in defense of those she loved.

A complete woman, did I say? No. Anne Prescott embodied completion for any person. I wanted to be like her. In odd moments, I even recognized that Holmes would have wished to share some of her qualities. Everything about her grew more focused, composed, and integrated, even the affection that she gave me.

At the same time, her mounting fury toward our enemies increased from a candle's light in the dark to a fierce blue flame that could melt metal. When we faced zombies again, I knew that the toll she would take upon them would be awful. She was relentless in training, earning even Mr. Uyeshiba's urging to take it easy.

One night at a lesson, Anne turned to Holmes and asked, "When do we go back to hunt them, Mr. Holmes?"

"That is not part of my plan just yet," Holmes said, buttoning his shirt cuffs.

"And why not?" I asked, for I saw the color rise in Anne's cheeks.

"I am not ready to go back yet," Holmes replied evenly. "I have insufficient information as of yet to identify where LaLaurie comes from or goes to with his zombies. I have crawled through miles of filth with O'Doole, looking for traces of the zombies' passing, but the conditions make finding clues near to impossible, and there are so many places to which the tunnels give him access. And as to expanding my searches, I will not risk any of those tosher lads again in searches which might expose them to danger." His voice rose as he spoke, to indicate the finality of his words.

"And you need not risk their lives, sir, when others stand by ready to take the risks," Anne returned, her back to Holmes and her eyes meeting mine. A shiver of fear ran through me as I anticipated the implicit violence of action against LaLaurie and his creatures. It would be deadly, brutal, and unremitting. Anne, Holmes, or I could be pulled apart—or worse, eaten.

Holmes reached out and turned her to face him, looking at me as well.

"I will not hear of any such thing at this point," he said. "It is rash, at best, to act without knowledge, which a more careful investigation will produce. At worst, it is suicide." His eyes flashed with intensity, and the tension grew palpable.

Anne pulled away from his grip. Her jaws clenched and she said through gritted teeth, "You are not my father, husband, or lover, sir. I am mine own, and I will—"

"Anne, please," I cried, restraining her and stepping between them. "I think it best to consider what Holmes has said. It will not be long before he identifies a path that will help us foil LaLaurie's plan. We simply must be patient. Remember, there is evidence that someone could hunt us down, retaliate openly."

She did not draw out of the grip of my hands, though I knew my strength would not hold her if she tried to. At length, when she did turn away from me, she crossed the room to fetch her hat and loose-fitting coat.

"Very well," she said.

***

Returning to the Oxford Street flat, we found "Anderson" gone and a note left on the table, which read, "Possible Parliament involvement. The L.S. convening. Come at once."

"What does this mean, Holmes?" I asked. "Surely no member of our own Parliament is involved. That's a preposterous notion. And who or what is the L.S.?"

Holmes studied the note, his brow furrowed. "It means that I must attend to this at once. Suffice it to say that the L.S. will work to see justice done to our foes—all of them. Watson, would you stay here with Miss Prescott and wait for O'Doole to take her back to her quarters at Magdalen?"

"Yes, of course," I answered, "but this is intolerable. You ask us to wait upon your plans, but you cannot or will not help us understand them."

"I'm sorry, Watson, Miss Prescott, but I am not yet at liberty to reveal certain aspects of those plans. I work with others at the present time. I must protect the confidence they place in me to keep their involvement secret. There are things afoot about which I must keep my own counsel until I am certain. Come to Baker Street tomorrow night, both of you. Perhaps then I will be able to disclose my thoughts to you more completely. Come with caution, though. The door will be unlocked; do not linger on the street or in open view."

Holmes began climbing down again through the trapdoor. "O'Doole, I'm sure, will be here shortly," he added. "He never misses a chance to act as your escort, Miss Prescott." And with that and a brief smile, he let the trapdoor close behind him.

Anne stood frowning, her arms crossed, staring at the trapdoor. I sat down with a tired thump on one of the flimsy chairs around that bare table, the oil lamp sending flickering shadows across the room. Anne spun on her heel and reached out to take my arm.

"Come with me!" she said, that fierce light in her blue eyes.

"What? Where?" I started.

"Back to those tunnels, Jack. We know how to get to them. We can leave here and emerge blocks away. If you can find us a cab, we can be there in less than an hour."

The urgency in her sweet voice melted the answering "No!" that my better sense urged.

"I feel it in my bones that we can find his damnable lair on our own, Jack. Just the two of us. We can move as silently as O'Doole or any of his lads."

"But we have no weapons," I protested, desiring to avoid dangers from which I could not defend her. As though she could see my resolve melting, her hands pulled me slowly to my feet, toward the trapdoor.

"And what can we accomplish?" I demanded, holding back as she tugged at me. I had never knowingly gone against Holmes's wishes, and I knew that this action would put us in peril.

But her face aglow, her strong hands on my arm, her urgency, all captivated me.

"We can act. We can look. We can do something, anything to relieve this horrible waiting. Please," she finished in a husky whisper.

I relented, and we took to the sewers.

CHAPTER ELEVEN

Between the two of us, we managed to find our way back to that tunnel where Spots and Bothers had met their gruesome end. My misgivings grew as we neared that place on this impetuous foray. But Anne led the way without hesitation, the flickering light of the oil lamp, which I held above us causing her shadow to dance over the filthy brick sewer walls.

We reached the place where the boys had died and stood a moment, looking about us. Mild rain showers had settled over London for the past two days, and more water was flowing here, washing away any traces of the boys that might have been left behind.

"O'Doole said that this tunnel is one of the main lines that empties into the river. If we push on a bit, I'm sure that we'll come to side passages, which we might explore one at a time," I offered.

Anne nodded, gave me an encouraging smile, and we set off, trying to keep to the ledge, where it remained in place. Along certain stretches, though, the ledge had given way to the rush of water and time, and we were forced to wade through brackish water up to mid-thigh.

Despite the heavy flow of water around our legs, we covered quite a distance between our entry point and the place where the boys had been killed. We pushed on quite a bit farther before we encountered another passage on our right, adding its weight of water and filth to the main tunnel.

"Anne," I whispered, a sudden realization gripping me with fear, "this line we've come down has had no breaks in it, no side passages emptying in."

"Yes. That's right, Jack. Why do you mention it?" she asked, stopping and turning a quizzical glance upon me.

"I think it means that the boys likely met their end down here because they got trapped without an escape. They simply could not get out, and," I gulped, "when they were slowed down by having to wade through that bit where the ledge breaks down, the zombies... ran them down."

"Oh!" she cried in a soft voice, pulling herself upright as though she had run into an obstruction. "Then we can't really go back that way, can we?"

"No. I think not. If we go forward, who knows when the next tunnel might join this one?" I said, doubt making my voice hoarse. "And if we are surprised by LaLaurie's creatures, we will likely suffer the same fate as those two hapless toshers. Damn it! I wish we had brought weapons."

Moving to me and taking me into a quick embrace, Anne said, "I'm sorry. My impetuosity has taken us into greater danger than I had imagined." Then she released me, before I could return her embrace. "But if we take this turning to the right, we will likely find areas to look into and also more places of escape. What do you say?" she asked, smiling.

"Yes. Yes, it seems prudent," I said, and started into the blackness of the opening on our right, against the rushing streams, which grew shallower. In a few feet, we were already on drier footing, though the stench did not abate.

Not having gone more than twenty yards, we approached the first bend in this side tunnel, and the tuneless notes of a pipe reached our ears.

"Jack! That piping..." Anne said in a fierce whisper, her strong fingers clutching at my shoulder.

"Can you tell which direction they are coming from?" I asked, fighting the panic. I wanted to tell her to run, but I could not determine the direction of the damnable sound. If I could do so, I would try to delay them enough to give her time to get out, though it would mean no escape for me. But the piping echoed so against the surfaces of those tunnels that it could have been ahead of us or behind us in the main tunnel. Its eerie tones bounced all around us, and both of us whipped our heads first one way, then another. The remains of Spots and Bothers loomed large in my mind, their poor bodies torn to pieces.

I heard a distant splash. I turned in the direction away from the main tunnel and caught the barest flickering of light around the corner ahead of us.

"They are coming from up ahead," I whispered. "Look, though, there just beyond the corner: there is a side tunnel some three feet up the wall. We'll make for that." Without waiting for her to comply, I grabbed her hand and headed toward the corner, where I stopped and peered around it, crouched, my head low along the wall.

Around another corner, some fifty yards from where we stood, we saw a stronger light flickering, outlining lumbering shadows moving toward us. Near where we waited, the tunnel they walked made a sudden, three-foot drop to the level of the one we occupied, giving the stream greater force. The approaching light grew brighter. We hadn't much time.

I doused our light and fairly dragged Anne to the opening. "Up, my dear, feet first. Worm your way back far enough to be in complete darkness, and then I will join you." I turned down the lamp wick, plunging us into darkness, and pushed the lamp into the opening.

To her great credit, Anne didn't pause to reflect on this choice, for the side passage stank worse than anything in the main tunnels we sought to quit. A thin stream trickled down out of it, and the stench of rotten food grew to a gagging intensity.

"Breathe through your mouth, Jack," she whispered, as I clambered up after her.

I wormed my way feet first toward her, and Anne's strong hands guided me to a spot alongside her, where she wrapped her arms around me, burying her face in my shirt front to blunt the stench. Her warmth surprised me, yet she shivered. I cradled her head against my chest, but she could not resist turning her gaze toward the tunnel mouth. We waited, watching the light grow in the opening a dozen or so feet in front of us, trying to breathe through our mouths but not loudly enough to be heard. I prayed that we were far enough back to avoid anyone's sight. Zombies, I hoped, would pass by such small tunnels.

Filthy water pooled around us. We shifted to let it flow on as the sounds of many feet splashing and that damnable, tuneless piping grew louder.

Then, two things happened at once. First, I jumped in startlement, for a rat ran over my leg and another right after him.

Second, out in the tunnel, I heard the piping stop and a coarse voice yelled an oath and screamed, before the sound of a loud splash: I supposed that whoever had been playing the pipe had not seen the drop and had taken it headfirst. I had never thought about the identity of the piper, but from his startled cry, I knew he was not a zombie.

Seconds after, a man's awful, gurgling scream echoed around us. The rats deserted us for the safer recesses of the drain, and in the flickering light, a grisly drama played out before us in that stage made by the opening of our passage. We had now no need to worry about our breathing being heard. The splashes of the piper running for his life, as well as the grunts of the zombies that followed him, filled the air around us. As he entered, stage left, two zombie men pounced upon him, and his shrill screams of panic turned into shrieks of agony.

We saw two more zombies leap into the picture and heard the sounds of their tearing and biting, mixed with the gurgling pleas of the piper, thankfully out of our sight.

A huge form, then, joined the action before us, as Alcee sprang into the midst of the attacking zombies with a harsh cry. "Venez, mes bêtes, venez! Vas-y, joue ta satanée flûte!" he called out.

"He is ordering them back and yelling for someone to play the pipes again," I whispered in Anne's ear, and she hugged me more tightly.

Another piper started an aimless tune, but Alcee quelled the blood-maddened zombies with his fists. I marveled at the enormous power of his bent body. When his creations set upon him, ripping at his long oilcloth coat, he snatched them up in his great hands and tossed them around the tunnel like meal sacks. They hit the brick walls with sickening, bone-crushing thumps as Alcee battered them away from the fallen piper, whose whimpering could be heard faintly as a sad descant to Alcee's roaring and the striking of his fists.

I glanced at Anne's face, thinking to see fear and horror registered there, but only saw her steady, wide-eyed gaze at the scene. Her hair and face streaked with filth, she was as vibrant as ever, for her brave spirit kept watch. The tension in her body told me that she wanted nothing more than to slide out of that tunnel and spring at Alcee, just to get her hands around his thick neck. I held her tighter, held her still.

In the tunnel, the drama came to a sullen end. In one hand, Alcee took up the body of the fallen piper by his coat collar; in the other hand, he lifted a zombie by one arm. I couldn't tell if the piper was dead, but the zombie's head had been smashed against the brick walls. Then Alcee started hurrying the zombies forward, grunting, "Allez, viens!" and the despicable chorus of the play passed in front of us. I counted at least eight creatures in the procession, along with an oily-looking beggar playing upon the pipe at their rear.

And I would have sworn that fellow's forehead was covered in a sweat of fear.

***

We waited a long while for the sloshing of their feet and the flickering of their light to leave us in the quiet, stinking dark, with only the chittering of nervous rats behind us. When those pesky rodents started to clamber over us again, I left Anne's embrace and crawled forward, hoping to find a dry lucifer in my vest pocket with which to light the lamp. One match did flare enough on a dry ceiling brick to get the lamp lit.

"We should go from whence they came," I said, when Anne hopped down at my side, "for I do not know which direction they took in the main tunnel, and I do not relish the idea of meeting them without any weapons."

"Aye, Jack," she returned, "and if we're lucky, we might be able to find where they came from." In the lamplight, as we moved toward the drop-off, I saw a cloth bag floating on the water near the tunnel we had just quit. The remains of a pouch of cigarette tobacco and a few strewn rolling papers floated about it.

"In the action, Alcee has lost his smokes," I said, stooping to pick up the items. But the bag, even soaked through as it was, had more weight to it than tobacco would.

"Anne," I whispered, "would you come and hold this lamp for me?"

Splashing back to my side, she held the lamp as I opened the drawstring of the bag.

"What have you there, Jack?" she asked, as I sent cautious fingers into the bag. I found a slick, meaty object and, half fearing what it might be, brought it up into the light.

"A large frog or toad of some sort. There appears to be another in the bag, along with some sort of dried plant material, though it is all gummy now," I said, peering into the bag. "These must be some of the basic ingredients in the voodoo ritual. Holmes found traces of amphibian tissue at St. Lazarus. With these better samples, he may well be able to track their delivery. This is a fortunate find."

"I trust you are right," Anne returned, studying the amphibian. "But that fellow is bigger than any English toad I've ever seen."

"I'm almost certain that this bag came out of Alcee's coat," I murmured, dropping the dead thing back into the bag. "I'll get these to Holmes. He has contacts who can help him trace the shipping of such things." I worried, though, that I would have to tell Holmes where and how I had found them, revealing that Anne and I had acted on our own.

"If you think it important..." she said, letting her voice trail away. She put a hand on my arm to steady herself. "I—I don't know what's come over me. I feel suddenly lightheaded."

Stowing away my evidence, I touched her cheek, neck, and forehead with the back of my hand, finding evidence of a mild fever.

"Do you feel well otherwise?"

"A bit achy, but not so bad," she replied.

"Come, we must get you home and dry," I said and led her away. I put my arm around her shoulder to help her if she grew faint again, and we pressed on. It wasn't long before O'Doole found us, which I knew meant only one thing: Holmes was aware that we had gone out on our own.

Jimmy led us back to his entry point and ran up the steel rungs to the manhole above. Anne and I looked up. We could see, framed by the round opening, stars shining in the unusually cold summer night.

Anne squeezed my arm and whispered, "I had a lovely evening. I'd kiss you good night, only..."

She didn't finish her thought, nor did she need to.

We climbed up to Commercial Street from O'Doole's entry point. O'Doole hailed a fellow driving a dairy wagon and cadged a ride for himself and Anne back to her quarters at the hospital. I gave him a sovereign and turned to make my way back to Oxford Street. The cold wind which blew from the east helped dry my clothes and reduce some of my sewer stench. At that hour, few people were abroad to notice me, and I was soon back at the Oxford Street address.

I did not expect to find Holmes waiting for me beside the fire, his oily clay pipe in his teeth and evidence of his having smoked for some time heavy in the air. But he was there.

I met his cold, angry eyes with as much fortitude as I could. He did not say a word to me. He nodded once, took up his hat and coat, and pushed by me to go down into the cellar.

"Holmes," I said, causing him to stop on the step. "You might wish to identify these substances, which I believe came from Alcee Sauvage's coat."

I pitched Alcee's cloth bag to him and turned back toward the fire. I expected something more from him than the banging of the trapdoor, which signaled his departure. But it closed with a finality that unsettled me.

Left alone in that dingy place, I cast about for something to do. The flush of success that I had brought back with me from my adventure with Anne Prescott lessened with the thought that I might have just alienated my closest friend.

The bottle of claret remained by the fire, though the chair, newspapers, and shoddy wooden table were all gone, suggesting that we were not going to be using this Oxford Street address any longer. I pocketed the note. Then I did the only reasonable thing I could think of doing: I doused myself with the claret to hide some of the sewer smell, stumbled out of the flat into the chilly summer night, and made my slow way home for all to see.

CHAPTER TWELVE

Mary did not bat an eye at my disheveled state when I returned home in the small hours of the morning. She was waiting in my surgery, wearing my dressing gown, as was her custom when she missed me, worried about me. When she heard my key in the door, she was there to draw me into her loving embrace, and I wished for nothing so much as that the earth would open and swallow me. That was an odd wish, given that I'd just come from the sewers and had found fearful danger there. All that Mary wished to know was that I was all right and to be told something about this case, anything that might help her see why I took such obvious risks and had ruined at least two suits of clothes thus far.

I told her as much as I could about Holmes having a client, Anne Prescott, who had lost her sister and fiancé to some sinister fellows in the East End who operated an awful, murderous network. I couldn't think of a rational way to explain the concept of a zombie to her. Mary listened as she led me to a bath and fetched for me a cup of soup which she had kept warm in the kitchen. I went to sleep, finally, with Mary's arm around me and a worry about Anne's fever that I could not shake.

***

I arrived early the next evening for my dinner with Holmes and Anne, and Mrs. Hudson left me to wait in Holmes's sitting room with a strong cup of tea. A cold rain poured on London again, and I thought of how the sewers would run heavy tonight. Clearly, I needed something similar to happen in my own soul. I desired to take Anne as my lover, though I had not done so—yet. Going against his orders, I alienated Holmes. Either of these realities, a month or so ago, would have been unthinkable. Both, together, I thought, were damning. Yet there was no rain in my heart and soul to wash me. I even wondered if Holmes would keep our engagement tonight.

I peered out the corner of the window, watching the street, thinking to see Holmes and Anne arrive. I jumped with a start, though, for the sitting room door flew open to reveal Holmes. Once he set eyes upon me, he slammed the door, which I had never seen him do in our time together. The Holmes I knew wasn't given to fits of pique.

"It is unlike you, Holmes, to let your emotions get the best of you," I said, facing him with what I hoped was a rational expression.

"Watson," he began, shaking his head and flinging his hat across the room, "I confess to being out of my depths here."

"About...?" I ventured.

"About what to do in a world where I cannot trust John Hamish Watson to honor his word, our partnership, and any regard for the safety of himself and my client!" he exclaimed, stalking toward me. "That is my problem, sir. I must ask myself if I can trust you, a question I have not had to consider since the first day of our acquaintance. And why? Because you cannot master your urges and desires! You might as well strip from me all I know of London as to have me question your integrity.

"I count on you," he continued, punctuating each word with scorn. "I teeter on the abyss of oblivion here, sir, and I put it to you, Watson: Can I continue to place my trust in your word and your good judgment, or must I quit this place and seek some living elsewhere?"

"What am I to say to such questions, Holmes?" I whispered, reaching behind me to find a chair. "Can I mean that much to your success? Your skills? That you would find it necessary to leave this place, your calling? Can one man ask such things of another?" I asked, not knowing the answer myself.

Holmes, too, took a seat and dropped his steely gaze to the floor. After a minute, he shook his head and murmured, "Yes. I demand a great deal too much from you, old friend, especially since you have found clues that will help me break open this case." He raised his eyes to me again.

"What? The frog, Holmes?" I asked.

"The entire contents of Alcee's bag, which I have been studying since I returned here last night," he replied with a heavy sigh. "I have not completed the investigation, but these items will likely lead us to LaLaurie and his current base of operations."

"What are the other contents of that bag, then?" I asked.

"The amphibians are specimens of the marine toad, *Bufo marinus*, an ancient species, which discharges a poison from its skin. Also in the bag were a small puffer fish and a rather large amount of human bone and ash. The other powder is jimsonweed, and it matches the stuff from St. Lazarus.

"With your findings, Watson, I think that I have a better chance of learning the means by which such specimens are delivered. All of these elements, acting together, form the basis, I think, of LaLaurie and Sauvage's voodoo ritual. They are quite revealing. I will know more about the provenance of the jimsonweed in a day or so, as soon as I can get the input of a certain botanist I know. I should be able, with a sample of the size you found, to identify where it came from as well as the place to which it was delivered. Thank you, Watson."

"I wonder where Anne—Miss Prescott is?" I asked. In my relief that Holmes had put aside his anger toward me, I had not noted until now that Anne was not on time for our appointed meeting.

"She was not well when we parted. She was feverish and weak," I added.

Holmes cocked his head and said, "Perhaps that is the sound of her entering the front door." We both waited as footsteps ascended the stairs to the sitting room. "No, that is Mrs. Hudson's step," Holmes said, rising to open the door before his landlady could knock.

"This just came for you, sir," said Mrs. Hudson, handing Holmes a telegram. He tore it open and devoured its contents in one swift glance.

"It is a message from Sergeant Magnus Guthrie, Watson, requesting that you and I come aboard the *Icarus*," Holmes replied, "me in the matter of a mystery and you for your medical expertise. I suspect that this visit will be quite off the record, as is the status of the *Icarus* at present, he says. A launch awaits us at the East India Docks. Guthrie says that the matter concerns the captain of that ship, and he is rather urgent in his request, claiming it a life-and-death matter."

Holmes rose and retrieved his wet cap and slicker.

"Mrs. Hudson, if and when our guest, Miss Anne Prescott, arrives, please urge her to await our return. She will need a good dinner, and I trust you will give her that. The good doctor and I must be off. That is, if Dr. Watson will honor me again with his trustworthy presence," Holmes added, turning to me.

"Of course, Holmes," I murmured, considering his offer as both an apology for his earlier anger and an answer to his question of placing trust in me.

***

In a short while, we were well on our way to the East India Docks, the wheels of our hansom cab bouncing over the rough cobbles of Commercial Road through a driving rain. We found Sergeant Guthrie pacing the wharf as the rain drove down upon him. Typical of his kind, Guthrie took little notice of it.

But Holmes said to me, "I hope you have your sea legs, my friend. The *Icarus* sits at anchor beyond Gravesend, in the deeper water of the estuary. This easterly blast seems like a portent of sorts, especially in early August."

Sergeant Guthrie shook our hands as we urged him back aboard the craft, ducked into the shelter of its pilot house, and steamed away from the dock.

"I cannot thank you enough, gentlemen," the sergeant confided in us as we sat under the minimal cover of the pilot house. "It's our Captain Suffield. 'E's as bad off as I've seen any man. Near lost his wits, I dare say, but not a man jack of us will report 'im as unfit. We love 'im that much. He's 'ard when 'e needs to be, but 'e's fair. A ship and its men need a strong 'and, and 'e 'as always been kind. Never a word out of place, like. Now, though..." He faltered and fell silent.

"Please, Sergeant. Anything you can tell us about the situation will help," Holmes said, seeking to steady the tough marine, who wrung his hands as though he fretted at the sickbed of his own father. I have seen similar conduct amongst many soldiers who are blessed with effective commanding officers, the sort who never expose their men to anything they would not face themselves.

"It started when last we were in port, sir, when MacGuire and I chanced upon you in that Mitre Square alley. We 'ad come ashore with Cap'n Suffield, whose old mum lives in a tidy place round

George Yard. I might add, Dr. Watson, that your note added a great deal to my defense in the Cap'n's eyes, since I 'ad missed the launch back to the *Icarus* that day."

"I'm very glad, Guthrie," I said, though in truth I was only thinking of my seasickness at that moment. I was grateful that, in the shadowy interior of the pilot house, neither Holmes nor Guthrie could see my face; I was sure it must be green. The launch belched black smoke from its stack, which only made my stomach more queasy.

"It was weeks into the mission, sir, though I cannot tell you where, and the 'ot weather where we was had took to makin' many o' the lads sick, like. In five years under 'im, I never saw Cap'n Suffield sick, but 'e took to 'is bed sudden, and when 'e left it, 'e raged like a tiger. None o' the lads 'ad seen anythin' like it, 'cept one old salt called Onyekachi, a black chap, a Jamaican, I think, who's been one o' Suffield's best 'ands since he took up the *Icarus* for Queen 'n country. An' what Onyekachi said made no sense at all, far as I can see: 'Key quote you yee amal bokor.'

"And now, Onyekachi won't talk to any of us. I'm supposed to be on watch now, but the lads sent me to get 'elp, off the record, like, and I turned to you."

Holmes's eyes brightened in the darkness as Guthrie spoke of Onyekachi. He turned to me and said, "Unless I am wrong, this evening's work marks another break in this business with LaLaurie. It is a good thing that we will have the chance to visit the *Icarus* as she rides at anchor. I doubt that we will be seen there, except by Her Majesty's men."

"I don't follow your line of thought, Holmes," I said. Guthrie, too, cast puzzled glances back and forth between Holmes and me. "Though I will be pleased to examine Captain Suffield."

"Onyekachi, Watson," Holmes explained. "He speaks, I would hazard a guess, some pidgin dialect of French?" I shrugged and nodded, as did Guthrie. "And in doing so, unless I am much mistaken, his cryptic comment means that he sees an evil bokor, a voodoo priest, at work behind the captain's condition. I cannot imagine there are many voodoo bokor in London at the present time, and I am quite willing to believe that Alcee Sauvage is the most likely name to put to that account. And, Watson, if my suspicion is correct, we may see by what degrees a man becomes a zombie. We risk much in going out of our usual routine, but we might also learn much about the ways of our enemy, at the very least."

Although it seemed tenuous to me, I knew better than to doubt Holmes's reasoning. Over and over, he had shown the uncanny ability to follow a logical thread of thought through a veritable skein of evidence. So, as we reached and boarded the metal-clad cruiser, I determined to trust Holmes and turn my full attention upon Captain Suffield.

After a few words with the commander of the watch, we were shown below decks to the captain's cabin. Suffield lay rigid, eyes open, fists knotted in the sheets of his bunk, as though he must keep his grip on it or else fly off the bed. He mumbled to himself through gritted teeth, and sweat ran off his face, soaking the pillow. The ship's doctor sat at his bedside, squeezing drops of water from a clean cloth into the captain's mouth.

In a dark corner of the small cabin, a shape moved as we entered, and a tall black man of middle years, dressed in the faded blues of a seaman, though shoeless, leapt to his feet. A mix of horror and fierce anger registered on his face, and he pulled a knife from his belt and placed himself in our way.

"Stand down, Seaman Onyekachi," Guthrie said in gentle tones. "These are the men I spoke about earlier. They've come to 'elp."

Onyekachi lowered his knife and folded himself back into the corner, mumbling something over a piece of carved ivory he held in his left hand. Holmes moved closer to his side, while I went to stand next to Suffield's bed.

Suffield had an intelligent face, sharp-nosed, with deep-set eyes. An imposing figure, just out of his prime, he was not tall but had the heavy shoulders and chest of a pugilist. Thick, rope-like muscles convulsed on each arm, even as he rested in his bunk.

"How long has he been like this?" I asked the ship's doctor, introduced to me as McCoy. He was little more than a youth, as fair-haired as his captain.

"Well, sir, he has run a fever for many days now, but he took himself to his bed three days before we dropped anchor. Before that, it was up and down, up and down. I don't mind saying, sir, that I do not feel able to help him."

"Nonsense," I replied. "You are keeping him hydrated, which is the first order of business when dealing with a fever. Will he drink of his own accord?"

"Once in a long while he will, when he relaxes his grip on the sheets and I see him sort of come back to us. For a time, those moments happened fairly often. This last bout, however, has lasted a day or more."

"What is it that he is saying?" I asked.

"Well, sir, as near as I can make out, it's the binnacle list—the list of men who need medical attention—from the day in the springtime when the captain last took leave of the ship," McCoy replied.

"Excuse me, Dr. McCoy," Holmes asked, "but might I ask what transpired before he took to his bed?"

"I don't like to say, sir," the young man replied.

"'S all right, Andy," Guthrie added. "These men are 'ere to 'elp us, not to carry tales back to the Admiralty. I've told them somethin' of it already."

McCoy nodded and whispered, "He beat Seaman Gilroy, sir. Which was the first time we ever saw the cap'n that irrational. Cap'n Suffield's a fair man, sir, and he makes his men toe the line, but he never, ever turned out to punish a man himself, and this was for a minor offense. Gilroy spat on the deck, sir, in disgust, like, with another man. And Cap'n Suffield just pummeled the fellow. Why, it took Guthrie and two other marines to pull the captain away from Gilroy. And that after the cap'n had complained of nothing but fatigue."

"When did his condition begin to degrade to this state, Dr. McCoy?" Holmes asked. I had never heard him so intent on asking medical questions.

"He asked me to examine him, sir, two days after his return from shore leave. There was nothing wrong then that I could see. Just a touch of flu, maybe, but that..."

"What, Doctor?" Holmes asked.

"I promised him I wouldn't say," McCoy mumbled.

"I think 'e would countermand that order now if 'e could, Andy," Guthrie said. "These blokes only mean to 'elp."

"Here, then," McCoy said, pulling aside the captain's shirt collar. Suffield's pale shoulder bore a wound we all peered at and knew: the marks of human teeth, upper and lower, stood out red, inflamed.

"He called it a love bite." McCoy chuckled a little at the remembered confidence of his captain. "He said he didn't want his men to have any knowledge about it, so I've kept mum. I didn't want to have the men think any way of him that might give them a cause to take liberties. The man has been on his missions for years now. Doesn't he deserve some private time ashore?"

"Indeed, McCoy," Holmes said, patting the young doctor's shoulder. "You have done well in telling us, and I'm sure," he said, looking at all of us in the room, "this knowledge will go no further. But what I am about to ask, I ask only at grave need: May I examine his personal papers? His personal log, perhaps?"

"That's a 'ard request, Mr. 'Olmes," Guthrie said. "A man 'as little privacy aboard a ship, and most protect what little they 'ave."

"I assure you, I seek only clues to unravel this mystery. But perhaps the captain will give his consent," Holmes added, pointing to the now-relaxed face of Suffield, whose eyes, rimmed red with worry, darted from face to face.

Onyekachi leapt to the bedside in front of me, and I gave ground to him. He took the captain's hand in his right hand and bent his forehead to touch it. Then he pressed the piece of ivory, still held in his left hand, with gentle insistence onto Suffield's forehead. From my position behind Onyekachi, I was able to see that the object resembled a mermaid.

The effect—if indeed it resulted from Onyekachi's ministrations—was instantaneous. The tension drained out of Suffield's body like water out of a sieve. All the while, Onyekachi muttered in his patois.

"McCoy, what does this mean?" I asked.

"I cannot say, Dr. Watson," he said, turning wide eyes on me. "Every time during which the captain enters a calm, Onyekachi treats him thus, though what he is doing, I cannot say. Now perhaps the captain will sleep for a time before another violent fit seizes him."

"Surely you do not think this is effective?" I asked.

"Strange things happen at sea, they say, Doctor," McCoy said. He laid his hand on Onyekachi's shoulder. "And it is the only thing I have seen to bring any relief."

Then, behind McCoy, Suffield suddenly spoke.

"Who... are... these men?" the captain sighed, turning his blue eyes toward us. He looked upon his own men as strangers. I struggled to recall a medical condition that would so quickly erase the memory of all those close to him. A fever that did so would likely have killed him already. A massive stroke might so impair his memory, but it would also show in some other signs of impairment, which McCoy had not reported.

"These men are here to help you," Onyekachi answered.

"Onyekachi," Suffield said, his voice fading with fatigue. "Do away with me, for God's sake. Let me go. I grow so tired of fighting. Just do what you know you must. You, only, know that this must... end... with my death. Send these men away before they, too..."

"No, Cap'n, sir," Onyekachi whispered. I leaned in to hear, as did Holmes. "No, no. I pray to Agwe Tawoyo to bring Ogou Balendjo, the healer, to stand between you and the bokor. When you better, we find him and kill the evil bokor. The Bon Dye, he will forgive all to rid his world of evil.

"You hold fast," Onyekachi said, showing the fronts of his scarred fists. The letters "HOLD FAST" were tattooed there, one letter to each of his fingers. "Agwe is here, always. I give him my coffee and rum every day, Cap'n. He save you, lead you back."

In the next instant, the worried look fled from Suffield's eyes, and his hands groped to catch onto any one of us. A groan escaped him, and then his eyes took on the soulless vacancy we had seen in the eyes of the zombies we'd faced in the alley. Onyekachi caught the captain's flailing hands in his own and gently pushed the old man back onto the bunk. He pressed his forehead against Suffield's again, and the captain subsided as Onyekachi whispered his heathen prayers.

The effect was marvelous and horrible: Suffield's vacant eyes fell onto Onyekachi's face and the tattoo which ran along his fingers. Then the captain ceased his attempts to escape and once again grasped the sweat-sodden sheet that McCoy replaced atop him. I saw his lips move as he again began to recite the binnacle list. Soon he had entered the rigid state in which we had first seen him, looking for all the world as though he held himself in check.

I stood helpless as this good man fought to hang onto his sanity. From McCoy's report, I saw that Suffield was getting worse. He fought a losing battle, with courage but with no hope of victory. I shuddered as I watched him struggle to hold onto his duty to his men, his ship, his mission.

"Each time of rest is shorter than the last," McCoy observed.

"I fear 'e won't last much longer, Mr. 'Olmes," Guthrie said in a low voice. "When that fit first took 'im, why, it was three of us it took to 'old him down, like. Cap'n might 'ave a few years on us, but 'e's as stout as any man aboard. Now... I just don't know 'ow long 'e can last."

"This man is fighting for his very soul," Holmes observed, drawing every eye in the room toward his face, for the truth of what he said fell hard on us all. A fear I did not wish to name caused a shiver to pass through me, something that threatened my soul as well.

CHAPTER THIRTEEN

"It is imperative that I look at his personal papers, especially any sort of journal or log he might have kept in his own hand," said Holmes. "I might not be in time to save his life, gentlemen, but the more we can learn about his movements before this started, the more likely we may identify the cause of this tragedy."

Guthrie looked at McCoy, who nodded his head in silent agreement. Guthrie went to the desk, which stood in the dark at the other side of the room, lit a small oil lamp and indicated to Holmes the material that lay scattered across the tabletop.

Holmes leapt to his work, taking in the materials one by one. The captain's personal log book had a locked cover. Holmes swept out a penknife and forced the lock. Guthrie fidgeted at his side, nervous at Holmes's intrusion.

"Here, Watson," Holmes called, beckoning me to his side. His finger poised first over an entry dated in early March. It read, "Received answer from E. Smith regarding shore leave. Things seem strained with her. Must see about spending time with her for the usual maneuvers while I am at Mother's."

"And here," Holmes directed, sliding his finger over comments about Suffield's various appointments with tailors and food merchants in the City. The entry he pointed out read, "On no account accept communications from E. Smith nor allow her near Mother. Emma's mark on me to remain hidden. Cannot believe it of her."

"Holmes!" I said in a fierce whisper. "Emma Smith? It's a common enough name, but if it is the same woman we saw at St. Lazarus, that's a concrete connection between the captain and LaLaurie, surely."

As I spoke, Holmes nodded, searched the next page, and found another entry. The earlier entries had been written in the smooth, flowing cursive of a man who took care with his personal journal. But in these last entries, the hand was crabbed, using block letters which were barely controlled. The last entry had only two words I could decipher, especially in the flickering light of the oil lamp: "shame" and "Gilroy." From what I could see, I could not be sure about the content of the entry. But the evidence of Captain Suffield's hand told me much about a man of sound mind falling rapidly into debilitation.

"Holmes, this looks like two decades' worth of senility compressed into mere months," I said. "I know of nothing, no disease process outside of a raging fever that goes unchecked, that produces such results. But that would have killed him before now. Something is destroying the man's higher faculties. With the degradation I see before me, I should think that the man who wrote these flowing lines, the man who was in a month's time reduced to this gibberish, should now be dead."

In the silence that followed this pronouncement, I could just make out the captain's fierce whispering of the binnacle list. I felt somehow that Suffield's repetition of this list—his listing of crew members who needed his greatest care—was the only weapon he had in the defense of his own mind. Suffield was holding with all his strength to his sense of duty, but that was being stripped from him all the same.

A voice came over my shoulder, causing me to start away from Holmes's side: "Agwe of the waves, he love this man, fight for cap'n, sea-father. Ki kote oute amal bokor?" Onyekachi asked.

Holmes stood and placed his hands on Onyekachi's shoulders. "I believe that we are looking for this evil bokor, Onyekachi. What do we need to do with this bokor in order to release the captain from his spell?"

Onyekachi's eyes narrowed as he focused on my friend.

"The bokor call the sea-father's soul from him to make him a slave, make him tzambi," Onyekachi whispered. "Bring me to him. I kill bokor," he added, drawing a wicked, thin-bladed knife from beneath his weathered blue tunic. Pure hatred of his faceless enemy showed in every line of Onyekachi's face and in his rock-hard grip on the knife.

"It will be better if you stay at the sea-father's side," Holmes said, returning the intensity of Onyekachi's glare. "Just now, your prayers are doing more good for him than your knife can."

They took each other's stares for a moment, Holmes the fiercely logical man and Onyekachi the fiercely loyal sailor. Onyekachi looked away first, and Holmes turned to me.

"Watson, we must act now," he said.

"I concur, Holmes," I replied, an uneasy sensation growing in my gut, "but we see no evidence of Devil's Snare, toads, or anything of the kind here. Can we really be talking about Alcee's involvement?"

Holmes said nothing, but his eyes held mine steadily, and I thought I saw something like worry or pity on his countenance.

"Guthrie, we must return to shore in haste," Holmes said, without looking away from me. "We must send an urgent telegram."

Then Holmes grabbed my arm, hauling me toward the cabin door.

"Come, Guthrie, lead the way," he said. "I'm sorry, but there is nothing we can do here. Watson, we must get back to Baker Street, to Miss Prescott, who, I pray, awaits us still. At the very least, a telegram might keep her there."

"But Cap'n Suffield, sir!" Guthrie cried. "Is there nothin' you can do for 'im? Can you at least tell us what is going on with 'im?"

"Your captain is going to die, my friend," said Holmes in quiet, serious tones. "I urge you to keep him here until he does. I fear that nothing more than what McCoy and Onyekachi are doing can be done, short of seeing that the persons responsible for this are brought to justice, which I intend to do."

"Mr. 'Olmes," Guthrie pleaded, "let me come with you. I've been 'elp to you before. I can't abide doing nothin', sir. The cap'n— well, sir, like Onyekachi says, 'e is our own sea-daddy and I'd strike any blow in 'is defense. I'll—I'll even give up me career if it means 'elpin' the man, sir, and you know Onyekachi would jump down a shark's throat for 'im. Please..."

"Guthrie, I need you to hold fast," Holmes said. "We'll take the launch back. For now, I ask you to attend your captain with your fervent prayers and your presence. There is much to do, and it goes far beyond the threat to Captain Suffield. You have placed yourself in enough danger already. Please trust me in this."

Guthrie, his warlike spirit crushed by the news that he must stand and wait, dropped his head. He nodded, though, and squared his shoulders, resolved to attend to his duties.

We left the ship in hurried stealth, avoiding the sharp eyes of the watch. Holmes urged the launch pilot to make all haste for the Limehouse Basin, offering him a sovereign if he would make the best speed.

Black smoke poured from the stack as we lent a hand at the shovels, piling coal onto the fire. Once we reached the smoother tide of the Thames, as the dark fronts of warehouses and low port buildings rushed by, my queasiness abated. I lost myself in the effort and in the thrill of the chase. When I looked at Holmes, though— Holmes leaning on his shovel handle, his face illumined by the fire of the boiler—I saw no excitement, only that grave sort of sorrow I'd seen in his gaze aboard the ship. I knew in an instant that his was a look of defeat, and it near stopped my heart.

"What is it, Holmes?" I asked. "You have the look of a man who goes to his punishment, not one who has been freshly released upon the chase."

"I see that you have not put the puzzle pieces together yet," he observed. "I cannot blame you, given your... attachment. It is a quality I should envy in you, dear friend, but I cannot desire it for fear that my heart would overrule my mind."

"If you mean that you think LaLaurie's plans are behind Captain Suffield's grave condition, why, yes, I have, in my own way, put that together," I said. "Other than that, I know only that we make all speed back to Baker Street and Miss Prescott."

But even as I spoke these words, a dark threat grew in me, one I did not wish to know or see, one which tainted the desire I had to return to Anne Prescott. It rose like a wave and threatened to engulf me. Anne and Suffield shared... something, and I could not bear to face it.

"Watson," Holmes cried, "think!"

I looked at him steadily, seeking to borrow his strength as I allowed the awful reality to enter my thoughts. The memory of the bite marks on Suffield's shoulder stood side by side with my recollection of tending to Anne's wounds after our first zombie encounter. I could not keep it away any longer.

"Anne suffered the bite of a zombie, as did Suffield," I said, my voice trembling with each word. "We have no choice but to see her as infected with the same vile contamination. Soon, maybe in weeks or months, she will share his fate."

Holmes nodded.

"But the voodoo, the ritual, Holmes!" I pleaded. "Anne has been through nothing of the kind. She..."

"We cannot know for certain, old friend," Holmes replied. "Perhaps Alcee Sauvage provides compliant subjects for LaLaurie's experiments. Perhaps, in the ritual, there is a way to control and enslave a person, creating a mind as tortured as we have seen in Suffield. Emil LaLaurie has, I think, found some way to spread this condition through disease. Do you recall those zombies you encountered in the alley? Do you recall their breathing?"

"Indeed," I said. "Some of them could hardly do so. Many of them coughed and wheezed as though they were dying of influenza."

"I have reason to believe," Holmes said, laying his hand on my shoulder, "that some poison that destroys their minds is passed from one person to another chiefly through contact, especially oral contact. It is taken into the bloodstream through saliva, through... a bite."

I stared at him for a moment, fighting against a growing sense of helplessness. The wave of fear washed over me, and I worked hard to maintain my sense of reason. I needed to think of some way to help Anne. She'd been feverish when last I saw her, when I'd had her in my arms. She had trusted me with her safety, and I had, without knowing it, already failed.

"God, no, Holmes," I pleaded, my mind scrambling for some way of escape from the terrible conclusion. "She was bitten, but it was a glancing blow, more a raking of the foul thing's teeth across her—"

I could not finish my thought. The curse had worked its way into our lives.

"She's strong..." I began. And then I thought about Captain Suffield's strength and how he suffered. Anne was just as strong, perhaps stronger, pound for pound, and in her training, she had become more like a living weapon. Were she to succumb to the violent impulses that had marked the course of the disease in Suffield, what a terror she would be.

My head spinning, I dropped the shovel and cast a hand behind me to lean on the gunwale. I saw, as well, the greater implications of Holmes's observations. This horror reached beyond my own loss into a much wider sphere. Soon, the zombie sickness could decimate London—all of England—all the world.

"If one can 'catch' this horror as in a strain of a new flu, why, it could be the end of—the end of all," I said. "Unless we find a way to stop it, it will not be just Anne, or Mary, or me. We have no way of truly knowing how long the disease takes to make its first symptoms known. It may vary from patient to patient..."

Thoughts of Anne's tired, feverish face as we had parted last night flooded through me. Even now I wondered if she fought the sickness, alone, unaware of what was happening to her. I could not watch Anne's face replaced by a soulless, decaying mask. The very idea threatened to unnerve me. Could I see that happen to anyone I cared about and survive?

"Steady on, my friend," Holmes said, squeezing my shoulder. "As you said, Anne is strong. We do not yet know how bad Anne's case is, but our first priority needs to be to find Miss Prescott and determine as best we may how we can help her in this dark hour. And, Watson, we must not lose touch with her again. We must keep her with us, somehow."

CHAPTER FOURTEEN

The launch hove to, and we landed. Then, keeping to the back ways, we ran through the dark, misty night toward Baker Street. The exertion of keeping pace with the deer-like Holmes gave me small respite from the horrors that possessed me.

Clearly, LaLaurie had infected Emma Smith. I remembered her sluggish manner at the infirmary. LaLaurie had been treating her. He had made her a carrier of his disease, perhaps in order to net further victims for Alcee's ritual. I marveled that anyone who called himself a man of science could proceed with so hideous an experiment, so poorly confined. It had already gotten out of his control and spread to Captain Suffield, perhaps even to his crew.

If the disease spread by contact, I grasped why Holmes had wanted Guthrie to stay on the ship. The idea of Royal Marines turned into zombies filled me with sick dread. Yet if, perhaps in the best scenario, it spread through saliva to blood contact, we would have time to combat it, and the new incidences that occurred would be less widespread.

Even those few of his creatures—I had ceased to think of them as men—who had weapons had tried to bite their victims. A zombie's bite might not kill, but it infected, a fate worse than death. The slow erosion of mind, of will, was a terror I could not face squarely. I fought to maintain my reason as I ran at Holmes's heels. But my chief fear was for Miss Prescott and for some way to treat her, to prevent the ruination of such a wonderful mind.

I struggled to think of ways I could perhaps treat the disease in Anne. After all, one Dr. Blundell had succeeded in transfusing blood

127

from one human to another nearly seventy years ago. In extreme need, that might be a remedy. I had seen it tried in field hospitals in my time in India. True, transfusions held as much danger as hope, but I determined that Miss Prescott would have every drop in my veins if she needed it.

"Steady, Watson," I murmured to myself. "Let's not shoot into the brown. Keep your eye on your target."

Soon, we crossed Marylebone Road, dodging the early morning dray traffic, and gained the relative secrecy of Marylebone Green. In the deeper shade of night, we approached Baker Street by skirting around the serpentine arm of the once-treacherous boating lakes in Regent's Park. The bulk of the South Villa sat stolid and dark on our right as we kept to the cover of the trees, though dawn could not be but an hour away.

As we neared the wall that would give us our first view of Baker Street two blocks away, Holmes signaled me to stop and drew me close to his side.

"Two men are keeping watch on the entrance to Baker Street," he whispered. "You can see their silhouettes under the lamplight, there, where the ground within the wall is high enough to permit one to peer over it without being observed." He pointed out two indistinct, dark lumps in the lessening dark.

"From there," he continued, "they can see the front of 221. I think it unlikely the men are there on some innocent errand. We must assume that my rooms will be the scene of a trap. Stealth, Watson, may help us more than a frontal assault. We do not know the numbers that face us, but clearly LaLaurie has been keeping tabs on our movements and seeks to trap us. Let us make our assault from the alley."

"Of course, Holmes. Lead on," I said.

I sought to follow Holmes's stealthy example. We stayed in the shadows of doorways and storefronts as we stole across Baker Street and made our way to Glenworth Street, the next street over from Baker Street. Then, passing through an unlocked garden path on Glenworth Street, we approached the alley at the rear of 221, which looked dark and sleepy. An enclosed grocer's wagon, drawn by a rather robust horse, sat parked near the back garden gate of Holmes's residence.

Holmes put out his hand and stopped me. His hand, pressed against my chest, trembled, and he strained forward, as though listening. I heard it then, too: that tuneless piping could barely be distinguished, but it came from within the house.

"LaLaurie and his servants, I fear, await us within. Let's take the higher ground. Up the drain pipe!" Holmes cried, springing to the nearest one. He clambered up its length, using his feet against the worn bricks, going hand over hand. With his sleeve drawn over one hand, he smashed out a window into his bedroom and called down to me in a loud voice, "Hurry, Watson! Arm yourself the best you can with what is here!" Then he swung himself into the ruined aperture, pushing away shards of glass so that they rained down into the alley.

I followed him up as best I could, but the climb was a severe test of my agility. I nearly lost my balance in the window, and Holmes's steely fingers found the front of my coat just in time and hauled me in after him. In a heap on the floor, I looked up. Holmes had his Gurkha knife, and the light of battle was in his eyes.

"I fear that LaLaurie has grown desperate after our sudden and public meeting with the Royal Marines. He means to run us to ground. Now, we take the fight to him!" he cried and sprang through the bedroom door. I found one nightstick of the kind constables use, as well as a longer, knob-headed blackthorn stick, and headed in after him.

As I stepped into the room, I saw Holmes frozen before me. At the door to the flat, Dr. LaLaurie stood with a pistol leveled at Holmes's chest. Behind him, crowding in the doorway, dark figures paced, and the tuneless whistle filled the staircase outside. The stench of them rolled, wave after wave, into the room. Even LaLaurie pulled a sachet from his pocket and held it to his nose.

"Not able to stand the smell of your own handiwork, Doctor?" Holmes chided. "I really am not surprised, though, that a LaLaurie scion would be behind this filthy business. I am sure that your mother would be proud of your efforts. Why, you've taken her primitive practices to a new low with your knowledge of diseases, haven't you?"

"My mother is no concern of yours, Mr. Holmes," LaLaurie growled. "I have waited to do this and will wait no more." He waved four of his minions into the room. "You are the worst kind of nuisance," he added.

Behind the shuffling zombies, who held their arms crossed on their chests, the huge, hooded figure of Alcee lurked, piping a tune to control the zombies. The threat of death hung in the air.

"I wish to assure you," Holmes said, "that I am the least worthy of the agents of justice who will fall upon you soon and take you down to ruin."

"Dear me." LaLaurie laughed, a high giggling sound without humor. "How you Englishmen do like to bluster!

"Now that I have found the right sort of host for my little experiments, I can refine my work. One day, medical science will acclaim my research on the nature and spread of diseases. And Alcee's 'undead' minions can be altered to serve much more lucrative ends. At your death, my work comes to fruition. I will avenge the losses to my family at last!"

Faster than I could follow, probably because my eyes were focused on the four zombies who stood drooling in front of us, Holmes stooped to his shoe tops, whipped out a throwing knife and launched it at LaLaurie's chest. LaLaurie squeezed off a shot in the same instant, but Holmes had already dodged out of its way, in a roll across the floor, which put him in front of me. The point of the knife buried itself in the doctor's shoulder. He went down screaming and dropped his weapon.

Moaning a cry of alarm, Alcee swept into the room and made for LaLaurie, who had plucked the weapon from his shoulder and hurled it aside. Alcee swept his master up in his arms as easily as he would a child. They must have descended the stairs then, but I never saw them go, for when Alcee had ceased his piping, the four zombies, each bearing a knife, leapt upon Holmes.

Swinging the nightstick in my right hand, I brought it down on the wrist of one zombie who had aimed two slicing strikes at my friend. He was much faster than any zombie I had seen before. The popping of the broken bone drew the creature's attention to his arm, so I kicked his left leg from beneath him and sent him to the floor with a blow from my blackthorn staff.

Immediately, another of them turned to focus on me, and I could see Holmes dodging and blocking the blows of the other two. I backed around the table that normally held the tea service as this fellow's knife slashed at me. He gnashed his teeth, his eyes barely able to focus on me, spittle flying from his mouth. Furniture fell; Holmes's chemistry table crashed to the floor in a rain of breaking flasks and retorts. Luckily, the alcohol-burning lamp there had not been lit.

As I parried the knife strokes with my stick, managing to smash one of my attacker's hands, I noted again that these were not the slow, shambling automatons of the sort who had attacked us in the alley. They also growled and grunted a good deal more, though their eyes still held no expression of hatred, fear, or even excitement.

I blocked a knife strike aimed at my stomach; I couldn't help but notice that many of this zombie's attacks were to my abdomen or groin. Plainly, these fellows preferred to gut their victims rather than stab them. I didn't want to think about why.

I heard shouts in the hallway, and I noted that Holmes had drawn his two attackers away from me. The fellow aiming his strokes at me overbalanced, and I caught his arm between my own arm and my staff, propelling him headfirst into the heavy oaken leg of Holmes's library table. I stomped on his neck, thinking to put him out of commission.

In the same instant, I saw Holmes sweep his knife clean through the neck of one attacker and deliver a thrusting kick to the chest of another. However, the first one I had knocked down rolled and tangled with Holmes's feet, taking him to the floor. Then Holmes's two attackers swarmed atop him, knives forgotten in their fists as, mouths opened, they sought for any exposed flesh into which they might sink their foul teeth.

"Holmes!" I cried and fell, for the zombie whose neck I had thought broken clutched at my legs with terrible strength. He already had his teeth set in the fabric of my trousers, despite the impossible angle of his head. The stout khaki ripped open, and his teeth were heading for the bare skin of my calf when I lodged the knob end of the blackthorn staff into his mouth, taking out teeth as I drove it home.

I jerked my legs from the creature's loosened grasp and brought the stick down twice, with all my strength, upon its head. I left the ruined mess of its brains on the tiles of the hearth and turned back, hoping to come to Holmes's aid.

Before I could reach him, I heard a woman's voice yell and then heard the meaty thwack of wood breaking bone. I lifted my eyes above the wreckage in the room and saw Anne Prescott, once again in men's clothing, standing over the two zombies who had taken Holmes down. A heavy rolling pin in her hand, her hair hanging loose, she stood, face glowing with exertion and, I think, satisfaction.

"Well met, Miss Prescott," Holmes said from the floor. Anne offered a wan smile and set a small wooden chair back on its feet, sinking down onto it. In the doorway, Mrs. Hudson uttered a short shriek and bustled to Anne's side.

"Oh, Mr. Holmes, I know I said that the safe room you had installed for me under the stairs was a needless extravagance, but I wish to take back those words," Mrs. Hudson said. "And I am grateful now that it will hold two in a pinch."

"How long have you been here, Miss Prescott?" Holmes asked, rising from the floor. He placed a steadying hand on her shoulder, as much to show his gratitude as to console or question her, I thought.

"I was late for dinnertime, but I came as soon as I could," she said. "I fear I have not been well since we got back last night."

I rushed to her side, dropping my stick. Along the way, I exchanged a meaningful glance with Holmes, and he nodded back to me as though to say, "I know."

"Mrs. Hudson, if you could find us some cold water," I said, holding the back of my hand to Anne's forehead and neck. "Fever, certainly. You said yesterday that your joints ached. Have you had any nausea?"

"Aye, Jack," she answered, turning her face toward me. I could see in her eyes that she was worried by her symptoms. She went on, "But I've never in my life had the flu, or no more than a wee touch of it."

"It may be that the stress you have been under has weakened your normal resources," I said, turning my eyes away from hers.

"I see that you are trying to travel incognito, Miss Prescott," Holmes said. "Have you been followed since last we saw you?"

"Oh, she did give me a turn," Mrs. Hudson interrupted. "I didn't know what to make of a beautiful young man at my door late at night."

"Mrs. Hudson, you'll be the center of scandal," Holmes teased. "Would you be so good as to bring us some tea with that cold water?" Having been gently reminded of her duties, Mrs. Hudson quickly went to fetch the requested items.

"Mr. O'Doole thought we were followed last night," Anne said. "After his observation, I thought it best to keep my goings secret. And this disguise is an easy one." I recognized that our efforts to keep our movements secret had been successful until our excursion.

Outside, constables' whistles could be heard converging on Baker Street. Deliberate, loud knocking on the outer door was followed by heavy footfalls on the stairs, and soon Constable Clary stood framed by the doorway, his red mustache bristling and his quick eyes taking in the scene.

Holding back a colleague, the constable said, "This is a right mess, Mr. Holmes, sir. We had suspicion of a burglary. Neighbors on Glenworth said that glass fell onto your back garden walk, so we came. I've sent a note along to Inspector Lestrade, as well. He likes to keep up with your activities."

"Quite right, Constable," Holmes responded, drawing him into the room. "You can see that we were outnumbered by this gang of thugs, whom I believe were in the employ of one Dr. Emil LaLaurie, late of St. Lazarus Infirmary. I have been investigating Dr. LaLaurie for unsound medical practices."

Clary gave Holmes a sidelong glance, clearly not knowing how to proceed in the face of such a thing. "Perhaps we'll just wait until Lestrade arrives to take over, shall we, sir?" he asked.

"Indeed," Holmes replied. "We should wait upon his sound judgment."

Holmes's comment raised an eyebrow on Clary's face, for the constable had seen Holmes disparage the inspector's intelligence to his very face on several occasions.

"Ahem. Yes, sir," Clary said. "I'll just await his arrival outside."

Mrs. Hudson bustled in around the retreating constable with a tea tray and a basin of cool water. Holmes guided Miss Prescott into my old bedroom with Mrs. Hudson in tow. He ordered Anne to retire and let Mrs. Hudson take care of her. Anne stopped at the door to my old room and asked, "And this was your own bed, Jack?" She gave a weak laugh as she passed into the room. Mrs. Hudson helped Anne recline on the bed and then closed the door.

"Holmes, I must do something for Anne as soon as possible," I said.

"I'm not sure what you could do. What are you thinking of trying?" he asked.

"Several massive blood transfusions," I answered, unable to face him.

"You are going to bleed her, Watson?" Holmes whispered. "Transfusions are awfully risky. In her present condition, if she is simply sickened with an ordinary ailment, a transfusion might make her worse."

"Even at the worst, I don't think that it would kill her, if we monitor her with care," I said. "And I'm afraid that her symptoms show..."

I could not finish the thought.

Holmes nodded in agreement and said, "Let her rest for the time being, then. See if a good sleep and Mrs. Hudson's care will set her back on her feet. As you say, Miss Prescott's strength is exceptional."

"So was Suffield's," I said. Holmes merely nodded.

"In the meantime, we must examine our attackers to see what we can learn about zombies. Quickly, Watson, let us look closely at the evidence we have before us, prior to Lestrade's arrival," Holmes said, turning to examine the bodies. "What is the first thing you notice about this fellow whose head I removed?"

"I noted at the moment of his death that he did not turn into a fountain of blood, as one might expect," I said. "As I look at him now, I see only a slow leakage of blood from his carotid artery. If your blow had snapped the artery, causing it to close, as will sometimes happen in a mechanical accident or an explosion, that might explain the lack of heavier blood flow. But that clearly is not the case here." I squeezed the end of the artery to express thickening blood from it, showing that it remained open.

Holmes had already moved on to the two creatures whose heads Miss Prescott had bashed in.

"The skin is still for the most part intact here, although the bones beneath it are well shattered—with a rolling pin, to boot. Quite a formidable opponent, isn't she?" Holmes observed, moving each man's shattered head with his foot. "I wish we could get a better look within," he added, stroking his chin. "I don't suppose you have a scalpel on you, Doctor?"

"I'm afraid not, old man," I quipped. "I left it in my other suit of clothes. Still, there is this," I said, tugging Holmes toward a darkened area near the hearth. He lit a gas lamp for better illumination.

"I think he will do," I said simply.

"Oh, I say, well done, Watson. You are our leading batsman!" Holmes exclaimed, kneeling to pull aside a wide section of the shattered skull of the zombie that had gone for my leg. He used a pen to open to the light the sides of the gash my stick had opened into the creature's head. "And here we see..."

Then, giving a start, Holmes turned a questioning glance up at me.

I had seen men's brains coming out of fatal head wounds. In field hospitals, I had sought to remove pieces of shrapnel or bullet fragments from men's heads. But this man's brains looked nothing like any I'd seen, wounded or whole. Necrotic and stinking, the diseased brain had gaping holes in it, as though something had bored through it.

"Holmes, this looks for all the world like a case of scrapie. Look at the way the tissue looks to have been eaten away," I observed, taking my memory back to medical school.

"Scrapie?" Holmes asked. "I don't think that I've ever heard of such a disease."

"Nor should you have. It is common only in livestock—sheep, as I recall—and if this is scrapie, it will be the first case ever reported in a human," I observed, prodding around in the zombie's skull. "No. Not scrapie. Look, it has done its worst work in the frontal lobe. I have no idea how any disease could work in this fashion. How could a disease attack specific parts of the brain?"

"Holmes," I gulped, turning toward him, "is this something voodoo does? It doesn't look like a natural pathology." My gorge rose at the thought of what LaLaurie had created. It sickened me to think of what might be happening at that very instant in Anne's body. Even if we could treat it, how much damage would it have already done?

I turned my panicking thoughts back to the subject on the floor before me. I palpated what I could of the hindbrain, which had showed the beginnings of similar damage, though nowhere near as advanced as in the ravaged frontal lobe. How long, I wondered, had this process taken?

"Yes," Holmes said at my side, observing and seeming to read my thoughts. "It is as though LaLaurie's disease turned this man into a weapon which will cease to function on its own within, what, another month?"

"It is hard to tell, since we do not know when these fellows were first—infected, treated, changed? Ghastly, but yes, if the condition of his frontal lobe had spread to the hindbrain, then death would have followed," I observed. I was trying to turn my thoughts to causes, symptoms, and treatments, as any good medical man should, but I could not fathom it.

"How has he done it?" Holmes mused. "Does the answer lie in those dangerous substances which Alcee employs?"

"I should think that jimsonweed and the toad poisons might alter a man's thoughts, make him pliable, open to suggestion, but I do not think that they would rot out his brain," I said. "But, Holmes, if LaLaurie's studies of infectious disease have become so refined that he can target the higher functions of a man's brain, the scientific implications could be monumental. But this sort of reckless science does no honor to LaLaurie. His experiments are yielding extraordinary results, yet they are so rash that they spill out of his control."

"Perhaps Alcee's voodoo rituals give LaLaurie a sort of control," Holmes offered.

"But why?" I asked. "What sort of revenge does LaLaurie hope to exact by ruining his awful soldiers?"

"Soldiers, you say? Watson, you are a marvel of insight," Holmes exclaimed. "I begin to see a pattern in this, and it leads me to a terrible realization: such creatures, dropped into an unwitting population, would act like a cancer on society, killing wantonly or making more of their kind before dying. In time, that would ensure near-total destruction. Remember Captain Suffield. Men who seek dominion might look upon this as the greatest expedience, holding it out even as a threat to those who will not bend to their will, once it has been shown to work.

"My God, Watson, think about the horror of zombies as a kind of shock force, at once lethal and expendable. Just think of the criminal or military implications of such a thing. There is no fitting word for this evil, voodoo or otherwise, when the ambition of those who wield it is so twisted."

I thought of the noble Captain Suffield and of my own dear Miss Prescott, and it threatened to unman me. How could mere men resist such a ruthless and powerful man as LaLaurie? Yet how could anyone stand by and not resist him with every ounce of energy in his body?

But how to stop it? My breathing had grown rapid, for the implications for Anne were there before me. My gaze turned to the door where she lay on my former bed, the disease, I feared, eroding her higher functions. Could LaLaurie's disease work that quickly?

"Steady on, Watson," Holmes said, seeing the look of terror on my face. He gripped my shoulder.

Then Lestrade's familiar voice called up to us. He came up the stairs at speed, another with him. I rose to my feet, pulling out my handkerchief to clean my hands.

"I came at Clary's summons as quickly as I could, Holmes, Dr. Watson," Lestrade said, clasping our hands in turn. "His report suggested a break-in, but this," he said, gesturing to the bodies on the floor, "looks like a slaughterhouse. My God, man. What has happened?"

I took a seat in my old armchair and searched my pockets for a pipe and some tobacco as I listened to Holmes recount the events that had led us to this sorry state. My own pipe, a brand-new Loewe Lovat which Mary had given to me on my birthday, came out of my pocket in two pieces, so I borrowed Holmes's black briar from the mantel. Breaking apart the fragrant Virginia tobacco helped calm me, though I loaded the pipe with shaking hands. I needed to remain calm.

Mrs. Hudson, ever the thoughtful hostess despite having been holed up while zombies shuffled through her home, brought up more tea, adding a plate of scones. She also bore a steaming bowl of broth, which she took to Anne. I marveled at this simple landlady, stepping over fallen horrors, shaking her head over the ruin of furniture, and wondering aloud who would ever get those horrible stains out of the rugs. I caught the constable's eye during all of this, and he shook his head and winked. It all gave me the effect of brief calm, even while we seemed to stand on the brink of ruin.

Lestrade listened to Holmes's narrative, making few comments and jotting items down in his notebook. Holmes omitted any mention of these thugs as zombies or the undead, which I realized was prudent. How could anyone accept what we had learned?

Lestrade asked, "And why is it that this Dr. LaLaurie would set thugs on you?"

"As I said, our investigation of his practice could ruin him," Holmes replied in truth. "And I do indeed suspect that he has a network of helpers of truly criminal nature."

"Were others here, aside from these fellows?" asked Lestrade.

Holmes told him of the men who had set a watch on the house.

"Seems they were laying for you," Lestrade said. "I'll have PC Winslow on it."

He motioned to Clary, who departed from his place at the door.

"And this one I know," Lestrade said, turning to another of the fallen zombies. "He was an arsonist by the name of Dattilo. He was a bad one; never wanted him for murder, though. Odd that he should turn up here. We lost track of him about four months ago now."

"Four months, and no sign as to his movements?" Holmes asked, catching at Lestrade's sleeve and shifting a quick glance to me. "He disappeared from his usual haunts?"

"That's right, sir," Lestrade said. "We wanted him for some bad business between exporters, down the docks. One fellow's imported goods—can't recall what they were—always seemed to catch fire before he could get them into his warehouse. Dattilo was a slick man with the flames."

Lestrade wandered to each of the other two corpses but didn't recognize either.

"I'm curious, Inspector," Holmes added, "about the identities of these other two, especially with regard to their crimes of choice, and about whether they, too, had gone missing of late. If you can find out such things, I should like to share in that information if possible."

"I don't see that as a problem," Lestrade said, "seeing as how they broke into your home with an intent to murder, although tracking their presence will be difficult. Some of these lads might have been in and out of different gaols when we had no eyes on them.

"But look here, Mr. Holmes, your keen interest in these men makes me curious. If I may ask, can you share more details of your present case with me? I've a feeling that we may do each other good in this."

Holmes did not reply right away, and I could read in his face the strain of doubt when he thought of telling Lestrade of LaLaurie's zombies. I confess that the thought of how to reveal such a thing had defeated me at every turn. None would believe the things I had seen in this case, I knew.

"I urge you to listen for word of Dr. Emil LaLaurie, late of St. Lazarus Infirmary," Holmes finally said. "But, because of confidences with one or two highly placed associates, I can tell you no more than that at present."

"Ah. I thought as much," Lestrade replied with a shake of his head. "But I must say that you look to be mixed up in something that's likely to get out of hand, Mr. Holmes, and you are going to need more than the good doctor here and some street Arabs to get you through it, if I'm any judge of the evidence. Just don't you forget the Old Bill, sir. We might be more ready to stand with you than you think. If you don't mind my saying so, I suggest that you and the doctor here stand down for a time in your investigation. I'll look into the LaLaurie chap and see if I can turn him up."

Lestrade and his associates, having taken up the bodies, departed with caution, for I had urged them to avoid contact with the blood of the fallen. I watched them cover those nightmare creatures, now truly dead, though they had been as good as dead for some time for all human concerns.

"What next, Holmes?" I asked, my need for action making me pace. "Is there nothing more we can do for Captain Suffield and his crew?"

"I can think of nothing at this point, except to be on guard in our movements. It appears that Captain Suffield is past our help. However, we must be on our guard: I do not think this the last attempt LaLaurie will make on us. Although we have won this skirmish, the war continues.

"For now, Watson, you should look to Mary's safety and get some rest if you can. I have sufficient guard on this place for now, and Mrs. Hudson will not stint in her care of Miss Prescott. Do look further into those desperate plans for Anne's treatment, should she show signs of succumbing. Tonight we learned that, in four months' time, an arsonist can be turned into an undead assassin. I would give much to learn how LaLaurie's disease and Alcee's voodoo ritual work together."

My gaze shifted to the door of my former bedroom, behind which Anne lay, her reason likely being undermined by LaLaurie's disease. I turned a pleading glance to Holmes, looking for comfort.

He held my glance and whispered, "Whatever comes of this, you are not to blame for Miss Prescott's fate, Watson. You must shake off whatever guilt you carry and know that you have done your best. For my part, I am sorry that I have caught you up in this business, though I would have failed already had you not been with me.

"It has taxed all my considerable resources. I cannot see far enough ahead to know how to thwart it, but with the evidence you and Anne have turned up, I have something more to work with. Given the virulence of LaLaurie's disease, I can tell you that we will likely see fatalities from this business for some time: months, maybe even years. A great evil has been unleashed on the world by this horrible blending of bad science and voodoo magic. It could bring England to its knees.

"But as long as I have you to fight at my side, I will work to undermine it," Holmes said. He yawned and stretched then, adding, "But for now, I must take some rest in this relative calm. Do you the same, my friend. I will send you a telegram by day's end, perhaps before."

I nodded, touched by his genuine concern for me, and took my leave, heavy-hearted.

CHAPTER FIFTEEN

At my failure to return, Mary fled to the safety of Dr. Jackson's residence, where I visited her now. I bade her stay for a while, until I knew more of LaLaurie's next moves. Mary demanded, though sweetly, that I explain the basics of this case to her, and I knew that she had the right. We settled in the Jacksons' reading room, amidst the quiet of the books.

"Mary, I am going to ask you to take what I say as true, though it will sound insane," I began.

A frown pulled down the corners of her mouth, and her brow furrowed.

"The men behind this case," I continued, "those who ordered the attack on Holmes and me, have a process, at once fascinating and horrible, whereby men—and women—are turned into unreasoning monsters. The word for these creatures is 'zombie.' It is a word from a primitive religion called voodoo, a religion which, when practiced by evil men, can reduce a person to a state lower than an animal's."

"I have heard something of it, but how is it possible, here in London?" she said.

"We believe some highly placed persons here might have an interest in it," I explained, "though this is only speculation as of now."

Mary sat quietly, looking at me, biting her lip. "The police would not believe you, would they?" she asked. I nodded at her keen insight. Mary's clear understanding served her well.

"No, and their involvement might even expose them to this infection. They would be victims in their turns, without months of training to prepare them, as Holmes and—and I have had. Though many constables are rough enough to deal with the physical demands, how could we convince them of the necessity? And how could we protect them against the terrible truth of the situation? Confronting one of these monsters is enough to unhinge a person. I—I often fear that my own response to them will drive me mad."

Mary rose from her seat and knelt on the floor in front of me, cradling my hands in hers. Her sweet eyes searched mine and she said, "I think that you were born for this. You may think that you are an average man—stolid, middle-class—but you, my love, are a man of action, a soldier first and foremost. I knew that when I met you and was drawn to it. True, your friend Mr. Holmes is extraordinary, but he would be nothing without you. And I will help you all I can."

She rose to her feet, kissed me, and led me to a bedroom in the upper floor of the Jacksons' residence. There she lay at my side, bidding me rest. Thinking offered little help, and I obeyed as well as I could, knowing that I must be prepared to treat Anne.

And may God forgive me for thinking of another woman as I lay in my wife's loving embrace.

***

Later in the day, I left Mary in the Jacksons' capable care and went back to my offices, where I found young Dr. Clancy Austin just finishing his notes on the last patient of the day. Austin, a fresh young doctor and protégé to Jackson, had agreed to step in for me, at Jackson's behest. Before he departed, I engaged his services for the foreseeable future, at least a month's worth, which pleased him no end. He left with promises to do everything in his power to build the practice as I would.

His case notes, as I went over them, were thorough and precise, which removed one worry from my mind, at least. Considering how close I had come to being bitten by one of LaLaurie's "undead," I considered that I must make arrangements for my patients should I become incapacitated.

I turned my thoughts away from my selfish fears and worries to the ravages of the disease LaLaurie had loosed upon London. If I did contract it, how much awareness would I have as the process chewed holes through my gray matter? Would I lose the guilt I bore over my desire for Anne? Would I recognize the love I would ruin? Erasing the higher functions first, if it did so, might be the disease's only mercy. If one were aware of the losses, how could such a thing be borne?

It was clear to me, given the different kinds of zombies I had seen, that much depended on the voodoo ritual used to make the subject pliable to the will of its master. However, the disease aspect made the zombie terminal: a temporary, malevolent weapon.

A knock sounded at the rear door of the house. Whoever had knocked must have scaled the garden wall, no mean feat.

"It must be Holmes," I said aloud, and ran to give him entrance.

I could see no one through the glass, and I surmised that Holmes must have hidden himself. Surely some action had taken place and he had come in stealth, seeking my help.

I threw open the door—and a huge fist pumped into my face.

I suppose that I must have flown backward with the force of the blow and landed in the scullery. I only experienced a sense of weightlessness and of floating in darkness, along with a fierce, brassy ringing in my head.

***

Waking with pain in my jaws and a throbbing head, I observed that I was in a rough bed, stripped naked, and with my hands and feet tied to the corners of the bed frame. Soft cloth had been bound around my face, over my mouth. I hoped it was clean. I wished it covered my nose, for the smell of sickness and unwashed bodies in the windowless room was overwhelming. The ceiling above me was stained with damp, moldy spots along its edges and in the corners. Meager light came from mismatched candles that stood on a spindly table near the door. I could see the back of Dr. LaLaurie as he lit another candle.

In the shadowy corner to his right, Alcee, cloaked and hooded still, grunted and pointed in my direction. Beside Alcee, I could see a woman seated in a chair, her dark hair hanging loose around her face and shoulders. I thought for a second that it was Anne, but then I saw from her fleshy, drooping shoulders that it was not.

LaLaurie turned toward me and smiled.

"So, you wake. Good. I feared that Alcee had hit you too hard," LaLaurie said, sitting beside me on the bed, one arm in a sling from Holmes's knife. How I wished that knife had found its mark in LaLaurie's throat. "I think that, perhaps, Dr. Watson, he is a trifle angry with you for taking away his Miss Prescott. He had plans for her. However, both of you, soon enough, will join our ranks of volunteers, Alcee's precious undead. In time, we will treat you to Alcee's mystical ceremony, to assure your compliance. You are a bold, strong man and will make a useful servant."

I pulled hard at my bonds, hoping a sudden lunge might break them. It did nothing.

"Ah. Do excuse the precautions," said LaLaurie. "We do not wish for you to disturb the neighbors."

I cursed him with black oaths under the cloth that bound my mouth. As I fought to speak my mind, LaLaurie raised an eyebrow, asking, "Have you a valediction? You are welcome to tell me, not that it will mean much." He tugged away the cloth over my mouth.

"Surely, as a doctor, you know that your work is out of control already, man," I protested.

"You must, in the name of decency, halt this before it destroys the very fabric of society."

"Do not think that I am a physician," he laughed. "No. Like my sainted mother and father, I am a scientist, and I take great pride in carrying on the work they started, work for which they were horribly maligned. Men despise what they do not understand, and my work will show the world what geniuses my parents were.

"Agreed, my studies fall outside the bounds of what one would call normal practice, for I have not turned a blind eye to what many call magic. Indeed, I am only now starting to grasp the chemical nature of Alcee's little pots of powder and dark, midnight herbs. In time, even the nature of these shall be clear to me. For I have found that the key to my success lies not in controlling the disease, Doctor, but in determining the nature of the host in which it resides.

"Here," he said, patting my chest, "is the laboratory in which my experiments bubble and stew. Here, within each infected host, lies the vengeance I enact on all for the sake of my family. And as I think of it, I wonder: What sort of undead creature will you become when our treatments are through? I wonder very much what my mother would have thought of what you will become."

"You are a monster, LaLaurie, a madman!" I cried, terror at the thought of my brain's slow rot creating panic in me. "If I could get free from these ropes, I would—"

His cold, easy laughter stopped my threats.

"But you cannot, will not, Dr. Watson. Surely you, a man of science and reason, see when you are beaten."

My bonds tightened the more I pulled on them.

"I fail to see how turning people into zombies will avenge any supposed wrong done to your parents. How will my death change anyone's ideas about your parents and their work? How can you see your work as doing so?"

"You, Doctor, and your troublesome colleague, Mr. Holmes, are just the sort of limited minds I oppose in my work, you who would thwart the work of genius with your petty concerns about what is right and proper. So sure that you are morally superior, you see yourselves as champions of justice, but you are mere obstacles in the road to greater knowledge. Now that I have vanquished you both, you will serve as mere signposts on that glorious highway."

"The same glorious highway your parents traveled?" I scoffed. "And if you wish vengeance, why here? Why Britain? Why not New Orleans, from whence your parents were driven?"

"Here, there, makes little difference," LaLaurie said. "I needed a patron for my work, one with the vision to see what I offer. The fact that he and others profit from my research matters little to me, for now I am granted freedom to pursue my lofty goals."

I saw, of course, that he was quite mad. Perhaps he had merely been warped by his parents' depravity. Perhaps it had been born in him. Either way, his need for revenge was mere delusion, stemming from that insanity. His sadistic parents had set him on this path long ago, I supposed.

I decided to change my tactics to see if I could appeal to him as a scientist, as he saw himself.

"How, then, do you manage to control your so-called experiments? How does your disease attack only the higher brain functions first?" I asked, trying to satisfy my own morbid curiosity as well as playing for time.

"Ah, so you have seen the effect of Alcee's piping after he treats them, um? Fascinating, is it not, what can be done when science and the dark arts work hand in glove, eh, Doctor? Really, I cannot answer you, for I do not know. The road to wisdom begins with those wonderful words, 'I don't know,' and frees us to dream."

"Or create Hell on earth," I spat back at him.

"But you must put such annoying questions out of your mind, for soon, you will have no choice, no mind, in point of fact. You will only have hunger, when the tune of the flute releases you," he said, smoothing the hair away from my forehead in a mockery of caring. "All such thoughts will disappear."

"A shame, really, a man like you falling into the blackness of the undead, but you have been so meddlesome," LaLaurie whined, wrinkling his nose in a childish gesture of pique. "I can only hope that you will be my best, most terrible creation yet. First we must infect you. Then Alcee will quiet your angry mind. He has been reminding me how bloodthirsty you are, and he cannot wait to add you to his circle of undead friends."

"You have lost control of your terrible creation, though, LaLaurie—" I cried, but was cut short when LaLaurie pulled the cloth back over my mouth.

LaLaurie gave me a confident smile and shook his head.

"Now, we have a little treat for you, the first of several," he said, gesturing to the woman.

Alcee hauled her from the chair and brought both woman and chair to the bedside as LaLaurie rose.

"Consider this a pleasant indoctrination into the realms of the undead," said LaLaurie. "I urge you to take what pleasure you can in it. Others who follow this woman will likely be less interested in lust than she is! We must give you a good dose, though, before Alcee begins. I wonder if a man of your strength will have the flu symptoms which the disease causes in so many. I trust, though, in your strength and look forward to you as my best soldier—that is, perhaps, until Mr. Holmes comes under my power. What a terror he will be, no? Then, what a joy it will be to watch you turn on those you love.

"Yes, take what delight you can from the little love bites. As she becomes more aroused, she may bite harder," LaLaurie whispered. "Close your eyes and think of Mary, or perhaps Anne, eh? Soon, when you close your eyes you will remember little, if anything.

"I'll leave you in the careful hands of Alcee and—is this one Martha?" Alcee, his hood thrown back, nodded, his face solemn.

"You see, I forget them so soon," LaLaurie said. "This was Emma's room before we had to let others dispatch her. What sport, eh? You English love your sport!

"I will see you soon, Doctor, though I will see less of you with each day. I look forward to tracking your degradation. I will note with care the way the condition grows in you. It will be an important study, although the outcome is beyond doubt.

"You should be glad that you will advance my knowledge, but, alas, of this you will have no awareness," he added in matter-of-fact tones, while I threw myself against my bonds, trying to get at him.

Alcee grinned at me and closed the door. Oddly, his face had no evil leer, though the widow's peak gave it a devilish air. He seemed, rather, as if he were doing me a favor as he turned his attention to the woman seated next to me, lifting her to her feet as though wanting me to see her full form. He ran his hands over her body as though in appreciation of the gift he offered me.

She might once have been a handsome woman, when she was young, clean, and untouched by this evil. Now, her fleshy face and arms spoke of her dissipated life. I wondered how she had fallen. She still reeked of cheap rum as Alcee placed her in the chair beside me. Maybe the need for drink had driven her to sell herself. And here, she had fallen prey to an even greater evil, reduced to her worst choice as her only function. Her eyes were as soulless as those of any of the zombies I had faced thus far, but her manner was more docile—for now, at least.

Alcee lifted the sheet from me and placed the woman's cold, rough hands on my stomach. Even as I flinched away from her touch, a moan in which deep sadness mixed with passion escaped her as she began to grope my body. I struggled, frantic to avoid her hands, but she was insistent and obviously experienced in arousing men. Her life on the streets had given her that knowledge, and it was all that was left of the woman she had been.

Whether or not she was able to arouse me—I thought it extremely unlikely given my terrified state—I still had a sudden horror that she intended to bite me first in an area that is most sensitive, as well as highly vascular.

In a fresh panic, I threw my body back and forth on the bed, trying to keep her from her single-minded desire. The ropes held me fast, though. I broke into a cold sweat with my frantic efforts. I knew I could not keep her from grasping me, and I did not think that my lack of arousal would matter to her. The point of my infection, it appeared, was at hand, and it was beyond any horror I had contemplated.

Still, if I moved enough, I might yet loosen the knots on my limbs and free myself, though I would still have Alcee to deal with. He stood back, clearly enjoying the spectacle of Martha's attempts to arouse me.

The door to the room burst open then, and someone flew at Alcee, hitting him hard enough to take the big man off his feet and ram his skull into the wall at the head of my bed. He fell back with a heavy thud. His attacker rained blows on LaLaurie's servant before Martha's cries of arousal got his attention.

Martha, intent on my body, took no notice of the intruder until he curled his left arm around her torso. Though she was not slender— a charitable guess would have put her weight at ten stone or so—the newcomer lifted her away from me, taking the sheet with her. The sheet then caught on the far side of the bed frame to my right, pulling the whole bed, and me with it, over onto its left side.

I hung there like a beast in a hunter's trap, observing the horror that greeted my eyes: It was Captain Suffield who held Martha, her feet off the ground. He no longer held back his desire to kill. With swift, hard strokes, he plunged a knife into her body again and again. Though Suffield's knife was clearly hitting vital organs, Martha responded with the same moans she had voiced earlier, as though she took pleasure in her death. I wondered if she would yet live, in her docile state, if he did not remove her head.

I would not have known Suffield except that his fine profile showed in relief against the light of the candles. He was wet and shoeless, stripped to the waist, with his once-bound hair flying in sodden knots around his head. Even in his sixties, he had little fat on him and exuded strength in every limb. Perhaps in finally giving in to the disease, he had regained every ounce of strength for which he had once been known.

Suffield fell backward with Martha in his grasp and turned in the air like a cat, landing atop her. She writhed, pressing her body to his. The captain brought his fist down on her forehead, and she lay still.

Alcee stirred and sat up, drawing the gaze of the captain. Suffield lunged for Alcee, who pulled back out of his way and fled the room. Suffield, snarling, wild, bounded after him.

I heard one door open, then another, then feet pounding in pursuit. Suffield was chasing Alcee, I reasoned, which put me out of immediate danger. I breathed a sigh of relief at my seeming reprieve. Still, I could not extricate myself, and there I was, hanging, naked with the removal of the sheet, the left side of my body touching the gritty floor. I had hoped that the turning of the bed on its side might serve to help loosen the ropes that held me. It did not. My bonds grew tighter as my weight pulled at them.

I'm afraid that I let out an unmanly shriek when Martha sat up, her disease-thickened blood oozing from her wounds. No longer interested in me, she stared at me, or through me, rather, and turned her head toward the door. I heard the outer doors open and close and footsteps coming back down the short corridor.

Suffield's wild figure filled the doorway again. He snatched Martha up off her feet, clasping her to his barrel chest. And as Martha embraced him like a lover, Suffield sank his teeth deep into her neck, tearing away her flesh. I closed my eyes against the sight but was forced to listen to the gruesome effort he put into his desire to feed. Looking again, I saw that she clung to him in a horrible parody of a lover's embrace, legs wrapped around his hips and arms clinging to his heaving shoulders. He passed into the hall with her and careened away, out of my sight. I could hear their movements and his grunting, moaning sounds mixing with hers.

Then I realized that the next sounds I heard would be his returning to dispatch me.

I thought about the scandal that my death in this situation would create. I only regretted that I would die without a fighting chance, trussed up like a sacrificial calf. The irony of such a death wasn't lost on me either. LaLaurie's observation about my bloodthirstiness came back to me, and I thought, with an odd sense of relief, that I would not meet my end through my desire to lose myself in combat. All I could do was await my end at Suffield's hands and hope that it came quickly.

In the meantime, the pain in my wrist and ankles grew. In desperation, I fought, again, to free myself, pulling myself close to the knot on my right wrist. With my teeth fastened on one strand of the knot, I pulled as hard as I could. The strand held, but when my teeth slipped off the rope, my head slammed into the frame and I blacked out.

When I regained consciousness I heard a voice, blessedly familiar, say, "I've found him! My word. Stay back a moment, please."

Holmes set the bed back on its legs and placed me on its top again. He draped his coat over my shivering body and began to cut away my bindings with his penknife. He glanced down at my face and favored me with a grim smile.

"Those who trussed you up must have feared you greatly. These ropes and knots would have held a wild horse in check," he said, patting my shoulder, placing my arms back to my sides. They protested, and I groaned.

"You may come in now," he called toward the door.

Anne Prescott peered around the door, her eyes wide, expecting the worst. Dressed in workingmen's clothes still, she offered me a wan smile as she came to Holmes's side. She bent down to embrace me, and I was heartened to see that she appeared to be her usual self, vibrant and strong. I started, though, as Onyekachi entered the room on silent feet behind her. In his tattered seaman's outfit, he looked quite out of place. His wide-eyed glance took in the room, as though he looked for any sign of his captain.

"Aye, Jack," Anne said, following my glance, "we have another volunteer for our small militia."

"Mr. Onyekachi turned up at my door last night with a note from Sergeant Guthrie saying that the captain had fled his ship," Holmes added. "Clearly, Mr. Onyekachi has his own agenda here, though I think that he will remain our ally."

"Did Suffield—" I started. "I mean, were there any—"

"Casualties?" Holmes answered for me. "Yes. Dr. McCoy died from a broken neck, I'm afraid. Guthrie is beside himself with grief over all this. I don't think we can keep him out of this struggle much longer. Unless I miss my guess, we will need both him and Onyekachi. Though I would do much to make sure that Guthrie doesn't sacrifice his career over this matter. The Royal Navy needs such men, men of courage and good judgment.

"And there is the matter of the other casualty on these very premises. Was there a woman here with your captors? She must have been, or she entered soon after. She was murdered. Her name was Martha Tabram. We were forced to wait until after Scotland Yard finished their investigation of the woman's murder, though I am sorry that we had to let you languish here while they blundered about," Holmes said, giving me an opening to tell my story.

Omitting only those details I did not wish Anne to hear, I gave Holmes every action from the time I'd been knocked unconscious in my home until the time I'd heard his voice in the hall. When I explained how Captain Suffield had entered and stabbed the woman called Martha, Onyekachi hung his head and wept bitter tears.

"For him, it is too late. May Bon Die have mercy on his soul and Elegba take him home," he cried. "I will kill this bokor, even with my last breath."

Then, grasping the blade of his wicked knife, he dragged the blade from his closed fist. Drops of blood fell from his hand, and I assumed that this sealed his blood oath to avenge his captain. I did not try to tell him that LaLaurie's disease, rather than Alcee's voodoo ritual alone, had claimed the captain. Instead, I took a mental oath of my own to avenge the wrongs of LaLaurie, whether or not he was insane.

"But where am I exactly, Holmes?" I asked, turning my thoughts to my present situation. I rubbed the abrasions where the ropes had bound me.

"In a fourth floor flat in George Yard, in a secret room which one must enter through a supposedly empty flat," Holmes told me. "I have an idea that the person whose name is on the lease for this place will lead us to LaLaurie's confederates. I shall ferret it out in time."

"It appears that Mr. Holmes sees what no one else sees," Anne added, turning an admiring glance toward my friend. "He had only to pace off the length of the rooms to determine that some space in the building was left unaccounted for. He reasoned that if you were here, you must be in that bit of extra space. Mr. Holmes thought it best not to involve you with the police investigation. It was just so hard waiting to find you."

"How long, then, have I been missing, and how did you know to look for me here?" I asked, worrying about Mary.

"As you no doubt surmise," Holmes replied, "Mary reported you missing. She returned home to signs of your struggle and came directly to me, which helped put me onto your trail, though that soon went stale. Onyekachi's visit preceded Mary's, so Miss Prescott suggested that we seek you in the places we associate with LaLaurie.

"And there, I think, either feminine intuition or Providence guided Anne's astute guesses, as it must have done in your joint venture into the sewers. We went to the place where she had last seen Tom McHugh, which put us in the neighborhood where the murder of Martha Tabram had just occurred. Here, with constables bungling about and destroying evidence on the lower floors, I made inquiries about the residents and found that the top floor, rather a decent place, is the home of Captain Suffield's aged mother.

"We left the premises, this handsome lad and I..." Here Miss Prescott donned her slouch hat again, smiling. "... lingered at a nearby public house, waiting for the officials to leave so that we might make a thorough search of this place. So, you see, several momentous occasions converged onto this spot, though no immediate facts connected them all."

"You were guessing?" I chided through a smile.

Holmes cleared his throat, nodded quickly once, and turned away. He then moved to the darkest corner of the room and brought my clothes to me, saying, "I think it time for you to return to Baker Street, old boy."

"Indeed, for there are several things I need to tell you about what I have learned," I said, nodding to Anne for her to step outside. Favoring me with a pretty blush, she smiled and walked out into the hall.

On the cab ride back to Holmes's flat, I kept silent, unwilling to reveal in front of Miss Prescott what I had gleaned from LaLaurie. Miss Prescott had removed her hat and let fall her luxurious hair in the cool night breezes that came through the cab's windows. The motion of the cab and the weight of her fatigue were enough to let her nod off into a gentle sleep.

"How came our friend to join you?" I whispered to Holmes. "When I left, she had taken to bed."

"She slept through the night and late into the day, arising well before any of the news began to arrive at my door," Holmes returned. "She seems much her old self, though I fancy that I can see some hint of fever about her still. Perhaps, with her native strength, she can resist the infection for some time. I think that the end will still come, though. Don't you?"

Holmes was likely correct, and I nodded my assent. "I think that I should go ahead with the transfusion," I added.

"Letting out the old and letting in the new?" Holmes returned. "A risky business."

"Yes," I said, "but a calculated one in light of the dreadful alternative. LaLaurie suggested that Alcee's magic helps with the zombie process in ways that even he doesn't grasp well. LaLaurie knew what the infection would produce in me, Holmes, but he also planned to have Alcee treat me, making me pliant. But if Suffield's actions tell us anything, Anne will indeed succumb to purely animal urges. I cannot bear seeing this affliction strip away her higher functions and leave her in the same kind of agony Suffield has felt."

Onyekachi, sitting at my side across from Anne, merely followed our conversation, holding the makeshift bandage on his hand.

Holmes merely nodded as we trundled along. Miss Prescott slept, her head down, strands of dark hair covering her face. As her robust figure slumped in repose, she looked like Martha Tabram, as she had sat in the room where I was bound. I shuddered at the passing resemblance and was grateful to see Anne revive and smile as the cab came to a halt.

Despite the sleepy aspect she had evinced during the ride, Anne was the first one up the stairs to Holmes's flat. She flung open the door, crying, "Mary, Mrs. Hudson, we have him!"

Holmes and I followed and entered to see Anne embracing Mary while tears streamed down the face of each. Even Mrs. Hudson dabbed at her eyes as she smiled.

Mary broke away from that embrace and rushed to my side, laughter mixing with her sobs of relief. She clung to me, shaking, and I to her. The others left us there. I had no words to tell her of my sorrow for the worry I had put her through, nor of my joy at our reunion.

CHAPTER SIXTEEN

The Baker Street rooms looked more like a barracks for a time, with Anne convalescing under the care of Mary and Mrs. Hudson, and with Onyekachi sprawled on a settee in deep, exhausted sleep.

Mary made use of O'Doole and Wiggins between meetings with their myrmidons. From their first meeting, a year ago, she had earned the admiration of Wiggins, who had always had an eye for her. O'Doole retained his affinity for Miss Prescott, so Mary set him to work fetching and carrying for her. Anne favored him with warm smiles, which brought color to his cheeks.

All in all, we were a strange and motley troupe, enjoying our comradeship despite the air of nervous anxiety that ran through most of our discussions. We were a stronghold under siege, it seemed, though we could see no enemies at our gates. Our enemies had found, in this horrendous infection, a way to threaten us even without being present.

"The fever still sits upon you, my dear," Mary told Anne, "and you have not had near enough nourishment in the past day. As a nurse, you really ought to know better. We need to get you into a lukewarm tub, clean you up, and feed you some strong broth. I know Mrs. Hudson is preparing some even now."

Bone weary, sore, and near famished, I chafed at waiting to have a sit-down with Holmes and offer him my observations on LaLaurie's and Alcee's creatures. It didn't help my mood that seeing Mary so involved with Anne sent shivers of guilt through me, but I told myself that whatever would be, would be. That Anne still had feelings for me, I could affirm in her words and actions. Seeing the sad smile on

154

Anne's face, though, as Mary embraced and fussed over me, sent a pang of sorrow through me, for Anne's eyes still held mine in love. I wondered if Anne felt as helpless as I in the face of our deep caring for each other. Anne's words and actions with Mary were as those of a sister, and the whole business set such a sadness in me that I could think of no cure for it.

Such a witness of Anne's noble and loving spirit, though, made me vow to get her through this. I would find a cure for her.

When Anne would rise and move about the room, though, her grace and strength made me dare to hope that without falling prey to Alcee's ritual and deadly potions, she could escape the curse. Blood treatments might help her fight off whatever infection tried to take hold of her. Already she no longer had any sort of flu-like symptoms, though she did have a slight flush of fever in her cheeks.

We ate, Holmes and I, while Mary tended to Miss Prescott. Onyekachi slept on, perhaps needing the peace of sleep more than food. Soon, our pipes lit, Holmes gave me his undivided attention.

"Tell me all, Watson," Holmes said.

"LaLaurie admits to having a patron," I said. "And his motives are those of a madman. He says he is bent on bringing honor to his family name, but that is the thinnest cover for the sick joy he receives from hurting people, if you ask me."

"Very like his mother, then?" Holmes asked.

"Indeed. His supposed knowledge of infectious diseases seems likely to stem from having been raised by sadists in a welter of sick science and voodoo rituals. He has created something more monstrous than his parents did together or apart. His patron must share something of LaLaurie's insanity—or be truly evil, despicable."

"Intriguing, and consonant with some information that has come my way," Holmes replied.

"You mean about the possibility of some parliamentary involvement? Don't worry. I removed that letter with the mention of the L.S.," I said.

"Yes, so I surmised when I went back to retrieve it," said Holmes. "I regret leaving in such a fit of anger. Please, do not press me yet about the L.S. The matter is out of my hands."

"Very well, Holmes, but if this L.S. contingency can provide you with information about LaLaurie's patron, I urge you to follow up. I'm sure that one member of this mysterious cabal of yours is a former prime minister. And another is a large man, fond of claret, possessed of an ironic sense of humor, and most often found behind a newspaper," I said, hoping that I sounded like Holmes in one of his deduction demonstrations.

"Touché," Holmes laughed, "and I hope that you will make his acquaintance soon."

I nodded my appreciation of his words and sought to return to more reasonable thoughts.

"My own findings, as LaLaurie's captive, have shown me very little that adds to the stock of knowledge that will lead us to LaLaurie's center of operations. Have your efforts been more fruitful there?"

"Yes, indeed, Watson. That cart horse LaLaurie and his associates left in Mrs. Hudson's alley provided me with two very fine shoe imprints. I have written an unpublished monograph on London's farriers, and I am certain the horse that left those tracks was not shod by a London smith. I shall know more in a day or two at the most, especially as other reports about the shipping of marine toads and puffer fish are due back."

"I hope when we have this information we can plan an all-out assault on LaLaurie's central location," I said, smacking the arm of my chair for emphasis.

"That would be a hasty move, Watson, for we do not know the identity or capacity of his benefactor," Holmes replied. "I beg you to remember that to attack, all out, in one direction might leave us vulnerable to a variety of retaliations, should his patron have criminal ties."

"But it will be a bold move, too," I argued, "like that which Anne and I took when we went into the sewers and found those clues. An audacious charge, even by our small numbers, might succeed because of its suddenness. It will not be expected, and we may be able to strike quickly enough to do great damage and derail LaLaurie's plans."

Holmes looked at me with his steady eyes. "The success of that action, though, might well cost our side a heavy price. And I remind you that our side is you, me, Onyekachi, and Anne Prescott."

"But you see how things are, Holmes," I insisted, my suppressed anger causing my voice to rise. "We are in a desperate fix. We need allies, and I can see none at hand. That is why we must attack unexpectedly."

"Indeed, I see that, and I have set such wheels in motion as to get us the allies we need. In a day or two, with greater access to information, I feel confident of having sufficient numbers to help us," Holmes replied.

"On whom are you calling, Holmes?" I asked. "The police? Surely the work you have done with Lestrade and Gregson has earned you enough credibility to enlist their support. But could they really help?"

"Watson, really," Holmes said with a huffing sound. "You recall how long it took you to grasp the idea of a zombie and believe it. And the police? They have nothing like your level of experience or your intellectual capacity. As it is, I am not yet cleared by my associates to let their names be known to anyone, even you."

I rose in frustration and paced about.

"Please, Watson, have patience," said Holmes. "And stay away from the window! Just a day or two more, and we will know when and where to strike. At that time, all that I know, you will know.

"You need rest, my friend. Take some rest here. All those you care about are as safe here as anywhere, under our wings, for the time being. The police provide a guard, still, on this place, even if they do not know the truth of why we need them. For a short time, we are safe. Rest, please," he insisted.

I do not remember my head hitting the pillow that night, and I slept long and hard, neither thinking nor dreaming until the approach of dawn brought an awful vision. As though in a fever myself, I tossed about in a dream of pursuing Anne through London streets and dark alleys. Ever she eluded my grasp, until she turned on me, her handsome features suddenly twisted into a bestial mask of rage. The dream ended when she plunged a long knife into my abdomen and ripped upward. I sat up shouting and clutching at my stomach.

My dream faded as Mary pressed her hands to my face and shoulders.

"John! It's me," she murmured in her low, soothing voice. "You are safe. It is just a dream."

"Y-yes," I stuttered," a dream." I reached for the carafe of water on the bedside table, gulped down two glasses and fell back at Mary's side.

"Shh," Mary whispered, stroking my forehead as I lay panting, shaking off the effects of the horrible vision.

"We must do more for Miss Prescott's condition," I whispered.

"Why, John?" she whispered back. "Is her condition worse than a mere flu? She is a strong girl and will likely cast it off soon."

"She has been bitten by one of the horrid creatures, my dear," I whispered. "And Holmes and I know that the infection spreads from one person to another by saliva to blood contact. I saw the most wretched effect of a single bite. It turned a worthy man into a ravening killer."

"Oh, God, no," Mary said, generous tears filling her eyes. "We must do more for her, then, if it's as bad as all that, John. We must. We—I—owe her that. Holmes told me how she fought them off at your side. But what can we do?"

"I think we might try a transfusion. We will have to bleed her, I'm afraid, as barbaric as that sounds," I said, wondering what Jackson or my other medical school classmates would say about it.

"She shall have as much of my blood as she needs," Mary offered.

"Perhaps," I said, wanting to ensure that Mary avoided all chance of contact. "It may come to that, but you do not carry sufficient weight to spare much of your own blood."

"Then I will not leave her side until she is well," Mary said, rising and putting on her dressing gown. She left Holmes's room to go check on Anne. I rose too, thinking to follow her though my aching joints protested, and I walked into the sitting room on halting steps.

It was empty.

"John!" Mary cried, emerging from my old bedroom. "She's gone!"

My eyes swept the room again. Holmes was nowhere to be seen, nor was Onyekachi.

I rang the bell for Mrs. Hudson, hoping to find anyone who was on the premises. I then ran to the head of the stairs as I heard doors open and footsteps approach from the back of the house on the first floor. It was Wiggins and O'Doole, pulling on trousers as they came. Mrs. Hudson came behind them, heading for the stairs.

"Where is Holmes?" I called, stopping them in their tracks.

"Is 'at all?" Wiggins asked, subsiding. "He left not ten minutes after you took to bed, sir."

That was like Holmes: indefatigable. I shook my head in acknowledgement, supposing my words had driven my friend into immediate action. I wished he had awakened me when he left. He knew we had to keep close contact with Miss Prescott.

"Did Miss Prescott or our friend Mr. Onyekachi go with him, then?"

Both boys started, then looked at one another and shrugged. Wiggins said, "Erm, not wot I knows of..."

"She 'adn't ought to be out and about, if you ask me," O'Doole offered.

I cast a look at Mary, who stood wide-eyed beside me.

"Oh, John, go look for her," Mary said, clutching my arm.

"I will, my love," I said, "but you must stay here and wait upon Holmes's return. I need you to send him after me. Let me write down the places in which I will seek her out."

"Not without some good breakfast in you," Mrs. Hudson called. "You won't last two hours without it. Just look at your color!" With that, she rushed off to the kitchen.

"She's right, John, you won't," Mary said. Though I chafed at the delay, I accepted they were right.

"You need to tuck into a good breakfast, too, for it might be a long day," I said to the lads. "Then, O'Doole, you'll go with me. Wiggins, you'll alert the Irregulars in a search for Holmes..."

They nodded and ran off to make their own preparations. I followed to give Wiggins some money to see to the provisions for his troops and then returned to the sitting room. Mary brought me my shoes and socks only; I had fallen asleep in my clothes.

Weariness and worry wrung a tired yawn from me.

"John," Mary said, sitting on the arm of my chair, "Miss Prescott, I think, is a very vulnerable young woman, no matter how strong she seems. Don't you think?"

"I quite agree," I said, fearing where this conversation might go. "She is in no shape to be out wandering. Someone might have seen her leaving here, for there are foes at work who are not zombies. Miss Prescott faces more dangers than the disease that I fear infects her." I worried about the marksman stalking Anne and Onyekachi and shooting them in some isolated place where they would not be found.

"What I mean is," Mary began, "that Miss Prescott has lost so much, and that you—and Mr. Holmes, of course—have done so much for her, become so important to her that, well, you need to be aware of how this could affect her understanding, her feelings."

"I quite agree, Mary," I said, allowing the truth of my own feelings for Anne to take a back seat to my need to begin her treatment. "My sole thought now is to get her back to safety, get her to my surgery, find some suitable blood donors, and begin to set her to rights."

I stood, and Mary embraced me. "None of us can lose you, John. Come back safe and soon," she said, giving me a kiss on the cheek and turning me for the door. As I left with O'Doole, I sought refuge in the idea that for once I had told Mary the truth, though I had not told all of it, for my heart smote me to think that Anne had left, and I might not see her again.

CHAPTER SEVENTEEN

Mary knew that I would start my search at Anne's old residence on Arnold Circus and make my way through Spitalfields back toward St. Lazarus. Along the way, I would leave messages at the other women's refuges where Anne was known. I hoped to end up at Mr. Hepplewhite's chapel. I hoped that Holmes would return and come to our aid.

***

It was a disastrous day. We found no sign of Anne or Onyekachi anywhere. I hoped that they would be together for protection, in case they came upon LaLaurie, Alcee, or any of their creations. I left notes for Anne on many doors and on message boards at Magdalen Hospital. I hurriedly asked after her at Urania Cottage and Cwmdonkin Shelter, only to be looked at askance by the staff, who were used to seeing men ask after women who had fled their violence. They rebuffed every request, no matter how I implored.

At day's end, O'Doole begged leave to search for Miss Prescott in his own way, and I returned, defeated, to Mary at Baker Street. As I stood on the steps, I desired nothing more than to gather Mary and flee, remove to some sunny clime, the south of France, perhaps, find a small home with a tiny bit of garden, and sit there in the pleasant sunshine until the end came. I have suffered the fatigues of work and wounds, but I had never experienced the tiredness of soul I knew at that moment. I considered that Holmes had failed in his watch over us, leaving as he had. I cursed myself for demanding quicker action, a demand which I was sure had sent him off.

Finding someone in London's immense sprawl is hopeless, if she does not wish to be found. Like a trackless wilderness or an equatorial jungle, London can swallow someone without leaving a trace. Even the most pleasant, fashionable city blocks have warrens of small, nameless lanes and shacks at their backs. There, the most desperate people take refuge. Wandering one or two blocks off shining Piccadilly Circus puts one amidst folk who live hand-to-mouth by any means. Into those places, persons can and do disappear.

As I stood on those steps, wondering how to proceed, the outer door opened, and Wiggins ushered me within with eager hands.

"He's back, Dr. Watson, though he don't look in no better mood 'n you do," Wiggins said. His quick steps allowed him to close and bolt the door behind me, slide past me, take the stairs two at a time, and open the sitting room door ahead of me. "Doctor's back, sir. O'Doole ain—isn't yet. Shall I make inquiries after Jimmy, sir?" Wiggins asked, as though Holmes were a superior officer and the lad were a hopeful subaltern looking for promotion.

I couldn't hear Holmes's response well, but I saw Wiggins smile, which told me that Mary had come to greet me. Wiping the sweat of worry away from my face, I brought up a smile for her.

Mary knew, of course, of my failure as soon as she saw me. Her embrace and kiss were brief but welcome. She drew me to my old chair.

"I will see to a fresh pot of tea for you two," Mary said, kissing me again, patting Holmes on the arm before she headed down to the kitchen.

"Do you think that Mary might now return home?" I asked Holmes. I knew her efforts to straighten and organize his bachelor's existence would be growing tiresome to him, especially with the pressure that was upon him—upon us all.

"As soon as it is safe," he murmured. "I'm dreadfully sorry that I was out when Miss Prescott and Mr. Onyekachi decided to leave. I'm sure we may count on the honor of Mr. Onyekachi for her protection."

"Really, Holmes, I must say I am disappointed you did not keep watch on them," I said. "Wasn't that our charge, to keep her where we could see her, help her?"

"Yes. It was. But the need for new information compelled me, though I gave those two an opportunity to go haring off, seeking revenge," Holmes said with a sigh. "I've never seen the need for revenge burn in someone as it does in Mr. Onyekachi, and I doubt anyone has greater cause for desiring it than Anne Prescott. I realize that my methods, working nearer to the bounds of law, are too slow for them. And also for you."

"You know me well. But the danger they are in, Holmes," I pleaded. "We must find them and help keep them safe. Given Captain's Suffield's timeline with the disease, there might yet be time to halt or reverse it."

"Perhaps, Watson," Holmes said. "But perhaps, too, neither of them wishes to be found or to admit any caution into their headlong pursuit. They are united by desperation. I doubt they have any shred of the sort of hope that burns in your manly heart."

"But, Holmes," I protested, "I must do something. I cannot stand idle as this evil endangers everything I hold dear."

"Nor will you," Holmes said, "for even though I failed in my vigilance over my guests, trusting to weariness to keep them in place, I believe that I have found the one clear thread that will allow us to unravel the fabric of our foes' designs."

"How, Holmes?" I asked, sitting upright.

"As you will gather, neither I nor my clerical associates at Scotland Yard, with whom I have worked for many of the past twenty hours or so, have been idle," Holmes said, drawing me over to his table, now littered with sheets of paper showing columns of figures. "Watson, in the growing depravity of this age, seemingly legal, mundane financial transactions will allow the tracking of many of the most nefarious criminal activities," Holmes said, warming to his subject. "But perhaps I go too quickly. Have you heard the name John Pizer?"

"No," I said, rubbing my eyes. Trying to find some commonality in the lists of figures, names, and dates that swam in front of me on those pages made my tired eyes burn.

"Pizer claims to be a humble shoemaker, but he is invested in many low-rent properties in East London. Suspicious enough for a man of limited income to rent out so many places, such as that flat in George Yard where you were held captive. Pizer's renting of that flat connects him in a concrete way to LaLaurie's enterprise. His own banking accounts amount to little more than a month's wages, and yet just within the past two hours I have seen bank receipts of quite large sums deposited into an account that Pizer has set up under the name of a company that supposedly exists along an empty farming lane near Northamptonshire.

"Scotland Yard has had its collective eye on John Pizer, whom they suspect of pandering. With Emma Smith and Martha Tabram as Pizer's 'tenants,' the police are searching for him in connection with Tabram's murder, and he has disappeared from London, seemingly. Since LaLaurie clearly has a plan in which he uses such women, I suspect that Pizer has gone into hiding with LaLaurie in Northamptonshire."

"Can you track these deposits and find the person who paid them?" I asked.

"Not in any official way, for they were all cash receipts. Luckily, my other associate, the newspaper-reading fellow, has means of doing so that are denied even to the police. We are near to finding LaLaurie's location," he claimed, an eager light in his eyes. "You should rest and regroup. I will take over the search for Miss Prescott and Mr. Onyekachi. Later today, you can take Mary home. I have arranged with Lestrade to have a heavy police presence in your slice of Paddington. He and Inspector Tobias Gregson have wanted Pizer for a while now on extortion and blackmail charges as well as pandering. Lestrade, at least, has agreed to my terms of cooperation, in return for his protection of my most vital allies."

"Very well, Holmes," I said, deflated. "But I do not know how you can bear such waiting when there is so much at stake."

I shook my head. Trusting Holmes had always been easy but was not so at present, since I remained outside of his confidence concerning our allies. Resigning myself, I left him so that I could help Mary gather our things to go home.

***

The next day, I busied myself with such preparations as were possible to undertake. I cleaned and oiled the Webley & Scott revolver and fretted over not having a more suitable side weapon, other than a bludgeon. A sharp blade that would remove a zombie's head was what I needed but lacked. I had no kukri knife like the one

Holmes carried, and under curtailed movements, I could not even contact Mr. Uyeshiba for the loan of a sword. I desired to keep his location secret even from the police, as Holmes wished.

On the fretful third day, I insisted on returning to work alongside Austin. Over the breakfast table, Mary hovered, casting quick glances at me, newspaper in hand, as though she would discern whether I could deal with this morning's news.

"Well?" I asked. "Has it started?"

"I fear it is so," she said, and handed me the *Times*. It was open to a middle page, alongside news of a more mundane sort. The headline read, "Fire in St. Lazarus Infirmary: Three Dead."

After I scanned the article, which only mentioned that the remains of three people had been found in the ruins—two men and a woman—I asked, "Has there been word from Holmes?"

"No, John," she answered.

"Well, the day is young, the sun is up," I said resolutely. "I will not give up hope just yet."

Fires in East London are commonplace, and while they might excite public interest, they do not hold it. This fire was just one of any number of recent blazes in the great number of derelict buildings that dotted Whitechapel, Spitalfields, and Southwark. No neighbors stirred abroad talking about it. Our empty street featured only constables wandering about. Even they would not know the identities of three bodies found in that fire.

Still, I paced. I fretted. I even broke Holmes's injunction to limit my movements and returned to Mr. Uyeshiba's dojo for further training. I begged the loan of a sword from him, but he scoffed, as he always did, at my ham-fisted ways and told me to stick to my club and pistol. He also scoffed at the futility of my worries.

Returning home, I could not free myself from the specters of dread which swam before my imagination. Had Anne and Onyekachi died in that fire? Who was the other man, then? Was it Holmes? Was it LaLaurie? If one of the men had been Alcee Sauvage, surely the *Times* would have mentioned his tremendous size.

I simply could not remain still. In frustration, I set out for Shepherd's Bush to find Lestrade.

"The two men found in the fire were petty thugs, known associates of John Pizer," he told me, his feet propped on his desk.

"They weren't burned as badly as the woman, so we knew them. We'd wanted them for questioning in the Tabram murder. They had been suspected before of assaults on women. As to the woman from the fire, we have little to go on: she was burnt beyond recognition in the very heart of the fire."

"Was the woman tall? As tall as I?" I asked.

"No, I shouldn't think so, Doctor. She might have been a bit over five feet, but as you know, a burnt body shrinks," Lestrade said. "But I have to say I'm curious about you being in such a lather about these poor souls. Is this something about that dustup at Baker Street? If it is, I need to know all you know."

Though my impulse was to take Lestrade into my confidence about this matter, something held me back. I shook my head and said only, "St. Lazarus was run by Dr. LaLaurie, who has some connection to that business. More I cannot say. Holmes has all the answers to your questions, but I'm afraid I cannot find him or Miss Prescott."

"Maybe Holmes is on Pizer's trail. He owes me that." A leering smile crossed Lestrade's face as he added, "Maybe those two went off together, eh? Old Holmes letting pleasure mix with business?"

"Preposterous," I scoffed. "Holmes never allows pleasure of any kind to interfere with his investigations."

"Well, perhaps the investigations were over, and they simply slipped away, being two people unattached. It does happen, doctor. Even the steadiest of men may wander from duty when a certain woman comes along. You've got to admit that."

"Yes," I returned in sad acceptance, though for a different reason than Lestrade had suggested. "I will admit that."

"There you go, then," he said, thumping his desk. "Case solved, without leaving the building!"

"Indeed," I grimaced, realizing I had exhausted help from official sources.

CHAPTER EIGHTEEN

That night Mary and I were awakened by a heavy pounding on the front door. We both hastened down the stairs, pulling on dressing gowns and slippers as we went. Mary reached the door ahead of me. She threw it open to reveal Onyekachi, Anne Prescott's unconscious figure draped across his arms. Their clothing was a bloody ruin. Anne bled from fresh wounds. Onyekachi's eyes stood wide, and the sweat of horror dripped from his brow.

"Bring her to the surgery," I exclaimed, ushering them both in and through my office into an examination room where I kept all my supplies.

Mary clung to Anne's hand, chafing her wrist to try and bring her around. Onyekachi hurriedly placed Anne on the table, saying, "I t'ink she have the tzambi sickness, the evil of the bokor, Doctor. She not t'inking right and fighting mad. Even I fear her."

Panic rose in me, and I fought it down. I barked at Mary to fetch warm water and bandages. I sat Onyekachi down in a chair opposite my desk in the outer room and asked him to tell me all that had occurred. I put the first question to him before I raced back to attend Anne: "Has Holmes been with you?"

He frowned and shook his head.

I turned back to my patient, intent upon treating her but uncertain, now that it came to the point, that risky transfusions of blood would help. Mary was at my side, having awakened Rachel to prepare food and drink for Onyekachi.

"Oh, John," Mary sighed. "What has she been through?"

"A veritable hell, I should think, my dear," I said, cutting away the sleeve of Anne's torn shirt. I recognized it as one of my own, which I had kept at Baker Street. The trousers were mine, too, belted and bunched around Anne's slender waist. I searched everywhere I saw blood on her clothing and gasped at what I found: her smooth flesh was bruised from heavy blows in many places. Indeed, her back had suffered so many blows so as almost to make it one bruise. But it was upon her arms and on one leg that I found the worst wounds: the marks of human teeth which had torn at her. And the older bite laceration on her arm stood out an angry red, as though from infection. I gasped at the horror.

"Is it as I fear, John?" Mary whispered at my side. "Have they infected her again?"

"Yes, love. They have," I answered, my voice hoarse with anger. "It looks drastic. If she has been reduced to unconsciousness by the disease, we may well have lost her." I didn't say that in that case we would soon have to dispatch her, and I had no idea how I could bring myself to do that.

"Still," I went on, "Mr. Onyekachi looks to be in similar shape, though he was not bitten. Perhaps she has swooned merely from her exertions."

"Yes, perhaps," Mary said, cutting away the trouser leg to expose the bite mark on Anne's right calf. She worked her way up one side of Anne's body, cutting away the clothing, and soon, as she washed and dressed the wounds made by knives and teeth, Mary wept softly.

"What is it, dear?" I asked, pausing as I treated the first bite with a fresh bandage.

"It's just that she is so fine and strong, so beautiful," Mary said. "And she is such a dear, sweet girl. She should not have to suffer so. It's wrong, John."

"Yes. Yes, it is, Mary," I replied, reaching across Anne's body to pat Mary's capable fingers. I found nothing else to say.

Doors slamming drew my attention away, and I ran to the office to grab my revolver.

Holmes stood framed by my office door.

"I have been on their trail since yesterday. You cannot think how glad I was to find that it led here," he cried.

"Where have you been, Holmes?" I asked.

"Liverpool first," he answered, "and then points south. Our forces are marshaling, and our assault will start soon, swift and sure.

It seems that others are of your opinion about the necessity of a bold strike."

"That would be Gladstone, yes?" I intuited, knowing the former prime minister resided often in Liverpool and knowing his concern for Anne Prescott and those like her.

"Yes. He has gained us some important allies. I returned to London yesterday, and young Wiggins found me stepping off the train in King's Cross. Since his report of the fire at St. Lazarus, I have been on the trail of these two, though I had little to go on. Pray, tell me all you know."

The idea of allies heartened me, to a small degree. I gave him a report of my few experiences and told him of Anne's grave condition.

Cold and dispassionate as ever, Holmes said merely, "Hm. I see. We have lost much, yet these two have brought some matters to rest. Shall I tell you of their exploits?"

But before he could begin, Mary's urgent cry of "John!" came from the examination room. Onyekachi with us, we ran to her aid.

We entered the room to see Mary backing toward us, her hands grasping the arms of Anne Prescott, who bore upon Mary with empty eyes and mouth open, head thrust forward to bite. I hardly recognized Anne as the woman who had fought at my side. Her wild countenance reminded me of Captain Suffield's when I last saw him. Much of her torn clothing had fallen away, but her aspect was that of a predatory beast, not a beautiful woman. She strained to reach my wife with her teeth and grasping fingers, as though she would tear her apart.

Holmes and I dove at Anne and bore her back to the table. Onyekachi sprang to our aid as we pushed her back onto the table, throwing himself across her body, clasping the table edges on either side to pin her down.

"Watson! Beware her teeth, man. A sedative! Rather a liberal dosage, I think, is in order," Holmes urged from his side of the struggle. Anne's legs flailed. Onyekachi trapped her arm as I released it.

Her upper body pinioned, Anne thrashed about. Her head lunged, teeth snapping at Onyekachi and Holmes. Holmes shouted her name over and over, trying to get her to recognize him. Anne's teeth gnashed at Holmes's cheek and missed him by a hair's breadth.

Those fierce blue eyes which had once shone with love for me started from their sockets, feral, inured to any softer feeling. My

169

thoughts ran again to Captain Suffield and his savage slaughter of Martha Tabram. Gasping, I plunged a needle into Anne's leg, horrified by what she had become.

Holmes caught a hand under Anne's chin and held down her head as the sedative began to take hold. Even when she fell unconscious, her breath came in ragged gasps, as though within her mind she continued to struggle.

"Have you any thoughts about our first steps in treating her?" Holmes asked.

Onyekachi stood, too, releasing his hold on Anne, as Mary returned with nightclothes to put upon her.

"Yes," I said. "I intend to take at least two pints of her tainted blood and replace it with healthy blood, each day for the next two days."

Holmes said, "I will give all I can spare, but I need to have each man at my side strong and able in two days' time. I have found LaLaurie's lair, the destination of those outlandish supplies, and I have found the source of Pizer's extortion money. It has all come together, and I hope that our bold move will catch LaLaurie off guard. Along with the small force I have conscripted for the fight, I hope to have you at my side, Watson. It will be a desperate venture. If we give of our blood, will we be able to endure?"

"I think so," I said. "But I fear we are too late. Look at her, Holmes. Surely we are on the verge of losing her!"

"We must all give what blood we can. Eat and build yourselves up quickly," I demanded. Holmes and Mary both turned stunned faces to me, but I began my preparations.

"You have my blood, too," Onyekachi offered. "I fight at her side and yours."

"Thank you, my friend," I said. "Would you be so kind as to tell us what happened to you and Miss Prescott after you left Baker Street?"

Onyekachi's tale was hard to follow, for he did not know street or neighborhood names. However, from what we understood, he woke first that night in Baker Street, thirsty for revenge. Once Holmes was gone, Onyekachi sought to follow him and begin his own hunt for Captain Suffield. Having seen Suffield degraded to the point of savagery, Onyekachi had taken upon himself the task of laying his captain to rest. However, as Onyekachi had hesitated at the door, trying to think of how to get back to the scene of the Tabram, Miss Prescott had joined him, claiming to feel perfectly well. Onyekachi, though he'd hated to ask for her help, had seen that her argument was valid: she could get him to anywhere in East London, where he had reason to believe the captain still lurked.

I conjectured from what Onyekachi told us that Captain Suffield had not been at liberty to roam London spreading havoc, as I had imagined. It must have been that Alcee had captured him. Like as not, Alcee was the only man with strength sufficient to control Suffield in his zombie state. He had taken the captain to the remains of his old altar in St. Lazarus. And that is precisely where Anne Prescott had found them, in the cellar.

Suffice it to say that Anne had led Onyekachi on a hunt of various locations before they had fetched up at St. Lazarus. Holmes may have a network of people whom he can employ to search the darkest parts of London, but Anne, having worked and ministered to the poorest people in the city, had a ready-made network of people who saw everything which went on in their streets and alleys. The hunters had sheltered with working harlots, beggars, and petty con artists, all of whom had benefited from Anne's help at the clinic or on her own time. Some of these people had seen Alcee capture the mad Captain Suffield and bind him in chains.

During this time, Anne had also armed herself with a butcher's meat cleaver, whetted to a razor's sharpness.

Before reaching the former infirmary, Anne and Onyekachi had encountered neither the zombies nor the doctor who had helped create them. Alcee, though, they had tracked to St. Lazarus.

Here, Onyekachi's story stopped for a moment, for the memory of the events that transpired in that place had driven him to tears. He mumbled prayers to Legba and Agwe Tawoyo for some time, on the verge of mental collapse. Poor, savage Onyekachi had come to the heart of the civilized world to confront its worst depravities.

Finally, he gathered his nerve and said, "We sneak down stairs through empty floors, and on first floor, Miss Anne, she find friend, Louisa, but dead. Oh, Doctor, don't make me say. Yes. I say, for two tzambis, they eating Miss Louisa on the floor. They eat inside her, her head and body, like wild dogs.

"Miss Anne, she make a choking sound in her throat, like she cries, but it turn into scream of angry and she t'row off these tzambis. I stand looking as she move, so quick, like water, fast, easy, but hacking them to pieces. She cut backs of legs so they not stand, first, then she butcher these tzambis. She take hands, ears, nose, then their... man parts. I try to tell her, tzambi feel nothing, but in minutes, her blade make these men into pieces. Then, she move to back wall, open door and drop into darkness.

"I follow her. Onyekachi never know such fear, but when I get to bottom in the dark, I see Miss Anne in light of fire on the bokor's altar. Anne kill tzambis—men, one woman. I see captain, held by chains where the bokor, he begin his chanting to claim all of captain's soul. I scream and the bokor, he run, letting captain go. I follow him as he leave through stinking tunnels. Anne come behind.

"The bokor, he escape and captain follow him, but bokor find wagon and get away t'rough streets that lead to water. Captain, like he smell water, head for docks and I follow. There, I catch him and take him into river. I—I do my duty and cut his t'roat, let the chains drag him down, to let Agwe of the waters have his soul, take him home.

"Now, I must kill bokor, but then I must die. Onyekachi sees too much and cannot live," he said, and wept bitter tears.

"What, do you think, my friend," I said to the shaking sailor, "made Anne so reckless, so willing to throw her life away?"

"She know that she would turn soon, that the bokor's magic was in her," he said.

"She knew?" Holmes asked, raising his eyes to mine.

"She hear you, in the carriage the night we come back after finding the doctor," Onyekachi replied. "She only pretend to sleep. Miss Prescott know she not have much time and wanted, like me, revenge for those she love."

***

As Onyekachi told Holmes his story, I proceeded to drain blood from Anne's veins, blinking back tears, pushing aside my revulsion for this medieval means of treatment. A slim hope, but as her skin grew ashen at the loss of diseased blood, I prayed that the healthy blood I put in would halt the spread of the disease, stem the tide of rot in her brain. I did not know if the transfusion would cure or kill her, as weak as she was.

Holmes went first as donor, and I prayed with all my might that his blood would have something in it, something which set him apart from other men, some intangible quality that might bring her strength she had never known. She would need such strength, if she was to recover from the horrors she'd seen—and done.

I used a saline solution by intravenous drip to help keep Anne from going into shock from blood loss. She remained unresponsive, but her color improved over the next day. I bled her a second and a third time, at a loss for a sense of how long I could continue this procedure or, if I did, whether it would halt the disease that gripped her. Without Alcee's poisons to cripple her thoughts, she might regain her reason. The horror that Captain Suffield had become, though, lingered before my mind's eye, and the images of my nightmare, where his figure had turned into Anne's, induced panic and dread in me.

Yet no one had treated Suffield as I did Anne. Perhaps, if we had reached him in time, we could have treated him so. I would not give up hope while I had a treatment to try, no matter how desperate Anne's case had become. I would work to save her. That fine and noble part of her that I had seen, and loved, was worth any effort on my part. Perhaps, just perhaps, if she could yet breathe the free air of her homeland as she recovered, she could forget the horrors she had lived through here. I would have it so, even if it meant her forgetting me completely.

***

During the course of my treatment of Anne, Holmes was often gone on errands, making complete his plans, but he told me nothing about them in detail. All I knew was that we would depart by train from Euston station on 30 August. Others would meet us in a specially commissioned car, and we would travel a short distance north. But of what we would face when we got there, and with whom we would face it, I knew nothing. I trusted in Holmes's plan and was prepared to take any risk to stop LaLaurie.

The evening of the 29th found Holmes and me sitting quietly in my outer office, with no words for each other. Holmes's keen eyes looked on me with proper worry. I was an emotional wreck.

We heard footsteps at the door and a soft murmur. There, leaning on Mary, Miss Prescott stood with my dressing gown wrapped around her. Mary had brushed Anne's hair, which lay over the shoulders of my gown. Anne's face, though bearing blushes of exertion, looked calm and rested. Mary hastened to lead her to a chair.

"Jack!" Anne called, holding out her hands to me.

I went to take her hands, and Holmes moved with me. I was grateful for his support, for I feared Mary seeing Anne's desire to embrace me. As we came to her, Anne addressed him as well and extended one of her hands to him.

Anne smiled, took our hands, and kissed them. "The men who have saved me," she said.

"I certainly hope so, dear lady," I returned, conscious that Mary had turned her eyes away. Mary murmured something about fetching us all some tea and left us.

"How are you feeling, Miss Prescott?" Holmes asked, kissing her hand with a bow and a flourish, I thought, to take her attention from me.

"I'm... better, I think, but my thoughts are so strange and muddled, Mr. Holmes," she replied in a tired voice. "I find myself thinking often of Katie and the shameful things she has done. Like as not, when she comes home, I'll give her a good hiding."

I know I started visibly. Holmes's glance grew more focused, though his smile never wavered. "You think that she deserves a sound spanking?" he asked.

"I'm sure of it," Anne returned, though she did not look angry. She went on in a calm voice but stopped in mid-sentence: "The idea of her, a woman of sale—but no, that cannot be. My Katie is—is gone, you say. Right?" She lay her head in her hands and breathed heavily for a moment.

"Yes, Anne," Holmes said, placing his hands on her shoulders, where Anne grasped them. "You've remembered correctly. It won't do to tire you much today. You have had a hard time. Just sit awhile and rest."

Anne hadn't mentioned the fate of her friend Louisa, and I wasn't about to offer her my condolence on the loss, but I noted her confusion about her sister. Likely, some damage had begun in her frontal lobe. I told myself that she could recover from this, though, in time.

When she turned her eyes back to us, I could see the tears pooling in them.

"I'm no better than Katie, with the things I've done," she sobbed, and the tears tumbled from her eyes. "Onyekachi has told you how I—"

"Your partner has given us an accurate description of what occurred, Miss Prescott," Holmes assured her, squeezing her hands. "Your actions are completely understandable, given your situation. You should not waste effort thinking about them. Soon, this problem will be over, and we can bring the plans of your former employer to a halt. Tomorrow, while you convalesce, Watson and I will lead the assault on his base of operations. Soon, when you are able, I have the name of an excellent surgeon with offices on Princes Street in Edinburgh. He instructs at the medical school there, and he tells me that he has need of a capable nurse."

Anne looked at me then, and though she wept still, she nodded and said, "Yes, Edinburgh. It's lovely there." She reached for one of my hands and squeezed it.

"You'll see, Anne," I said, bending down to look into her eyes. "This will pass into an unpleasant memory in years to come." I stood, still holding her hand, but she rose to her feet and drew herself to me. It was an intimate embrace for one so sudden, and she kissed me softly on the lips. As she drew back from me she said, "And I am well enough and will be better soon, so that I can return the love you have shown me."

The sound of Mary's gasp drew my eyes from Anne's face. Mary, I supposed, had previously intuited the nature of Anne's feelings for me. Perhaps she had also suspected that I returned those feelings. Now, though, she knew for certain.

"Mary!" I cried. Anne returned to her seat and dropped her head into her hands again as I left the room in search of my wife. I saw her retrieving her coat from the front hall, and I strode to her and placed my hand on her arm, Holmes a step behind me.

"Do not touch me!" she hissed, snatching her arm out of my grasp. "She has talked much in her sleep, and at every turn, she has asked for you, her 'Jack.' I—I don't—I don't want to see you. Leave me alone."

"Mary, please," I protested. "She is a very sick young woman..."

"No woman is sick enough not to know when a man loves her," she retorted and walked out of the door.

"I'll see that she is safe, Watson," Holmes said, taking his hat from the hall stand. "I think perhaps Anne could use a little mild sedation and further rest. Look to her and then get some rest yourself. We will leave at first light."

***

When I returned to my surgery, I found that Anne had gone back to her room. Onyekachi was just coming back down the stairs, having watched her fall asleep.

"Do we still go with Mr. Holmes in the morning?" he asked, his eyes wide with apprehension.

"Yes, my friend. We have done all we can for Miss Prescott now. We must turn our attention to Dr. LaLaurie."

I sent him to get some sleep and turned to my bed, my mind whirring with fatigue, confusion, and anxiety. I thought sleep would never come. My thoughts were all for Mary's safety, mixed with the hope that Anne had been cured. Sorrow and guilt weighed heavy on my heart, but I finally sank into uneasy slumber.

***

A light kiss awakened me, and I turned, thinking to see that Mary had returned. But Anne Prescott lay beside me under the sheet.

"What? Anne?" I gasped.

"Shhh," she whispered, and kissed me hard. Rolling atop me, Anne looked down at me. The warmth was back in her eyes. Her sure hands unbuttoned my shirt, removed my belt, for I had not thought to change into nightclothes.

My hands found that Anne wore nothing at all.

"Please," she moaned. "Onyekachi says that you will be gone in the morning on this next mission. You might never return. If Mary doesn't need to be with you tonight, I do. This might be the last time I see you, and I want you to know how much I love you, my Jack."

I'm sure that Anne recognized the ready answer my body made to hers, for her kisses and caresses led me to where I had long desired to be: at one with she whose body, mind, and soul had drawn me to her since the first day I met her. There comes a point when worry and fear drive a man past the point of caring about consequences. I lost myself in the warmth of that night, thinking that tomorrow might be my last day, so desperate was our plan.

I fell asleep with Anne in my arms, where she lay warm, secure, and whole. I remember her sweet smile, the hair falling in her face, as I drifted off to sleep.

***

I awoke to Holmes shaking my arm. I sat upright, looking around. Anne was gone. Looming behind Holmes, I finally recognized Sergeant Magnus Guthrie, though he, too, was dressed the same as Onyekachi, in plain clothes of heavy cloth. Without the scarlet tunic of the Royal Marines, I scarcely knew him. Guthrie, also like Onyekachi, carried a navy cutlass and a stout truncheon on his belt. He also wore a Webley & Scott pistol in a shoulder holster such as the one I use.

"Watson," Holmes said, "We're marshaling."

"Yes. Yes," I cried, "I'll be right down."

I dressed in haste and ran down the stairs, where Holmes waited at the open door. Mary stood at his side, smiling at him.

"Mary," I said. "I am grateful that you have returned."

The glance she turned on me was kindly, if diffident, and she said, "I have a charge to keep here. I will be here when you return. How long I am here after that, we will have to determine."

All I could do was bid her farewell.

CHAPTER NINETEEN

And with that, we set off. My thoughts ran from the heights of my elation at the memory of being with Anne to the depths of sorrow and guilt at Mary's parting words. Like all soldiers, we knew that this mission could claim our lives, or worse yet, leave us all infected with LaLaurie's disease. But we raced through the dark streets of London to embrace whatever awaited us, each perhaps cherishing the notion that some of us might make it through.

I scanned the three faces beside me in that heavy brougham. Holmes, eyes alert, seeing everything we passed, thinking, likely, of every step he'd take. He leaned forward, straining to get to his goal. Guthrie's face, with its thousand-yard stare, gave away no clue of his feelings about the combat that awaited him. He was detached, relaxed, and yet somehow lethal, competent in the business of war. Onyekachi sat with hands folded and shaking in his lap, lips mumbling prayers to Elegba. He alone invited my sympathy, for he had seen too much to bear and looked only for a way to end his misery at the loss of his beloved captain.

None of us spoke, and I could not break that silence.

We had no provisions with us, so I assumed our journey would not be a long one. Holmes, his keen eyes staring out into the darkness, appeared to be thinking over some serious matter, for his brows were drawn down in fierce concentration.

I learned of our destination after we pulled up to a street in back of Euston station. As we left the brougham, Holmes turned to the driver and said, "If I do not send you a telegram before midday today, you will know what to do. Correct?"

The driver scoffed once and uttered an odd, high-pitched giggle, a giggle I was sure I'd heard before, as he drove away.

"Holmes, that was Anderson, the newspaper-reading fellow!" I gasped, stepping close to Holmes so that he alone could hear me.

Holmes shot a smile in my direction.

"His given name is Mycroft. The family name, he shares with me," he said through his crooked smile.

"Your...?" I started, trying to think of what I had gleaned about Holmes's family.

"Elder brother," he finished. "The most brilliant yet sedentary man in this kingdom, I'll be bound. You must know, Watson, that before he stirs from his home or the Diogenes Club, Britain must stand upon the brink of ruin. But take heart, for his power is in his mind and his reach is great."

"Oh," I managed, and then Holmes turned and took off.

He ushered us into a narrow gateway between two businesses that backed onto the tracks leading north from Euston. Soon, we encountered a stout gateway, which Holmes opened for us, letting us onto a railway siding on which sat a single sleek engine with one long passenger car attached. We were waited upon, I could see, for the engine was at full steam, like a Thoroughbred spoiling for a race.

Within that rail car, I saw enough to surprise and humble me. Guthrie moved amongst the men there, shaking hands and grinning. The greetings of the men were the only sounds of merriment that whole day long, as far as I recall, but they were grim greetings of a kind I knew, the good-humored, rough talk of soldiers.

Guthrie had five companions, all armed as he was and clothed similarly. I knew by intuition that they were Royal Marines, likely his bunkmates from the *Icarus*. One lad must be Corporal MacGuire, for he was surely twenty stone of muscle, topped by a solemn, grim face. His eyes, like Guthrie's, took in everything and nothing, simply waiting for the onset of battle.

"Gentlemen," Holmes called to them as the car doors slammed and we lurched forward, "Sergeant Guthrie has briefed you, but there are several points I wish to stress before we get to our destination.

"We will have a short, hard march of an hour or so when we exit this car. Thanks to the kind assistance of this gentleman, whom you no doubt recognize"—here, the tall, stately form of Gladstone stood up at the rear of the car and took a bow—"we will have the opportunity to undertake this mission in the greatest secrecy, though the action will be hard and bloody.

"Today, we will face a great number of implacable foes who will not hesitate to kill us. If we few can succeed, though, and capture the men behind this business, we will save England from a catastrophe of unimaginable proportions, for the plague of zombies that our foe, Dr. Emil LaLaurie, is ready to loose upon us would be the poison that wipes out our people."

The men looked on, having been briefed on the nature of zombies, information they had taken in with only a few wry grins and shakes of their heads.

"I can see that the terminology we use promotes your disbelief," I added. "I was the same way until I faced many of the creatures in a Whitechapel alley. They have no compunctions about killing anyone, and if you do not seek to kill them as fast as you can, you will die today—or worse."

"I have no doubts about what Mr. Holmes and Dr. Watson have said," Gladstone added, leaning on a much-worn axe handle to steady himself as the train rocked. "When he convinced me of the seriousness of this threat, I determined to fight it in any way I could, as is my duty as God's servant on this earth. For this man LaLaurie has created an abomination, a disease that has claimed the lives of countless innocents, like your own Captain Suffield. And though these men whom you will face today have likely never desired to become the plague creatures they are, if you put an end to them, you will have done the work of angels. May Almighty God anoint each of you and keep you safe!"

Surprisingly, MacGuire then stood and said, "I know that my companions and I have been briefed that we are to kill these zombies, as you have named them, but I must believe that any man can be saved. We have all been on special missions like this, for which we will never receive public recognition, but I have never sought to take another Englishman's life, and I always think that a man, no matter how corrupted, has a chance to change. Is it not so with these men, the zombies? Are they beyond even the grace of God?"

"Yes, they are, in human terms," I answered, "though I hope that the Almighty's grace will cover them along with us. The disease, the evil that has claimed them, has no cure for those who are completely taken by it. It will be an act of mercy to end their horrid existence. LaLaurie's process destroys the victim's brain, and no man can call his life his own when his very mind is stripped away.

"They are no longer men. He has made them weapons of terror. They no longer know of human decency. I do not think that they are capable of learning or changing. Each one is capable, though, of killing at will and spreading his disease to anyone into whom he can sink his teeth."

I told them what I had witnessed in the actions of Captain Suffield and watched as their faces went pale. They nodded their heads and exchanged glances one with another, and even MacGuire nodded at last, though I could see that his generous heart wished that it were not so. The only warrant he needed came from having seen what had happened to Captain Suffield.

***

The train rolled on, and the men sat with heads bowed. When I could, I dared to think about what life might be like with a woman such as Anne Prescott at my side, for clearly last night she had chosen me and graced me with complete intimacy.

I recalled the words she had whispered to me in the dark: "I never thought that I would find a man like you, a man who could love all of me the way you do. Your gift to me is a life that a woman might only dream of in this world. I know that I have brought you the pain of inner conflict, and I love Mary for her sweet nature, too, but Jack, you and I, together, why, it is the stuff stories are made on, a dream come true, my love, a dream that lives in the waking world when two people believe in each other. It is the cause for which I would gladly give my life. Come back to me, Jack. Come back." And I had assured her that I would.

I was forced out of my reverie by the sound of pistol chambers opening, the hiss of long blades coming out of scabbards. I observed my comrades checking weapons, adjusting belts and the leather guards on their arms and legs. They worked in silence, making sure that the tools of their grim trade were ready, as soldiers will on the eve of battle. I did the same, turning my thoughts away from Anne's embrace and Mary's sorrow and anger to my own weapons and my own captain, Sherlock Holmes. I prayed, as all soldiers do, that this mission would not prove my last. Even if it should, I prayed that it would save my beloved England from this terrible plague.

I noted that Holmes bore, in place of his kukri knife, one of the katana that we had seen in training. As he called my attention to the wicked-looking thing, with its scabbard and pommel of dull, midnight black, I recognized it as the sword Mr. Uyeshiba called Mustard Seed. Perhaps it had recognized Holmes as its true master. If so, it had made a good choice. It was a fearsome weapon, and I was glad that it had not come to me. I shivered at the sight of it, though I did not know why.

Holmes then produced for me another katana.

"The sharpest of all blades, Watson," said Holmes. "A loan of sorts from Mr. Uyeshiba. It was all I could do to dissuade him from coming, though we could have used his help. His importance among my secretive allies is too great to risk him."

"He is vital to the L.S., then, I assume. Well, we could certainly use him," I muttered, recalling Uyeshiba's speed and striking power. "He is much more suited to such a weapon than I am. Still, I will be glad to have it should the cartridges run out." I hung my sword on my belt in place of the cutlass I'd been given, wondering how well I could wield it.

***

Holmes moved away from my side and spent the last few minutes of the journey trying to convince Gladstone to stay with the train and await our arrival—however many of us returned—at the Banbury station. The Grand Old Man only smiled and demurred, saying that if his career ended today, he would have it so.

"I can think of no greater blow to strike in God's name on behalf of the victims of this madman than to give all in this cause."

Holmes simply said, "Yes, sir. You know of our plans. So I trust you will keep up with them." Gladstone smiled, shook Holmes's hand and removed the leather cover from the head of his well-used axe. Popular reports said that Gladstone's axe had felled a great many trees. He took a whetstone from his dungarees pocket and ran it along the keen edge.

***

The train ground to a halt in the dark before dawn. It left us in a field fresh from the harvest, south of Banbury, an area of well-kept plots and hedgerows, rich land for tilling. It was odd to think of London's worst corruption having its source somewhere in these quiet, wholesome fields, where the damp winds carried the scent of autumn approaching. Yet Holmes had found that LaLaurie's exotic supplies all made their way here to Northamptonshire, to Brompton Castle, where lived a Parliament member with a doubtful reputation. Even now, I leave out his name, for the sake of his heirs.

Holmes was sure, since John Pizer was involved, that this peer of the realm hadn't dreamed of backing such a horrid operation on his own. Under threat of Pizer's blackmail, he lent his support to the scheme that would, Holmes was sure, cost his life and his family's reputation.

We started out, falling into a short column of twos, running toward the dangers.

Holmes knew the area well, for he led us through shallow spots in the streams we came upon and generally kept us under cover of trees or fence rows. We gave a wide berth to any farm house or outbuilding. Soon, I saw light within the upper rooms of Brompton Castle.

We ran on. Soon, we were forced to wade Sor Brook and swim the broad moat that surrounded Brompton, holding our cartridges and pistols out of the water. I doubted that we possessed ammunition enough to settle this matter with firearms. I imagined countless zombies waiting for us, but I had no idea of the odds we would face. Brompton, a magnificent old estate, could hold many of LaLaurie's creations, too many to contemplate.

Having forded one stream and swum the brackish castle moat, we were chilled quickly by the pre-dawn breezes, but the marines took no thought of their comfort and with swift hands began the work of getting us over the wall. Working with grappling hooks and stout ropes and using MacGuire's massive frame as a ladder, two marines, Gilhooly and Winthorpe, helped haul me up to the top of the formidable, ten-foot-high wall. There they secured themselves and spun both ropes into one. MacGuire amazed me by hauling up his own huge bulk hand over hand. Holmes, Guthrie, Adams, and Gunn surmounted the wall a little farther on.

I noted that Onyekachi and Gladstone had not reached us, having fallen behind in the run. They would follow us, since Gladstone claimed earlier that he knew the area. I was certain that Onyekachi would not desert him. We left ropes in place and turned our attention to the enclosed space within the castle walls, now a sight that would sicken any Englishman.

The stench greeted us first. The stately dwelling lay dark to the left, except for a light in the window of an upper hall. The lawn enclosed by the castle walls should have been spacious, park-like. Torches shed glaring light across the once-lush grass, now filled by a low, rambling, wooden structure with no windows. Unpainted, raw, and reeking of corruption, it transformed the once magnificent green space into a cesspool.

The wooden building's tarpaper roof, more than twelve feet high, sagged already in places, though even in the dark the building's wood looked new-cut and unfinished. The charnel stench emanating from it, made visible in the ooze of mud and filth around its foundations, told me that LaLaurie's creations filled it.

My eyes burned with tears at the image before me, a sign and symbol of what the rogue American witch doctor wished to do to England. Unless he was stopped, no castle or fortress would be safe. Would Buckingham Palace, in time, suffer the pestilence of zombies, I wondered?

At no time in my life had I so desired to close with my enemy and destroy him utterly, yet I had no idea where to look for him, though Holmes had assured me he was here. I feared that I might lose my chance to face LaLaurie and take him down, despite my physician's oath. This one man, I did desire to harm.

The marines near me pointed to their ears and looked to me or Holmes for a sense of the piping tones we heard. I had come to expect it in the presence of zombies. The tuneless whistling, now emanating from the wooden structure, made the creatures docile.

I could not see who piped that awful tune, nor did I care. I had seen what happened to the fellow who piped for those undead, and I reasoned that such a man had lost all honor, to sink so low. I wondered how many such men had joined the doctor's staff, and I counted myself fortunate to have these marines at my side.

Zombie moans and groans rumbled like distant thunder. I could see no sentries on the two doors of the foul structure. Only the tuneless piping kept the foul creatures within, I surmised.

"When the music ceases, those creatures within will turn to ravening animals. They feel no pain and do not stop for what we would see as a mortal wound," I whispered, watching Gilhooly and Winthorpe exchange doubtful glances. "Crush their skulls by any means or remove their heads from their shoulders. Show no hesitation."

With that, we leapt down from the wall, our landing silent on the soft turf. My unit ran to meet Holmes and his three marines. Guthrie, landing farther along the wall, ran straight for the entrance to the building as Holmes, Adams, and O'Hara waited for us.

"Guthrie!" Holmes stage-whispered, trying to bring the big man to heel. Guthrie tripped and sprawled flat, sliding in the mud. A short, brazen clanging arose from within the structure. He turned a pale, mud-spattered face to us and the wire that had tripped him. The piping stopped. Sudden, deadly silence enveloped us.

A small man bearing a pipe in one hand, his other hand clutching his hat to his head, burst from one of the double doors, whimpering as he fled. Guthrie lay where he'd fallen, shifting his glance between us and the dark opening. That odd quiet held us all for a few short seconds before the other door flew open and disgorged Hell.

CHAPTER TWENTY

The zombies boiled out of the building, an evil regurgitation. The foremost leapt onto Guthrie, pounding, rending, jaws snapping.

"To him, lads!" Holmes shouted, and I drew my revolver. I put two shots in the first zombie head that rose above Guthrie's struggling form. I didn't take into consideration whether the shots were safe. There was no time.

Guthrie rolled away with the remaining two zombies latched onto his sword arm and opposite leg. He gained his feet, and with a frantic spin, he dislodged the zombie on his arm. I put another bullet into the head of the fellow gripping his leg. Guthrie took the head off the one he had spun away as it lurched back at him.

"Give a little ground, men," Holmes called over the zombies' approach, "but form pairs and take them as they come!" At my side, Adams and Winthorpe sought to push the zombies away; already they were being overcome.

"Do not pause!" I yelled, cleaving the head of one zombie that was clawing at Adams's back. "Cut them down, cut them down!" I kicked the legs from under a tall zombie that loomed over me and sent another bullet home, but there was no time to set up any sort of line.

Holmes, MacGuire, and Guthrie forged ahead into the pack of shambling figures that poured out of the double doors at us. The massive strength of the two marines toppled zombies over each other. Twenty, thirty figures, many naked, limping, with suppurating wounds, had already surged out of the black recesses of that evil maw, eager for our blood.

Holmes slid between the heaving bulks of MacGuire and Guthrie, making himself the point of a wedge. He gained two steps on

Guthrie and MacGuire and plied that dreadful black sword. Bright blade moaning as it cleaved the air, it flashed through the zombies' rotting flesh, laying a ghastly harvest at his feet. Guthrie laughed and cheered and dealt lethal blows of his own, as did the dour MacGuire. Yet zombies surged past them.

Guthrie battled on, tireless, stomping, shooting with his left hand and caving in skulls or lopping heads with the cutlass in his right. MacGuire stood silent, teeth bared, battling with truncheon and saber. He had yet to draw his revolver, for he had moved to the center of the open doorway, just behind Holmes. Holmes was ever in front of him, and the lad would not risk a shot passing through a zombie and hitting his captain.

"Good lad!" I roared, battling to a place near his side. Adams and Winthorpe, standing well off to my left, were slower to take the sort of action needed; they fought, but only in a defensive manner. I could hear them encourage each other and shout to Gunn and Gilhooly for help.

I had no time to think of their plight, but on reflection, I'm amazed that they could face the savagery of the zombie attack, for as always, it was remorseless, implacable, a wave of grasping, tearing hands, gaping mouths, and empty eyes. Those younger fellows had never faced enemies so careless of themselves, so focused on just destroying life. I had time to think only "God help them" and strike at any zombie that came near me, with O'Hara at my side.

But soon, with bodies piled around us, we stanched the tide of zombies that rolled out of the doors. Holmes, procuring a torch from beside the doorway, leapt into the black interior, Guthrie at his back and MacGuire behind them, hurling bodies away from the doorway.

Gilhooly screamed behind me, and Adams, I think, shouted his name. I cast Gilhooly a glance and saw that the zombie he had impaled with his cutlass had drawn itself forward onto the blade and sunk its teeth into Gilhooly's neck, blood spurting out in a wild spray.

The smell of that young Irishman's fresh blood seemed to quicken the actions of the creatures. I saw one that Adams had kicked to the ground turn and spring upon Gilhooly, crushing his skull with a two-handed blow that surely shattered its own bones.

It took no notice of its own injury, but buried its maw in Gilhooly's head to eat the poor lad's brain. My gorge rose in disgust, and I put a bullet through that creature's head—too late. Adams, Winthorpe, and Gunn needed no other provocation. Tears streamed from my eyes as we redoubled our efforts, and we soon cut down the rest of the horrid crew before the doors.

Holmes called from within the building, "Watson! I need you!"

I holstered my pistol and entered the door with a call to the others: "Take it to them, lads! Within!"

I stopped short upon entering, for I saw Holmes standing not far from the doorway, confronted by partition walls within the structure that created what must have been a series of connected avenues within the building. I imagined that the piping had kept zombies marching through that hellish maze, since they never seemed to rest.

"We are too few to search out every corner here, and I can half see and hear many more of them fighting to get to us. I've had a look from the top of this partition, and I cannot see any way to confront them all at once as I had hoped," Holmes admitted, breathing heavily. "Set fire to this building, Watson, from the rear."

Collecting Winthorpe by his arm, I replied, "This place will go quickly, Holmes, with its fresh timber and tarpaper roof. Do not go too far within."

I ran, with Winthorpe at my side, around the far side of the building and found our path blocked by an oak that had been carelessly felled to make room for the structure.

"Cut branches as we go, lad," I called to Winthorpe, drawing my own sword and taking several branches in an instant. I soon had more than an armload from the venerable old tree.

Though Winthorpe's cutlass was nowhere near as sharp as the katana, we soon had more fuel than we could carry, so we made for the back of the building. Off to our right, at the bottom of another short tower in the castle wall, I could see what looked like a jumble of garden implements, so I made a dash for it to see if I could find any accelerant to aid our fire.

Stepping within, though, I first found not one but two corpses, obviously castle groundskeepers. They had been dead for months, I saw, but they had also been consumed as Gilhooly had: Their skull cavities had been scooped clean and their stomachs ripped open. Again, I fought off the urge to vomit.

Forcing myself to scan the shelves, I found two cans of turpentine. As I ran back to join Winthorpe, I vowed to avenge those two sons of the soil, as well.

At the back of the building, Winthorpe had his hands full, for three of the creatures had breached a low opening on the rear wall, looking for a way out. He stood in their midst, fighting desperately, not giving ground, though outnumbered.

I stopped and drew my pistol, taking one with a headshot and knocking the other aside with a shot to its neck. Winthorpe finished that one with a backhanded chopping stroke of his cutlass and felled the third with his truncheon as I ran to his aid.

We had a fire to set. As Winthorpe spread the dry branches along the base of the wall, I shot several more of the vile creatures as they tried to worm their way out of the hole the others had clawed through. They came headfirst and were easy targets. Three shots, and then their rotting flesh stopped the hole. I jammed as many dried branches around them as I could, anxious to see them burn.

Winthorpe took one can of turpentine and splashed one side of the wall, while I did the other. Soon we had a blaze going all along the back wall, fed by the dry brush and the turpentine. Within seconds, it reached the tarpaper of the roof. Its sudden, intense heat forced us to step away, and I feared that it would spread so fast that our men might well be trapped within.

"Dr. Watson," Winthorpe called to me, "one of them bit me." He held out a bloodied hand.

My heart sank, and I looked into his wide eyes. He was a golden-haired youth, well above six feet, with the build of a rugby forward. I'm afraid that I trembled at the thought of what would likely happen to him.

"Here," I said, pausing to make a tourniquet from my pocket handkerchief. "This will have to be tight enough to make your hand numb, but we must try to keep the infection from spreading." I knew that with his heart pumping as mine was, the disease had likely already gotten into his bloodstream. Here was another who would need transfusions as soon we returned to town.

"Take heart, lad. I have seen the process halted, even reversed," I said, thinking about Anne. I had every reason to think that we could help him, and I tried to encourage him. The look on his pale face, the wide eyes and trembling jaw, told me that he thought of the bite as a mortal wound. He nodded his acceptance of what I had said, though, and we returned to the front.

There, all our men were once again engaged, but now things had changed. I had forgotten the sort of undead that had attacked Holmes and me in the rooms at Baker Street. That class of zombie was faster, and they used weapons.

They had evidently decided to show their more cunning abilities. As more of the slower, shuffling zombies emerged from the maze-like lanes in that darkness, the quicker ones sprang out amongst them and began to wreak havoc. Gunn and Adams were both down with massive wounds from the razor-sharp knives of the faster zombies.

These faster zombies were much more lethal. I had no idea how many of those we would encounter here, though by this time there must have been a hundred zombies strewn about the grounds in front of that shed. How many more there were, I could not imagine.

The fire, though, would take care of a great many of them, for it roared over the building as though it, too, were eager to rid the world of this plague. I prayed that we would not be caught in its onslaught.

The fighting went on like mad, as Gunn's and Adams's bodies were dragged back to lie beside Gilhooly's. Guthrie fought in silence, with greater cunning now, treating every new threat as one of the more able zombies. Winthorpe ran to his aid.

Already, MacGuire had felled several that had come flaming out of the dark lanes within. He cast their bodies back within the flames as two of the swifter ones pounced down toward him from the tops of the partitions. MacGuire caught each one by the neck as it fell and then slammed their heads together with such force that the creatures went limp, skulls smashed, before he cast them back into the flame.

I had been looking for Holmes, but in vain. But as flames raced along inside the roof of the structure, leaping onto the beams over which the tarpaper had been nailed, the flash of Mustard Seed's blade shone for an instant. Holmes was scrambling atop the partition walls within, three of the swifter zombies copying his every move. He was so close to the flames that his coat smoldered.

I took aim and fired at one of the zombies that chased him, sending it crashing back down into the flames, which roared to greet it. Guthrie followed my example and shot the next one as Holmes bounded down and rolled out the door.

The third zombie, though it missed its dive at Holmes, fell straight upon Winthorpe, burying its two knives into either side of the poor lad's neck. Winthorpe managed to keep his feet, though, and bearing the fast zombie's weight, he rushed into the heart of the flames.

Guthrie shouted his name. With a bellow, Winthorpe pushed harder, knocking partition walls down, bearing his attacker further into the inferno. Guthrie yelled the lad's name again and started to look away. He turned back then, took aim, and sent a bullet through the back of Winthorpe's head as the doomed lad crashed to his knees in the heart of the fire. The zombie, trapped, howled and thrashed in the hungry blaze.

Holmes was at my side, though, hauling on my jacket. "Come, Watson, we must take the keep. There, I believe, we will find our quarry." To Guthrie and MacGuire he called, "Hold them within and get those doors closed as soon as you can. Let none escape!"

"O'Hara," he added, "you're with me. Make haste, man!"

O'Hara had knelt beside the bodies of his slain friends, but he leapt to service at Holmes's order. He paused only to sweep up two more pistols and jam them into his belt, then followed behind us.

The heavy oaken doors to the keep stood open, so we mounted the stairs inside. Holmes went in front, and I begged leave of one of the extra pistols O'Hara had in his belt. I had sheathed my long sword and stashed the truncheon in my belt, where I could get to it easily. In a stairwell, I would need pistols.

Pausing to reload as Holmes approached the door into the upper room of the keep, whose light we had seen from the fields, I watched from below as he worked the latch and pushed open the creaking barrier. In an instant, one of the faster zombies pounced on him and buried its teeth in the left shoulder of Holmes's coat.

Pushing O'Hara aside, I fired and took that one down, though the report of the heavy round in that stone enclosure left a ringing in our ears I can sometimes still discern. O'Hara stopped and clapped his hands over his ears, but Holmes dashed forward into the room.

When I gained the entrance, pistols leveled, I saw Holmes fending one creature off with his left hand while he swept through another's neck with his whistling blade.

When I shot the one at his left hand, he turned to me with a grim smile. His face was lined with fatigue, and his coat front and both sleeves had been reduced to bloody tatters. The room, though, was empty.

"I think, now, that we make for the great hall, but we will have to go in darkness," he called, looking for O'Hara and then beckoning him on.

As we searched along the unfamiliar passages, making always toward the center of the great house, the only light we had was from the blaze of the outbuilding. Flames covered it and shot up into the gray pre-dawn. The smell of burnt bodies would be awful, but I hoped, foolishly, that we had destroyed them all.

As we gained a hallway into which a light shined from the room we would enter, Holmes stopped to make sure that both O'Hara and I were entering with two pistols drawn.

"I would imagine," Holmes whispered, close to both O'Hara and me, "that LaLaurie and Alcee are within, with the peer. They will be armed, but if shooting starts, take care not to hit their hostage. He has already paid the price for the lack of good judgment that put him in Pizer's power. Pizer, I imagine, will be there as well, for he still has an interest in maintaining his tight hold over so powerful a family as this. Go with care."

Peering into the partially open door, we saw LaLaurie pacing to and fro in the light from a flickering hearth, his hands behind his back. Beside him, a middle-aged man whom I surmised must be the member of Parliament, Pizer's victim, sat bound and gagged, the sweat of fear and fatigue rolling down his face.

Behind him stood a short man with dark hair and mustache, whose eyes watched every move LaLaurie made. This, I assumed, was the blackmailer, John Pizer. He looked more like a shopkeeper than a criminal, fidgeting in his ill-fitting suit. He didn't appear to be armed. Every few seconds, he turned from LaLaurie to glance at the figures of several swift zombies—the last of the doctor's stockpile, I hoped with grim satisfaction—who stood chained together in the darker recesses of the room. I assumed that Alcee was behind them, where I could not see him.

Holmes pushed the door the rest of the way open and strode into the room. O'Hara was on his heels, pistols leveled at LaLaurie's head. I rushed in behind them. But when I passed the door, it swung closed, and a stout walking stick crashed down across my arms, knocking free both of my guns. A huge hand and arm shot round my throat, cutting off my wind.

Alcee had me.

Holmes and O'Hara backed into the nearest corner at my surprised choking sounds, and O'Hara turned one pistol to take aim at Alcee's head. Though I thrashed about with all my might, the bokor held me easily in his grasp, chuckling low at my useless struggles. As twisted as his torso was, he stood no taller than I did. He far outweighed me, though, and my efforts to kick him or stomp on his foot were futile. His strength terrified me, and I could not breathe enough to order O'Hara to take the shot.

With both hands on Alcee's heavy arm, I hauled down on it enough to croak out, "Shoot him!" But LaLaurie had drawn his own pistol and aimed it at Holmes's head in the same instant.

"Let us end this now," LaLaurie growled. "Break his neck, Alcee!" He cocked the hammer on his revolver and took steady aim at Holmes.

I caught a flash of something that reflected the firelight before me for an instant, and a knife thrown with remarkable skill thudded home into Alcee's knotted shoulder, near my ear. Uttering a startled cry, Alcee dropped me. Rolling away, I scrambled to find my pistols in the shadows on the floor. LaLaurie fired but missed a dodging Holmes, only to take O'Hara in the shoulder. O'Hara fell, cursing and seeking to get a handle on one of his pistols again.

In the moments that followed, LaLaurie released his remaining zombies from their chains and they spread out into the room. Pizer yelped and fled at top speed into the darkness of the hall's far corner, pausing only long enough to take up a thick portfolio from a tabletop. He disappeared, and with him, I thought, went LaLaurie's research notes.

From the other end of the hall, then, I heard a thundering voice roar, "The Lord is my rock, and my fortress, and my deliverer. My God, my strength, in whom I will trust!" The sounds of heavy blows falling punctuated every other word.

I looked around one of the chairs and saw Gladstone, his stance wide and strong, wielding his great axe as though he would fell an entire forest. The axe whistled in a deadly arc around him. Two zombies fell, their heads rolling across the floor toward us. At Gladstone's side, struggling to reach beyond the zombies, Onyekachi fought with truncheon and cutlass. It had been one of his knives that had pierced Alcee's shoulder.

The six creatures were no match for our friends, though I saw Gladstone take a knife wound to one arm. Onyekachi broke free of the pile of zombie bodies, struggling to disentangle himself from the dead hands that still clutched him. His eyes never looked away from Alcee Sauvage.

LaLaurie dashed toward the door we had entered, propelling Alcee before him, and fled, even as O'Hara's shots from the floor chipped the stone of the doorway.

Holmes, springing to my side, cried, "Watson! Are you able to move?"

"Yes," I croaked. "After them!"

On our feet once again, we left the room in pursuit of our quarry, though I was still dizzy from Alcee's chokehold. We pelted along the hallways, pausing to test for open doors through which our enemies might have escaped. We found that they had been forced to retrace our steps.

Expecting that they would be met by MacGuire and Guthrie in the yard, we trusted that we would have them cornered, but we met our men coming up the stairs.

"Has no one passed you?" Holmes cried.

"None, sir. We came when we heard the shots," Guthrie cried.

"Up!" Holmes shouted, looking to the ceiling of the keep.

It took only a few seconds to find the dark, narrow stairs that led up to the topmost battlement. From there, the only escape would be a harrowing plunge into the moat, but we knew our quarry to be desperate and willing to take any chance to flee our grasp.

As we neared the open trapdoor, the dark blue of the morning sky above us, LaLaurie sprang into view and fired his five remaining rounds at us. They ricocheted amongst the stones, clipping me in the arm and Holmes along his ribcage. MacGuire and Guthrie threw themselves flat on the stairs behind us and escaped all the bouncing missiles, though they bore cuts on hands and faces from the stone chips that flew in all directions.

I shot at LaLaurie, who skipped away from the opening, and then Holmes passed me, leaping out onto the top of the keep. I climbed high enough to cover him from the ladder.

We had them. They stood with the short battlement wall of the tower behind them.

LaLaurie sheltered behind Alcee, who stood tossing a knife from hand to hand. His long face was set in an evil grin. His shoulder, pouring blood, suggested that Onyekachi's thrown knife had found an artery, yet the bent giant stood firm, muttering incantations. We would not take him alive.

LaLaurie placed a foot on the battlements, ready to leap into the moat below.

From behind, I was plucked aside as Onyekachi sprinted past me on the ladder and sprang in front of Holmes. Onyekachi chanted, "Yemaya, take away his power! Agwe Tawoyo, avenge my captain!" as he rushed the huge bokor, ready to give all to avenge poor Suffield. Alcee's knife met Onyekachi and plunged into his side. It was not enough: Onyekachi's headlong rush bore the big man over the edge of the short battlement, and they pinwheeled down to splash into the dark waters.

Lunging out to the wall, pistol ready, I sought to get a shot at Alcee, whom I feared would overpower the fierce sailor. In the water, though, Onyekachi was more than a match for the bigger man. Though Alcee stabbed at him repeatedly, Onyekachi dove and swirled like a shark. As Alcee cast about him, Onyekachi rose one last time behind him and drew his knife across the big bokor's throat with a shout of triumph.

"For my captain! Die, bokor! Die!" Onyekachi screamed in final vengeance, and Alcee, his hands clutching in vain at his gushing throat, grew still. The water around them darkened with their mixing blood as Onyekachi let Alcee go. Onyekachi lay back on the surface of the dark water, his cries of victory growing weaker. I could see Alcee's knife protruding in our friend's chest as he lay on the surface, blank eyes staring at the sky. LaLaurie, who had watched the struggle at our side, cried "Alcee! Mon frère!" as Alcee sank.

MacGuire plunged over the battlement to come to Onyekachi's aid, but his shipmate was dead before he could get to his side. As MacGuire dragged Onyekachi's lifeless form to the moat's edge, we turned our full attention back to LaLaurie, who held his empty pistol at his side and backed away from us until his legs pressed against the short battlement.

I raised my pistol, looked into the mad eyes of Dr. Emil LaLaurie, and said quietly, "Did I not promise that my revenge would be swift?"

"Watson, no!" Holmes cried, pulling my arm down. "We need him. His knowledge can help us, surely. If we have him, we do not need his notes, Watson. Think of those you must help, man."

Lowering my revolver to my side, I replied through gritted teeth, "Very well, Holmes. He lives, for now, though I will follow him to the gallows to make certain of his death."

"Ah, so someone you love is infected?" LaLaurie sneered. "Precious Anne, perhaps? But I would rather d—"

LaLaurie stopped. His body jerked as something struck his chest. At the same instant, I heard the crack of a distant rifle. Magnus Guthrie yelled, "Down!" and pulled us to the cold stone in a tangle.

LaLaurie clutched at his chest, mumbling something I could not hear clearly. He looked down at where blood from a bullet wound gushed out around his fingers. It spread out from his hand in a growing patch of red. I looked up from below, watching LaLaurie's legs buckle under him as he sank.

"The marksman!" Holmes shouted. "He has tracked us!"

"I'd know the sound of a Martini-Henry rifle anywhere," Guthrie cried, his face pressed to the cold stone.

LaLaurie lay in front of us in a widening pool of his heart's blood. His eyes, staring, wild, looked toward us, bloody froth bubbling from his mouth. He would die in seconds.

"Maman!" he murmured. "Mor... iar... ty assass...ine... a... moi..."

Then the sight fled from his eyes and bright blood stopped his voice.

The effect of his words stunned me, as when a sharp blade slices flesh so fast, so deep as to cause only shock, no pain. Holmes's eyes turned to mine. We were inches apart and had both gasped in the same instant. LaLaurie's dying words had claimed that Moriarty had just murdered him. That name we knew and had reason to fear. We had no doubt that he meant Professor James Moriarty. Holmes's eyes clenched shut, and he rolled onto his back, his shaking hands covering his mouth as though to stifle a scream of panic.

"Holmes, am I correct? Did LaLaurie just say, 'Mama, Moriarty has murdered me'?"

196

Holmes nodded his head and whispered, "Fitting, I suppose, that his last thoughts were addressed to his mother, a woman as evil as Moriarty but far less cunning. I had searched for some evidence of that arch-criminal early on in this business and found nothing to identify his presence. What other criminal is so powerful, so shrouded in darkness, so far- reaching in his plans? Blind! I have been blind!"

In my slow thoughts, I saw the picture unfold before me. Moriarty, the arch-criminal, was LaLaurie's patron. Moriarty had used LaLaurie as his catspaw and had now cast him aside. When I did not kill LaLaurie, the marksman did, as he had tried once before to kill us on that warehouse rooftop. We would not find the marksman. He would be long gone by the time we descended this turret, for Moriarty had planned it all, with the horrible, cold thoroughness that Holmes claimed made Moriarty the foremost criminal mind alive.

Holmes lay, his eyes staring in horror at the pale dawn sky over him. "Always ahead of our plans," Holmes moaned, striking his fist on the stone surface. "Controlling a network of known criminals. Deep financial resources. Ah, Watson, how could I have been so blind to the truth staring at me? We are undone!"

Thinking back to the zombies we had killed at Baker Street, I muttered, "Likely enough, he gave up a number of his criminal agents to LaLaurie's 'research' when it became plain that the best zombies were those of a criminal nature."

"Very likely," Holmes whispered. "And he employs many, many more. He is an abstract thinker, a mathematician, Watson. Even now, he has foreseen our next actions and works several ways to counter them. We are undone."

Whatever hope I had for myself shriveled in the fire of those horrific words.

Part Three.

"Awash in the Evil Tide"

CHAPTER TWENTY-ONE

Holmes secluded himself with Gladstone immediately to alert the former prime minister that he and other members of the mysterious L.S. lived under the same level of threat from Moriarty that we did. The rules and conditions had changed in the deadly game we all played. Holmes emerged from that meeting with darkened brow but resolute attitude. Gladstone dealt with the unnamed, victimized member of Parliament.

Horror made me numb, but I did as Holmes had bidden me. Guthrie, MacGuire and I searched the house for LaLaurie's case notes but turned up nothing but two slips of paper, lying near the door through which Pizer had escaped. Both were torn from pages, little more than scraps that one might pull off a handy sheet to mark a place. One had a street address, "8 Victoria," with no city mentioned. The other read, "S. Holm." I pocketed them, thinking they would be of little use.

I patched up our hurts with numb hands and heart, thinking of Moriarty so far ahead of us, not daring to imagine what we might face upon our return to London. We could not return to London quickly enough. I feared to think what Moriarty had already done to strike against us.

Most readings of the sniper's presence pointed to Moriarty working his plan before ours, circumventing what we had come to Brompton to do. Wiping out more than a hundred zombies seemed scarcely worth it if the evil genius behind it all was willing to let them go with such ease. He evidently had what he needed and had been able to do whatever he wanted in London while we were here. Holmes had been right about the danger of this sudden, bold move against LaLaurie. Our seeming courage had exposed us where we were vulnerable. That very thought sickened me with dread, even as we stood in seeming victory at Brompton.

At Banbury Station, I watched Holmes dispatch a telegram to his brother. Though our abject failure threatened my ability to reason, my first fears were for Mary's safety, especially after the emotional blow my affections for Anne had given her. Anne, if she continued in her recovery, could defend herself, should an attack come. Mary, though, relied upon me as her defense—or she once had, anyway.

We planned our return as best we could. Holmes kept my attention on the needs of the moment, for my thoughts kept drifting back to my worries about my household coming under attack from Moriarty's agents. I knew a police presence remained around them, but I had little confidence in the dear Old Bill, and it waned even more in the face of Moriarty's ability to foresee our plans.

I simply had no way of knowing what he intended, and neither did Holmes. We could only guess that he would carry on his criminal commerce with the results of LaLaurie's sickening experiments. Like as not, Moriarty had his own collection of the deadly creatures with which to work his plans. Holmes reminded me that every single criminal action Moriarty undertook had several outcomes that were not readily visible but would serve his ends.

"That is why I sent Mycroft a telegram. He can move his agents into place to protect those closest to us. I suspect we will be greeted by one of Mycroft's agents at King's Cross."

"But this Moriarty bloke," Guthrie observed, "is 'e really that powerful? I can't imagine that 'e'd be so little known, if 'e 'ad such influence as you suggest, Mr. 'Olmes."

"Who is a more fearful enemy, Sergeant: the bold warrior who rushes at you headlong, reckless and desperate, or the careful, meticulous tactician who finds the moment of your least awareness and greatest weakness to attack in silence?"

Guthrie replied, "Then this bloke knows our strengths and weaknesses and 'ow to use 'em."

"That is Moriarty, and that is why we do not know how to meet him next. His next move is nearly impossible to guess," Holmes replied. "He has planned each step, as well as alternatives to each move, long in advance, with several variations in place for the ways in which we might counter him.

"And he does so in the insulated secrecy of a lair we cannot find. Clearly, London is his base, but not any one place in the city. Watson and I have found that his resources allow him great reach, even to North America, and the goods that I tracked to Brompton Castle show that he has been active in South America in pursuit of this zombie-making venture. One of his men, Pizer, was able to gain a corruptive influence on a member of Parliament. And I suspect he has even brought men of criminal influence quietly into England. He is the most brilliant, cunning, and deadly foe imaginable."

"So all we can do, sir, is react to what we find next?" MacGuire asked, to which Holmes nodded his assent. "Then how do we arm ourselves, sir, for the next action?"

"I do not know whether you should count yourselves as part of it yet," said Holmes. "Your participation in last night's action was at Gladstone's direct request to the Admiralty. I have shared information with you about Moriarty, for you have now earned his ire, having opposed his plans. I do this only to forewarn you, and you should avoid even the mention of his name around others. He will not forget you, gentlemen. Nor shall Watson and I, but Moriarty's ill favor may yet claim each of us, in secret or direct action."

"I know that I speak for the corporal 'ere, sir, when I ask if we can join you in this action, if our superiors allow it," Guthrie said. "I cannot think of any Royal Marine who would not."

"We would be thankful for your help," Holmes replied. "But please recall how this mission arises and ends in secrecy. You men have seen what's at stake; indeed, you have lost friends to the zombie threat that Moriarty wields like a weapon. Can you imagine the panic that widespread knowledge of zombies would create? Given the careless ways he handled it, LaLaurie's disease process could yet infect any number of innocent people.

"I say all of this to indicate that it might be a losing proposition to join us, but win or lose, Watson and I must carry on against Moriarty's plan. We will welcome your aid if your superiors see fit to have you join us. It will be perilous."

"So, we wait and see what King's Cross holds in store for us," I stated with a heavy sigh, knowing that my concerns lay beyond King's Cross, where Mary and Anne awaited me at home, not realizing the danger in which I had left them.

The heavy early morning traffic of arrivals at King's Cross diminished by the time we steamed onto a siding away from the main platforms. It took only seconds, though, to recognize the huge figure of Mycroft Holmes standing in the warm drizzle that had settled over London. Beside him, shifting from foot to foot in an impatient jig, William Wiggins waited. We leapt down to greet the unlikely pairing after a troubling utterance from Holmes: "Mycroft has come. This cannot be any but bad news, gentlemen."

As Holmes had said, his elder brother stirred from his flat or from the Diogenes Club only in situations of national peril. Mycroft's long face, below his umbrella, was set in a grim scowl, and I knew to expect the worst.

"The good news," Mycroft began as we approached him, "is that my agents have detained several French, Italian, and German persons whom we believe came into Britain on criminal business at the behest of Professor James Moriarty, though they will not confess to us his plans. They seem to fear him more than any lawful prosecution."

"'Seem to fear,' Mycroft?" Holmes said. "You do not often deal in 'seem,' brother."

"Yet I am left with that, since our usual methods of persuasion have yielded no other results," Mycroft offered, dipping his head in recognition of his brother's understanding. I wondered if the usual methods of persuasion included torture, and I did not see it as unwarranted.

"But the bad news...?" I said, waiting breathless to hear what I suspected.

"Ah. Yes. You should proceed home immediately, Dr. Watson, while I think my brother and these two soldiers should proceed to the area of the former St. Lazarus Infirmary. We have received reports that several of LaLaurie's creations have been terrorizing the local residents. This may be false information, but we must take no chances. Doctor, Wiggins will accompany you. I have left a brougham at your disposal just outside the station. I urge you to make all possible haste."

"Tell me, Wiggins, what awaits me in Paddington," I demanded, once we started away from the station.

Wiggins would not meet my gaze, but he sighed and said, "Your missus was gone from the house when I went 'round this mornin' early. Miss Prescott was, too, sir. Your home is a wreck, but I left there without knowin' anyfink more." Since he had always held Mary in highest esteem, I took from his sullen attitude toward me that he had gleaned something of what had transpired between Miss Prescott and me. I accepted his as the first of many disappointments my actions would create.

Two constables stood outside my home as we arrived. The door was open behind them on a dark and empty house. It was my home, but it was not. It had been violated. The carriage had not halted when I leapt out its door to fly past those men, with Wiggins on my heels.

I cried, "Mary? Anne?" as I entered my home, made instantly foreign to me. I could have been running into a newsagent's or a bank, so unfamiliar the place had become. Here was the first physical indication of Moriarty's actions while we were away. Invading my home, Moriarty had taken it from me. In a sense, I had allowed him to take it—take my loved ones—from me. Yet I still did not know who had borne the brunt of my supposedly heroic absence.

The door to my study had been shattered. Someone had battered it down. Broken pieces of crockery crunched under our feet. Shards and pottery dust trailed down the hall into the kitchen. The hall stand where I always placed my hat, coat, and walking stick had been broken asunder. My greatcoat, which had hung there when I left, was gone, as was my good bowler.

My office had been ransacked: furniture broken and hurled into corners. Books lay scattered on the floor, and my surgery notes drifted amongst the wreckage of my overturned desk. When the door to the examination room within opened, I let out a cry of alarm, so overwrought was I.

Austin stepped through into the midst of the devastation, his head bandaged and one arm in a sling. He limped toward me, holding out his good hand.

"John, come with me. Mary is within," he said, his voice hoarse.

"Is she—?" I faltered, thinking the worst. "Is Anne—?"

"No. Mary will mend. The worst harm is that which she took in her heart, seemingly," he answered in low tones, looking at the floor, withholding the censure of his gaze. He beckoned me into the room but did not follow and did not mention Anne.

The examination table lay empty, I'm glad to say, but Mary perched on a stool that sat beside it. Her hands lay bandaged and folded together on its surface. I wondered if she had been praying and expected her to rise and face me.

She did turn her eyes to mine and offered me a sad smile, so I went to her side and sought to place my hands on her shoulders. But she rose and moved away from me, holding her arms across her abdomen. Her face bore a bruise on each cheek, as though she had been struck and backhanded. The sight of it turned my thoughts red, and I swore under my breath at the name of Moriarty. I would hound that man to the bitter end. I would make him—

"It was Anne," Mary whispered, shaking away my thoughts of the hated name. "Who else did you expect? You brought this upon us, upon me, John. You could have treated her anywhere, removed her to Baker Street or St. Bartholomew's—anywhere—but you had to have her here, to replace me. I'm not surprised that her name was on your lips as you entered the house."

"My first thoughts were for you, Mary," I answered, truthfully, though my brain reeled. It could not be. Anne had improved before I'd left. She had been on the mend. Holmes had arranged a billet for her in Edinburgh. She was recovering.

No.

"Your first thoughts," Mary said. "A man's first thoughts are predictable. I cannot find fault in it, really. She is—was, I guess—a great beauty, vibrant, stunning. I suppose your first thoughts betray your love for her, but I must bear my share of blame, too. She was lovable, endearing, needy in such a way that I, too, was drawn to her, though I saw when I first met her that she was in love with you, my heroic husband. Now, this." Her voice broke.

"Won't you tell me what happened?" I asked, hoping to hear something in the facts that might offer me some hope. Mary's words echoed and rang in my head. She was right. I could have treated Anne elsewhere, but I had wanted her near me. I had brought this upon us, upon Mary. This devastation rested on my shoulders.

"I would rather hear what you have to say first," she said, folding her arms across her chest.

I took my seat on the stool she had vacated. She stood trembling on the other side of the table, her eyes tired but attentive. I told her of my failing on the night we had left. Had it only been a day ago? It seemed forever ago, in a time so distant that it could not be recaptured. I spoke to

Mary honestly about Anne's coming to me as I rested. I told Mary that her own words at our last parting had been such that I had thought she would leave me. And I told her of the success we'd had at Brompton but of the outcome that had left it all in doubt.

Mary uttered a bitter laugh, a sound I had never heard from her before. I could not bring myself to share with her the true depth of my fear of Moriarty.

"Yes. Your first thoughts," she said as her grim laughter fled her voice. "And the great campaign ended up achieving nothing? Nothing for you and Holmes, anyway." She paused and fixed me with an angry glare before she went on. "Well, I'm sorry, John, but your precious Anne is gone, and you shan't be rid of me yet.

"Anne Prescott is not now the woman who was your client, nor the person who had come to know you as 'Jack.'" Mary's voice came low and rough. "She has become something less than human, like a beast of some sort, but one bent on revenge, I think.

"You see, sometime after you left, I went to Anne's bedside, intending to turn her out of this house. I found her still asleep but in a turmoil. The bedclothes were ripped by her struggles, and she cried out for Tom and Katie, and yes, for you, her 'Jack.'" Mary uttered the name with venom.

"But when Anne awoke from her dreams, I did not recognize her. I had thought her weak, but she rose from her bed like an athlete, took our Rachel by the arms and flung her across the room as though she were a doll."

"Was Anne able to say anything?" I interrupted.

"Yes. She called Rachel a wicked, sinful whore." Mary hurled the words back at me, causing me to start. "She clearly thought Rachel was sister Katie. When I confronted her, thinking that perhaps she was in a waking dream, she—well, she treated me in the same way. She thought that I, too, was Katie. The very idea!

"Luckily, I was able to escape into the hallway and get Anne to follow me. I ran down the stairs before her, and though I locked myself in your office, well, you can see what she did to the door. When she broke in, she fell, and I escaped with Rachel into the street and away. We made our way to Dr. Jackson's residence. Later, I learned from the police that the others came and took your Anne Prescott away."

"Took her away?" I cried. "Who were they, Mary? Where—"

"How could I know that? They ransacked your office, I assume, or Anne did, on her own. I do not know, and I do not care!" she shouted back at me.

"My God, Mary," I said in stricken tones, "how ghastly. I had no idea. I thought that she was—"

"Cured, and waiting for you to return? I think I know what you thought, though I must confess that after hearing some of her ramblings in her sleep, days ago, I was more interested in her recovery and removal to Scotland.

"Oh, yes, I know what you thought. But in that time, the fear grew in me, John, that should she recover, I would lose you to her. I could not compete with her beauty and her passionate nature. If she had been recovered this morning enough to walk, I would have been glad to have her gone, even if you had followed her, as I suspected you would after I saw the way you returned her affections. I hope that those embraces were worth the pain they brought, John."

Grief and shame gripped me hard. The memories of those golden moments with Anne broke open my heart and showed me the wretch I had become. I had seen the eyes of Wiggins, of Mycroft, of Austin, looking at me and knowing my failings. I swallowed hard and took a deep, steadying breath, though reality hit me hard: Moriarty's men had taken Anne Prescott, and I could do nothing for her. However, Mary had survived and was safe, though I believed I had lost her as my wife.

Mary turned from me, clearly struggling with her anger. She began to pace the room in agitation, looking anywhere but at me.

When she went on, her voice shook, recalling the waking nightmare. "I never dreamed, though, that Anne would disappear in front of my eyes and become that thing, that fierce creature. And now—now she—" Mary broke down in weeping and could not go on.

I said nothing and watched as Mary wept. Time stopped in that eternity of grief and pain that bound us together still.

Minutes or hours later, I could not tell, Mary mastered her tears and claimed, "If you do abandon me, John, I must still claim some rights as your wife and hope that your treatments can have good effect. I came back here this morning to demand some justice from you, for I thought at the very least you could give me that, but now..."

Here Mary paused, giving a frantic tug at the bandage on her right hand. She wasn't bleeding. But Mary thrust her unbandaged hand into my face. I thought that my heart would stop at what I saw there: the distinctive mark of Anne's teeth, fine and straight, showed on either side of the fleshy outside palm of Mary's hand.

"Perhaps you should take two pints from me today, instead of from the one you love," she said.

Her eyes poured her anger and pain into mine, and all I could do was accept it as earned.

Chapter Twenty-Two

Within two hours, Holmes had returned with the two doughty marines. There had been no signs of the undead in the area, and Holmes had brought his men to Paddington as quickly as he could to support me. I had a quiet word with him after administering a mild sedative to Mary so that I could begin her treatment.

"Watson, I..." Holmes started, and stopped as suddenly as he had begun. He stared into my grief-stricken eyes, unable to do or say anything that would lessen the sting of guilt and loss.

At length, he said, "If I can do anything—a transfusion for Mary, anything—please let me know. I wish to have a quiet word with Austin now, for I assume he was here when Moriarty's men captured Anne. We'll find her, Watson."

Austin was seated in the kitchen but seemed to want to be elsewhere. The look in his eyes reflected back to me the reception I would get from my colleagues and neighbors when the truth of this all came out. Holmes went in to speak with Austin, and as I left, I wished Austin well. I was glad that Moriarty's men had not killed or taken him. I found small relief that I had kept him from landing on Moriarty's list of those he had used to hurt our cause.

With as much tenderness as I could muster, I began Mary's treatment. My supplies had been scattered, but it took little time to set them to rights. I did note that every surgical scalpel I possessed was missing.

Taking two pints of blood from Mary's veins left her color ashen, though she appeared to be in a comfortable sleep. The first transfusion, though, which I took from Rachel, reacted poorly in Mary: she emitted a low moaning noise and woke briefly to say that her back was in spasms of pain. I was forced to put her back on the saline solution to keep her from going into shock.

In a moment, I heard a knock at the door, where Magnus Guthrie stood, smiling, baring his brawny arm for me. "I understand that this brave lady requires some blood. Please, take mine. McCoy, our sawbones, figured me for the fellow whose blood goes with anyone's."

"Thank you, Guthrie," I said. "I'm sorry that you have had to endure all this. I realize what you must think of me, with this sordid business of my, um, association with Miss Prescott coming to light."

He gave me a rakish smile and replied, "Well, sir, I never figured you for a wanderin' sort of bloke, but you're a soldier through and through, aren't you?"

"I suppose I am," I said, thinking that he commented on my moral failings as being like a soldier's. "I'm certainly no exemplar of any kind."

"No, sir," he shot back. "I meant that your sense of honor will see you through, like any good soldier's. I saw it first time I met you, same as I recognized the sound of that rifle shot that took Dr. LaLaurie. I'd know a Martini-'Enry report anywhere, and I knew you to be a man of honor, sir. Why, any man might wander a bit in error. Comes with the territory, so to speak, especially in a fightin' man like you. And anyway, with the sins on my own 'ead, who am I to judge any man? But, you see, Cap'n Jack, it's your honor that will bring you through, steel true, blade straight."

I dropped my eyes to the floor, knowing that he was being kind to a man who had fallen short of the mark and was offering him a way to aim higher.

"MacGuire's another good one for blood, sir," Guthrie changed the subject as I prepared his arm. I nodded my thanks, knowing that I would have use for the big man, too. Soldier's blood for Mary was appropriate, given what she had been through and what she would likely yet endure.

With Mary's treatment well under way, I joined Holmes in the kitchen with Austin. Austin claimed that a force of some ten men had arrived at the house in the morning, just after Mary and Rachel had fled, with Anne raging through the house looking for Katie. Austin had retreated out into the back garden but had seen enough to know that Anne had turned on those men as she had Austin and Mary. They had subdued her with their numbers and bundled her off into a large black carriage. Austin clarified that these men had ransacked my office, taking what they wanted as quickly as they could.

"Moriarty seems to have chosen Anne Prescott," Holmes sighed, "in conjunction with LaLaurie's findings about the best hosts for the zombie disease. Remember how delighted he was at the prospect of you as one of his creations?"

"True," I said. "But they got her out of here, out of any place where she could endanger others. I'm glad, to a degree, that she was gone when Mary returned and that your injuries are no worse, Dr. Austin."

He dipped his head to me in acknowledgment, though he still refrained from meeting my eyes.

Mary rested in the faithful care of Austin, who had returned to the surgery to watch over her. A night's rest and proper nourishment was necessary for all. Holmes moved through it all, eating, resting, and conversing with ease, as though he had little care for any matter except news of Mary's condition. I had nothing to report and would not for days, months maybe. Though I consulted calendars and my notes, trying to find some aspect of the disease's process that I could describe and track with certainty, I stood thwarted at every turn.

I had a paltry amount of information with which to work. LaLaurie had said that the disease process depended upon the nature of the host. The timeline of Suffield's symptoms was months longer than Anne's, though she had suffered a greater number of infectious bites in her foray with Onyekachi. Had the transfusions caused some greater, more aggressive response from the disease in Anne? What would early and repeated transfusions do to Mary? I had no good idea, but I clung to the idea that the fresh infections had done the worst.

Holmes, perhaps picking up on my agitation, asked me to accompany him on his first foray into the East End on the hunt for Anne Prescott. Perhaps it was too soon—I was not sure I felt up to it—but I went with him anyway, one early morning after one of Mary's transfusions.

"We must assume that Moriarty wishes to use Anne as a weapon," Holmes said as we took a northerly tack up Brady Street. "If my brother's findings are correct, we can assume that Anne will demonstrate the effectiveness of a zombie as a weapon. She will impress his clients, I think."

We alighted from the cab at the Whitechapel Road corner and walked a few minutes in silence, as I thought miserably of the fate Anne might face and considered again the possibilities for averting it.

"I'd give a great deal to have LaLaurie alive for questioning about now, though I would be happier with just his notes," I said at last.

"Indeed," Holmes grunted, "which was likely one of Moriarty's motivations for having him killed and making sure that Pizer took the notes away with him. Our great enemy planned every step, for LaLaurie was clever but not strong enough to have resisted determined questioning for long. Moriarty removed his liabilities, namely LaLaurie, once he gained his own control of the zombie process."

"How are we to proceed, then? What are we doing here?" I asked.

"Looking for any clues as to Miss Prescott's movements, if Moriarty has started to use her. One finds clues by looking, Watson, as I looked at the draft horse's shoes which led me to a farrier in Banbury and thus to Brompton Castle," Holmes explained. "We will look for clues as to Miss Prescott's movements and whereabouts. Today, we start with her rooms."

"Ah, yes," I said in bitter tones, "the rooms to which you moved her, away from my amorous advances."

"We make for her new lodgings, in Tent Street, where she stayed this summer, as arranged by Adam Hepplewhite," Holmes replied, maintaining his stride, ignoring my guilt.

I kept up as best I could with Holmes's long stride until he came to a sharp halt as we gained the entrance to a long alley connected to Buck's Row. He waited a moment, watching the movements of several men down that dim lane. As I looked also, I saw four constables gathered together near a doorway a block or so down its length.

Then, three more constables came jogging along from different directions, converging on the very corner where we stood.

As they passed us, Holmes called out, "Hargreaves! What business have you on Buck's Row, sir?"

One of the bobbies halted, stopping and turning a quizzical stare in Holmes's direction, while the others ran on. "Do I know you, sir?"

"You are only known to me through a relative of mine, Bert Tiller, who has said much about you in honor and good faith," Holmes replied, all smiles and gentlemanly manner. "I wonder what brings so many of London's finest to Buck's Row so early on the first of September."

Hargreaves pushed his helmet farther back on his head and looked closely at Holmes, saying, "Why, I must thank Bert when I see him. He's a hard man to read, is our Bertram. I must say that you two could well be brothers. The resemblance is uncanny. But I'm here now, sir, on the murder of a... a dressmaker. Ghastly business. Not something that concerns you, or Bert, or your friend here. Best to push along and give my regards to Bert."

Hargreaves turned and followed his mates, having dispensed with curious onlookers in the time-honored tradition of the Metropolitan Police. And Holmes did "push along," walking even more quickly than before up Brady Street.

"So Bert is a friend to policemen as well as dockworkers?" I asked, puffing along at Holmes's side. He ignored the comment, so I asked, "Do you think that Anne going missing has something to do with that dressmaker's death?"

"I do, Watson, indeed. I believe Anne may be responsible for this murder. Hargreaves, as you no doubt realize, said 'dressmaker' as a way to indicate that the murder victim was a prostitute. I think that Moriarty knows Anne to a great degree. It seems so, at any rate, for if he means to use Anne, he knows about her lasting anger with Katie, who took to prostitution. Likely, then, that he will target prostitutes as Anne's victims."

"We must go more quickly," Holmes added. "Can you manage a brief run, old fellow?"

"I will try to keep up," I replied.

Running reminded me of the aches and pains I still felt from our set-to at Brompton Castle, but I recovered some of my stamina and forgot my soreness by the time we reached Anne's rooming house. It was a quiet, out of the way place, on a courtyard that ran a short loop from one end of Tent Street to the other. The lodgings beside it were rather run down, but the overall look of the place said it was honest, clean, and simple.

The landlord showed us up to Anne Prescott's rooms, finding we were confederates of Adam Hepplewhite. Holmes had presented the man with one of Hepplewhite's calling cards as well as one of his own.

What we saw in that room shocked the landlord so much that he fled the scene.

Moriarty and his men, I guessed, must have brought Anne to this place. It must have been after her murder of the dressmaker, for I saw traces of blood everywhere. The furniture was minimal—a frame bed, a table and chair, and a small mirrored dresser—but it had all been savaged and marked with patches of drying blood. One set of marks, low on the wall nearest the bed, showed the word "Jack" scrawled in blood. I blanched and bent to touch it, only to have Holmes snatch my hand away.

"Careful, Watson," he said, then added, "We are late in coming. Others have been here before us."

Here he drew my attention to the wreck of the dresser. There, in the crevice of the mirror's frame, rested a folded note addressed "Sherlock Holmes." No other thing in the room had escaped destruction. The note had a neat, almost pristine appearance to it as unsettling as the damage to the rest of the room.

Holmes inspected it for a moment with his glass before he lifted it out of its resting place. He opened and read it, then turned it several times in the dim light after he had absorbed its message.

With a heavy sigh, he turned it over to me, saying, "It is worse than I had feared, Watson. Our efforts today will prove to have been in vain. Moriarty himself has been here. He toys with us."

I held the note in shaking fingers and watched Holmes turn and leave the room. I followed him as he returned to the landlord's residence, but I left by the front door, not waiting for him, and took a moment to read the missive when I reached the street.

MY DEAR MR. HOLMES, AND, OF COURSE, "JACK," DR. WATSON:

FIRST, I WISH TO THANK YOU FOR LIBERATING ME FROM THE UNNECESSARY BAGGAGE OF THAT TIRESOME AMERICAN AND HIS GIANT FRIEND. TRUE, HIS RESULTS ARE INTERESTING TO SEVERAL OF MY ASSOCIATES, AND IN MY OWN WAY, I SHALL MAKE USE OF THEM, PERHAPS EXPANDING ON THE MANNER OF HIS PET DISEASE IN THE INFLUENZA OUTBREAKS I HAVE PLANNED FOR THE WINTERS OF THE NEXT COUPLE OF YEARS. THEY ARE ALWAYS SO EXCITING!

I REALLY MUST THANK YOU, TOO, FOR ALLOWING YOUR CLIENT, MISS PRESCOTT, TO FALL SO EASILY INTO MY HANDS, ESPECIALLY WITH A BRACE OF DEAR JACK'S SCALPELS. REALLY, I HAD THOUGHT YOU MORE CAREFUL, MR. HOLMES. MISS PRESCOTT IS A WONDERFUL ASSET TO MY WORK AND WILL ALLOW ME TO PROCEED ACCORDING TO MY ORIGINAL PLANS, REGARDLESS OF PIZER'S INEPTITUDE.

I DOUBT WE SHALL EVER MEET, FOR I AM BUSY WITH THIS ENTERPRISE AND HAVE LITTLE TIME OR PATIENCE TO DEAL WITH SUCH PREDICTABLE OPPONENTS. YET I DELIGHT IN WATCHING YOU SCRAMBLE ABOUT. PLEASE, DO CARRY ON! I WILL SOON CONTROL THE HEART OF YOUR EMPIRE WHILE YOU WASTE YOUR TIME.

J. M.

Those words held me in place. I had no command of my feet, and my breathing grew ragged, shallow. Holmes, standing now at my elbow, placed his hand on my shoulder and said, "Come along, old fellow. We have much to do."

"Where do we start, Holmes? We are beaten," I said, breathless. The thought of Anne Prescott within Moriarty's immediate control horrified me, let alone his offhanded reference to spreading LaLaurie's version of the zombie flu as though it were a game of sorts. It all unbalanced me. I grew chilled even in the bright sun. I could see no way to escape Moriarty's plans or the disasters that would fall upon us. Anne had my surgical knives. She had likely already murdered a woman with one of them.

"What can we do, other than wait and watch?" I cried.

"We have not lost our ability to reason, Watson," Holmes said, pulling at my sleeve. "And we have not ceased to act. Plus, we now have this," he added, plucking the note from my shaking fingers. "Where Moriarty contents himself with power as he perceives it, we have knowledge, commitment, and the awareness that we act in a just cause. Let us press onward."

"Certainly, Holmes," I replied, resolved to do whatever I could, hopeless though our cause might be. "But where? How?"

"This paper bears a distinctive quality I can trace, I'll warrant," Holmes said, "as do the ink and the pen nib used. We will begin by searching out our sources. Moriarty might think he has us beaten, having taken one of our pieces, but we have not reached the endgame yet.

"We will do our best to find and control Miss Prescott, old fellow, but first, we must pay a visit to Lestrade and Gregson in the Yard. It is time that we cease to move in the shadows—"

"Yes... of course," I said, struggling to shape the words. I felt dizzy, and a growing blackness seemed to surround me. Holmes's face swam before my darkening eyes, his strong hands grabbed the shoulders of my coat, and I spun to the ground in a lazy, dizzy motion that seemed to go on forever.

CHAPTER TWENTY-THREE

Moriarty taught me—taught all of London—the meaning of terror in the coming days.

After a brief recovery from my collapse, Holmes and I returned to our haphazard search for Anne. Holmes plied every network of informants available, from his force of street lads to match girls to beggars. From several of these nearly invisible folk, we knew that Anne Prescott had murdered a prostitute on Buck's Row. She had been seen by eyes that are never acknowledged.

Moriarty ran rings around us. He had indeed transformed Anne Prescott into a dreadful puppet. Pulling her strings from so far above that we could not see him, he let her kill at his whim, and we could do nothing to stop him. Though the weather, strangely cool all summer, warmed in September, I knew a bitter wind, an east wind, was coming. Its name was Moriarty, and when it arrived in full, I felt it would topple everything.

After the Buck's Row murder of Mary Ann "Polly" Nichols, Holmes found one of my missing surgical knives not far from the scene of the crime. The police had missed it, of course, in their heavy-handed inspection of the crime scene. Though Holmes would not say it, I knew that Moriarty had very nearly managed to implicate me, even as I rested in my bed, for my name was engraved on all my surgical tools. I had become a mere pawn in the chess match between Moriarty and Holmes, waiting for a hand I could not see to move me or capture me, to whisk me off the board. The tension robbed me of sleep, of hope.

Annie Chapman died a week later, and we concluded from the manner of her death that our own Anne had done the evil deed. Our forces, aided by Guthrie and MacGuire, on loan from the Admiralty, proved ineffective, for we had no idea from whence Moriarty would move. Holmes had traced the notepaper Moriarty had used to London Hospital. On the eighth of September, we secretly searched London Hospital and found no trace of him. That night, Anne Prescott sliced Annie Chapman's throat and mutilated her torso. When we emerged from our nightlong search of the hospital, we could hear the distant constables' whistles breaking the dawn as they found Chapman's body in a back garden off Hanbury Street.

I had never seen Holmes so focused, so determined to out-think his foe, but we were always behind in Moriarty's game, as though he changed the board and the conditions of the game even as we played. It galled Holmes and tested his patience and mettle more than any other of the cases we had worked together. In much of his earlier work, Holmes could solve a mystery from his sitting room when all the facts were given him. Here, we had facts in mutilated bodies and crime scenes, but even Holmes could not predict Moriarty's next move based on those details. We only knew that Moriarty could use Anne to kill at his whim.

We reasoned that Moriarty used each murder as a demonstration of his zombie "product" to potential buyers. What we could not know was the identity of his next victim. Now, with our enemy having no certain base of operations, we could only wait each night, guessing where Anne Prescott, the terrible marionette, would appear.

It did become clearer, though, that Moriarty would target only poor women of the East End. Most of the victims were labeled as prostitutes because they had accepted money for sexual favors, but this was a common condition amongst the grindingly poor female residents of the East End. Without rent money, after all, one might sleep on the streets, an increasingly lethal prospect.

And many a young man from a well-heeled family in the West End looked to the East End for his pleasures outside of matrimony or a proper and proscribed courtship. Moriarty wasn't the only one who used that population for his pleasure, though his preferences were more twisted. East End prostitutes were expendable. They were ready-made victims.

Holmes, however, made me see this reality in a new light.

"I am convinced by Moriarty's thoroughness of planning," he said to me on the night of 30 September, after a frustrating month of nightly failures to track Moriarty's movements, "that he chooses his victims with great care from a predetermined list. His method only appears random. He is a mathematician, after all. I think his desire is to eliminate specific women, as he did LaLaurie. I would wager that each victim must have a connection to the network LaLaurie created, for LaLaurie's weakness was his lack of control over his subjects. Moriarty takes care to leave no traces of himself behind."

I leaned against the window of the Brown Bear pub on Leman Street, where we sought to blend into the shady crowd on the late-night streets. Holmes and I were waiting for one of Inspector Abberline's associates, DCI Reid, to walk by. Abberline had been tasked with the case and appeared to have had no success, which frustrated Reid. Holmes had earned the trust of Reid in a past investigation, and Reid was helping Holmes with fresh details of the murder scenes.

"But that group of women whom we can associate with Tabram, Smith, Nichols, and Chapman is exceedingly large. Thousands, I should think," I replied.

"We must work, though, on the assumption that there is a connection between them, in order to predict who is next on Moriarty's list," said Holmes. "Do you think that Mary is well enough to assist us?"

His request caught me off guard. Mary had improved a good deal in recent days, though her manner to me was chilly, as I knew it might well be. I fully expected her to leave me when she felt her strength return. Holmes's asking about her help seemed to come out of the blue, as though he grasped at straws, like the rest of us.

"I can ask her, Holmes, but why? How could she help?"

"She and Adam Hepplewhite can work with the charitable interests who seek to help such women on a regular basis. With the material he has collected from Magdalen, Urania, and Cwmdonkin, he is ready to begin this work, but he could use help with its analysis. I know that Mary has expressed an interest in charitable work on behalf of fallen women."

"I will ask her, but..."

Holmes turned his keen glance back to me then. "I apologize, old friend, for I recognize that your situation with Mary remains uncertain." He turned his collar up against the irritating drizzle.

"I almost think that Guthrie or MacGuire should ask her," I said. "They have all three become pretty chummy, as those two stout men have been contributing their blood to Mary's treatments."

"Hmm, yes. They do have a good rapport with her. Perhaps we should collect them and seek their input. They loiter now not far from Abberline's headquarters, awaiting some stirring of the constables. The hour grows late; it is after one o'clock. I think Reid will not favor us with a visit tonight. Let us go find our friends. We are doing no good here."

We paused long enough to chat with O'Doole, who had been patrolling the underground in the vicinity. O'Doole told us that his lads were "spooked" by something happening just east of our location, but he had not heard of any specific actions that indicated the presence of the large, black brougham seen leaving the other murder scenes. It had been seen before, and we reasoned that Moriarty used this vehicle to transport Anne and his clients. Hopeful of catching on to some police actions in the matter, we hurried off to the Leman Street station to see if we could glean any information.

At our arrival, we found all in chaos, groups of constables running in opposite directions. Guthrie and MacGuire ran to meet us, their faces registering near-panic. As we neared them, Guthrie held up two fingers.

"Two," he said in low, hard tones. "She killed two tonight, almost equal distances from this very spot, sir."

The news hit us like the blow of a hammer. That dreaded east wind blew in my soul. Moriarty knew our motions and played his cat-and-mouse game with cruel glee.

Even as we stood listening to what Guthrie had heard in the mad scramble of constables, Holmes looked at me, his eyes wide with disbelief.

"Moriarty knew we stood outside the Brown Bear, planning, this very night," Holmes murmured, and I saw that his usually steady hands were shaking. "He found or placed victims on either side of us, just out of our reach. He might not have seen us directly, but he knew what we were about. He mocks us, Watson."

We gathered news in the next two days about the horrendous events, as did the rest of London. Newspapers gave us the names Elizabeth Stride and Catherine Eddowes as the two victims of the 30 September murders. The Central News Agency claimed to have received, days before, letters from the murderer, who called himself "Jack the Ripper." That name was easy to attach to the earlier murder of Annie Chapman as well. Moriarty held all of London, then, in his terrifying grip, making our plight even worse.

Holmes retreated from me in those few days, bent on finding something like a pattern in Moriarty's plans. I went home to try to convince Mary to lend us—Holmes, at least—her help. Mary and I had exchanged few words during the course of her treatment, and I had asked Guthrie and MacGuire to speak to her. Before they could arrive, though, Mary approached me on her own as I sat at breakfast in our kitchen, the *Times* in my hands.

Mary stood behind me, scanning the newspaper headlines over my shoulder. When I read the name "Jack the Ripper," I recognized Moriarty's hand in it. I tossed the paper aside in frustration and put my head in my hands, despairing. If one of my scalpels were found at one of the murder scenes, even the slow-moving police would not hesitate to connect Jack the Ripper to Dr. John Watson. Moriarty's threat settled in my stomach, a cold, sickening weight.

Mary took up the discarded paper and read the article. Her frown turned to a look of cold fear, and she said, "John, is this evidence of the hand of Moriarty? Does he mean to implicate you in these horrible killings?" Mary, always insightful, knew the answer, of course. Her voice was quiet with dread.

"Yes," I whispered.

Mary continued, "His men took your surgical knives. Other articles I've read suggest that the murders are being done by a medical man... because of his knowledge of human anatomy." She shook her head in disbelief. "I can't believe that a man could be as evil as this Moriarty."

"A man, no. Moriarty, yes. He enjoys this whole business as a game of sorts that he plays against Holmes. I am merely a way to distract Holmes from the business of finding him out. I know that Holmes does a thorough search of each murder scene for any evidence that implicates me. He doesn't mention it, but Guthrie and MacGuire have told me of it."

"But, John, Moriarty's actions are monstrous," Mary said. "Is there any aid I can give you to thwart this?"

Her words brought me a flicker of hope in that moment of darkness. I knew exactly what to say: I told her of Holmes's plan for researching the connections between the women we knew who were part of LaLaurie's network of zombie plague carriers and the supposed Ripper victims.

"Holmes—and I—hoped you would help us," I finished.

"When do we start?" she asked.

"As soon as we get Holmes's request," I replied, heartened.

Mary nodded her head and said, "I am more than ready."

"Does this mean that you and I... that we will..." I feared pushing the matter too far.

"It means, husband, that I am still your wife, and that I am more than willing to fight an injustice in any way I can," she exclaimed, and left the room. It was not a pardon, but it wasn't a verdict, either. I could hope, at least, that it spelled a truce between us. Her demeanor, her very posture, told me that she still knew deep anger at me, however.

When Guthrie and MacGuire came a short time later, they too bore news of unlooked-for hope: Jimmy O'Doole's second in command, a round-faced, bright-eyed tosher named Harvey Brewer, had reached Holmes with incredible news. That sewer lad, watching from the drains, had witnessed the murder of Catherine Eddowes. Holmes awaited us at Mr. Hepplewhite's chapel, where he would take young Brewer's report.

When we arrived at St. George's, where Holmes and the Reverend Hepplewhite had assembled all of the relevant records, I met the youthful Mr. Brewer. With the added bulk of Guthrie and MacGuire, the tiny kitchen was beyond its capacity.

We arrived while the lad was in mid-report of Anne Prescott committing the second murder. Holmes beckoned us to his side to listen.

"So, Harvey, your confederates alerted you that they had seen the black carriage heading your way," Holmes summarized for us.

"Yes, sir," the lad said in the clear tones of someone used to speaking in front of others. "It must have been a fast strike, sir, for the growler was in and out of the Berner Lane area in a heartbeat."

"Yes. Moriarty was demonstrating both speed and thoroughness, likely to impress a possible client. Catherine Eddowes was killed and mutilated in the way we've seen with the other murders. And Elizabeth Stride was killed by a single slash of her throat, made by a sharp blade," Holmes said, looking at me. He handed me a bloodstained scalpel, which I tucked away in my breast pocket with a shaking hand. I doubt that any other took note of his action, but it told me that Holmes had been out all night searching for clues at the scene of each murder.

"Yes, sir," Brewer confirmed. "Lookin' out from a loose manhole cover, I saw her murder old Kate. She cut her throat, right enough, and then..."

The lad dropped his gaze to the floor, and Mary went to his side and hugged him around his shoulders, stroking his mop of unruly dark hair.

"You need to repeat the details, my son," Hepplewhite said. "May I infer that you knew Catherine Eddowes?"

"Yes, Reverend, I did. Knew her from Cooney's Lodging House, where she, Alice, and Martha would room together from time to time. They were all lively ladies, sir, ma'am, no better than they ought to be, Mum said, but good-hearted. We're all sinners, livin' under God's mercy, right, Reverend? Kate used to sing to us little ones, when our Mum was gone, she did. But she'll not... sing..." Heavy tears cascaded down the boy's round cheeks at the memory of a woman's kindness so brutally silenced.

"Harvey," Holmes asked in a soft voice, "was that Martha Tabram?"

The lad nodded his head. "Yes. And Alice McKenzie. They had quite a few regular friends. All went to the same clinic, when they needed it. Sort of looked out for each other, sir."

Holmes shot me an excited glance.

"Would you recognize their names again, if you saw them?" Holmes asked.

"I think so, as Jimmy might. Little John Limeberry, too, sir. Most of those ladies were good to us little ones."

Holmes drew Mary and Reverend Hepplewhite together. "This is our chance, unlooked for and surprising, but our chance, indeed. I need you two to pore over these records and try and determine which women might have had some lasting associations with the women whose names we can connect with LaLaurie's work. Look for any connections you can: shared addresses, work party lists, and those arrest records I have brought."

Holmes turned his attention to Guthrie and MacGuire, saying, "I need you to go with Mr. Brewer, as soon as I have heard the last of his report, and find O'Doole, Wiggins, and the Limeberry lad. Bring them back here as quickly as you can, and then arm yourselves. Tonight, we go on the hunt."

Holmes and I then listened to the rest of Harvey's report, sparing the lad the need to detail the horrors he had seen. Holmes's chief interest lay in what happened after the crimes.

Brewer was succinct: "Several hard lads came and tackled Anne Prescott, sir, pullin' her off Kate's... corpse. She fought hard and managed to stab one fellow and sink her teeth into another man's leg before they got her covered in heavy canvas. They wrapped chains around it all and carried her away.

"Then, a tall spare man came, and two more with him. Those two blokes were from the States—I could tell from their accents—and they was askin' of the tall one how soon they could take her—meanin' Miss Anne, I guess—back with them. The tall one answered, but I couldn't tell what he said. See, he was bendin' down... cuttin' away part of... the corpse's insides. And then they all left in that big black growler. I'd been watching, quiet, like, and when they left, I ran, sir, and tried to find O'Doole, and, well, here I am."

"And a fine piece of detective work you've done, sir," I said, shaking the boy's hand as Holmes patted his back.

"We will get you some tea and refreshments, Harvey, and then, if you will take your ease here for a time, we've less strenuous work for you. Watson," Holmes said, turning to me, "this is our chance. If we can get a list of names and locations, we will have a better idea of our quarry's next attack. If this earnest young man heard right, we must face the fact that Anne and, I presume, other zombies, will be exported. Do you still wish to take Anne alive?"

I hesitated only a second before saying, "Yes, I do. I must try." Mary turned a bitter glance in my direction but nodded.

Even with the guilt I carried about my feelings for Anne, I could not tolerate that she should be taken, in her condition, to foreign shores. True, we would never be together, but she had believed in me, needed and confided in me, loved me. Even if I recognized that I should never have countenanced those feelings, she had ever been a true friend. I would free her from Moriarty's awful slavery, even if it caused Mary to hate me more. Love, even misplaced love, demanded this of me.

Holmes set me to work alongside Mary and Adam Hepplewhite. Together, we began to search for the identities of those who were most likely on Moriarty's list of targets. Holmes absented himself, shrugging off my recommendations that he rest and find refreshment. I worried that the strain he put himself under to best this foe would be too much for even his iron constitution.

Like as not, Holmes had been hard at work with his brother Mycroft, who must have worked just as tirelessly behind the scenes to bring down Moriarty's criminal network. Clearly, Moriarty knew our whereabouts at most times, but no marksman had shot at us as we came and went from St. George's Chapel. I did not doubt that this was due to Holmes trying to track Moriarty, with the help of his brother and of those in the secretive L.S. who aided Gladstone in his unofficial efforts. They were likely making Moriarty more careful. It was as hopeful a time as I can remember of those dark days.

Later, with the help of the boys who had lived among and known these women, we had a list of names that could all be related through the past several years. Emma Smith and Martha Tabram, whom we knew to have been LaLaurie's victims, were the key. Frances Coles was on the list, though her whereabouts were unknown, as was the issue with her constant friends, Ruth Bracksieck and Mary Kelly. Clovis Porter and Jane Slead, two younger women who had moved to the East End within the past year, had been somewhat constant in the company of Coles and Annie Chapman. They had been arrested in a minor altercation in which they had sided with their friends, and their opponent in the fight had been John Pizer.

With them, Rose Mylett and Elizabeth Stride were mentioned. Mylett and Eddowes had shared the George Yard flat with Smith when they had first started to work the streets. Most importantly, Jane Slead had roomed with both Eddowes and Stride at different times and had been in treatment at St. Lazarus, where Stride's common-law husband had caused a public disturbance and been detained a year ago; the physician in charge, LaLaurie, had not pressed charges.

Holmes studied the results of our research and came to a quick conclusion. "Perhaps, because of her closer friendship with the other women, Moriarty will move against Jane Slead next," he said. "It is conjecture, but sound enough. Since Wiggins knows her most recent location, we will cast our nets there tonight."

For his safety, I asked Adam Hepplewhite to escort Mary home and bade him remain in Paddington, for Holmes had secured from

Lestrade another constable or two to watch my residence. It was more protection than that provided by his chapel. The Reverend smiled and made light of my worries, though. He said he would return to his chapel, where we would find him close if our need pressed us.

Mary did not look at me as she left with him. Besides her emotional turmoil, I knew she had given much to the effort of the day and was tired. I hoped that Austin would give her something to help her rest. But any road I had to such a rest would be a long one.

CHAPTER TWENTY-FOUR

Wiggins procured for us the address of Jane Slead and her husband. They turned out to be a rough-looking couple from the Dales. With the promise of ten pounds sterling, it took little convincing to get them to leave their lodgings, such as they were, and return home to Yorkshire. We stayed behind, watching them take their meager belongings and the money which would send them on their way.

Mrs. Slead had confirmed that John Pizer had sought to become her procurer, though she and her friends had refused his efforts. Mrs. Slead also confirmed that the other women on our list who were known to her had some connection to St. Lazarus Infirmary or to one another, and she revealed that she and her friends had often sought their clients at a pub called the Frying Pan, not far from the Sleads' present home. Given the times they usually worked the area, she helped us plan our actions to trap Anne, who would likely be set upon them.

"Well, Watson, would you prefer to wait here in the flat or take to the streets between here and the Pan?" Holmes said, referring to the popular pub.

"Meeting her at all, as she is now, would terrify me, Holmes," I confessed, "but I have to, and I suppose alone is better. She might recognize me."

We each wore protective leather gauntlets and leggings under our outer clothes, as we had when we'd invaded Brompton Castle. With my nightstick, I thought that I might be able to subdue Anne in close quarters. Holmes and I had coils of silken rope ready to bind her, if possible. Holmes had his deadly black sword and I my revolver, though, if all chance of her capture was denied to us. Neither Holmes nor I spoke such thoughts aloud.

Holmes said, "Very well. It is still several hours until midnight, and we might well have a long wait before us. We know little about how Moriarty's teams control Miss Prescott, other than covering her in canvas and then setting her loose on her victims. I shall scout the area between here and the pub, seeking out trysting places and other dark corners where Jane and her friends have been known to work. O'Doole and Guthrie are nearby, two streets over—under, I should say—keeping an eye on a low house often used by Alice McKenzie and others. Wiggins and several of his lads have vantage points on several rooftops. You should have a minute's warning, perhaps two, should Anne show in this area tonight."

As Holmes left, he paused halfway out the door, looked me in the eye and said low and hard, "Remember, if she is too far gone to know you, Watson, take a clear shot—please."

"Look after yourself," I returned, placing a chair against the back wall and turning off the gas lamp behind me so that the only light in the room came from a streetlamp outside. I drew my revolver and checked its chambers, then placed it on the floor beside me. I looped the coils of silken rope with which I would try to trap her hands.

After a while, my head sank onto my chest, and though my shoulders and back stayed tense to keep me in the chair, I did sleep, for the tension of the hunt had worn me down. I dreamt of that young tosher, Brewer, in a pulpit, exhorting me and faceless figures around me to keep watch for the return of the bride. I thought that odd, for the Parable of the Ten Virgins and their lamps, in the Gospel of Matthew, exhorts us to wait upon the bridegroom. In my dream, I asked Brewer if I was right. He ignored me.

With Brewer's last loud shout of "Repent!" and the sound of his fist pounding the pulpit both ringing in my ears, I awoke and saw Anne in the room with me. I had not heard the door open, and I saw no sign of its having been broken.

The coat she wore slid off her shoulders to the floor, and she stood before me in men's trousers—mine, I guessed by the loose fit at her narrow waist. A white shirt, poorly buttoned, hung loose too, and its front and rolled-up sleeves were dark with dried blood. In her right hand, she held one of my long-bladed scalpels. Where the bright metal still showed among the bloodstains, it reflected the light from the streetlamp, which seemed to burn brighter than before.

Her feet, shod in shiny black leather, made no sound as she moved toward me. I stood then and called to her, "Anne! It's me, Jack!" and she stopped. I moved to my right, so that some of the light from the street would shine on my face. She turned with me, the blade in her hand shaking, and I saw her wary eyes cloud for a second. She shook her head, making the coils of her hair swirl through the darkness. On her chin and long, smooth throat, I could see—and begin to smell—the dried blood that stained them, rubbed away in spots by her rough handlers.

"Anne, do you know me? Anne?" I pleaded.

Her eyes did clear, though, as they returned my gaze. She blinked several times and shook her head again, and when she met my gaze a second time, I saw something of Anne Prescott for a moment, some memory of her true self onto which she could grasp. She lifted shaking fingers to my face, and she shook her head once more, hard, as though to clear it.

"Yes, Anne. It's me, your Jack. Please let me help you," I whispered, tears spilling down my cheeks.

She tracked one tear with her fingers. Her lips, still caked with dried blood, moved. She shook her head again, as though she would twist it off through sheer force and gasped at the effort. Coming close to me, her hand on my cheek, eyes wide with fright and a faraway sadness, her own tears welling, she whispered with effort, "J-Ja-Jack? Save me, p—pl—"

Footfalls sounded in the hallway outside the door, and she flicked a glance in that direction, then turned back to me, the light in her eyes gone cold, feral. It was not Anne looking out at me. She caught sight of the rope I had begun to extend to her in my shaking hands, and then in her eyes there was something I had not seen in any eyes except those of the zombies that had first attacked us and most of those we had met in that awful shed at Brompton Castle. I could not name it.

She dropped her chin then and sank into a fighting crouch, my long scalpel raised, its edge glinting in the feeble light.

"This is my death," I thought with a shock.

O'Doole burst into the room, the tall strong form of Guthrie behind him, and then Anne blurred in front of me. I could barely see her cross the six feet or so between where she had crouched and my friends at the door. I yelled "No!" as her right hand flew and slashed across young O'Doole's throat.

Guthrie cried out and caught the boy in his arms as the force of the blow sent O'Doole reeling backwards. A dark spray of the boy's blood arced across the room.

Anne, spinning on her right foot, struck Guthrie in the face with the heel of her left foot, a strike so powerful that it took both him and O'Doole to the floor of the hallway, where they fell into the path of two more men rushing into the scene. Moriarty's agents, I reasoned, come to collect Anne. I heard the clink of chains. The first was a man of bold profile under his bowler hat. As he struggled to get into the room, shoving Guthrie and O'Doole away from him, I dove back to where I had sat, scrambling to find my revolver.

Anne kicked the man in the bowler hard in the stomach. The second man dropped the canvas and chains and rushed through the door toward her, gauntleted hands extended, tackling her. He took her to the floor. Though he was a big fellow, with a face scarred by many fights, Anne rolled with him, turning his greater weight under her.

She came up atop him and pinned him to the floor. Then she sank my scalpel into his neck, and his spurting lifeblood darkened a yet-unsullied white patch on the front of the shirt she wore. The man thrashed in his own blood, and his gurgling shrieks sounded as Anne sank her teeth into his face, tearing away a mouthful of his cheek.

I raised my pistol and fired, but Anne was too quick for me, rolling away from the figure on the floor. The deafening report drew the first man's eyes to me. I fired at him, too, but the round tore through the doorjamb beside his head.

Anne screamed "Jack! Jack!" but it sounded more like the cry of a great cat enraged at being forced from its kill. The flesh from her victim's face fell from her mouth as she screamed. She turned and threw herself out the window.

I heard men shouting in the street below. The fellow in the bowler dragged himself out the door, crawling over Guthrie, who had bent over O'Doole, trying to hold his hand over the boy's throat. I saw Guthrie make a grab for the man with his bloody hands, but Moriarty's henchman delivered a savage blow to Guthrie's face, and he fell back.

I sat staring at the awful scene before me, at the two pools of dark blood spreading on the floor of the room and hallway. Holmes sprang into the room, the cry "Watson!" coming loud and urgent.

"Here, Holmes," I growled, pushing myself to my feet.

When he saw me rise, he took in the scene of the room, reading the action he had not seen. He stooped and picked up my greatcoat from the floor where Anne had dropped it, then removed my scalpel from the man's neck. Rousing Guthrie, he ordered, "Take O'Doole with you. Go out by the back stairs. Watson, move. Follow me." As we left, I heard men coming up the front stairs and the neighing of a team of horses.

The shrill whistles of the constables reached my ears, not too distant, calling each other to the scene as we pelted down the back stairs.

"That fellow in the bowler is one Albert Vollimer," Holmes said. "The police want him for a murder involving black magic rituals, some year and a half ago. It doesn't surprise me to see him as Moriarty's associate. He is likely the new bokor."

"Yes. I fear that he has put Anne through the ritual," I whispered in reply. "Some evil seems to possess her. Holmes, I—I had no chance..."

"I know, Watson. I see what she has done. We have no earthly way to save her."

"I must try," I insisted, drawing Holmes's hard glance.

"But, Watson, she..." Holmes began. I knew from his glare that he needed me to think, as he did, that Anne was too far gone to save. I had to try, and Holmes didn't like it.

Outside, we met MacGuire and Wiggins, who beckoned us to a muffled wagon that waited in the alley. Holmes had provided a means of escape. We all piled into the back as it trundled away.

O'Doole's lifeless form lay on the bed of the wagon. The scent of a fire not very far away caught in my nose, completing the feeling of desolation that had come over me.

The driver halted at the end of the alley, pausing long enough to let a constable dash by in front of us on his way to the house we had just left. We made our escape with the only sounds the muffled wheels of the wagon, the bagged feet of the nag, and the sobbing of Wiggins, holding O'Doole's dark head in his lap.

Gladstone met us within the dark stable on Glenworth Street. As we disembarked, I was shocked to see that our driver was Mycroft Holmes.

I listened to Gladstone's report about having set L.S. resources to the task of hobbling Moriarty's financial empire. Their success, Gladstone said, would force Moriarty into more desperate action. I heard him warn the Holmes brothers, "Moriarty will move openly against our members. The L.S. leaves London in your hands. I will not be far."

After their brief conversation, they made ready to leave us. Guthrie and MacGuire would go with them, taking poor O'Doole's lifeless body.

Before he departed, Gladstone took me aside and said, "It was a noble effort, Doctor. You did your best, and you gave two people an occasion to begin again. I will do what I can to help these people, all of them, and take them out of harm's way." He paused and dropped his eyes, though, uttering, "We know now that we cannot save Anne Prescott. She is lost to us. But we cannot lose you, too. Please follow Holmes's words to the letter, my friend. We shall prevail."

"Yes, sir. Thank you, Mr. Gladstone," I murmured, before he left with Mycroft and moved to take his seat in the brougham with the others.

Holmes guided me to a low door in the rear of the stables, a door which opened onto a dark stairway and a tunnel that would lead us to the cellar of Mrs. Hudson's home. The tunnel reminded me of the catacombs once used to house the dead, and I wondered how many corpses I would create by having tried to rescue Anne Prescott. Poor Jimmy O'Doole's surprised face swam before my mind's eye. The look in his startled eyes before he died will haunt me forever, I fear.

Holmes hurried me through the house to the front door, where he hailed a hansom cab. Before I got in, Holmes put his hand on my sleeve and stopped me.

"Watson, return home and gather your household. You must leave England, all of you, at once. We are on the verge of Moriarty's awful retaliation. I—we—have asked too much of you already. Given the events of this night, I must ask you to go. Leave London, and do not let me or anyone know where you go."

"Holmes? You are sending me away? I... I can't believe it," I protested, remembering how he had expressed his need for me in his work. Then it occurred to me: they knew that my first wish was to save Anne Prescott. "Holmes, I must—"

"You must save yourself and protect those who depend upon you," he stated, his hand gripping my arm. "You are likely Moriarty's first, best way to hurt me, to hurt our cause. If he removes you, he knows that I will not have my best comrade, so you must remove yourself. Please, Watson."

He turned away from me and said hoarsely, "It is asking too much of you to kill her. I must. To track her, find Moriarty's base of operations, we will have to live a life in hiding as Moriarty does, fight him on his terms, and take his weapon away."

He released my arm and stepped back toward the door of 221.

"Watson, Moriarty killed Adam Hepplewhite. Gladstone told me. Moriarty burned the chapel to the ground with Mr. Hepplewhite inside. Moriarty watched us, intercepted that telegram I sent as soon as we deployed our forces.

"I will not risk you and Mary or your household. I have Guthrie and MacGuire and our Irregulars, and we have no families through which Moriarty can strike at us. We must fight on in secret."

Holmes's pleading tone compelled me to go, though I wanted to protest that I needed to stay with him and finish this fight. It was not in me to run from it, now that the chance was given me. I left, though, anxious to relieve him of the burden of myself and my loved ones.

I stepped inside the cab that would take me back to Paddington. The east wind in my heart blew hard and bitter. It did what terror always does: drives us apart, convinces us that we are alone and all is lost.

My front door stood open as we approached. Something was amiss. I saw no constables. A single light burned in my study. I tossed three sovereigns to the driver, bidding him wait, no matter what he heard, for I would have need of him. I pulled my revolver at a dead run from the curb. Stepping quietly into the dark opening, I heard Austin's angry voice within my study: "Why, what is the meaning of this, sir?"

I rushed through, revolver drawn, colliding as I did so with a man who had his own pistol leveled at Austin's head. As he stumbled forward, this man managed to pull the trigger, but he had pitched onto my desk, the muzzle of the weapon meeting Austin's shoulder. The report was muffled, but not Austin's cry.

I fell upon Austin's attacker, bringing the butt of my pistol down upon his head not once but twice. Footfalls could be heard coming down the front stairs, and I turned my revolver toward the door, only to have it pointed at Mary and Rachel, both pale and clutching their nightclothes to their breasts. Rachel screamed and fell, while Mary breathed a shocked, "John!"

"Mary, you and Austin will leave at once," I ordered. "Rachel, you will lock up this house in the morning and return to your mother's home with a month's wages. Mary, you and Austin must take passage to Ireland, preferably in the west, where you will be noticed less. Take whatever funds we have in the house, which should see to your safe exit, accommodations, and return—"

"If we wish to return," Mary said, her voice cold and her gaze colder.

"As you say," I replied. "But now you must make haste. Every instant of your delay will increase the opportunities for Moriarty's men to kill you. They will not hesitate, once they learn that this man has failed in that mission."

My need to remain, despite Holmes's pleas, burned white-hot in me. The barest semblance of a plan was unfolding in my head.

I dragged Moriarty's agent into our back alley, not knowing or caring if he were dead or alive. In the former case, he would be found in a day or so by another resident. In the latter, he might return to finish his work, and I would take him, force information from him.

The others fled before the fierceness of my resolve. With Austin bundled into my best long coat and dress hat, Mary in her traveling clothes, I sent them away in the waiting cab with their scant luggage. The thudding of the front door had a finality to it that made me think I'd never see either of them again.

Then I gathered my supplies and hid myself in the cellar. Angry, hurt, and full of the need to fight, I refused to leave Anne in Moriarty's hands, to let him sell her into murderous bondage. I did not know how many days of life she had left, but I had a plan to try to save her.

Hiding in my cellar, when I heard Rachel close and lock the house from the outside, I went again through the plan desperation had given me.

We had learned from young Brewer that Moriarty might let those men from America take Anne with them. Holmes, fighting a war of attrition, seeking to preserve the lives of the women targeted by Moriarty, would have no time to consider this. I, however, could investigate the means by which Moriarty planned to send Anne away. Though Mycroft Holmes was likely at work on this, I determined to take up this chase myself, incognito. I knew my chances were no greater than his, but his agents lacked my resolve, my commitment, my burning need.

The time waiting to move was the worst. I fell to wondering if my blows to the head had killed Moriarty's assassin. I lay down on the cold camp bed in my cellar and waited for any sound of his or another's entry, which might allow me to trap him—or her. I waited for two days, living off tinned meat, biscuits, and water from the cellar pump.

No one came. Moriarty's man must have fled, and I dared hope that Austin and Mary had found safe passage elsewhere. With the house empty now, to all appearances, I gambled that Moriarty no longer had an interest in my house. It was to my person that he wished to do damage.

Unshaven, far less clean than I wished, I exited my cellar in the dark of a rainy night, intent on working my plan in the morning, hours away. My rational mind challenged me with questions of what I would do if I learned the location of Moriarty, for storming a stronghold on my own would be foolish. The only chance I had was to confront Anne, as I had once before, and wrest her from his captivity. If the shock of a more violent assault upon her had defeated for even moments the evil force which possessed her, I had to believe that she could be freed.

Yes, it occurred to me that any demonic entity that held her would not bend to my will alone. I have never been deeply religious, but I did trust that God would not countenance such an injustice. Anne had never had a chance, a choice to resist the evil that held her. Certainly, her actions and mine were ones many would label immoral. But through my intervention and faith in the ultimate source of justice, I would seek for her that choice, even if it was only to let her die.

With every day that passed, her poor brain would be deteriorating more. I had no idea how long she might still retain some shred of her former self, deep within, but I abhorred every day for the torment it caused her.

That day, I checked shipping offices of every kind for vessels bound for New York or Boston. I was rebuffed all day long: passenger manifests were not divulged to reckless-looking men.

As I traveled through the city, I saw signs and heard stories of the "Jack the Ripper" fears that possessed London. Many people were fleeing the city as the Ripper madness created more public panic. The police, as usual, remained baffled, and several police stations had been burned by angry crowds. My thoughts often returned to Holmes and my friends, who nightly lived in the midst of that madness. I feared that they would run into the rough justice of the many Whitechapel vigilante gangs. Stories ran rampant about strangers, especially foreigners, being set upon by men driven to extremes of panic.

The newspapers didn't help, either, suggesting that it was only fallen women who needed to fear the Ripper. The whole of the East End population saw this as proof that the poor were not thought worthy of protection. People had to look out for themselves, their families, friends, neighbors. As I crossed the city, in every office, before every door, I was a stranger and therefore suspect.

At last, however, my search paid dividends. As I took a meal in a pub near the wharfs, I overheard two men nearby talking about a merchant ship, the *Holmia*, out of Finland. Something stirred in me, some insight, perhaps born by my need to seek God's justice. I knew that name. I had seen "S. Holm" written on one of the two small slips of paper I'd found in Brompton Castle. It was a desperate hope that gripped me, but it was the only hope I had, and I was forced to believe that I was led by the same just Providence I trusted to deliver Anne. Dressed as poorly as I was, I dared to approach the men.

"'Scuse, sir," I said in my best West Country accent. "D' you mention a ship called the *Holmia*? One of my mates said he booked passage on her, bound for New York. D' you know how I might get on her? It'd be worth standin' you each a pint o' cider."

"Aw, lad, ye'd best head back to Devonshire an' face whate'er awaits ye as take that crossin', for the gales will be up hard, an' ye dun't look to have strong sea legs," replied one of the men.

I accepted the joke at my expense, looking like a country bumpkin, but they let me join them and soon had fresh pints in their rough hands. I told them that I was fleeing my wife, on account of having had a dalliance with her sister, which wasn't that much of a stretch from the truth. I let them chide me over those two pints for a quarter of an hour, and finally they relented and gave me the address of an office where I might yet purchase a ticket on the *Holmia*.

The hour grew later, and I did not fancy being abroad late in the dock area for fear of running into any of the mobs of men. So I returned home in a roundabout manner, determined that I would accost Mycroft Holmes after visiting the offices of the Finnish Ship Lines first thing the next morning. My plan gave me hope that with this information, Mycroft's agents might gain access to ship lists through unofficial channels.

Under cover of darkness, I retrieved better clothing from my closet, and the next morning, I stole away in the pre-dawn chill. Forced to loiter over a meager breakfast, I waited not far from the offices of the Finnish Ship Lines, waiting for them to open. Once they did, I presented myself to a smiling clerk as one hopeful of making the Atlantic crossing at all speed on the *Holmia.*

"Sir, the passenger berths are filled, and we haven't much cargo space to spare, either," the clerk answered. "I'm afraid, sir, that we have nothing for you."

"Ah," I said, with a knowing shake of my head. I feared that my five days' worth of whiskers made me look rather shabby, but I played at being something of an academic, as was my quarry, Moriarty. I played a hunch that he might use his real name. "My colleague, Professor Moriarty, told me to expect as much. Oh, excuse me; I recognize that you cannot divulge your passengers' names. Forgive me, please."

"Yes," he said with a nod and a smile. Did his smile suggest I was right?

I played another hand. "I might yet be able to convince one of Professor Moriarty's associates from New York to give up his berth for me, although I know the ship sails in a short time."

"Yes, sir, she sails in a matter of only thirty-six hours or so. And the gentlemen from New York seemed quite anxious to depart, sir, as is most of London, these days."

"Yes. Dreadful business, these murders," I said, rising and preparing to leave. With my shaking hand on the doorknob, I played one last gambit. "I suppose that they have arranged shipment for the live specimens later, perhaps in the spring?"

"They must have, sir, for the *Holmia* has no live specimens on this voyage, though the laboratory materials they are sending will take up quite a large portion of the cargo hold."

"Indeed, the packing crates looked to me like oversized coffins," I remarked, as though I had seen them. I pulled a gruesome face for his benefit, and it disarmed him.

"That was the impression I had, too, from the shipping manifest," he finished with a laugh. "Good luck, sir."

I gave him a pleasant wave and closed the door as carefully as I could to disguise my hasty departure. With this information, I was sure that I could barter for the chance I needed.

And Mycroft Holmes was the only one who could give it to me.

***

After crossing town afoot, each step hardening my resolve, I approached the door of the Diogenes Club, within which sat many of the most powerful men in Great Britain, men at the very heart of British commerce and law. At the service entrance, I begged a cook to ask for someone to take a message to Mr. Mycroft Holmes. I waited a quarter of an hour on the cold steps, feeling rather vulnerable to view. Soon, a stately, white-haired fellow in his vest and shirtsleeves, and wearing a white apron, came out, his brow furrowing as he studied me. He introduced himself as Mr. Holmes's valet, Stevens.

I smiled at him and said, "My name, sir, is Dr. John H. Watson, and I am desperate to see Mycroft Holmes."

"My word. You don't say," he whispered, eyes squinted. "I know your name, sir, but I had thought you far removed from these shores."

"That was the notion, yes, and I'm glad that some think it accomplished. My need, however, is urgent, and I must have Mycroft Holmes's aid. I have valuable information to barter," I explained. "Would you do me the honor of passing along my request to see him?"

"Certainly, sir," he said, his hand moving to rest on his chin. "I, er, must ask you to remain here, if you will. I'm sure he will wish to speak to you, but the club has quite strict rules about admittance."

***

In the Diogenes Club, through which I was soon escorted in secrecy, a strong sense of England yet prevailed: orderly, stolid. Elsewhere in the building, the business of running the Empire went on. High court judges, captains of industry, and heads of state

238

occupied secluded seats in that great, quiet common room off the entrance hall. I doubted if they had experienced the effects of Moriarty's terror campaign as had the man in the street. Perhaps they were too well insulated from it by their power. I almost desired that they should taste the fear that gripped common folk, but I dismissed that idea as unworthy.

I thought about Anne's eyes, the last time I had seen them. She had asked me to save her from her unholy plight. I closed my own eyes in an attempt to gather my thoughts, for I could not lose myself in fearful reminiscence.

I heard Mycroft's voice at the door behind me.

"I must say that the beard suits the obvious desperation of your visit, Doctor," he said, extending me his large hand to clasp. "But you need not barter information to get my help. We all thought you gone. I know Sherlock does."

"Does he?" I replied in gruff tones, angry and shamed that Holmes had sent me away. "The beard is, perhaps, a passing thing, but it serves to deflect attention away from my more-sought-after face. I am glad to hear that our ruse worked.

"And if I need not barter, then you may have my information: in less than thirty-six hours, sir, I believe that Professor Moriarty will take passage to New York, along with his associates and his ghastly cargo, aboard the *Holmia*."

Mycroft nodded his head in appreciation as I explained my investigation.

"And now," he asked, "is your intent to join my brother, despite his wish to send you away to safety? What are you prepared to do?"

"I cannot join him yet," I said, "and if possible, I would ask that you refrain from telling him that I am back, at least until tomorrow. I fear that he will think of me as a liability, but I am here to end the threat of Anne Prescott, in one way if not another."

"She will kill you, Doctor," Mycroft said quietly.

"I am prepared to risk that, and if need be, I will give her the death that she deserves," I said.

He sighed and nodded, accepting the situation and the risks we all shared.

"Where she is, we do not quite know," he explained. "However, if you are correct about the *Holmia*, a matter I should be able to determine with my connections, we will be able to pin down Moriarty's departure point and take him and his associates before they leave.

"This is commendable work," he added, "which, I'm sorry to say, we have not had the wherewithal to do. Well done."

"I seek no commendation, only information, sir. We haven't much time," I replied. "I know that I cannot storm a location that Moriarty and his men hold, but if you can tell me whom Holmes and company are seeking amongst the unfortunate women from whose ranks Moriarty has chosen Anne's victims, and where those women can be found, I will try to find Anne in that way. I did so once before."

"But how, Watson?" Mycroft asked. "She killed Jimmy O'Doole the last time you sought to detain her, and she would have killed you except for the arrival of my brother. And last night, she murdered MacGuire, fell on the poor lad's back and cut his throat. She took a piece of his neck in her teeth before she bolted. Guthrie is beside himself with grief."

"I—I have no time for grief," I said, swallowing the loss of that fine young man as yet more tinder to fuel my fires. "I must do what I must do. With your help, sir, I will do it better and seek, if nothing else, a way to make amends for my failings."

Mycroft stared into my eyes and I into his. I trusted he saw my clarity of purpose. I set the worth of my own life at a pin's fee. My love for Mary, Holmes, my country, even Anne, had driven me to this end. It was an honorable end for me, even if it came to my death.

"You must seek Clovis Porter, then, or Mary Kelly," he sighed, breaking the tension between us. "I can give you the addresses associated with them. Only three remain in London: Clovis Porter, Mary Kelly, and Rose Mylett. Some, like Coles and McKenzie, have gone to ground on their own, and they appear to have reached a place of safety, for we can find no trace of them. Mylett is extremely cautious, too, and seems to have found a way to keep herself hidden.

"And you must take these," he said, gesturing to the table behind me, where lay the sword I had used in our assault on LaLaurie, along with a box of fifty rounds for my revolver.

"But, Watson," Mycroft continued, "the Anne Prescott you knew is gone, irrevocably. She eats parts of them, Doctor. She ate the chunk that she tore from MacGuire's neck, man. I do not think that there is a shred of her left in that superbly animated corpse. Would it not be a mercy just to take her life, through any means?"

"Yes," I said. "But I must try, hoping beyond hope that something can be done for her. I—we—owe her that. She was taken from under my roof, and I was not there to prevent it or protect her."

I picked up the ammunition and grasped the lacquered scabbard of the long sword.

"Yes," Mycroft whispered, "I can see that. And the Empire owes her something, even if it is only a clean death. I trust that you or my brother would do the same for me. I know that Sherlock and his men, even Gladstone, have agreed to that for one another, should they become infected."

We had said our all. However, before I left, Mycroft advised me to seek out a rather legendary, notorious fellow by the name of Tobias Schneckt, who frequented a pub called the Grapes, on Narrow Street near the Canary Wharf.

"A well-known procurer?" I asked.

"Not as such," Mycroft replied. "His racket is protection, for working prostitutes, for the most part, but his own protection is his greatest concern, I believe. Sherlock has tried to recruit him but has been too busy in the hunt to commit resources to doing so. And Schneckt is rather cautious. If you can find him, he will almost certainly know more about these women's movements, but it will be dangerous to you, I think."

Mycroft outfitted me with his own large oilcloth coat, for it hung low enough to cover the scabbard of the sword beneath and was wide enough to allow me to carry the pistol and another box of cartridges, as well as a nightstick as the last line of defense.

"You haven't more time than the rest of this night, sir," Mycroft said, shaking my hand and leading me to the rear exit of the Diogenes Club. "I cannot keep vital information from Sherlock, though I will take such time as is required to determine the validity of your information about Moriarty's plans to leave these shores aboard the *Holmia*. We must not lose any opportunity to catch him. However, I will tell my brother of your return at my first opportunity, which will likely be in the early morning.

"In the meantime, try to avoid getting yourself killed," Mycroft went on, a crooked smile on his lips. "After all, Department Zed will require your services."

"Department what?" I asked.

"Zed," he quipped. "Z for zombie, don't you know. I thought it rather fitting that our little organization should have a name."

"We have an organization?" I said in return. "I should think another name would be better, if we are to have one."

He shrugged his shoulders as though the matter were out of his hands. Likely, members of the L.S. were behind the name. I could only shake my head and make ready to leave.

CHAPTER TWENTY-FIVE

Within two hours of leaving Pall Mall, I had hitched rides far enough across town to take me nearer the Thames and a decent walk from the Grapes. I was grateful to find several banknotes and a pocket full of change in Mycroft's oilcloth to add to my diminishing funds.

Once at the Grapes, I took a place at the bar and ordered one of London's finest ales. I also told the barman that I was interested in meeting Tobias Schneckt.

"Right, sir. I 'spec you are. Well, when you've finished yer pint, like, step around to the rear o' the prop'ty, to his office," he said, with enough deference to make me doubt him. Holmes had spoken of the rough justice in these quarters an eon ago, when this horrible case had started in Mitre Alley. I recognized a setup.

Upon finishing my pint, I tipped the barman with a shilling and a touch of my cap and set out for the meeting. As soon as I had left the light of the street, rough hands set upon my shoulders, taking hard grips. "Easy, guv," a deep voice beside me purred.

I relaxed, but when the fellow on my left pushed his handful of my coat further into the dark, I took his wrist to capture his momentum and stepped forward, low and strong, turning my hips as I did. This took him off his feet and propelled him into the unsteady legs of his companion on my right. They both went down hard as I hauled my pistol out and held it on them.

The sound of clapping was heard ahead of me, and Mr. Tobias Schneckt, I presumed, stepped into the little bit of light we had.

"Well done, sir," he said, his nasal voice cheerful. "I see that you are a man of some accomplishment. Have you come looking for employment? In these harrowing times, I have more people leaving my service than seeking it. No one wishes to face the Ripper, you know."

"I wish to face the Ripper," I replied, "and my mission is to end that threat."

Schneckt favored me with a doubtful smile and turned to his fallen men.

"Get up," Schneckt commanded them, "and kindly escort this man to my table. I like a good story, and this fellow seems to have one."

Back inside, my companions of the alley now solicitous for my comfort, I had a fresh pint thrust into my hands and the earnest, oily countenance of my host beaming at me across the table. The business of the Grapes went on around us as though we were invisible. In fact, I thought I remembered seeing this fellow at this same table as I had entered earlier. The patrons took no notice of us, though Schneckt's table sat in the middle of the floor.

I went to the heart of the matter.

"I am looking for Clovis Porter and Mary Kelly. I have their last known addresses here," I said, showing Schneckt the information Mycroft had given me. "This is a matter of great urgency, Mr. Schneckt. I have just hours to find them and, if possible, save them from the hands of the Ripper."

"You know who he is, then?" he whispered, his eyes wide with worry and fear, his hands trembling now as they toyed with his glass of rum.

"I know what tracks and kills these women, yes, and I know why," I replied. "And I mean to stop it."

"If you do, you'll be the toast of London, sir. Might I have the privilege of knowing your name?" he asked, putting on a pleasant, if anxious, smile.

"Call me Jack," I replied.

That froze him on the spot.

"Are—are you—?" His eyes went wide, but even as he started to ask the inevitable question, I was already shaking my head.

"No. I am not the Ripper. If I were, you and your companions would be gutted and lying in the alley," I said, sitting back enough to draw the razor-sharp sword two inches from the scabbard and snick it back home. "I aim to end this terror, and you are the man who can help me do so. Be honest, please, for I have no time to mince words, nor do I have money to offer you, short of these notes," I said, drawing several folded bills from the oilcloth pocket.

His hand pushed the money back to me, and it was his turn to shake his head. I wondered if he would be sick, since he had gulped a rather large swallow of rum and looked to be turning a bit green.

"I do keep an eye on all the girls, sir, as it is my business to give them what protection I can," he said. "And I would be best served in my business, sir, by the Ripper's removal. But the two girls you mention, um, Mr. Jack, sir, well, they are by way of being awfully independent young women, especially Mary Kelly. Clovis, though, she is really pretty fresh to the trade, sir, and keeps company with young gents from the West End, you know. Rather proud, in fact, though she's a decent enough lass in her own way."

"And will this address get me to her, Mr. Schneckt? I have mentioned that I am in rather a hurry, have I not?" I kept my voice low and calm, confident now that Schneckt desired what I offered.

"The one you have is rather old, though it might work," he said, looking at the addresses Mycroft had written down for me. As he did so, Schneckt drew a ledger from a cloth shoulder bag beside his chair. "Let me see..." he said slowly, opening the volume and thumbing through its well-worn pages.

"Yes. This one, I think, is where you will find her tonight and tomorrow, on Princelet Street, not far from the Ten Bells." Schneckt wrung his hands, perhaps to make them stop shaking, and jotted the Princelet Street address down below Porter's other location. "But I know, too, that Miss Kelly, though she has never used my services, has a standing engagement on this night of the week with a gentleman in the Edgware Road. She'll likely be back at the Miller's Court address in a day or so. When she returns from her Edgware Road engagement, she most often works out of the Bells," Schneckt said. "As I said, a comely but willful girl. It is hard to track her."

"Thank you, Mr. Schneckt," I said, ready to make my departure. "Your help has been invaluable. I will report this to my fellows," I added, thinking that I might yet introduce this slippery fellow to Sherlock Holmes, if I made it through this night.

"I rather think that you will be the Ripper's next victim, which seems such a waste to me," Schneckt observed. "If you know him, why not just set the coppers on him? Better yet, why not throw your lot in with my lads? You'll be sure to find him if you keep company with those girls, for there's folks seek them out every night."

I realized that he knew of Holmes's efforts to find and protect the women from our list. If he had heard of Holmes's efforts, it would not be long before this matter reached the ears of the press. That would ruin any secrecy that Holmes, or I, still had.

"There is more at stake here than you know, sir," I replied, rising. "You would do well to keep knowledge of my visit to yourself."

"Gladly, sir, for they say that one ought not to contradict a lunatic in his mania," Schneckt replied, putting his book away and giving me cautious looks from his shifty eyes.

***

I took my leave of Schneckt, taking a northerly heading on Commercial Road at a brisk jog. I turned my focus to my journey to the area of the Ten Bells and Princelet Street. Schneckt had given me a good description of Clovis Porter, a vivacious girl with a sweet face, a raucous laugh, and a generous figure who wore her black, curly hair piled atop her head. Going with care and staying just a block or so off of Commercial Street, I reached the pub in a little less than an hour, with the cold drizzle running down the neck of Mycroft's oilcloth.

Moriarty and company would go after Porter tonight, since they likely knew that Kelly was out of the area on this night of the week. If Schneckt knew, likely Moriarty did. I intended my warning to Miss Porter to be quite convincing.

From the open door of the Ten Bells, I had a good view of the pub layout, but it was crowded with patrons, and the noise was great. Within, though, I heard a braying laugh that sounded promising. Stepping further in, my hat low, the laugh rose again, and I saw the black curls bobbing in time with it at a corner table by the windows to the right. I turned on my heel and walked outside in that direction to get a better view of her.

She sat in the company of two well-dressed young men, who were plying her with drink. The young men looked as if they were delighted by the prospect of using her for the night, and though they looked to have little harm in them, I grew angry at the thought of

246

what Clovis Porter had become, would become, with many more nights like this. Her lads eyed each other over her loud laughter, thinking that the fun was about to start.

They left with her between them, her giddy steps faltering and black curls bobbing, making for Princelet Street, with me half a block behind them. The traffic was light, so the sound of the heavy vehicle coming along behind me drew my attention, and I gasped when I saw it. I had been right about Moriarty's awareness of Kelly's movements.

Black and massive, the vehicle could hold many men, and it slowed as it neared the trio of revelers. My heart sprang into my mouth, and I nearly shouted at the trio to run, but the brougham picked up speed and hurried past them.

The brougham took a right turn several blocks past Princelet. I knew that I had only minutes before they sprang the trap.

Thus far, none of the supposed Ripper victims had been found with any other bodies: no clients of the fallen women had met their ends. Moriarty would wait for the chance to take Porter alone. He was careful in demonstrating the effectiveness of his prize zombie, and I wondered if one or two of his clients were within the brougham to witness the act or at least its aftermath. I shuddered to think of the mind that would plan, let alone enact, such a thing, but I could see it before my eyes.

I picked up my pace, silently thanking the heavenly powers that had brought me to Mycroft and Schneckt. I might well save Porter and confront Anne, as I desired.

As the trio of Porter and her two would-be lovers approached the front of the flats, I called to them. They stopped, their smiles fading as I jogged toward them. One of them said in a rather squeaky voice, "Push off, mister. This one is ours tonight." Clovis giggled.

"No," I called back, maintaining my heading toward them, "tonight I send you home to your mothers, bloodied but alive."

As I came to them, the young fellow who had called to me put up his guard, as though to defend his lady's honor, and I flattened him with a strike of my right palm to his forehead. My momentum and weight, for which he was no match, took him down hard, and his mate was calling, "Hey! I say! Stop! We mean no harm!" as he ran to his fallen companion.

"Then do none," I said, taking Miss Porter by the arm. "Go home and do not come back."

The young men ran back in the direction from which we had come, casting nervous glances over their shoulders to make sure I didn't follow them.

I dragged Clovis Porter into the darkness of the doorway. The flat was on the ground floor, which would aid Moriarty's planning. Miss Porter had said little except to giggle and bleat once or twice as I dispatched the two youngsters. But now, she crooned, thinking me another customer, "Oooh, you're a strong lad. And I like men with beards. They tickle so." Here she fell into her raucous laugh.

I opened the door and led her to the flat number that Schneckt had given me. We entered the flat while she asked, "So, what do you like, dearie? I hope it's not too rough. A little ro—"

"Silence, you stupid child!" I said in a fierce whisper. I had my hands on both her upper arms, and as she began to rub against me, I thrust her back to stare into her eyes. "Listen!"

Her face wore a dreamy smile, and she was pretty. The drink and abuse had not touched her yet, beyond her wanton attitude.

"My name is Jack," I growled, "and unless you do as I say, your life, as foolish as it is, will be over tonight."

The name "Jack" reached her, against the tide of gin, and her eyes went wide as she began to whimper. She started to collapse from fright and drunken confusion, but I held her up. "Listen!" I barked at her again. She bit her lip and tried to control her fright. She stood on her own, though she trembled and sobbed.

"Do you know anyone in the flats above this one?" I had to shake her to get her to answer me. "Is there anyone on the top floor, two floors up, whom you know well enough to go to them now for protection?"

"M-Mister and Mrs. W-Willis," she managed to get out. "They—they invite me to dinners Sundays. My papa knew them f-from school."

I took all of the money I had about me and thrust it into her shaking hands. It was enough to keep her going for weeks.

"You go to them now," I growled, leaning close to her, "and stay with them. Do not leave until tomorrow. If either you or they wish to inform the police, do so in the morning and tell them everything, as much as you like. And then go back to the place from which you came. Do not come back here to London, to this life. Do you understand?"

She nodded, her eyes going even wider in fright.

When I released her, I watched her spring up the stairs, two at a time, like a country lass running up a hill on May Day. I waited until I heard the voices far above me and a door closed with a bang.

Then, leaving the door of Clovis Porter's flat ajar, I waited.

I took cover behind the door, for I had made the mistake last time of letting Anne confront me first. My plan, simple as it was, demanded that I get some control over Anne before she knew I was there. If Vollimer and his henchmen arrived first, I would shoot them down in the doorway without a second thought. I recognized that this would be an act of cold-blooded murder, and I knew that I would accept the consequences, whatever they might be. I had promised that I would do my all, and I intended to.

A step in the hallway made me grow still. The door pushed open with a slow creak. The second or so that passed seemed an eternity. When I gauged from the shadow on the floor that Anne waited there, I lunged with all my weight and strength and hit her with the door. She fell with a gasping snarl. I shut and bolted the door to prevent any departure or entrance and leapt toward Anne's tall form, sprawled on the floor. I kicked the wicked blade out of her hand before I did anything else.

The brief daze I had given her faded in an instant, and she gathered her legs beneath her to spring at me, as I'd known she would. A jungle cat could not have pounced more quickly or with more ferocity, but I managed to dodge to the side and a deliver a hammer-like blow to her forehead, so as not to break my own hand. Down she went to the floor again, full on her back, her head snapping back onto the wood of the floor, and she grew still for a second.

I knelt at her side and scooped her up in my arms. "Whatever you are, by whatever name in the annals of Hell from which you are summoned, I banish you in the name of all that is holy!" I cried, trusting to the powers of good to defend me.

"Anne, Anne!" I cried then, "Come back to me now. It's Jack. I'm here to take you away from it."

And to my great relief, her body went limp in my arms, her eyes closed, and her breathing grew more regular, calm. I chafed her wrists and, with light taps to her cheeks, called her name over and over. I did not know how long I had until her handlers tried to make their entrance.

Something, maybe the urgency in my voice, reached her. The doorknob rattled. Anne's eyes opened to tiny slits, and she struggled to make them go wider. One eye focused first, then the other, and they tracked to my face. That was Anne Prescott's gaze. She was not my Anne, but she was her own, herself in that instant.

Her left hand struggled to rise and touch my face. Her mouth worked, but she could form no words. LaLaurie's disease had taken her ability to speak. Still, I sought to get whatever remained of her out of the hell in which she had been trapped.

The ghost of a smile formed on her lips. Her eyes, focusing and unfocusing, stayed on my face and tracked her fingers as they touched my face. The well of sadness and loss in that glance broke my heart. She retained some knowledge of her state, though she was helpless to break free or resist the evil that held her. Though her hair was in strings, clotted with old blood, her clothing foul with it, and her body a thin wreck compared to that of the vibrant woman who had fought at my side, I saw the tattered remains of her noble, beautiful spirit in her fading eyes. Tears formed in my own eyes as I gazed at her.

I would never again be her lover. I knew that I should never have dishonored her by letting it happen in the first place. But as her friend, as one who loved her generous, sojourning heart, I could grant her a reprieve from torment and let her die, let her reach her own peaceful end.

The sound of rhythmic chanting rose loud in the hallway. Blows struck at the door. A violent shiver ran through Anne's body. A gurgling cry came from her throat, and her eyes went wide in terror. She arched and plunged with such violence that she dropped away from my arms and onto the floor, and her eyes shut as though fiery pain tore through every nerve.

She grew still. A snarling rose from her lips, and the left hand that had caressed my cheek now struck me with savage force, knocking me onto my backside. The chanting went on in the hall, and I yelled "No!" and drew my revolver, firing three times through the door. Men scurried away.

When Anne's eyes met mine, they were not her own anymore. She drew her legs beneath her and crouched like a beast before me. The demon-haunted eyes stared at me.

Yet she stayed still, quivering so hard I feared that her bones would break. Her head shook back and forth fast, hard. Anne fought against her captor, I thought. Yet she remained in a crouch on the floor, with only the ragged nail of her left index finger scratching at the floor.

"Anne!" I cried, tears streaming down my face. The only reply she gave was a screeching snarl, and whatever entity controlled her broke free from Anne's fading control and lunged across the floor toward the long, thin knife, scooping it up with one hand even as she planted a hard kick to my chest, sending me backward onto the floor. Stunned, I dropped my pistol. She landed on me, knees pinning down my arms, knife raised, and I knew that my death would be swift.

Through my tears, I smiled at her and whispered, "Goodbye, my dear Anne."

But the stroke did not fall. The knife quivered in her hand. She looked at the shaking hand and arm and screamed at it. It would not move. She tore the knife from the stiff fingers with her other hand and raised it to strike again, but again it would not fall.

With a terrifying scream that rang through the house, she leapt from me and kicked through the door, setting upon her handlers. Their sudden cries of pain and terror led out of the house. How many they were, I had no idea.

Rising to follow her, I retrieved my revolver, and as I looked at the place where her fingernail had gouged the floor I saw, as though written by a child, the words "kil me," her last plea to me as she had fought her hardest against the beast within. I had failed, but she had not. With that horrible thing in her, she could not die on her own. I had to take her life.

I rose then and stumbled out the door to the vacant hallway, my pistol drawn, intent upon releasing her with one shot. Neighbors' shouts rang through the thin walls all around me, and doors were opening as I found my way out to the street. I was in time to see the brougham round the corner, gathering speed as I stumbled after it. I passed an alley opening, and a strong hand grabbed me by the collar; the steel of a pistol barrel pressed into the hollow at the back of my head.

"Gotcha, my lad," the voice of Magnus Guthrie said, close to my ear. And I collapsed in his grasp. Failing to recognize me, Guthrie let me fall on my back as others approached. He trained his pistol on my forehead. Holmes came then and called my name. I'd wondered if I would ever hear him again.

"Watson! Watson!" Holmes cried, pushing Guthrie's revolver away from me. "My God, man, can't you see? It's Watson." I looked up into the intense eyes of the world's only consulting detective as he looked into mine.

"Yes, I'm back," I whispered, "and determined to take Anne Prescott's life."

CHAPTER TWENTY-SIX

Soon I sat in an open coach, rattling away to the east. The venerable Mr. Stevens of the Diogenes Club drove us, and Holmes and Guthrie rode with me. Holmes had listened as I'd told him of my findings, and he did not ask me about Mary's whereabouts, for which I was glad. I had enough on my mind. I think he recognized my intent. He only said, "I am glad to have you at my side once more, old friend."

"More to the point, Holmes, if what I have learned is correct, we will know soon where to apprehend Moriarty within the next twenty hours or so. Have you had any contact with Mycroft since yesterday afternoon?"

"No, Watson, but word might yet reach us tonight. Mycroft knows where to find us. We are on our way there now."

Within a short while, Stevens drew the coach to a halt before the ruin of St. Lazarus Infirmary. I fear I stood gaping at it, for Holmes hopped down from his perch and led me around what would have been the back of the place, now just a pile of brick and charred beams. He took a quick turn and beckoned me down a set of steps into a dark opening, recently cleared and swept. I opened the door and heard the click of a revolver hammer in the darkness ahead of me.

"Holmes?" I whispered, half turning and raising my palms in surrender. Beside me, Wiggins's young voice cried "Blimey! Is it 'imself?"

"Yes, William. You may stand down," Holmes said, pushing in around me. "Watson is back in the very hour of our greatest need."

I was greeted by many voices calling my name in welcome. They were a sorry-looking bunch, but I was glad to see them and hear the stories of their efforts to protect the women Moriarty had chosen as his victims.

It wasn't long before a small lad, the John Limeberry of whom Harvey Brewer had once spoken, brought a note from Mycroft Holmes. His keen-eyed brother surveyed its content in the flickering light. "McCall Brothers warehouse, on the Isle of Dogs," Holmes announced, with every eye in the room upon him. "We are assured that Moriarty means to be there at the turn of the tide, later tonight."

A cheer broke out from the ragged throats of all there, though I urged them to quiet themselves.

"Mycroft has identified Moriarty as being on the *Holmia* passenger manifest?" I asked.

"Yes, through one of the aliases Mycroft's agents have found in their search of Moriarty's financial resources," Holmes replied, grasping my hand. "Watson, you have done it!"

Without pausing for further comment, Holmes, Gladstone, Guthrie, and I departed, letting Stevens take us to the Diogenes Club, where we would make our final preparations.

***

The wintry dawn passed as we were ushered into an upper meeting room of the Diogenes Club. Holmes assured me that with all that had been leading up to this day, his brother would be awake, and he was correct. Mycroft ordered us a breakfast which we consumed with relish. Mycroft and Stevens prepared a map so that we could plan our routes.

We set our plan and acquired Mycroft's aid. Gladstone, Guthrie, Holmes, and I would lead the assault on the location we had deemed to be Moriarty's departure point. Mycroft promised to have Stevens in an open coach near the center of the Isle of Dogs, standing by to move us at speed to another location if need be.

"I will also alert Scotland Yard that Moriarty might be taken as he tries to leave England, either tonight or tomorrow, at Plymouth, when the *Holmia* makes her final call before the crossing," Mycroft added.

"He is too cunning. I do not think that any official agency will apprehend him," Holmes muttered. "And certainly, you will not get the Metropolitan Police to mobilize before high tide tonight. Watson is back, having done what we could not as we endeavored to remove Moriarty's intended victims to safety. We must keep Moriarty from leaving these shores, at all costs."

Holmes and I were, again, of the same mind.

***

Later, as the day's light faded, Holmes and I made a fast approach toward the warehouses at the side of the Thames. We came down Manchester Road as fast as we could, me remembering that the Isle of Dogs, stretching away to our left, had once been labeled "the killing fields." But the cold night and impending horror of our plan did nothing to lessen the fire within me.

A boy cried out not far away, and one of Wiggins's Irregulars, a boy called Nowicke, sprinted toward us in the gloom, followed hard by a man in a dark overcoat and bowler hat. Holmes dashed forward and scooped up the lad as I dodged into a spot beside the man's path, my right arm sweeping forward, catching him just below the chin as he reached me. He left his feet and crashed to the cobbled street, going limp as his head met the surface with an audible crack.

When Nowicke had regained his breath, he pointed back the way he had come and cried, "It's that third one along, sir, the one that says McCall Brothers shippin', sir! Wigs and the tosher and me, we came up be'ind it, where a boat 'ad just docked, like, and there were big 'ard lads after us in no time. 'Urry, 'urry, sir!"

With orders to circle around the block and go back east to find Guthrie and Gladstone, we sent Nowicke off at another run and made for the warehouse. Its upper floor gave scant light to the street.

Moriarty was there. I could feel it.

Mr. Uyeshiba always claimed that a sword was no weapon but an extension of a man's soul. We started together, me trying not to flap and clank, wondering how a piece of hammer-welded steel could be anything but a weapon. I had no time to wonder more, for as we came upon the warehouse, I heard Wiggins's young voice pipe "Help!" at the same time that Brewer called out, "Oh, no, you don't!"

We turned beside the building and sprinted hard for the dock at its rear. I drew my pistol and ran toward the sound of their struggles. The two lads were holding at bay three men, agents of Moriarty, who were trying to make their way onto the dock, where a broad steam launch lay at anchor. The boys stood together, Wiggins on the left, down on one knee, training his pistol on the foremost man, while Brewer brandished a cutlass in their faces.

Our footfalls sounded on the boards of the dock as we set upon them. They turned, and I brought the butt of my pistol down on one fellow's head, dropping him cold, while the other lunged at me to take away my firearm. None of them, I saw, were armed.

Holmes dispatched his man with a swift kick to the groin and a chopping stroke to the fellow's shoulder, which broke his collarbone. He then took the fellow who was threatening to push me over the edge of the dock in a choke hold from behind and soon had him silent on the dock.

"Bind these men," Holmes barked, causing Brewer to run toward the waiting launch and haul away a length of stout rope. "Wiggins, are you hurt?"

"Blighter tried to hinge me knee backward," Wiggins said, standing and putting weight on it with caution. "You served him right, though, Mr. Holmes. Got 'im right in the nadgers!"

"Make sure that these three do not get free to follow us into the warehouse, you two. Enter that warehouse only if we call for you, agreed?" Holmes ordered.

"Yes, sir," they said in unison.

Turning to me, he said, "Watson, go back to the west side of the warehouse and see if you can gain entrance there. I will take this approach. Soon, Guthrie and Gladstone will be trying to make their entrance from the east. We must help them."

I sprang away, hurrying back to the low door on the west wall. I tried its latch, only to find it locked from within. When I heard Gladstone's voice rise to a hoarse shout within the building, I took a step back and kicked the door down, plunging ahead into the feeble light within, my pistol ready.

The stench hit me first and caused me to stop. Then, the sight of moiling bodies filling the room, struggling to get to Holmes on the south and Gladstone and Guthrie on the east, spurred me into action.

The room was stacked with wooden boxes, as long as coffins but wide enough for two bodies each. The cargo, though, was now seeking to fasten its collective teeth into my comrades. I could not tell how many zombies were in the room, but I fell upon the mass of them, shooting at zombie heads that came under my sights. They turned upon me then, and I was soon battling for my life.

My six shots gone and six zombies down, I swept out the sword and set to work, lopping off arms, legs, or heads as they came within my reach. The sword did not yet feel like an extension of my soul, for it strained my shoulders and back with each desperate stroke.

I could not believe how many zombies there were; it seemed as if everything before me was a wall of savage faces, some mutilated beyond recognition. Everywhere I looked, mouths gaped, blades slashed, and bludgeons hurtled toward my head. I dodged, trying to set them in a line, as my training had shown me, but I would no more take one down than I had to reset the line, dodging as much as striking.

Yet, at every strike, I tried to take one down. Already I had taken off three heads with the sweeping blade, razor-sharp, and their thick blood coated it.

As I spun again, I ran into the side of the familiar black brougham, the door having just closed on Moriarty and another man, similarly dressed, whom I had never seen before. One of his American clients, I supposed. Moriarty likely intended to show off his prize, Anne, to this American before they took ship.

The two black horses in the brougham's traces began to rear and plunge, making the vehicle rock, as they neighed and balked at the smell of so much foul blood. I kept my feet and fought on, trying to get near the carriage door in order to open it.

A stout arm reached around my neck from within the brougham's interior, lifting me off my feet. I kicked out at the zombie that clawed at me and clung to my arm as I tried to turn my blade to strike at it. With several awkward kicks, I managed to knock several other zombies down and keep them from biting me. But, my air cut off, I knew that I would not be able to struggle long.

Then I heard Holmes shout "Watson!" and he leapt through the air before me, the keen blade of his fell sword, Mustard Seed, whistling, glistening in a lightning arc. He aimed a stroke at the arm that held me, and it let go. I heard a very American voice exclaim, "Damn the man!" as that American drew back. Holmes's sword cut through the door as I dropped away, and he had to set his feet and wrench it free, for the wagon hurtled forward.

"Stop them!" Holmes yelled. Several zombies swarmed onto him as, oblivious of his personal danger, he rushed to my aid. As he spun to deal with them, his sword arm thrust upward, and three of them stood without arms. Even as I scrambled to reach the traces of the brougham, I saw him sweep the heads off of each stunned zombie with strokes so fluid that they looked leisurely. I hacked at the harness and earned a lash along the right side of my neck from the driver's whip, but I could not stop him from waving his team forward. I did the best I could to grasp the harness, even dropping my pistol to do so.

To my great delight, Guthrie leapt atop the horse on the far side, pulled his revolver and fired twice at the driver. The second shot took that man in the shoulder, and he tumbled over me, into the two zombies that pulled at my coat. The smell of his fresh blood set them on him, and I heard his screams as they tore at him.

But the brougham rushed out through the doors, into the dark. Moriarty was away, again.

Finally we stopped, leaning on walls or on our weapons, breathing hard. The fight, while successful, had taken too long, and we all knew it. Moriarty and his American client were well on their way to Mary Kelly's Miller's Court address by now. I hoped that she had gained some sense from the lads' attempts to warn her and had kept away. Still, if we could get to Stevens and his wagon, we might overtake the heavy brougham.

Gladstone assured us that he would stay at the warehouse and look after the lads until we could send help, and the three of us sprinted away, seeking Stevens, who we knew waited for us another block or so away. The still warehouse and business buildings were dark around us, as a bitter cold river fog rolled along the streets.

Young Nowicke emerged from a black alley and rushed to meet us.

"Mr. Stevens is late, Mr. 'Olmes," he said. "Accordin' to Wiggins, that wagon should 'a been 'ere long ago, though I think I 'ears 'im now."

The lad's sharp ears had picked up faint sounds from the fog-enshrouded dark. He pointed, and soon we saw the open wagon approaching, the driver muffled to his ears against the wet chill. I holstered my pistol and slid the sword back into its scabbard, ready to leap aboard, but Guthrie's sudden cry held me back even as I neared the wagon, hands reaching to lift myself aboard.

"Crikey! That ain't ol' Stevens!"

The driver whipped up his horse then and bore down on all of us in the street. He pulled a pistol from within his coat and commenced firing on all three of us, as Holmes, Guthrie, and Nowicke leapt away. His shots went wide, and the first one, aimed at my head, ripped away my bowler but missed me, though the shock of the round made my head throb.

It did not stop me from getting a hand on the wagon as it leapt forward. Grabbing the shooter's trouser leg, I hauled him toward me with all my might, pitching him down to the cobbles face first. Guthrie, who by then had pulled his own pistol, quickly shot three times, striking the man twice in his chest and once in his head.

Holmes stood over the driver, looking down at the ruin of the man's skull. Together, Holmes and I rolled the dead man onto his back, his blank eyes open still, blood pooling around him, finding the dark cracks between the cobbles.

"Vollimer!" Holmes cried.

"The bastard must have waylaid Stevens near here or at the Diogenes Club," I said.

"I must assume that is correct, Watson," Holmes replied. He looked down the road in the direction Moriarty had taken. His thoughts were obvious: too much time. "I fear that we must consider Mary Kelly's life as forfeit, if she was at Miller's Court tonight. The question is, where is Moriarty bound now?"

"If 'e means to try and catch the *'Olmia* at Plymouth tomorrow, 'e might be bound for King's Cross station," Guthrie said. "Surely we can stop 'im if we leave now."

"No, not King's Cross," I said, my mind working quickly. "He has not dealt us his final blow, I think."

With no hope of saving Mary Kelly, I forced my thoughts to be brutal, focused only on stopping Moriarty. Holmes's eyes, bright with intensity, seemed to approve of the rigor of my thoughts.

"He cannot be done, since he has opportunity to hurt us yet," Holmes said. "But how do we guess his next step, take his next dare? What path do we take to confront him? You see it, Watson; I can tell. Speak your mind, man!"

"He is always a step or two ahead of us," I cried, giving voice to the intuition that rose like a red dawn inside me. "The Diogenes Club, Holmes."

"Yes, Watson. You have hit it. Remember his letter we found in Anne's room? 'To strike at the heart of the Empire,' he wrote. If there is one place where he can bring ruin upon us and the Empire, it is the Diogenes Club!"

"Holmes, we must fly. Moriarty's last trump in this will come only if you are too late to stop him. He strikes blows in stealth, hoping, relishing the thought of your discovering it," I said, certain that I read Moriarty's cruel logic in this.

We leapt onto the wagon as Holmes whipped the horse into a gallop. Holmes had recognized his own thoughts in my words, and now, nothing except Anne Prescott would keep us from thwarting Moriarty's plan. The wind of our passage tore at us as we raced for central London.

The streets of Pall Mall, where the icy fog lay quiet and calm in this late hour, resounded with the speed of our flight. Several shrill whistles erupted in the night behind us, constables alarmed by our reckless passage.

Holmes halted a block away from the club, and we sprinted the last block toward the nondescript door behind which the elder members of Britain's leading families sat in supposed safety. And even as we approached, my heart near leapt from my throat, for shots struck on the pavement around us.

"They hold the door against us!" Holmes cried. "Volley fire, men!"

Holmes went low, up the small set of steps, casting away the night-black scabbard of Mustard Seed as Guthrie and I emptied our chambers at the doorway over his head. I did not know whether any of the enemy's shots had hit him. But as Guthrie and I gained the short steps, Holmes cast himself through the doorway, and I heard men's angry curses and cries as Guthrie followed him. I plunged after them.

The club's entry hall had been half glass, starting three feet or so above the floor. Our shots shattered this glass, allowing Moriarty's men to fire from behind the cover of the low remaining wall.

I nearly fell over the body of a man shot down in the hallway. Two men, also claimed by our volley of fire, lay slumped over the partition. Another well-dressed man, the American, judging by the long Colt revolver useless in his fingers, staggered and fell back into the common room, clutching at his throat, where Holmes's blade had passed through. Before me, Guthrie, his cutlass and truncheon moving too fast to follow in the dim light of the hall, fought two men at once. One sagged toward the floor from a blow of the truncheon. A shot rang out and Guthrie fell back, but not before he had run the other man through with the cutlass.

Holmes sprang into the common room, sword drawn, with me at his heels. He halted, though, for before him, Mycroft was down on his knees, hands bound behind him.

Moriarty stood beside him, a syringe filled with dark liquid pricking the skin of Mycroft's neck.

And so I had my first look at Moriarty, at his wide brow and deep-set eyes, and I hated him. That long, sardonic face wore a look of insane, evil glee. His eyes danced as he looked at us.

Moriarty had a man remaining. On the other side of Moriarty stood John Pizer, holding before him a figure wrapped from head to toe in dark, stained canvas, bound with a metal mask around its face and chains wrapped around its slender form. From Pizer's smile, I could tell he thought his side had the upper hand.

My gaze went back to that tall man in the center, his face lean like Holmes's, his eyes just as bright with intelligence. Yet there was something else there, a dazed look, as if a descent into madness had claimed him long ago.

"Damn you, Holmes," our enemy said in an almost cordial way. "You have proven to be a fine match, though you might say that I have your queen and several other key pieces." He gestured behind him, showing us at least three members of that august club bound in a similar way to Mycroft. Several men also lay unconscious on the floor of the common room behind him, club members who had resisted his entry, no doubt.

"But you see that I have the last move," Moriarty went on. "And, as is obvious, your queen has long been playing on my side of the board."

Holmes lowered the sword in his hand, but I noted that he let it turn in his hand, edge up.

"You must know that we have you beaten," Holmes said. "You have no more immediate allies other than this shoemaker, who looks ready to bolt at the first possible moment."

"Mr. Pizer and I have many allies still," Moriarty replied. "All I have to do is push this plunger and your brother will become one of us. You see, LaLaurie's meticulous records helped me to know that blood drawn directly from the liver of one of his infected specimens is the quickest way to turn a man into a weapon. I can get another to do the ritual business, since, I presume, you have dispatched Mr. Vollimer.

"True, zombies require a bit of control to use safely, but I think you have seen that they are most effective and easy to create. I have a stockpile of this elixir, which I can offer to the highest bidders—and, yes, Mr. Holmes, there are many. Once Mr. Pizer releases your precious Anne Prescott, I have only to depress my thumb to demonstrate my superiority and let her deal with you."

Suddenly Holmes moved, sliding forward and bringing Mustard Seed up in a whistling arc that nipped through the steel needle at Mycroft's neck. Moriarty, good as his word, depressed the plunger, but the deadly poison merely squirted onto Mycroft's collar. Moriarty let out a sharp cry and staggered back, away from the next sweeping stroke of Holmes's sword, aimed at taking the man's head from his shoulders.

Pizer tugged the strap in his hand, letting the metal mask, leather bonds, and canvas cloth drop away from Anne Prescott. And both he and Moriarty backed into the common room, away from her reach.

Anne stood for an instant, blinking, her glance shifting from Holmes to me. No trace of the Anne I loved was left in those eyes.

What can a man say when he has beheld the face of a loved one degraded beyond the point of enduring? What can he say of the horror of seeing great beauty ruined and gentle kindness turned into demonic rage?

"Help us," I prayed, knowing that even at our best, neither Holmes nor I was a match for this demon-haunted woman.

Anne blurred into motion, so lethal that it took my breath away. I lunged at her as she turned to Holmes. She spun, taking my weight around her center, flinging me into the room, and I lost my weapons.

I heard a window crash behind me and saw that Moriarty had pitched Pizer through one of the windows of the common room to the dark street.

Then I heard Holmes's cry behind me. Anne had ducked under his stroke and kicked his legs from under him. I heard the sickening crunch of her strike and saw his knee hinge sideways. Anne stomped at Holmes's leg as he fell and sought to roll away. Mustard Seed tumbled out of Holmes's hand.

Then I saw that Anne held one of my scalpels in her right hand, the last one for which I had to account. It flashed as she scrambled atop my friend and raised it in her right hand for the killing strike.

I don't know where I got the speed, but I threw myself at her, grasping her right hand. Though I caught it, she still managed to slash Holmes's arm, raised in defense. Clasping my arms around her, I rolled her away from him. With a strength and agility I could not match, she slipped through my grasp and sprang to her feet, two yards away. I sought to roll away, too, though labored with fatigue and fear. I had to try and reach her, somehow, to find Anne within.

"Anne!" I shouted. "Anne Prescott!" Her eyes knew me for a split second and fought to focus on me. Her knife hand wavered. Yet, in the next second, a horrid scream broke from that once lovely throat and nothing of Anne Prescott showed in the feral eyes that met my gaze. The demon within her grinned at me. Those evil eyes went wide, as though with sick delight, and that soulless voice screamed "Jack! Jack!" in such piercing tones that I blanched before it. It was as though raw evil had come up from the pit of Hell to cast that name, the remembrance of my own failing, into my face before it claimed my life.

"Watson!" Holmes called to me, pitching his sword to me from the floor. I caught the hilt of Mustard Seed in both hands, needing it but hating what I had to do, even as Anne launched herself at me. I spun hard to meet her, my only thought in that moment to deliver her from the evil that enslaved her body and what was left of her mind. She was in the air before me, her blade ready to slash my throat, but the speed of my stroke was, for once, faster. Every ounce of compassion I knew, I put into that stroke: all my love for Anne, for Mary, for Holmes, and for the country I loved.

And Mustard Seed's blade passed through Anne's neck with barely a pause in its speed, shearing through even the tangled black hair. The tresses floated out to follow the blade as it finished its deadly arc out of its shattered host, trailing the dark mist of the demonic presence behind it. Stinking of Hell's pit, the mist roiled in the air for a second before it dissipated and was gone.

***

Mary Kelly also died that night, a most horrible death. The scene of her murder was a nightmare of savage butchery. But it was the last of the Ripper murders, though that fact gave me small comfort.

Even with Anne's death, I knew that we were not finished with the deaths by zombie attack. Moriarty had done his work too well, though we had stopped—for the time being—the worst he had thought to do.

Gladstone called me a hero when he welcomed me into the L.S. Its actual name is the Logres Society, and someday the other stories of my exploits in its service, along with Holmes and Guthrie, will clarify its mission and history. That fabled sword Mustard Seed, I'm told, chose me as its master the day of Anne's death, though I see myself as ill-suited to its use. However, if my life proves so long, I will pen the accounts of my use of it in Department Zed, the protective arm of the Logres Society in England. As per Holmes's wishes, though, I will withhold these tales from the public until after our deaths.

As to Anne Prescott, I had her remains cremated and took her back to Scotland. Alone, since Mary had not returned to me, and with Anne's ashes at my side in a simple urn, I took the train to Edinburgh, left the Princes Street station, and made the hourlong trek up to the easternmost promontory of the Salisbury Crags. The locals call the place Arthur's Seat.

There, on a cold afternoon of misty winds blowing into the Highlands from the North Sea, I let Anne's ashes fall. I prayed then, as I do now, that she is at peace, even as I carry on without her the work I seem destined to do. I am honored and humbled to do so in her memory, at the side of Magnus Guthrie and of that magnificent champion of justice, Mr. Sherlock Holmes.

The End.

ABOUT THE AUTHOR

M.J. Downing is a native of Louisville, Kentucky. Born in Shively in the spring of 1954, he was raised in Okolona. M.J. resided in the Highlands for twenty years before marrying his wife, Amy, and moving to Valley Station.

M.J.'s interests are in this order: God, who is *the* Mystery; family, Amy and daughter Mackenna; writing stories; reading, everything from comics to criticism; playing guitar, all things Celtic; working out; walking; watching movies; travelling; and the comforts of home. He is a certifiable Tolkien geek and will wear you out with it, if given any encouragement.

For employment, M.J. has been a firefighter, a construction worker, a tobacconist, and many other things. Since 1983, he has taught college writing and literature classes, spending the last quarter century doing so at Jefferson Community and Technical College, Southwest.

FOR A FREE, EXCLUSIVE, SHORT STORY BY MJ DOWNING, VISIT HIS WEBSITE AT

http://www.downingplace.com/

FOLLOW MJ DOWNING ON FACEBOOK

https://www.facebook.com/markstories54/

CPSIA information can be obtained
at www.ICGtesting.com
Printed in the USA
LVHW091425200619
621858LV00001B/193/P